P9-CDG-640

AUG 2 5 2008
II 29

DEC 2 7 2009

Withdrawn

Pearl Sydenstricker Buck wa[s] Virginia and taken to China as the turn of the century. The daught[er] Presbyterian missionaries, she lived wit[h] family in a town in the interior instead [of] traditional missionary compound. Buck gr[ew] speaking Chinese as well as English received most of her education from her m[other]. She received an M.A. from Cornell and t[aught] English literature in several Chinese unive[rsities] before she was forced to leave the count[ry] 1932 because of the revolution.

She wrote eighty-five books and is the widely translated American author to thi[s] She has been awarded the Pulitzer Priz[e] William Dean Howells Award, and the [Nobel] Prize for Literature. She died in 1973.

Dragon Seed is streaked with tragedy, but Mrs. Buck's best work, the juice of life strongly through it; humor and passion ar[e] here, appropriately muted but not dead. [The] people live close to the earth and their lives take of the vigor and fertility, its patience, its eter- nal self-renewal. . . . As ever, Mrs. Buck's style is deceptive, for it is simple and yet equal to all the complex things required of it.   —*Books*

The author could hardly have suspected when she was writing *Dragon Seed*, the potency of its future appeal. The period in which the public is reading this book is precisely the right period. As war propaganda, the message which this book brings is terrific.   —*Christian Science Monitor*

Mrs. Buck is. . .quite ruthless in showing us what the unprepared common people of China had to endure from their conquerors, and, deeply acquainted with the nation she writes of, she is able to let us share their fears and weaknesses as well as their extraordinary dignity and courage.
      —*The Spectator*

NORTHVILLE DISTRICT LIBRARY
212 W. Cady Street
Northville, MI 48167-1560

Other Novels by Pearl S. Buck

All Men Are Brothers (*translator*)
East Wind: West Wind
The Good Earth
A House Divided
Imperial Woman
Kinfolk
The Living Reed
Mandala
The Mother
The New Year
The Pavilion of Women
Peony
The Promise
Sons
Three Daughters of Madame Liang

DRAGON
SEED

Pearl S. Buck

MOYER BELL
Kingston, Rhode Island & Lancaster, England

Published by Moyer Bell
Copyright © 1941 by Pearl S. Buck.
Copyright © renewed 1984 by Janice C. Walsh,
Richard S. Walsh, John S. Walsh, Henrietta C.
Walsh, Mrs. Chico Singer, Edgar S. Walsh,
Mrs. Jean C. Lippincott, and Carol Buck.

All rights reserved. No part of this publication may be reproduced
or transmitted in any form or by any means electronic or mechani-
cal, including photocopying, recording or any information retrieval
system, without permission in writing from Moyer Bell, 549 Old
North Road, Kingston, Rhode Island 02881 or Moyer Bell c/o
Gazelle Book Services Ltd., White Cross Mills, High Town,
Lancaster LA1 1RN England.

Fifth Printing, 2006

**LIBRARY OF CONGRESS
CATALOGING-IN-PUBLICATION DATA**

Buck, Pearl S. (Pearl Sydenstricker),
1892-1973.
Dragon seed / Pearl S. Buck.

p.   cm.

1.China—History—1937-1945—Fiction.
I. Title.
PS3503.U198D7   1992
813'.52--dc2040092   91-40092
ISBN 1-55921-033-8 pb.   CIP

Printed in the United States of America
Distributed in North America by Acorn Alliance,
549 Old North Road, Kingston, Rhode Island 02881,
401-783-5480, www.moyerbellbooks.com and
in the United Kingdom, Eire, and Europe by
Gazelle Book Services Ltd.,
White Cross Mills, High Town,
Lancaster LA1 1RN England,
1-44-1524-68765, www.gazellebooks.co.uk

NORTHVILLE DISTRICT LIBRARY
212 W. Cady Street   JUN 1 7 2008
Northville, MI 48167-1560

3 9082 10867 2786

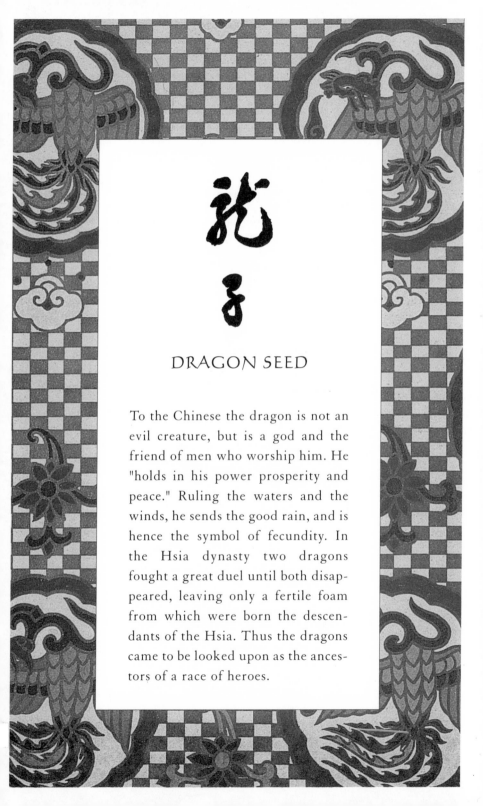

DRAGON SEED

To the Chinese the dragon is not an evil creature, but is a god and the friend of men who worship him. He "holds in his power prosperity and peace." Ruling the waters and the winds, he sends the good rain, and is hence the symbol of fecundity. In the Hsia dynasty two dragons fought a great duel until both disappeared, leaving only a fertile foam from which were born the descendants of the Hsia. Thus the dragons came to be looked upon as the ancestors of a race of heroes.

I

L ING TAN lifted his head. Over the rice field in which he stood to his knees in water he heard his wife's high loud voice. Why should the woman call him now in mid-afternoon when it was not time to eat or to sleep? In the further corner of the field his two sons were bending over the water, their two right arms thrusting together like the arms of one man as they planted the rice seedlings.

"Ho!" he shouted. As one man they stood at the sound of their father's voice.

"Is that your mother?" he inquired.

They listened, two sturdy young men. He felt his belly move with pride at the sight of them. They were both already married, and the eldest, Lao Ta, had two sons, the youngest now only a month old. Lao Er, the second, had been married four months and his wife was beginning to fret. Besides these two, Ling Tan had his youngest son, Lao San, who at this moment was sitting on the water buffalo grazing somewhere on the round grassy foothills along this valley. There were also two daughters in his house, only one of whom was left to be wed. The elder he had given to a merchant's son in the city whose walls could be clearly seen from behind his house.

At this moment his wife's voice came too clearly for any mistaking. She bawled at him heartily over the fields.

"You old bone, where are you? You deaf-and-dumb!"

"It is our mother," Lao Ta exclaimed. All three men grinned at one another, and Ling Tan put into the water the sheaf of rice seedlings he was holding in his left hand.

"It is throwing away money to stop in the middle of the afternoon like this," he said. "You two, do not stop!"

"Free your heart about that," his eldest son replied.

The young men bent again to their work and with each swift thrust of their hands into the muddy tepid water they planted a green seedling. Their feet sank into the rich mud under the water, and upon their dark bare backs the sun was warm. Beneath the wide woven bamboo hats upon their heads they talked.

These two sons of Ling Tan's were good friends and had always been from the moment they could remember themselves. There was less than a year between their births, and they had always told each other everything. Even marriage to two separate women had not separated them. These women they had been discussing when their father called, and to them they returned when he went away. They were still so young, these two men, that their own bodies and what they ate and drank and what came into the day and the night were all stuff for wonder and talk. So far as their thoughts yet went, the world was bounded by the green hills around the valley where their father's land was, which was to be their land, and the center of the world was the Ling village, wherein all who lived and died were their kin and had been for hundreds of years. Even that great city was only their marketplace. When there was a harvest of grain or vegetable or fruit they went there and sold their harvest, and that was all they knew of the city, or cared to know. Since their sister, born just after them, was now married to a small merchant in the city, they sometimes blamed themselves and said they ought to go and see their brother-in-law, but they seldom went. There was enough to busy them on the land.

Under their hats they now talked, without abating one whit of swiftness in the thrust of seedling into mud. Behind them was

4

the watery empty field and in front of them the even rows of green seedlings standing firmly upright.

"Can a man tell when what he plants in a woman takes root?" Lao Er asked his brother.

"It is blind planting," Lao Ta said, laughing, "and so it must be done over and over again. It is not like this planting we do in the light of the sun. Does she struggle against you?"

"At first, but now never," Lao Er said.

"Leave her alone for three days and then behave as though it were the first planting," Lao Ta told his brother. He went on in manner of the elder to the younger. "When a man plants his seed, the soil must be prepared. That is to say, the seed must not be thrown down anyhow. All must be made ready and only when it is ready may the seed be cast. Nor must the seed be scattered as the wind blows weeds. It must be thrust deep into the earth, so- and so- and so- "

Each time that he repeated this word he thrust his bare dark arm down into the wet earth and planted a sturdy seedling.

Lao Er listened to this with all his heart.

"I am an impatient man," he said, half ashamed.

"Then it is your own fault if you have no son," his elder brother replied. He threw a sly look at his brother, whom he loved, and his full mouth twisted into a smile. "When you are a year married, you will find the son more important than the mother."

"But how she frets," Lao Er said. "Every month when her flux comes she curses it."

They laughed again, seeing, both of them, the young high-tempered girl who was Lao Er's wife. The elder brother's wife was quiet and plump and if she had a temper, she kept it secret. But Lao Er's wife was like a western wind. Wherever she was she stirred all around her. Lao Er had loved her the moment he saw her.

Lao Ta loved his wife too, but not, he knew, with his whole

5

being. That is, he could delay his going to bed until other and older men had yawned and stretched their muscles and given over their loitering at the tea shop in the village or about the square in front of the small temple. When he came home if his father were still awake he could stand gossiping on the threshing floor in front of the house. There was no haste in the way he loved his wife. She would be there asleep in his bed where she had early lain herself down, and he had only to go to her.

But Lao Er's wife was restless and full of mischief, and Lao Er never knew where she was until he had her safely beside him. Every evening he was torn between the watchful eyes of the other men, ready to laugh at him if he were the first to break away from them, and the desire in him to know where she was. Jade, he called her, though her full name was longer than that. "Jade!" he called the moment he came into their room. Sometimes she was there and oftener not. He seldom found her twice in the same place in the house or out of the house and never waiting for him in his bed. He longed to know if she loved him, but he had not dared to ask her, lest she laugh at him, she whose laughter, like her anger, was always too ready and too clear. He fell silent, wondering where at this moment she was in the house. In the morning she had come out into the fields and she helped him to plant rice, but after the noon meal she would not come.

"I want to sleep," she had told him, and threw herself on the bed in their room and went to sleep before his eyes. He longed to lay himself beside her and dared not, because his father would upbraid him for lying with his wife in the daytime, when rice seedlings were waiting to be planted. So he had gone off leaving her sleeping, her high-cheeked little face as pretty as a child's. But how long did she sleep and then what did she do? He cast a glance at the sun. It was still too high. He sighed, and went on with the planting.

. . . Under the matting roof which he always put over his courtyard in summer Ling Tan was listening to a stranger. He

6

was a peddler of Shantung silks and grass cloth, one of those men who make their living by travelling south with their goods in spring and selling them to Southerners and then carrying back with them in early summer the thin silks of the South such as are not woven in the North. He had now from the North only a few pieces of grass cloth so coarse that he knew none but a farmer's wife would buy them and so he had left the city to go out among the villages. Thus he had come to this house because it was bigger than most farmhouses and because he saw at the gate a pretty young woman idling.

She seemed unwatched but she was not, for the moment he came up to her and spoke, the mother, Ling Sao, came out from behind the gate and said to him sharply:

"If you must speak to a woman, speak to me and not to my second son's wife."

"I was only going to ask her where her man's mother was," the peddler said hastily. He perceived in one glance of his eyes that this elderly woman was a strong managing mother, and the head of her house. "I am on my way north to my home," he said, "and I have left only a few feet of good grass cloth for summer wear and they told me in the village that you were the most discerning woman in these parts—"

"Put out your cloth and put in your tongue," the wife said.

He hastened to obey her, though he laughed politely when she said this, and in a few minutes they were quarreling heartily over the price of the grass cloth.

"I have put the price at a gift," he argued at last, "because there is to be war this summer in the North."

The cloth fell from her hand.

"What war now?" she asked.

"No war of ours," the man replied. "It is the little dwarfs from the East Ocean, who always like to fight."

"Will they come here?" she asked.

"Who knows?" he replied.

7

It was then that she went to the door and called for her husband to come.

Now Ling Tan listened to the peddler as they sat at the table under the matting roof of the court. Under his feet the stones were cool. It was a pleasant court, warm with sun in the winter and in the summer cool. An ancestor of his had sunk a small pool in its center and had planted a lotus in a jar. This lotus now bloomed with six flowers, deep red in the center where the yellow hearts were. The table was set here in the summer and here they ate even when it rained, for the matting held off the water. At the table he sat with the peddler while his wife poured them tea and then took her seat on a bench a little to one side. She was making shoes. The sole was thick but she had a long iron needle. When it held fast in the cloth she seized it in her strong white teeth and jerked it through and pulled the hempen thread after it. Ling Tan always turned his eyes away when he saw this for it set his own teeth on edge, though, because he did not know why, he had never told her so.

"You say the East-Ocean dwarfs have killed some of our people?" he now asked the peddler.

"In the North they have killed men, women and children," the peddler said.

He lifted his bowl and drank the tea and stood up. "I must reach Pengpu tomorrow and so I part from you," he said. He was a common looking fellow as peddlers are, his talk worn smooth with much use in many places.

Ling Tan did not stir. "What is the outlook?" he murmured to himself.

But since he asked no one, no one answered him. The peddler shouldered his pack and bowed and went away, and Ling Tan was left alone with his wife in the court. She went on sewing and he sat there looking around at his house. The walls were of ancient brick and the roofs were low and tiled. Inside the house the partitions were of brick laid single between beams of

8

wood and first plastered with earth and then washed white with lime. Here his ancestors had lived and died and he had been born, the only son of his parents, and here his three sons lived and his grandson.

The afternoon was still and hot. The hearts of the lotus flowers quivered. In the silence he heard his grandson cry. Ling Sao rose and went into the house and he sat alone. He had a good life, he thought. He was lucky that his share of the earth was near a great city, near the big river, in a valley set under hills from which the water ran down even in dry weather. There was nothing that he desired that he did not have. He was neither rich nor poor. In his house his only dead child was a girl. He himself had never been ill. At fifty-six his body was thin and strong as it had been in his youth. He could beget sons as well as ever if it had not been that his wife was past it. An old woman in the village teased him often to buy a concubine through her but he would not.

"I have my sons," he had told the greedy old woman only yesterday.

"A man cannot have too many sons in these times," she had said. "What with wars and guns and all these foreign things, who can have sons enough?"

But he had only laughed. Except that she bore no child, his woman was as good as ever and better because she knew him to the core of his being. He was satisfied and he had no wish to begin over again with a young girl. Besides, peace flew out of the house when a second woman walked into the door.

He struck the table with his hand, swallowed the tea that was left in his bowl and stood up and tightened the strip of blue cloth that was the girdle about his waist.

"I go back to my work!" he shouted. No one answered him, but he expected no answer, since they were only women who heard him, and he went his way.

In the field he was pleased to see how near his sons were to

9

the end at which he had been working. Another good hour and by sunset the field would be done. This was the last field and with it all his rice would be planted and his family fed for another year. He bent his back again and saw his own face dimly in the brown water, a thin face square at the cheeks and the jaws. He could always keep his hat on easily because the string caught firmly under his square chin. There were men in the village who had to hold a hat string between their teeth because their chins were slopes. But he was not one of them. And he could close his mouth over his teeth decently and need not always be agape as his third cousin was, who was nevertheless a good man and even a little learned, with sense enough to read the meaning out of the magistrate's proclamations on the city wall.

Ling Tan himself could not read a word. He had never needed to read. Sooner or later, he always said, a man heard everything. If it were good news he heard it quickly, and the more slowly he heard bad news the better. He had not sent his sons to school, either, and for this he had not yet been sorry, no, not even when from the schools in the city the young men and women students came into the villages to preach that today every man and woman should read and write. Looking at those pale students, he still thought to himself that he saw no reason to believe what they said. He had his own ways and he kept them.

Now in the field he did not speak to his sons nor they to him until the work was done and they met at the last seedling thrust down. Then they straightened themselves, the three of them, and pushed their hats off their heads to hang down their backs.

"What did our mother want?" Lao Ta asked.

"There was a peddler from the North and he brought news of a war," the father said. It had been an hour since he had thought of the matter and by now it seemed of no importance to him. The North was far from here. He measured with his sharp eye the lines of the seedlings, green against the brown water. The shadows they cast made a straight black line. His sons' right hands were as steady as his own. He wiped his face with the end of his girdle and said to his second son:

"Go and buy a little pork at your eighth cousin's shop. We will have it tonight with cabbage."

"Let me go for him," his elder son said mischievously.

Ling Tan gazed at his two sons and he saw that Lao Er's face was crimson. "Now what is between you?" he asked. Lao Ta laughed and would not speak, and the younger grinned like a silly boy. Their father smiled. They were still children, these two!

"Keep your cursed secrets," he said, laughing. "Do I care what you do?"

He turned homeward, very content, and a moment later saw his second son slip into the gate of the courtyard before him. Whatever it was that made him hasten from work at least it was in these walls, Ling Tan thought. It did not occur to him that it was his son's own wife that made him so quick.

. . . Lao Er went into the room that was his with Jade. She was not there.

"Jade!" he called. There was no answer. "Jade!" he called again. He made his voice low. Perhaps she was hiding. Sometimes she hid and came out only when he was distracted, to laugh at him. But though he called yet again, she did not come out. The room was empty.

He felt the fear he always did when he could not find her at once. Had she run away from him? He went into the court to find his mother. She was not there and he went into the kitchen. The wooden lid of the cauldron was steaming with the evening's rice and so he looked behind the great earthen stove. There his mother was crouched, feeding the dried grass into the firebox. He could not for shame ask his mother where his wife was, and so in pretense he made his voice angry.

"My mother, why do you feed the fire? My worthless one ought to do it for you."

"Worthless indeed," his mother replied. "I have not seen her since the sun was in the middle of the sky. These young women! The matchmaker cheated us. It comes of having their feet free. When I was a girl our feet were bound and we stayed at home. Now they run around like goats."

"I will find her and bring her home and beat her," he said and felt so angry that if he had had Jade before his eyes at this moment he would have beaten her.

"Do it," his mother replied. Then her small shrewd eyes lit with laughter. "Only make sure first, my son, that you are able! Women are not so easily beaten, now-a-days!"

She laughed a dry silent laugh and spread the grass sparsely over the flame. Ling Tan was not a poor farmer, and her own father had had rich soil to till, but she had been well taught that, rich or poor, in any house there should be no waste of food and fuel and cloth. When she wove a piece of cloth and cut a garment from it, the scraps of the cloth could lie in the palm of her hand. This the matchmaker had guaranteed and it was true. But it was hard to find such young women now. Orchid, her elder son's wife, had feet bound in childhood, but the revolution had come before the work had been finished and her father had commanded her feet to be unbound, even as Ling Tan had refused to allow his own two daughters to have their feet bound.

She sat feeding the grass into the stove, leaf by leaf and blade by blade, a twig or two, a stalk, while she meditated upon her sons' wives. Good or bad, sons' wives could make the home happy or miserable and upon them depended the old. Sons could not be trusted, because in a house women were stronger than men. Thus, she thought, who could believe that her second son would beat Jade when he found her?

"He will not beat her," she muttered into the flame. Her husband had beaten her twice in her youth, once in anger and once in jealousy, but he was stronger than his sons. Nor had she suffered the beatings calmly. She had pounded him with her fists and clawed his cheeks and bitten the lobe of his right ear so deeply that the marks of it were there still.

"Who bit you there?" people asked him even now.

"A hill tiger," he always said and always laughed. She had come from a village in the hills.

But Jade—could any man beat Jade? She sighed and let the fire die and rose. Her knees were aching but she paid no heed to it. She lifted the lid of the cauldron and sniffed the rice. It was fragrant and nearly done. She fitted the lid firmly. There was no need for more fire—the steam would finish the cooking. She yawned and reached for the rice bowls that stood on a shelf in the earthen chimney. Part of a fish left from the noon meal would make meat, and the cabbage left she would stir into the rice. Fish cost nothing, for they had fish in their own pond and it was only needful to drop the net into the water.

She set the bowls on the table in the court, put down the chopsticks, and then went into the room where she and her husband slept. He was there, washing himself in a bowl full of cold water. They did not speak, but over the face of each of them came a look of peace. She sat down and taking the silver toothpick from her hair she picked her teeth slowly, gazing at him as he washed. She thought calmly that his body was as good now as it had been the first time she looked at it, hard and thin and brown. He moved quickly and with full strength, washing himself, wringing the cotton towel, which she wove as she had woven nearly all the cloth they used, and wiping himself dry. He was a clean man. There was never a smell nor a stink about him. When he opened his mouth to laugh in her face sometimes his teeth were sound and his breath came sweet. There was his third cousin whose breath was like a camel's.

"How do you sleep at his side?" she had asked the cousin's wife only the other day.

13

"Do not all men stink?" the woman had replied.

"Not mine," she had said proudly.

"Now I will have my supper," Ling Tan said suddenly. He drew on his loose blue cotton trousers and knotted a clean girdle about his waist. Then he remembered the pork. "I sent the eldest for pork," he said. She opened her eyes wide. "We had half a fish left from noon."

"I will have the pork," he said loudly.

"Have it, then," she replied and rose to go out to prepare it. When she entered the kitchen she saw the pork already there on the table, lying upon a dried lotus leaf. She seized it and examined it, always ready to be cheated by their eighth cousin, the butcher, though she never had been. The man was afraid of her and respected Ling Tan, and though he had his poor meats, as any butcher has, he knew where to sell them. This pound of pork was as good as could be had anywhere, the red and white in layers under the soft thick white skin, and she could find no fault with it. She chopped it quickly with garlic and salt and rolled it into small round balls and dropped them into boiling water. She had a deft hand at cooking and Ling Tan had not smoked more than two pipes before she was ready.

From the kitchen door she shouted to her eldest son, "Your father is ready to eat!"

Lao Ta came out of his family room, washed and clean, his child in his arms.

"We are here," he said.

Ling Tan coming out of his door shouted for his second son.

"He will not hear," his wife bawled from the kitchen. She was stirring the cold cabbage into the boiling rice. "He is looking for his woman."

From the court came laughter, the laughter of two men whose wives never ran away. The mother dipped the rice into bowls and brought them out and laughed with them, and at the door the eldest son's wife came and stood buttoning her jacket.

"Let me, mother," she begged for courtesy, since she did not move. Then she laughed because they were all laughing, though she had not heard why. But this household was always laughing at something and being an easy kindly creature Orchid laughed without stopping to find the cause for their laughter.

And as they sat down the third son came quietly into the gate, leading the water buffalo by a rope through its nostrils. He was a tall silent boy not yet quite sixteen years of age, and nobody spoke to him when he came nor did he expect it. But he caught the quick careful look of his mother's eyes and his father's glance. Both looked at him to see if all was well, and Lao San knew what they did not, that he was the son they loved best though most uneasily, because of his temper. In many small ways he took a child's advantage of his two older brothers, but they allowed him, doing no more than cuff him over his shorn head if he teased them. But toward his parents he was often wilful and ready to be sulky, and as little as possible did they command him to do anything, and Ling Tan purposely let him take the buffalo to the hills that he might have the rebellious boy away from him. Thus he was spared the need of dealing with his waywardness.

All of this was because Lao San's face was so beautiful. This third son indeed was so beautiful that his parents had from his birth prepared themselves for his death at any moment, for how could the gods not be jealous of such beauty? He had long eyes whose pupils were black as onyx under water, and the whites were clear. His face was square and his mouth full and the lips cut square and full as a god's are. His great fault was his dreaming indolence, but they forgave him this as they forgave him everything, and it was true that in the last two years he had grown as fast as in any other four. Now he dipped up water out of a jar and into a wooden bucket, and standing just outside the court among the bamboos there he washed himself and then came in and took his place at the table.

15

It was a sight to make a man's heart strong, the father thought to himself, looking at his sons. Lao Er's place was still empty, but he would come sooner or later, and then the table would be full. Upon his knee Lao Ta held his baby son and now and again he put into the child's little mouth, pink as a lotus bud, a morsel of rice he had chewed fine and soft. The evening air was growing cool and the lotus flowers were closing for the night. There was silence everywhere except for the sound of the loom in the weaving room, where Lao Tan's younger daughter was still at work and would work until she was called to her meal.

The mother threw down an armful of straw for the buffalo to eat. The yellow dog came in fawning and humble in the hope of food. This dog was as bold as a wolf before strangers from whom it expected nothing, but now before its master it was mild as a kitten, and it crawled under the table to wait for scraps. Ling Tan put his feet upon it for a footstool and felt the beast's stiff hairs against his bare skin and its body warm beneath his soles. He bent and threw down a good lump of fish in sudden kindness to this one who was also of his household.

. . . In the fields about the house Lao Er was still searching for Jade. The sun had not yet gone down, and its long yellow rays lay like honey on the green. If she were there he could easily see her blue coat. The wheat was cut and the rice still short and there was nothing to hide her. But she was not there. Then she must be somewhere in the village. He cast his mind quickly over the places where she went—not the tea shop, because only men were there, and not to his third cousin's house, for the son of that house was of his own age and had wanted Jade for his wife in the days when the old woman who was matchmaker for her was searching out the best husband for her. This fourth cousin had seen Jade one day as she stood at her father's door in another village, and had loved her then. But so had Lao Er already seen her and loved her, too, and between the two young men there had grown a great anger and they hated each other, and took

16

every excuse for quarreling. The thing came to be known in the village so that everybody kept their eyes on the two, ready to shout out and leap forward to part them if they flew at each other.

Nor would Jade say nor did she yet say which of the two she wanted. She shrugged her thin shoulders and would not speak when her mother asked her, or if she spoke she said:

"If they both have two legs and two arms and all their fingers and toes, and if they are not cross-eyed or scabby-headed, what is the difference between them?"

So her father put the whole choice upon which man's father gave the best price for Jade and the two young men begged and harried their own fathers and threatened to kill themselves if they could not have her, and so destroyed the whole peace of the two households that Ling Tan met his third cousin one day at the tea shop and took him aside and said:

"Since I am a richer man than you, let me give you thirty silver dollars for yourself and then I beg you to tell your son that my son is to have this girl, otherwise we cannot find peace."

The cousin was willing, for thirty dollars was as much as he could earn as a scholar in half a year and so the thing was settled and Lao Er was betrothed to Jade and as quickly as he could bring it about, he married her. But the strange thing was that he could not forgive her in the most secret part of his heart because she had not chosen him against the other, and he had not yet dared to ask her why she had not. Sometimes in the night when he lay beside her he planned that when he knew her better, when she had opened to him her heart, he would ask her:

"Why was it that you would not choose me when the choice was put to you?"

But he had not asked her yet. Though he knew her body so well, her he did not know, and so there was no peace in his love for her, and all his love was still quick and full of possible pain.

He went swiftly now toward the village and without seeming to do so, kept his eyes wide for a slender girl in a blue cotton coat and trousers, whose hair was cut short about her neck. He had fallen into a fury that day not twenty days ago when he came home and found that Jade had cut off her long black hair.

"I was hot," she said to his angry eyes.

"Your hair was mine," he had cried to her, "You had no right to throw it away!"

She had not answered this and then when he saw that she would not speak he cried at her again, "What have you done with the long hair you cut off?"

Still without a word she went into their room and brought out the long loose stuff. She had tied the thick end of it with a red cord, and he took it from her hand and laid it across his knees. There it was, straight and smooth and black, a part of her which she had wilfully cut off from her life. He felt the tears suddenly come to his eyes, as though for something he had possessed which had been living and now was dead.

"What shall we do with it?" he had asked in a low voice. "It cannot be thrown away."

"Sell it," she had said. "It will buy me a pair of earrings."

"Do you want earrings?" he had asked in surprise. "But your ears are not pierced."

"I can pierce them," she had said.

"I will buy you the earrings," he had answered her, "but not with your own hair."

He had taken the hair then and put it into his own small pig-skin trunk where he kept his best clothes and the silver neck chain he had worn as a child and one or two more of his own things. When she was old and the hair on her head was white, when he was old and had forgotten how she looked now, he would take that long hair out of the trunk and remember.

He had not yet had time to buy the earrings. The rice plant-ing had kept him busy from dawn to dark until today. Now as he pretended to saunter through the village, his eyes sharp and his wits flying ahead of his feet, he thought that if he found her doing no naughty thing, he would go tomorrow into the city and buy those earrings, and tonight he would find out what she wanted them to be. Still he did not see her. He began to be frightened because he did not see her anywhere and his thought took hold of that young man who was not yet married to any woman, because he was still peevish at having lost the one he wanted. He went toward his cousin's house and there was his cousin's wife at the door. She was a large pig-shaped woman and she stood with her bowl of food held to her face and she supped out of it as though it were a trough. He would not mention the name of Jade in her presence.

"Are you eating, my sister-cousin?" he asked politely.

"Come in and eat too," she replied, taking the bowl from her face.

"I cannot, though I thank you," he replied. "Are you alone at home, then?"

"Your cousin my lord is eating, but your cousin my son is not home yet."

"Ah," Lao Er said, "where is he?"

"He went toward the city, or said he was going there when the sun hung over that willow tree. I do not know where he is now," she answered.

She put the bowl back to her face and he went on. By now his heart was beating wildly. If Jade were with this cousin of his, he would kill them both and lay their bodies in the open street for all to see. His blood came rushing up the veins of his throat and swelled into his cheeks and eyes and his right hand twitched.

At this moment he drew near to the open land before the village tea house and here a crowd had gathered, as there often was to see some passing show of actors or jugglers or travelling merchants with foreign goods. Today it was not any of these, but a band of four or five young men and women, city people he could see at once, who were showing some magic pictures upon a sheet of white cloth they had hung between two bamboos.

The pictures he did not see, for at this moment his eyes fell upon his cousin, sitting on a wooden bench where the crowd parted. He was so sure that Jade was with him somehow that he looked to see if she were at his side but she was not. For a moment he was taken aback, and all his hot blood turned cold and he felt faint with weariness and hunger. When he found her, he thought, he would beat her anyway even if she were doing no wrong, because she was not where a woman should be, at home and waiting for her husband.

At this moment the voice of a young man who had all along been speaking now came into his ears and he heard it.

"We must burn our houses and our fields, we must not leave so much as a mouthful for the enemy to keep him from starving. Are you able for this?"

No one in that crowd spoke or moved. They did not understand his meaning. They could only stare at the picture upon the white cloth. Now Lao Er looked at it, too. It was of a city somewhere of many houses, and out of the houses came great flames and black smoke. The people looked and said nothing. And then before his eyes Lao Er saw one move and leap up and it was Jade. She flung back her short hair from her face.

"We are able!" she cried.

Before all these people she cried out and he was afraid. What were these words and what did they mean? And what right had she to speak so when he was not there?

"Come home!" he shouted at her. "I am hungry!"

She turned and looked at him and seemed not to see him. But his shout had brought the crowd back to their village and to their even life. They stirred and yawned, and men stretched themselves and muttered that they were hungry, too, and had forgotten it. One by one they rose and began to saunter home and Lao Er nodded to his cousin, though he was still angry because he could not find fault with him and he waited for Jade. He would not be mild with her, he thought, watching her out of the end of his eye because he was ashamed to look full at his wife in the presence of others.

"Do not forget that what I have shown you are true things!" the young man called but no one heard him. There Lao Er stood until Jade came near and then he began to walk away, seeing out of his eye's end that she was following him. He did not speak to her until they were well away from the village and then he made his voice surly.

"Why do you shame me by showing yourself off to everybody?"

She did not answer this. He heard her steady tread in the dusty path behind him. He went on, his voice as loud as he could make it.

"I come home my belly roaring like a hungry lion," he cried.

"Why did you not eat, then?"

He heard her voice behind him, clear and mild.

"How can I eat when you are not in your proper place?" he shouted at her without turning his head. "How can I ask where you are? I am ashamed before my own parents not to know where my wife is."

This she did not answer at all, and at last he could not bear not to know what she was thinking, so against his own will he turned his head and met her eyes full, ready and waiting for that head of his to turn. She was laughing. The moment their eyes met the laughter burst out of her and all the strength of his anger went out of him like wind from his bowels. She took two steps forward and caught his hand and he could not pull it from her grasp though he still did not want to forgive her.

"You use me very ill," he said, his voice now as feeble as an old man's voice.

"Oh, you look so pale and so thin and so ill-used," she said, her voice rich with her laughter. "Oh, you are so to be pitied, you big turnip!"

He did not want her laughter and he did not know what he

wanted but it was not her teasing laughter. The moon that had been a shape of white cloud was turning gold in the darkness and the fields of water were full of frogs' voices. In his hand her hand lay like a little beating heart and he put it to his neck and held it against the hollow of his throat. He wanted some huge great thing for which he had no words. His words were always too few for his need, enough for the things of his usual life but not enough for this.

"I wish I were a man of learning," he said thickly, "I wish I knew words."

"Why do you want words?" she asked.

"To ease myself," he answered, "so that I could tell you what I feel in me."

"What do you feel?" she asked him.

"I know," he said. "But I have not the words."

They stood facing each other in the narrow path between the rice fields, for the moment out of sight of any house. A great willow hung its long green strands about them. Lao Er put his hands upon her shoulders and drew her slowly until she was against him. There he held her for a moment and she did not move. They stood alone in the quiet evening and closer for this moment than they had ever been.

"But I, too, am not very learned," she said in a whisper.

"Is that why you do not often speak to me?" he asked her.

"But how can I, when you are always so silent?" she asked in return. "Two must speak, for understanding."

He pondered this for another moment, his arms loosening their hold upon her. Were they both waiting for each other, expecting each other, and neither knew what to say until the other spoke first?

"Will you tell me everything in you if I tell you all that is in me?" he asked.

"Yes," she said.

His arms dropped. Without touching her he felt nearer to her than he ever had.

"Then tonight we will speak together," he said.

"Yes," she said.

Her voice was so soft that it was not like Jade's voice, but he heard it. She put her hand into his and they walked on and came toward the house. Only when they came to the gate did she take her place behind him again.

In the court the men had finished their food and at the table his mother and his elder brother's wife were eating and with them his younger sister.

"You were a long time gone," his mother cried. "We could wait no longer."

"I want no waiting," he replied. And to his wife he said roughly so that none might think them shamefully in love, "Fetch me my food in a bowl and I will eat it where my father and brother are."

And like any proper wife Jade filled his bowl and gave it to him before she took her place among the women. She too had forgotten what the young man had said at the temple, though while he was speaking she had thought that she could never forget it. She took up her bowl dreamily, her heart too quick for hunger. This man to whom she was married, tonight would she know what he was?

Ling Sao spoke to Jade as she rose from the table.

"Since you did not cook the meal, you may clean after it."

Jade rose at her mother-in-law's voice.

"I will, my mother," she said.

So rare was it for her to rise thus, so soft her voice was, that the mother stared at her in the twilight and said nothing as she went toward the gate of the court.

"My son must have beaten her after all," she thought, and stepped through the gate.

Outside upon the threshing floor Ling Tan sat on a bench

23

and his sons sat near him upon the hard beaten earth. The youngest was curled on a bundle of wheat straw asleep. She stared hard at her second son. He was eating with great joy in his food. There was no sign on him of anything except joy.

"He did beat her," she thought and was glad to think he had. The best marriage was where the man could beat the woman, and she was proud of her son.

. . . Who could have believed, Lao Er asked himself, that a man and a woman could come closer together through speech than through flesh? Yet so it was with them that night, with Jade, his wife, and with him.

At first he felt so strange when he lay down beside her that he was abashed. "It is only Jade," he told himself and yet it seemed to him that she was more strange to him than she had been on their wedding night. The flesh he could see and comprehend but what was hidden behind her pretty face and her smooth body? He had never known. Now he did not want to touch her, only to listen, to hear. He waited and she lay silent.

"Are you waiting, too?" he asked at last.

"Yes," she said.

"Who will speak first, then?"

"You," she said. "Ask me what you will."

What he would? There it was in his mind, and it ran out to the end of his tongue.

"Do you ever think of my cousin who wanted you, too?" He blurted these words.

"Is that what you want to know?" she cried. She sat up in bed and drew up her legs and sat on them crosswise. "Oh, you are silly! Is that what has been curdling in you? Then no- no- no- and however you ask me I will say no!"

His head swirled as though it were full of a whirlpool of water.

"Then what are you thinking all day when you go about so

silent, and what do you think of at night when you do not speak all night long?" he cried.

"I think of twenty things and thirty things at a time," she said. "My thoughts are like a chain and one is fast to the other. So, if I begin thinking of a bird, why, then, I think how it flies, and why it can lift itself above the earth and I cannot, and then I think of the foreign flying ships and how they are made and is there any magic in them or is it only that foreigners know what we do not know, and now at this moment when I think of that I think of what the young man said before the tea house, how those ships fly over the cities in the North and crush them down and how the people run and hide."

He broke this chain of her thinking. The cities of the North were far away.

"Why did you go there today?"

"I sat and sewed on your blue coat. Then I had no more thread and your mother had only white. So then I went out to buy some of the blue thread. When I went to the village there the people were."

He broke in again.

"I wish you would not go on the street alone."

"Why?"

"Other men will see you."

"I do not look at them."

"I do not want them to look at you. You are pretty and you are my wife."

"But how can I stay always in the courtyard? These are not ancient times."

"I wish it were those times. I would like to lock you up."

"If you locked me up I would not eat and then I should die."

"I would not let you die."

She laughed. "But still these are the new times and I will come and go."

"Does any man ever speak to you?"

"Not more than to another he knows."

They fell silent again and then he began. "Tell me what you thought of me when you first saw me."

She plucked at the blue and white flowered cotton cover of the bed. "The first time I saw you I cannot remember."

"No, I mean when—after we were married."

She turned her head away. In the moonlight he could see her forehead and small straight nose, her lips, the lower one a little behind the upper, and her full chin.

"I was glad you are taller than I am. For a woman I am too tall," she said.

"No, you are not."

She let him say this and did not answer.

"And then what did you think?" he asked her.

Now she hung her head. "Then I wondered what you thought about me."

"But you knew I wanted you," he said.

She lifted her head suddenly. "And then I wondered—if we should ever talk together. Were we to be to each other only what others married are? Yes, and would you care what I am or only that I gave you children and made your food? And was I to be yours or only belong to your house? Will you learn to read? There are things in books to know. Will you buy me a book? . . . There—that is my secret. Instead of the earrings, buy me a book! It is why I cut my hair off. I was going to sell it to buy a book. Then I was afraid to tell you, so I said earrings. It is a book I want."

She leaned over him in her anxiety for him to hear her.

"A book!" he said. "But what have people like us to do with books?"

"I want only a book," she said.

"But if you cannot read?"

"I can read," she said.

26

Now if she had told him that she could fly like a bird, she could not so have astonished him.

"How can you read?" he cried. "Women like you never read!"

"I learned," she said, "a word at a time. My father sent one of my brothers to school, and from him I learned a little every day. But I have no book of my own."

He thought about this a moment.

"If this is what you want," he said slowly, "I will give it to you. But I never thought to see a woman read in this house."

So they talked on, half the night through, until they were drowsy with weariness.

"We must sleep," he said at last. "Tomorrow's work must be done. And if I am to go to the city, too, to buy the book—"

He stopped and held his breath. For now she curled down beside him as he spoke, and put herself close to him as she never had. It was so sweet, this movement of her own will toward him, that he could not say another word. It was the sweetest instant of his life, better by far than the first time he had taken her on his wedding night, for this was the first time she had ever come to him of her own will. Why had he been such a fool, he asked himself, as not to know before how a woman's heart was made? But none had told him. He had stumbled upon the knowledge out of his own discontent that even marriage had not given her to him. Now he possessed her because she gave herself to him.

When he slept that night he knew as surely as though a god had been in him that out of this night she would conceive a child. Out of this night a son would be born to him.

II

Now Lao Er had often bought goods for his father, because of all three sons he was the one who was most at his ease in the city. The father never entered the city gates if he could help it for he said his breath would not come in and out evenly once he was there, and his wife would not go often because she said the city people all had a stink to them. This Ling Tan himself would not wholly allow, because he said each kind of human flesh had its own smell, and then she said that if this were so, she would stay with her own kind of flesh that lived in the fields and ate its meats and vegetables fresh and not decayed from long lying in markets. The eldest son was too trusting a man for the city and he believed what city folk told him, and the youngest was too young and Ling Tan would not often allow him inside the city gates, lest he learn evil. So it came about that Lao Er was the son who did the city business, who took eggs to the corner shop at the Bridge of the South Gate, and who weighed the pig's meat when they killed, who carried to the rice shops their surplus rice after each harvest.

This he had done for years enough so that now when he came through the great gate he did not feel frightened or abashed or trip one foot over the other for staring as most countrymen did. He walked in with his head up and his face clean and a decent blue coat and trousers covering his body. He did not

28

wear socks because it was summer but he put on a fresh pair of straw sandals that he and his brothers wove out of rice straw in the long winter evenings, and he smoothed down his short black hair as he came into the first busy street. He knew where to go for his business, and when he talked to the men in the city he did it with sharp cool sense and yet with good country courtesy. If he were given a bad penny by the eggman who bought his eggs, he took it and said nothing to the man's face but he took care the next time he brought in his eggs to have all very fresh except three rotten ones. Since three eggs were anywhere bought for a penny when the man found these three rotten he perfectly knew why they were there, and knew that Lao Er could discern a bad penny as well as he a bad egg, and so the two understood each other as well as though they had spoken, and there had been no need for anger between them. By such means Lao Er had come to be respected among the people he knew in the city, and so he respected himself there.

But today when it came to buying a book he knew no more than a child. He went to a certain street where booksellers had their wares out on boards set on benches and stared awhile at them. Except that some were large and some were small each book looked like every other. Seeing how long he stood there, one bookseller after another asked him what book he wanted and he had always to say he did not know. He was ashamed to say he wanted a book for his wife, because this would make her seem strange and unlike other women, so he pretended it was for himself.

Now without exception these booksellers were small old weazened men who had once been scholars or teachers in little schools, men who had not succeeded well, and so had sunk to the selling of books for merchandise. But none of them so much as imagined that Lao Er could not read. One by one they put out their wares saying, "Here is a good one full of laughter about the foreign devils," or "There is a pleasant dirty tale of a

29

nun and her lover," or they said, "Here is the *Three Kingdoms* if you have not already read it and who has not?" They tossed the books before him and still they looked alike to him. He picked up by chance one that had a bright pink cover and said, "What is this one?"

"Why, what you see," the bookseller said carelessly, pointing to the letters on the back.

Lao Er laughed, shamefaced. "The truth is I cannot read."

That man could not believe what he heard. "Why then do you buy a book?" he inquired. "Why do you not buy sweet stuff or a toy or a piece of cloth for a new coat or a silver earpick or anything except a book?"

His voice was so full of scorn that Lao Er was angry. "I will buy a book, but it shall not be yours," he said sharply and turned away. He would go to his elder sister's house and if her husband were at home he would ask him what was a good book and then he would come back and buy it from the table next this old man's and before his very eyes.

He strode off down the crowded street and across three others and came to the shop where his sister's husband was the master. It was a shop for foreign stuff, full of all sorts of wares, foreign flashlights and rubber shoes and bottles of all kinds, cakes and foods in tin boxes, and garments of knitted yarns in all colors and pens and pencils and dishes and framed pictures of fat white women with round blue eyes. Usually Lao Er could spend all the time he had looking at one thing after another in the cases locked under glass tops, but today he went straight through the shop to the court behind where his sister lived, and the two clerks knowing him let him pass.

There he found his sister's husband holding his last child on his knee as he leaned back in a rattan chair fanning himself. The man was fat for his age and he was now naked to the waist, his body soft and pale as a woman's. Around his pale smooth wrists were rings of flesh and his fingers were fat and pointed.

All his friends cried that he was getting rich since he ate and drank so well, and he laughed and let them think it.

"Ah, my wife's brother," he cried when Lao Er came in. "Sit down—sit down!"

He raised himself a little, but not more than he needed to do for the younger brother of his wife, and he bellowed for her to come.

"Here is your second brother, mother of my son!" he bawled.

She came running out, her coat loose at the neck and her round face cheerful as it always was.

"There you are, brother," she shouted at Lao Er, though he was only a few feet away, "and how are the old ones and all the others? And why does my sister-in-law never come to see me? Is she with child yet? Why, what a puny man you are!"

She threw out these words one after the other like bubbles from her full red mouth, laughing between them and with them until words and laughter were all mixed together. Then she ran back and brought out some foreign cakes such as came from the shop and she poured out fresh tea for him.

Then Lao Er told all the news and toyed with the child and listened to his sister's husband tell how good business could be if only the students would not preach night and day against the buying and selling of foreign goods, since left to themselves people never asked where goods came from, and what had business to do with such matters as students and love of country. When all had been said then he could put the matter of the book to his brother-in-law.

Now this brother-in-law, Wu Lien by name, could read because he was a city man and his father and grandfather had been city men before him. But each in his generation had taken for his wife a woman from outside the city walls and this was because women in the city after a generation or two grow soft and sleep long in the day and sit late at night gambling with bamboo pieces, and will not suckle their own children and are too easily willing for their husbands to take concubines. And so Wu Lien had read plenty of books in his youth, and even now he read them often when the day was hot in summer or when in winter it was cold in the shop and the best place to sit was beside a brazier of coals in his own room. He put the child down from his knee and spoke gravely as a man ought when he speaks of letters.

"There are books for every need," he said. "It must first be asked why the book is wanted and who is to read it. If a man wishes to read it secretly and for his own private pleasure there are books for that. If he is tied to his house and cannot travel and he longs to travel, there are books for that. If he likes to think of poison and murder and dares not commit such deeds himself there are books for that. For what is your book wanted?"

Lao Er grinned half in shame and then made up his mind to tell the truth.

"Why, here it is, brother," he said. "I married my woman thinking her like any other one, and now I find out she can read and yearns after a book. She cut off her long hair to sell, even, that she might buy a book and without telling me why when she did it. So, instead of a pair of earrings I had promised her, I said I would buy a book for her, and that is why I am here today. But how can I tell one book from another?"

"You should have asked her what she wanted," Wu Lien said and Lao Er agreed.

"But I never thought of such a difference in books," he said.

Wu Lien pondered the matter a moment and then he turned to his own wife who sat there listening to all this with her mouth open. "You are only a woman, mother of my son," he said, "and if you could read what would you like to read?"

The idea of reading set her to laughing behind the hand she always put in front of her face when she laughed because her teeth were black.

"I never thought of it," she said. But when she saw her city

32

husband look at her with impatience on his fat face she took her hand away and made herself grave and considered what he had asked.

"When I was a child in the village," she said, "I used to hear the old one-eyed man who told stories tell about certain robbers who lived near a lake. When he told them, every one, man or woman or child, they all leaned forward to hear what would come next and when he paused at some point where a man lay caught in a trap or a battle was about to be fought and passed his basket for pennies, they rained into it like hail on a ripe rice field."

Wu Lien looked at her proudly.

"You have hit on exactly the right book," he said. "That is the one, my brother," he said. "It has everything in it, and all the women who deceive their husbands are punished and the righteous prevail. It is a naughty book sometimes, but the naughty ones are always punished and go down in battle before the others. The name of the book is *Shui Hu Chuan,* and it is full of righteous robbers. Yes, I read that book when I was a small boy and I could read it again."

He began to pull his fat underlip, smiling as he did so, and remembering the pleasure he had once had in the book. Lao Er rose and repeated the name of the book and thanked them and bade them good-by and was making his way through the shop, now crowded with many customers, when he was stopped by the sound of quarreling voices. These voices shouted so loud and so suddenly that everybody stopped buying and turned their heads toward the wide door of the shop. Lao Er found himself held there by an army of young men with rocks and sticks in their hands.

In front of them was their leader, a tall young man who wore no hat and his long hair fell over his eyes. He brushed it away and shouted at a clerk to open a case. When the clerk delayed, he took up the rock in his hand and crashed it through the glass of the locked case.

"Enemy goods!" he cried in a high voice.

He put in both his hands and lifted out watches and pens and trinkets and threw them into the street, and the moment he did this all the young men rushed in and began to break the cases and to throw out the goods, and a great groan went up from the customers at such waste of good stuff, though there were some who seized what they could get and made off with it, and as fast as the stuff was thrown into the streets, the people there fell upon it. When the young men saw this they were twice as angry as before and they rushed out and beat the people with their sticks and cracked their heads with the rocks they held until the people fell back. Then some of the young men stood guard over the goods that the others threw out and set fire to ·them, and shirts and coats and blankets and knitted goods and hats and shoes went into the fire. All around the blaze the crowd stood, their hungry eyes fixed in horror upon such waste but no one dared to say a word. Lao Er stood there, his mouth hanging open at all he saw, but he, too, did not dare to say a word. His brother-in-law did not come nor was there any sign of a clerk left now in the shop, and who was he, one man, to speak if these did not? He watched until his heart was sickened and he went away.

He was halfway to the city gate before he remembered that he had forgotten to buy his book, and so he turned back to the street of booksellers and went to the table next to the little bitter man and asked for the book. The bookseller tossed it to him, a thick old book dirtied with many who had read it.

"A dirty book like this must be cheap," Lao Er said, looking at the spots of grease and black.

"So it might have been a few days ago," the bookseller said, "but in the past few days many of the students have come to buy this book who never read it before. Ask me why and I have no answer. I do not know why they do anything, those young ones. They are like drunk men and as for the women—" He spat on the stone on which he stood and rubbed it with his foot.

"What is the price?" Lao Er asked.

"Three silver small pieces," the bookseller replied.

Lao Er stared in horror.

"For a book?" he shouted.

"Why not for a book?" the old man retorted. "You spend as much on a piece of pig's meat and you eat it and it is gone and what is left is waste. But a book you put into your mind and there it lies and you can read it over when you forget it and think of it longer and out of it who knows what you will think? You might think yourself to fortune."

So Lao Er reached into his girdle and took out the money and paid it, and then was angry because the old man next who had been watching all this time smiled sourly and said,

"If you knew the name of a book why did you not speak it? I have that book." And he took it up, clean and whole, from his table.

In spite of his anger Lao Er could only go on, saying as he went, though he wished he had the clean one, "I had rather have the dirty one from him than a clean one from you after this morning, you turtle's egg," and so he went homeward.

And yet he had not left that street before he thought he ought to go and see his sister's husband's shop again and how they did and if the ruffians had gone or not. So he wound his way there once more and when he reached the place the shop was boarded up and only a heap of ashes lay in the street. A few beggars and children searched these ashes for buttons and bits of metal but the people came and went about their business as though they had seen this sight many times before.

He stood asking himself whether or not he should go in and see whether the ones within were well or not, but before he did so it came to him that he ought first to think of his own parents

35

and their distress if he should be tangled in this trouble, and the more especially did he hesitate because upon the boards there were scrawled in white chalk some great fierce-looking letters. He stared at the letters a long time but nothing came from them to his mind, and at last he turned to an elderly, learned-looking man in a long black robe who happened at that moment to be passing.

"Sir, will you tell me what these letters say?" he asked.

The man paused and put on his horn-rimmed spectacles that he drew out of his bosom pocket and pursed his lips and read the words a few times to himself. Then he said:

"These letters say that what has happened to this house shall happen to every like house that sells enemy goods, and if it is not enough, life itself will be taken from those who sell or buy enemy goods."

"Sir, thank you," Lao Er said in alarm. The words were as fierce as they looked, and he knew that in duty to his parents he ought to leave this spot at once and hasten to the safety of his own home, and in no way let it be known that he had any kinship to this house. This he did, and under his arm he held the book for Jade, wrapped up in the strip of blue cotton which he wore otherwise around his neck to wipe the sweat from his face if he were hot. These were strange days, he thought to himself, when in a morning one could see what he had seen. He made haste to leave the city where such things could happen and he hurried home and he was glad for the peace of the fields and the clear calm sky.

When he came home he gave the book to Jade, but even the book was forgotten today in what he had to tell them all. There in the courtyard they all listened to him and Pansiao, his youngest sister, stopped her loom and came out too to hear. When he had heard all, Ling Tan drew on his water pipe a while. Then he spoke.

"Did you ask what was the name of this enemy?"

Lao Er's face went slack at this question.

"Curse me for a fool," he said, "I never did think to ask who the enemy was!"

And he was dazed for a while at his own stupidity.

. . . But all that happened in the city was very far from these who lived in this house. Night fell there as it always did and they ate and made ready for sleep as on any other night and each felt in his own way that here on the land nothing could be changed, whatever folly the city people committed against each other. Ling Tan and his wife talked together for a little while before they slept, anxious for their elder daughter, and Ling Tan said he wished that he had given her after all to a farmer with half the promises that Wu Lien had made. But his wife would not agree to this.

"She is no longer of our house," she told her husband, "and what happens to her is her husband's business now since she has given him two sons. Tomorrow if they are in trouble they will find a way to send us word and then we will see if there is need to worry."

He listened to this and willingly put his worry aside, and soon over these two stole the quiet of the house in which they had lived so many years and the quiet of fields they had tended so long, to which they trusted for food and for all they needed. Whatever befell, the earth which they owned was theirs and would feed them.

And Lao Ta in his room where he lay on his bed with his wife while she suckled her child to sleep told her what he thought of the thing that had happened to his sister's husband.

"Such things come of foreign learning," he told her. "These students, nowadays, they do not know the ancient righteousness and they have no measure whereby to measure themselves. This seems right to them today and that tomorrow and they do not know that one man's mind cannot say what is the true right

37

for another. No, in their pride of a little learning they rush out to do evil like this."

"We will never let a child of ours go to those schools," his wife murmured, and fell asleep with the babe still tugging at her breast.

"We will not," he agreed and lay thinking further. He thought slowly and with difficulty and sweated at it as though he were plowing a rough field behind the water buffalo. At last, having made a thought, he spoke it aloud for his wife to hear. "A man should stay in his own house," he said, "if he stays in his own house and does the work he knows how to do and cares for his own, who can destroy him? If every man so behaves himself, what enemy can prevail against the nation?"

He waited for his wife to agree with this but first there was only silence and then came the sound of her gentle snore. He felt a little angry that his wisdom was so wasted but he was too good-hearted a man to wake her as some men would because she slept before he did, and so he let his hard thinking subside, and soon the quiet of the house stole over him too, and he slept.

And Pansiao, who spent her days at the loom, who never went to the city, she could not imagine the thing she had heard and it was so strange it went out of her mind like a dream told. In the house she had been kept a child. She was the last born and born indeed so late that her mother had been ashamed. To conceive, to bear a child when Ling Sao was more than forty years old had made everyone who heard of it smile, and in the village the women called out to her as she grew big:

"What vigor, old one!" and they laughed and said, "a good sow is not too old as long as she litters."

This shame had put a cloud upon the child, and since in the village, nothing was hidden from anyone, Pansiao knew that her birth had brought mockery upon her mother. Her very name carried the mockery, though this had not been meant. Ling Tan's old third cousin had chosen for her the name Pansiao, or Half-

38

Smile, a pretty name, though one too bookish for a farmer's daughter. But the cousin could not deny himself the pleasure of such a name and Ling Tan had let it pass, thinking the matter of small account since the child was a girl. But when the villagers heard the name they put their own meaning into it. "Half-Smile—Half-Smile," they said with laughter, and thereafter the name could not be changed.

Now, as Pansiao grew, she had grown like her name, and she was a gentle, half-smiling, half-sad young girl, never feeling herself wholly welcome anywhere, and eager, therefore, to do all she could to win welcome. But she was often weary, not being as strong as her mother's other children, and so tonight, though she had listened with wonder to what her second brother had to tell, once she had laid herself down to sleep, she slept.

And Lao Er and Jade, too, had already forgotten. For she had opened the book and by the small light of the bean-oil lamp on the table she began to read the characters slowly aloud and Lao Er listened and watched her pretty lips. It was magic, he thought, that her eyes could pick up these letters which to him were like bird marks on the paper and her eyes gave them to her voice and her voice spoke them to his ears so that he could perfectly understand them.

He understood them and yet what filled his mind was his delight in Jade and in watching her eyelids moving up and down the page and the little finger with which she pointed at one letter and another. She read softly, singing the words out as a story-teller does, and he was suffocated with his pride and his love and had to tell her so, lest he burst himself.

"I hope no evil lies ahead of me," he said, "because I am so wicked I love you more than I love my parents, and if there were food enough only for them or for you, I would give it to you and let them starve, and let the gods forgive me if they can for it is the truth."

She looked up from her page and then her face went red and white and her voice faltered and she put the book down.

"I cannot read when you keep watching me," she said, and her smile trembled on her lips.

"But since I cannot look at the book and know what it says, I must look at you," he said.

And she, to divert his mind from shaming her and making her shy with his love, took this moment to cry out. "Oh, and I forgot I was going to teach you to read, too," and so she put the book on the table and made him bend over with her and repeat after her the characters at which she pointed. He was obedient and did as she said, but all the time his mind was out of his body and hovering about hers, and he learned nothing. When at last they went to bed together he had forgotten the day as though it had never been and this house in which he was born was his world.

Of all the ones who lay in that house only Lao San, the third son, was thinking of what his brother had seen. His bed was a bamboo couch in the main room of the house because there was no room for him to have for his own, though his father promised to add a room for him and his wife when he married. Upon this couch the boy lay restlessly turning and not able to sleep, imagining to himself the young men who had destroyed that fine shop. Who were they, and who was the enemy they cried against? It came to him that there were many things in the world that he did not know, and he wondered as he often did how he could learn them if he stayed on and on in his father's house.

He grew tired of turning at last and he rose from his bed as he did sometimes when he could not sleep and went into the shed where the buffalo was tied. The great silent beast had lain himself down on the earth for the night and the boy pulled some straw out from under its muzzle and curled himself against the warm hairy body. This dull familiar presence calmed him and he too fell asleep.

By the time that the late summer dusk grew into darkness the house in the midst of the fields was as silent as one of the graves of the ancestors. But it was no grave. It stood full of life, sleeping but eternal. An aged and crooked moon shone down upon the water in the fields and upon the silent house, as hundred years upon hundred years the moon had so shone, when it was young and when it was old.

III

THIS Ling Tan was a man who lived his life both wide and deep, though he seldom stepped off his own land. He did not need to wander, since where he was there was enough. Thus under the skin of the land which he tilled as his fathers had before him there was the body of the earth. He did not, as some do, own only the surface of the earth. No, to his family and to him belonged the earth under their land, and upon this possession Ling Tan used often to ponder. What, he would ask himself in the long pleasant days of lonely plowing, or longer tilling against weeds among the young crops, what lay beneath this soft black skin of the earth in which were held the roots of his seedlings?

He had once in his youth dug a well for his father and for the first time he had seen what lay under their fields. First there was the deep thick crust of the earth, fertile and loose with the tilling of his forefathers and with their waste which they poured back into it year after year. This earth was so rich that almost it was quick enough to spring into life of its own accord. Fed for growing and nurtured for harvest, it lay hungry for seed as a woman is, eager to be about its business.

This earth he knew. But under it was a hard yellow bottom of clay, as tightly packed as the bottom of a pan. How did that yellow bottom come there? He did not know nor did his father, but there it lay to catch and hold the rain for the roots that needed it. And beneath that yellow clay was a bed of rock, not solid, but splintered and split into thin pieces, and between these was grayish sand. And under this bed was still another, strangest of all, for here were pieces of tile and scraps of blue pottery and when Ling Tan dug the well, he even found an old silver coin of a sort he had never seen before and then a broken white pottery bowl and at last a deep brown jar, glazed and whole and full of a gray dust. He had taken these things to his father, and father and son they had looked at them.

"These were used by those from whom we sprang," his father had said. "Let us put them into the tombs with your grandparents." So they had done, and then Ling Tan went on digging and out of those depths clear water spouted forth one morning like a fountain, and never to this day had the well failed.

Yet beneath that river, he used often to muse, this earth of his went on. Others had owned it and lived on it and had become part of it themselves, for it was a common saying of the old men in the village that if a man could dig deeply enough in his own land or any land, he would find, five times over, the roots and ruins of what had once been great cities and palaces and temples. Ling Tan's own father's father in his time had once dug deep for a grave for his father, and had found a small dragon, made of gold, such as might have fallen from the roof of an emperor's palace, and he had sold it for enough to buy himself a little concubine he craved. Ill luck it was, too, so the story had come down from generation to generation, for that woman was evil and robbed his house of peace and goods and he was helpless whatever she did because he loved her and through this love they all but lost the very land they had, and would have lost it if his old wife, seeing what havoc was about to fall upon them, had not given the concubine timely poison. Even then it was evil enough, for the man, when his concubine was dead, killed himself, but at least the land was still his sons' possession. But after that it was always told that the concubine was somehow faery

43

and that the dragon was no true dragon but a fox spirit that had entered into the body of the pretty girl the man loved too well.

Whether all this was true or not, there the land was, and it went deep down beyond fountain and river and rock and as long as he lived it belonged to Ling Tan as far as it went down and to his sons after him.

The whole earth, he had heard, was round. This at least a young man had told who came preaching of many curious things to the village one summer's day. He came, he said, to help the common people and to do them a good deed by what he called teaching, and because the people in the Ling village were courteous and kind they were willing to listen, especially as it was a feast season and they were not working. So they listened to tales of the roundness of the earth and to the wickedness of flies and the young man showed them pictures of flies as large as tigers, which he held up for them to see. The women cried out when they saw flies so big but Ling Tan told them afterwards to calm themselves, since it was only in foreign countries that flies were like that. Here they were small harmless things that a man could pinch between thumb and finger if he wished, but who cared whether they lived or not, since they had no sting and did no hurt?

That the whole earth was round he found it hard to believe, and he often thought of that young man, a good young man and doubtless a pilgrim of some religion, doing a penance for his soul by walking from one village to another preaching his knowledge. Thus when Ling Tan found among his melons a round one he would think, "That is as the earth is." But what he could not comprehend was how, if the earth were round, men on the bottom side could walk. Yet when he talked of this in the tea shop one evening, his third cousin said that it could be true because he had heard that the people on the other side of the earth did all the opposite of what it should be done. Thus, he said, their children were born with white hair that grew dark as they grew older, and they pushed a saw away instead of pulled it to them, and they put cloth on the floor instead of on their beds, and all they did was reasonless and mad. So, he said, it might be true that they even walked with their heads hanging down and liked it.

Of such things Ling Tan mused as he tilled his earth and it moved him to laughter to think that somewhere very far below the spot where he stood his land went on and on until at last foreigners stood on it and doubtless planted seed on it and took their harvests from it as though it were their own.

"I ought to ask them for my rent," he would think and grin until one of his sons seeing him grinning under his big bamboo hat called out to know why he was merry, and then Ling Tan said:

"I have just thought that on the bottom of this land of mine somewhere a foreigner reaps his grain without asking me and I could have the law on him if I knew how to tell him so."

His little black eyes sparkled and his sons laughed with him. Not one of them had ever seen a foreigner close, though in the city there were some scores of them living peacefully and doing their business. Ling Tan had once asked a man who served in a foreign house and who had come into the country to search for fresh hen's eggs if his master walked head down or up, and the man had said, up, as he did, and Ling Tan respected the foreigner the more for learning wisdom when he came here. But the foreigner on the other side of his land grew to be a joke in Ling Tan's household, and if the soil grew dry he would pretend to grumble that the foreigner on the other side had drained it, or if his turnips came up smaller than they should, he said the foreigner was pulling at the roots. By this means all the household came to have a friendly merry feeling toward foreigners everywhere, though truly they knew none except in this merry fashion. And yet because of it, if a strange man had come to the house and said he was a foreigner, Ling Tan would have asked him to come in and sit down and drink tea and eat a meal with them.

But Ling Tan owned not only the earth as deep as it went beneath his feet but he owned the air above his land as far as it went up. The stars over his land were his stars and beyond them whatever there was was his. Of them he knew nothing for none could tell him of the heavens. To him the stars were a handful of lights, lanterns, jewels perhaps, toys and decorations, things for beauty rather than use, like a woman's earrings. They did no harm and what their good was he did not know except that he was glad they were there, else the sky would have been too black above his head at night.

But sometimes he thought they followed the moon, perhaps, or splintered themselves from the sun. For that there was enmity between sun and moon in the sky everybody knew. Two or three times in his lifetime this enmity had blazed into battle and sun would try to swallow moon or moon would swallow sun, and then everywhere people were frightened and shouted and cried and screamed into the sky and beat gongs and hollow drums and empty rice cauldrons or whatever they had at hand to make a noise. After the noise grew great enough the sun and moon would give heed to it and slowly they drew apart and went back to their own ways again. But if they had not heard the commotion from the earth, they would have fought until one had downed the other somehow, and then half the light from heaven would have perished, and worse if the sun had lost and been swallowed by the moon. But whatever the stars were, they were his, Ling Tan thought, if they were above his land, and he used to wonder if in another life his would be the power to reach up and pull a star down and hold it in the palm of his hand, and if he did would it burn there?

Such were Ling Tan's thoughts and they were mingled with others that had to do with the cost of grain and the measure of his harvest and whether or not he ought to divide the land among his three sons when his time came to go into earth himself, or ought he to let the eldest have it and the second help him. But if he did this then would there be food enough for the third one when he married and begat his own sons and then would they not quarrel because their bellies were not full? For Ling Tan knew out of his common wisdom that when men have land enough to give them food they have nothing to quarrel about beyond the small things that a night's sleep can change. But when land is the cause of quarrel men will quarrel to killing each other.

He put the matter to his eldest son one day, not because he felt himself old and beyond work, but a man's years are lived when they are lived and there is a time for everything, and now was the time to plan and to think while his mind was strong in his strong body.

"Can this land feed three men and their wives and children after I am gone?" he asked his eldest son.

Lao Ta was at that moment drawing water out of the well by rope and bucket and he drew it up and drank first and then splashed what was left over his bare shoulders and arms.

"It can, if you ask me if I am willing to have it so," he said. "For I will eat less meat if my brothers will and live in peace with them."

More than this Ling Tan did not ask because he was satisfied with the answer and with his eldest son's honest looks. He could leave the land to him and know that whatever it bore this eldest son would divide equally among all, and if the others did not like it, they could go elsewhere and Ling Tan's dust would not stir in its sleep, because he had done well enough in his time.

. . . To such things as stars and sun and moon Ling Sao gave no thought. What, she would have said, had they to do with her? The house was full of matters she must think about and manage and mend, and its lives all looked to her. Thus her

47

smallest grandson as month followed month did not know which was his true mother, the one from whose soft breast he drank, or the strong big woman who took him often and carried him astride her hip while she came and went, and fed him with sweetened rice from her lips. Mother and grandmother were one to him. And her sons, though Ling Sao wanted them married and married early so that there need be no foolishness in the house, still she knew that no young woman could be to her sons what she was, and she loved to hear their voices, now the voices of men, call to her as once they had called in little childish piping, "M-ma!"

"Yes, my meat dumpling!" she always answered, and no one thought it strange that so she answered even to her eldest son, himself a father, when he came to her to get a button mended or the thong of a sandal secured. For Orchid was one of those women who when they have given birth are in a daze at what they have done and she could think of nothing but her last child and she would sit idle staring at him and listening to him breathe while he slept and think that she was busy and too busy to tidy their room or to sew a rent in her husband's coat or to make a shoe sole. For this the mother cursed her secretly and complained about her to her husband.

"That Orchid," she grumbled one night in bed, "she has this last child and now she has no time for anything else even the elder one. And if it were not for me our son himself would starve and go in rags like a beggar. She can do nothing but sit and look at the child, though he is still so small that put him anywhere and there he lies. What when he crawls and walks and what when there is a third and a fourth? Why, when I had a child I counted it nothing. Do you remember how I tended the fields and cut the wheat and harvested it and bore the second child and how I put the two of them in a tub and did my work and no ill came to them? But she—oh, the last child's breath will

48

stop if she does not see it come in and out, and the child might swallow a mite of dust out of a beam of sun falling upon it!"

"There are not many women like you," Ling Tan agreed, half asleep.

"And Jade," Ling Sao mourned. "What use is Jade to me? Her mind is on that book our second son brought her. Yes, when her child comes—"

Ling Tan woke up. "Is Jade to have a child, too?"

She pursed her lips in the dark. "Her flux has stayed itself ten days beyond its usual coming," she said solemnly, for, being a good mother to her sons, Ling Sao knew it was her duty to question her sons' wives of such things. "And what she will do when the child comes if she has not finished reading that book I do not know." She went on, "She will hold it in her hand, I swear, and let the child be born anyhow. It was an evil day when a book came into this house, and there is nothing so bad for a woman as reading. I had rather she took to opium."

"No, not opium," he said. "I saw that curse in my own old mother and never will an ounce of opium come into this house."

"Well, then, not opium," his wife agreed. For she knew what ill had befallen this house when Ling Tan's mother in the forty-sixth year of her age had begun to smoke opium to soften a pain she had in her womb. Food and clothing, she cared nothing if she had neither, but the opium she must have, and she lay with her eyes half shut night and day, dreaming and sleeping and waking only if they tried to cure her of the habit. Nor had they heart to try very much, for the pain grew hard and strong in her and only with opium could she draw her breath. Seven years the thing had gone on and more money had been wasted in the buying of opium than had been spent in food or clothing, and worse than that, for in those years opium was made a forbidden thing by the magistrates and if any bought or sold or used the stuff he took his life into his hands. Ling Tan's father knew this, and so he forbade his son to buy it and he himself went to secret places to get it, telling no one, and it came to be so dangerous a thing to do that each month or so when Ling Tan's father knew he must go yet again to buy he arranged all his affairs with his son and warned him that if he did not come back he must not go out to search for him, because he would be in prison and beyond any hope of rescue and Ling Tan must behave him as though he were dead and remember that it was his duty to live on.

Time and again the two looked at each other knowing that it might be the last time, and not so long as he lived would Ling Tan forget that brave wrinkled face looking into his as his father risked himself yet once again for his old wife. He was glad at last when within three days a cholera carried both of them off and his mother first, so that his father could die in peace, knowing that his son had not to make the dangerous journeys in his place. So opium was for Ling Tan the destroyer of all peace, and he rejoiced when it grew yet more difficult and dangerous to buy and always more forbidden until now it was a thing scarcely ever heard of that any but the very rich could smoke an opium pipe.

But when Ling Sao took to brooding over her children she could not easily give over. Now her mind ran on in the peace and darkness. "And that little daughter of ours," she said. "What will we do about the weaving when Pansiao is married? She is in her fifteenth year and it is time to be thinking of some one for her, and Jade ought to learn the loom in her place. Now it is your duty to tell our second son so, and you must tell the eldest son that his wife shall help me more in the house, for when I am gone she will have to take my place, and Jade ought to learn to tend the weaving, and when we find a wife for the last boy, we must find a good strong one to work in the fields with him, and so every part of our life will have the one to tend it when we are not here."

Ling Tan did not answer, for by this time he was far gone in sleep. Nothing so soothed him to sleep as the sound of his wife's voice talking of house and child. She went on, tempted the more by silence and no answer from him.

"And though I said we need not worry about our eldest daughter since she is no longer of our house, still I do worry, because after all I gave her birth and suckled her, and I wish I knew how she was and if her husband has his shop in order again and how it is with them all. Curse me that I cannot rid myself of worry even about her!"

Now Ling Tan snored and so told her that she could expect no answer from him, and she fell silent, and thought how when it came to the bottom of anything she had to do it herself and she could never understand why it was that men were children their lives long for all their windy talk. When a thing had to be done in the house a woman must do it, and she made up her mind that tomorrow, though the rest of them starved, she would walk into the city and see for herself how her daughter was and especially the two little children.

"And if I see any young new-fashioned students there spoiling my son-in-law's shop, I am not afraid," she thought. "I shall go after them myself and beat them and jerk their noses, and what can anybody do to me, who am only an old woman?"

Thus planning she comforted herself and fell asleep in peace.

... The moment Ling Sao woke she remembered what she had decided to do, and she rose long before any other awoke and began to set the house ready for her day's absence. There was not a thread of daylight yet in any window and the stars shone as large and soft in the black sky as though it were midnight, but she knew by her inward measure what the hour was. By the time she was dressed and the house swept and the rice washed it would be near cockcrow.

So it was that just as she had given the rice its third washing and put it into the cauldron and covered it with water she heard the cocks calling from village to village to each other. Ling Tan would stir in his sleep at this noise and though he did not wake

51

at cockcrow he never slept so deeply afterwards, knowing even though he was not awake that soon he must rise for the day.

It was too early still to light the fire, so Ling Sao went creeping into the bedroom and brought out the little box where she kept her combs, and she set this open beside the candle on the table in the court, and rubbing off the small mirror that she could see clearly she began to comb and oil her hair so she might enter decently her daughter's house. She scarcely needed a mirror, for she had all her life smoothed her hair back in the same way, braiding it when she was a girl and wore a fringe over her forehead, and then rolling it into a knot when her mother had pulled out her fringe the day before her wedding. The hair went back of its own accord now and scarcely needed oil, it lay so smooth by habit. But she tied it with a strong red cord before she knotted it and then smoothed it back with the oil she made herself from the shavings of the slippery wood of a certain elm tree put into water. This done she twisted the knot over her long silver pin that had the blue enameled ends, the same pin she had as a part of her wedding goods, with two rings and a pair of earrings and an earpick with a toothpick on the other end and this she always thrust into her knot ready for use when she needed it.

When she had finished her hair and washed her face and rinsed her mouth she no longer needed the candle and it was time to cook the rice for the morning meal and set out the salt carrot and the salt fish to go with it to send it down. One by one they got up in the house and Jade and her second son were always last. She allowed this yet for a while, for the first year of their marriage was not finished yet, but when it was finished she would tell them that they too must rise with the others to work.

Not one of them but saw the moment they looked at her that she was ready for some unusual thing today. She had on her best undercoat of white cotton cloth, and her newest shoes with the heels turned down because they were still tight in the toes and she had put her gold earrings into her ears.

Ling Tan stared at her when he saw her.

"What now, mother of my sons?" he asked.

"I fell to thinking in the night," she said, "and so I thought to go and see the elder girl after all and find out how she is and the children and their father."

"How can you go into the city alone?" he asked.

Ling Sao tossed her head at this. "Do I fear any man?" she asked.

So she ate her food and called out to her daughter and her sons' wives what they should do while she was gone. "Orchid, you must tie your smallest son to your back and get your hands free for once and you must prepare the food, and, Jade, you shall keep the fire going for her so that the smoke will not harm my grandson's eyes, and as for Pansiao she must weave as she ever does, except that if your father wants anything, child, then you must answer his call, for the other two have their own husbands, and as for you, my third son, if you want anything ask your sister. The tea must be kept hot in the basket, and do not put any food by for me, for I will eat myself full at my daughter's house and enough to last me until tomorrow. She always buys some extra meats for me, or sends out and fetches in sweets and dumplings. I shall eat enough for two days."

They all listened to her, and Ling Tan went into his room and brought out some money for her to spend, which she made much show of refusing.

"Why should I waste our good silver? Be sure I will not take it! Keep it to buy seeds with in the autumn. Besides, I want nothing. If you give me a gift I cannot say I want anything."

But Ling Tan pushed it toward her laughing, and so in the end she took it as she had planned to do from the beginning and as he knew she would. If he had not given it, she would have asked for it, but since he had been so courteous, she felt she too must reply with courtesy.

So at last she was ready to go and they all came with her to the door to wish her a good day, and she set off with a few presents tied into a white handkerchief to give her daughter, six hens' eggs and a handful of ripe peaches and some dried persimmons.

The sun was well up over the mountain when she set out at her usual steady walk, but not high enough in the sky to be hot. It would be hot, though, for there was not a cloud to be seen, and no wind rippled the water in the rice fields. But she was eager for the day, hot or no, because she was hearty enough to like a day now and then different from others, and she liked to go into her daughter's house and see what was new, and to feel the two servants respectful before her because she was the mother of their mistress. That what they gave her was anything like what they showed the mother of her son-in-law was not of course to be expected, yet it was enough to make her know that she was not a common visitor.

She was still so early that every now and again she passed a neighbor carrying his vegetables or straw to the city markets and every now and again one shouted to her to ask her how she did and how her old man was and where she was going. To every one she answered cheerfully and asked him of some small thing she knew of in his household, and all this made the walk seem quick to the city. Nevertheless, the sun was very hot when she entered the deep shadows of the city gate and she was glad of the coolness, and she sat down on a melon vendor's little stool and ate an early melon, though afterwards it made her a little sorry, too, for it lay green for a while in her. But she stopped again and drank some hot tea at a small shop to send it down, and when it was down she felt well again and so at last she came to her daughter's door.

The shop was open and the two clerks there, but not all the cases were full nor was all the glass mended. She went about looking for what used to be there and she saw that much of it was gone. What was left were such cloth and small goods as

54

could be bought in any little village shop. All the bright things, the strange foreign things, the lamps and lights and toys and straw hats and rubber shoes, the cups and bowls and dishes with flowers on them of a foreign color were gone. She knew then that the loss here had been very great and that her daughter's husband had not dared yet to make it right, and he must fear trouble to come.

So with her full lips pursed together she went back of the shop and found all worse than she had feared. Her daughter's husband sat slack in his chair, his flesh so fallen away that with the fat gone he looked as though his skin were a garment too big for him. Never had she seen such once-fat jowls hang down in such dewlaps, or a belly once full so overhang itself like a windless bag. He lay asleep when she came in and her daughter sat beside him fanning him. When she saw her mother she made a sign for silence and dared not give over fanning.

Ling Sao bent to whisper in her daughter's ear. "Is he ill that he looks so slack?"

"Ill with bad luck," her daughter whispered back. "He cannot eat."

Now Ling Sao knew very well that when a creature, man or woman or beast, cannot eat his food he is on his way toward the grave, and she was frightened at the thought of her daughter a widow so young, and so she stole into the house and without stopping to look at the children or to greet her son-in-law's mother, she rolled up her sleeves and went into the kitchen and pushed aside the servant who stood at the stove.

"Mend the fire for me," she told the woman with such will that the woman obeyed even without greeting. "Begin it small," Ling Sao commanded her. "When I bid you, let it burn up quickly for the space of a hundred breaths. Then make it small again."

Out of the eggs she had brought and with some bits of meat and onion she found in a bowl on the table she made a dish so fragrant with goodness that Wu Lien, waking a little to brush off a fly, smelled it and opened his eyes.

"What is that fine smell?" he asked.

"My mother has brought some new eggs from the country and she is cooking them," his wife replied.

"I can eat them," he said.

When his wife heard this she ran into the kitchen at the moment that Ling Sao was lifting the eggs into a bowl and she seized the bowl.

"He wants them," she cried, and took up some chopsticks as she ran and she gave the bowl to Wu Lien.

Now Wu Lien had eaten nothing or as good as nothing since the day his shop was ruined, and because he was a man who filled himself full three times a day by habit, his hunger was gradually rising in him though he had not known it and thought himself as low as the first day. Here was this good food under his nostrils, eggs such as a city man does not know from birth to death, and he plunged in his two chopsticks and did not take the bowl from his face until it was empty. Ling Sao and her daughter stood watching him, and the two women's eyes turned to look at each other in their pleasure and then back at him again. When he brought the bowl down empty they laughed, and then a great belch of wind came up out of him and they laughed again.

And Ling Sao cried, "I know why I felt I must come here today, and my old black hen who lays an egg once or twice a month laid an egg four days together and the yellow one two eggs, one day after another, and so the gods work their will. Now you are well." She turned to her daughter, "Fetch him the hottest tea he can drink and he will be as good as the first day he was born."

While her daughter did this she sat down and shouted for the youngest child to be brought to her, for Ling Sao was a woman who never felt herself whole unless she had a child on her knees or across her hip, and so while she held her daughter's youngest child naked except for his wetting cloth in her hand under him, she watched Wu Lien drink his hot tea and his last wind came up and while this was going on she talked to him for his good.

"Whatever the ill, you ought not to stop your food or to let your flesh waste away," she said. "You must remember that you have parents and sons and no man belongs to himself but to these before him and after him. If he lets himself be destroyed, or if he destroys himself, the proper relationships are broken off and the nation will fall."

Wu Lien opened his eyes heavily at her. "Who knows but that the nation must fall anyway, old mother?" he said sadly.

Ling Sao looked at her daughter, not understanding such talk.

"That is all he thinks about," the young woman said. "Over and over again he says the nation will fall."

Ling Sao fanned herself briskly. "The nation is nothing except the people and we are the people," she said. "You, Wu Lien, ought not to consider that one day of ill luck can overthrow you. You must buy more goods and put in your foreign things again and call upon the city to protect you and so take heart."

But Wu Lien only groaned. "I have bad news to tell," he said, "I have saved it in myself for these three days—four days tomorrow, it will be."

Ling Sao interrupted him. "There you have been wrong," she said. "To keep ill news in your belly spoils the liver and dries the gall. Anger and sorrow and ill news—all must come out, for the body's health."

"It is not my private ill fortune," Wu Lien said. "This is ill news for the nation. The East-Ocean enemies have sent their ships to the coast nearest us and their soldiers have stepped upon our land and our soldiers have met them but we are not strong enough for them."

Now Wu Lien knew when he said this that the minds of the

57

two women could not comprehend what he was saying. They had never been away from this city and the countryside around; and to them the two hundred or so miles that lay between here and the coast were like two thousand. They had never sat in a train nor even in a foreign spirit car nor had they been the seven miles to the river port to see a foreign ship. All they knew was that once, years before, these foreign ships had let their guns out against a wandering army in this city, because they held some foreigners, and in the country Ling Tan's household had heard the distant guns like thunder and they had often talked of it, until they forgot it.

"Do you remember those guns you once heard?" Wu Lien now asked. "There are now such guns at the coast, laying waste that city there."

"I remember them," she said comfortably. "I was scraping out the rice cauldron with sand and it clattered in my hands and rang an echo. I cried out to my old man that it was an earthquake. But in the end no harm came of it."

"Harm will come of this," Wu Lien said, groaning. For he was a merchant and twice each year he went to the coast to buy his goods and he knew the city there very well, and he could see what was ahead of him now. The students who had destroyed his goods were only the forerunners of the evil to come. He dared not buy any more such goods, and if he did not, what had he to sell in his shop that could not be bought anywhere?

"Comfort yourself," Ling Sao said. "The sea is very far away, and even the river is far enough. What can they do to us?"

"They have flying ships," he said. It made him angry that these two women would not be afraid and he wanted to make them share his own fears. So he went on to sound as fearful as he could imagine. "Those flying ships can come up from the sea in two hours and let their eggs down on us and burst our house apart into dust and what can we do against them?"

"You shall all come to our village," Ling Sao said stoutly, "I

58

always did say a city is a place full of danger. I can see this little meat dumpling every day if you live in our house. . . . Oh, Heaven, I ought to die!" This she screamed forth suddenly because at this moment the little boy she held let out his water and she, listening to Wu Lien, had forgot to hold the cloth to him and down the water came upon her best coat. There was great commotion and her daughter leaped forward to take the child but Ling Sao would not give him up and they struggled over him.

"No, curse me," she said laughing, "what do I care for his little water? He is not the first child that has used me so, and it will dry in a breath or two."

In the midst of this commotion Wu Lien's old mother came out from her room where she had been sleeping, and so Ling Sao must spring to her feet for that, because Wu Sao's place was above hers, and so she gave her greeting.

"Here I am troubling your household again," she said loudly, "but I heard of the shop and I came to see for myself. Now I tell your son that he is not to let himself be so disturbed. A man ought to eat for his parents' sake, and he with no father, he ought to remember you, Elder Sister, and take care of himself, because his flesh is yours and not his own."

Now this mother of Wu Lien was a woman so fat that she could not walk more than the three or four steps from one place to another and she was too fat to try to talk, because her voice had grown into a whisper, so she nodded and smiled and sat down. As soon as she sat down she began to cough, not as a person ought to cough, but with a deep shaking rumble that made her eyes stand out like fish bladders and her face turn purple. When this began Ling Sao's daughter ran for red sugar and Wu Lien leaped to pour tea for his mother and the maid servant came running out of the kitchen to rub her back and her neck, and what with the child and this old woman by the time quiet

59

was come again, that which Wu Lien was saying had been forgotten, and he did not say it again in his mother's presence.

Instead he excused himself, telling them that he must go into the shop, for suddenly it seemed to him in his anxiety that he could not bear the presence of women. This Wu Lien was not a stupid man. He read a newspaper once or twice a month and he went to the largest tea shop in the city and he listened to all that was said there of what happened everywhere. He knew, therefore, what it might mean if the things he had heard were true. He felt the more fearful for he himself did not hate the East-Ocean people and he saw no good in war at any time, for his business would be ruined and many others with him. Only in peace could men be prosperous, for in war all was lost. This country of his was not like some others he had heard of, where only in war was there work enough to be done. He had often sat listening in the tea shop to those who talked of things they had seen in foreign countries, and this he held was a main difference, that in foreign countries war was a business, but here it had never been.

Now, suddenly weary of all the women's commotion in his house, he made up his mind that he would go to the tea shop for awhile, where for shame he had not been since his shop was ruined, and so he dressed himself in his room, seeing with grief how loose his trousers were around his belly and how long was the tie to his girdle. When he went out he took another way than through the room where the women sat and he went by a side street instead of the main one, and when he came to the tea shop he sat at a small side table instead of the one in the center where he usually sat with his friends. All of them, he knew, must have heard of his shop, and none had come near him, and so he did not know how he stood with them, whether he could still be called a good merchant, or whether he was a traitor. So he waited to find out what he was.

It was not long before he heard. For a little while it seemed good to him to be back here in the place where all were men and where there were no children and women to disturb the talk. But today it was not as usual. The place, though full of men, was silent. In silence men sat and drank their tea, or if they spoke it was only to exchange a few words, and then to fall silent again. Little meat was eaten and there were no full tables of noisy sweating men gorging themselves on good foods and emptying their wine cups to each other. They were all dressed neatly and quietly and none laid aside his coat because he was hot and to let his sweat flow. Instead it seemed as though they were cold with fear.

In his place he sat waiting to see if any would greet him. He ordered some green tea and when a careless small waiter brought it to him and wiped out the bowl with a foul black cloth he had not the courage to reprove him. Instead he blew in it and rinsed it out with the hot tea and drank a bowlful slowly, watching for an eye to catch his. If he were greeted, all would be well. If he were not, then he must know his name had been put up for a traitor. For these students had their revenge not only in destruction but they would print in newspapers and post on walls and on the city gates all those whose goods they had destroyed and call them traitors.

At the moment that he filled his bowl for the second time he did catch the eye of a man he knew, one of his own guild, with whom he had often feasted and drunk tea in this very place. Had all been well, the man would have shouted to him and Wu Lien would have bade him come to his table. But the man's eye slipped over him as though he were a stone.

"I am a traitor," Wu Lien thought heavily. So quickly had the world about him changed that what a few weeks ago was good business today was traitordom.

The tea in his mouth changed to salt water and he put down his copper coins and got up and went away. Down the street at the same book stalls where Lao Er had bought his book he stopped and bought a newspaper, and stood there reading it. That city on the coast, he read, was set afire and in the blaze the armies now fought. He read and groaned aloud to read the name of one good shop after another gone and ruin everywhere. Why it need be so he had no idea. A bare month ago there had been a small trouble in the North. For years there had been head-long talk by students against the East-Ocean people, but what good business man had listened to them? He and his kind prospered and once in a year or so he met an East-Ocean merchant or two who were full of courtesy and kindness, though their tongues were stiff when they spoke any language except their own, and in courtesy he had learned enough of their language to do his business with them. He had no quarrel with them then or now, and what was their quarrel with him?

He felt so bewildered standing there that the old bookseller asked him if his belly pained him or if something were wrong with his vitals. He shook his head at that and folded his paper and went a roundabout way to his house and entered again by the way he had come.

There through the opened window he heard the women's voices still clacking and he shouted for his wife and when she came running he bade her bring his food here that he might eat in peace and when he had eaten he would go into his shop and take inventory of what was there.

"I shall buy no more new goods," he thought sadly. "I am ruined, I and my house, and as long as I live I shall not know why, or why what I have done honorably all my life is now held against me for a crime."

Of this Ling Sao knew nothing. She ate heartily of her daughter's meats and she examined the children from head to foot, and when the old woman went to sleep again and she was alone with her daughter she inquired concerning all her affairs so that she could gauge the measure of her daughter's happiness and success in this house.

"Does your husband like you as well as ever?" she asked her daughter.

"If anything, more," her daughter replied laughing. "He calls for me whenever he wants anything, and it is I who serve him. He gave me a new piece of silk for a coat before the shop was looted and now he says he wishes he had taken much more from the shop and given it to me. He says I am such a woman as he would have asked for had he had the chance to ask."

"But does he go out at night?" Ling Sao asked again, pursing her lips. She did not tell her daughter so, but she knew that if a man speaks too well to his wife she must take care also, lest he speak out of an ill conscience of some sort and praise her to make amends.

"Never," the daughter replied with pride, and so the mother's heart was set at rest. For she never forgot that there were in the city women of a very different kind from her daughter. This daughter was an honest hearty woman who could never even put paint on her face without getting it askew so that anyone could see it, and she was already growing plump and her bosom was full for her last child, and Ling Sao knew that city women keep their bodies thin as snakes, and they have no breasts, and so daintily do they spread their paint and powder that they look almost as though they grew themselves like that except that all know there are no such women.

So at last the end came to a very pleasant day for Ling Sao and she made ready for the walk home again, and in her handkerchief she tied some cake her daughter gave her and she took a last swallow of tea and smelled the two children's cheeks and squeezed their small bodies once more and called farewell to Wu Sao who had spoken only twice all day, once for food and once for tea, and nodded to her daughter, and so passed through the shop where Wu Lien was. But since there were other men there, too, she only bowed to show she knew her manners and then went down the streets.

Never, it seemed to her, had the city looked so prosperous as it did this evening. The shops were full and busy and the streets noisy with vendors and the people came and went laughing and talking. The wind had died down and the night was hotter than the day had been and already there were those who had moved their beds out on the street to sleep there and were now eating their evening meals where they could watch all that went past them. There was laughter everywhere and loud calling back and forth and no one stopped to ask if he knew another's name, but he called anyway and made a joke and to Ling Sao it seemed that all were as merry as though they were of one blood.

"So we are of one blood," she thought in comfort. "People of Han we are, and if these people in the city have their own smell, why, we have ours who live outside the city wall, but still we are all of one flesh."

And so walking homeward and smiling to herself she fell to thinking of a thing she had heard, how foreigners have hair and eyes of any color they happen to be born with.

"I do pity them," she thought, "for if it were I and I could not be sure if what I gave birth to would have black hair and eyes as humans do, how could I give birth? I would cast the child too soon, I know."

So she went on home, and saw how all the fields were fertile. The rice fields were dried and the young rice was beginning to head and there was the promise of fine harvest. All was well with the land and when all was well with the land then everything was well.

At home she found them waiting for her, and each one had done as she had bid. The day away had made her glad to come home again and as she looked from one face to the other, each seemed better than she had remembered. Even Jade seemed better and she looked at that pretty young face and thought, "How can I blame my second son for loving her too well?" And of Orchid she thought, "A soft good soul and I must not be so hard

64

on her." And she took her own little daughter's hand and looked at the calluses that the threads had made and said, "Tomorrow you shall not weave. Let the loom be idle a day, and rub some oil into these hands."

When Ling Sao was mellow and kind the whole house seemed full of health and they all sat enjoying it like heat from a gentle fire or like sunshine that is not too hot or like wind that is not too cold. And thus while they sat and while they ate together, peace filled them, and they listened to all she had to tell and she talked and talked and yet with all her talking she forgot to tell them what Wu Lien had said.

One by one they went to bed until there were left only Ling Tan and she, and when they had made the home right for the night, the dog outside the gate and the third son's bed made and he asleep in it, and the buffalo tied, they too went to bed. Not a sound was over the land except the quiet croaking of the frogs in the ponds. Side by side they lay, and since she had been away from him for a whole day Ling Tan felt his belly move with warmth toward her and he reached out his arms toward her.

"My good old woman," he whispered. "You are the best old woman in the world."

And so even to him she forgot to speak of war.

IV

How then could Ling Tan be prepared for the next day? It was a day like any other. He had slept later than usual in the morning and discovering it he leaped out of his bed. His wife was already up and he heard his eldest son in the court, washing his face and rinsing out his mouth, and the mother was calling to the others to get up because it was day again. A day like any other it seemed, and so they sat down to their morning food, and he directed his sons each to his task for the day. If there was any difference at all it was merely that today he wanted the buffalo to plow and not go out to the hills for grass and so he told his youngest son:

"When you have eaten, take the beast and tie him to the plow. It is time for the second planting of green cabbages."

There was no other difference. The day was clear, and the skies cloudless. Three days ago there had been rain and it was too soon to look for it again. He would plow today and plant to-morrow and the next day there might be rain.

So he went out to his work and his sons went with him and in the house the women set themselves to their tasks and as he went out he heard Ling Sao say to Jade, "Sit before the loom a while and I will show you myself how the threads go and what the shuttle does, and Pansiao, take care of my elder grandson for me."

These were the only differences. He went out and while the

66

sun moved upwards he pushed the plow from the back and his third son pulled the unwilling beast from the front and so the work went on. In the next field his sons went through the rice, pulling the weeds and hoeing the drying earth. When his eyes wandered up and down the valley he saw in every field men like himself and his sons. They were his neighbors and his friends at like work. The year was good. Rain and sun were in proportion to each other, and already the harvest was in full promise. He had nothing to wish for which he did not have, and what he had was enough for any man.

Then how could he be prepared for what he saw? It was at mid-morning that he heard the noise of flying ships. He knew the noise, for now and again he had heard it, but never had it been so loud as this. He looked up and he saw the sun shining upon the silver creatures in the sky, not solitary as he had always seen them before this, but many of them and moving with such grace as he had only seen before in wild geese, flying south across the autumn sky. For one moment he thought these were wild geese out of time. But they came not from north to south, but from east to west, and they came too swiftly for geese.

In a moment they were all but over his head. He had stopped as soon as he saw them and so had every other man working on his land, and they stood, their faces turned upward not in fear but only in wonder at such speed and such beauty. That these were foreign things all knew, for none but foreigners could make machines like them. Without envy and with only hearty admiration Ling Tan and his neighbors watched these silver birds high in the sky and small.

And then they saw a silver fragment come out of one and drift down while the ships went on. Down the silver fragment dropped slanting a little toward the east, and it fell into a field of rice. A fountain of dark earth flew up and this they all saw, still without any fear or knowledge. In simple eagerness to see the thing they ran toward the field, Ling Tan and his sons among the rest, to look for the thing that had fallen. They could not find it. One or two bits of metal they did find, and there was the hole, and the man who owned the field laughed as he stared down into the hole.

"I have wanted a pond on my land for ten years and never had time to dig it and here it is," he said joyfully, and they decided together that such was the purpose of these machines, to dig ponds and wells and waterways where they were wanted. Thirty paces the pond was one way and a little longer the other, and every man paced it off to make sure and envied the man in whose field it had fallen.

So busy were they in this that it was not until their first wonder was over that they thought to hear and to see what was now going on. Then one man did hear over the city these same sounds that had made this hole, and he looked up and saw over the city wall a good three miles away, the rolling smoke as though of great fires. One by one peaks of smoke rose into the still air, slowly, for there was no wind, and they curled upward like black thunder clouds.

"Now what?" Ling Tan called, but no one answered, for none knew. They stood together, so alike in their blue coats that one man looked like another, and watched. Eight fires over the city wall they counted and one small one to the side, and as for the flying ships, they thought them lost in the flames, until suddenly they came soaring back again out of the dark smoke, but this time very high, so that they were only as big as stars in the top of the sky, as they glinted against the sun. Then they turned with the sun and were lost.

Nothing could they make out of the smoke that still grew no less, and every man went back to his work with wonder in his heart. But it was not a market day and since the good weather held and it was time for the cabbage planting before rain came, no one took time to go that day to see what the smoke was and

68

by sundown the smoke was pale and all but gone and so they went home to eat and to rest for the next day's work.

"If the thing is big enough to talk about we will hear of it before we are dead, and so there is no use to go to the city for it," Ling Tan said to his sons as they went home, and they all laughed. And at the supper table they envied together the man who had a pond dug easily in his land.

In the night, in that part of the night when the new moon sinks, when there is darkness until dawn begins to break, Ling Tan heard the dog growl. However deeply he slept he woke instantly if the dog growled, for the beast had been taught to warn the house if anyone came to it by stealth. He heard it bark loudly once or twice and then there was no more barking but he heard a hand beating at the locked gate. He lay a moment pondering what this could mean. If it were a stranger the dog would still be barking. It must be therefore that the dog was suddenly killed or else it was no stranger.

Now there is no man with his full wits in his skull who will get up in the black of the night and open his gate not knowing who stands at it, and so Ling Tan woke his wife and then held her fast to keep her from running out before he decided what to do. For she was an impetuous woman and, as she always said, she feared no man and if there were knocking at the gate her only thought was to open it and see who was there.

"By such haste many a good man full of healthy blood has been felled before he could open his eyes," Ling Tan said, holding to her arm with both hands.

So after a moment's talk while the noise on the gate grew louder they both got up together, and by this time the whole house was roused and their three sons were out of their beds too and so they all went to the gate together, Ling Tan carrying the lighted bean-oil lamp in his hand. Whether to speak or not was the next matter. He decided not to speak but to listen, and what

69

they heard was the dog fawning and whining with joy and not anger.

"It may be he has been fed some sort of good meat," Lao Ta whispered.

Then they heard a voice speaking, and to their astonishment it was a woman's voice.

"Are my father and mother dead, too, that they hear nothing?" These were the words that came clear and loud over the earthen wall, and as soon as they were spoken all knew whose voice it was and Ling Sao ran forward and pulled at the gate.

"It is our eldest daughter," she cried. "But why is she out of her good bed now?"

She threw open the gate and what she saw and what they all saw was beyond what they would have said could be. There stood the eldest daughter and Wu Lien, each with a child, and there was old Wu Sao, on her feet, but dazed as though she did not know where she was or what had happened to her, and they had besides a few bundles of clothing and a teapot and a piece of bedding and a basket of dishes and a pair of candlesticks and their kitchen god.

When the eldest daughter saw her mother and father she broke out into loud crying.

"We are all but dead," she sobbed. "We might have been dead had we been ten feet nearer to the street. The two servants and the clerks lie buried in the ruins. The shop is half gone. We have nothing but our bare lives in our hands."

They all pressed into the gate as they spoke and Ling Tan locked it quickly behind them. Bandits, he thought, bandits had broken into the city. It had not happened in a hundred years, but in ancient times it had happened that robbers out of the hills had swept down and into the city.

"Why were the city gates not locked?" he asked.

"How can city gates be locked against the sky?" Wu Lien asked. He set down the youngest child and looked at himself.

In the long walk the child had wet him up and down until he looked as though he had stood under a rain spout. He looked at himself miserably for he was a man chary even of a child on his knees until it had learned its manners.

"What do you mean?" Ling Tan asked him, holding the lamp high and staring down at him.

"The city was bombed—have you heard nothing?"

"Bombed?" Ling Tan repeated. The word was one he had never heard.

His daughter burst out. "The flying ships came over the city this morning. Well, we gave them no heed, for we were all busy at our affairs, and then I remember one of the clerks called out of the door that it was worth coming to see for there were so many of them. Heaven saved me for I was at that moment suckling the child and I did not run out as I would have done, and my man was still sleeping and so was his mother and the other child was playing at my feet but the two serving women ran out and then I heard such a noise—*pu-túng!* I jumped so that I tore my nipple out of the child's mouth and the earth shook under my feet and such screaming as came from everywhere at once and I screamed and the lime flew from the walls of the house and a beam fell across the table. But that was not the half of the noise. The shop—father and mother—the shop trembled and the north wall fell into a heap, and half our goods are buried there, and the two clerks, and one of them newly married and the other such an honest young man that where shall we find one like him again?"

"What is the use even of an honest man if there is no shop to put him in?" Wu Lien groaned.

All this time Ling Sao's mind was struggling with what came thus into her ears but it was not to be understood and so she gave it up and thought only of those things she could understand, how here in the dark of the night were her child and her

71

little grandchildren and their father and the dazed old woman, all weary and hungry and frightened, and so she cried out:

"We shall find beds for you all, and, Jade, you must light the fire for tea, and, Orchid, drop some wheat noodles into water, and let them eat and sleep, and in the morning we can set ourselves to understanding what is wrong."

To herself she said that it must be more mischief from those students who had first ruined Wu Lien's shop, for she thought it was only his one shop in all the city that was now newly damaged from the skies.

But Jade knew better. She said not a word but she went into the kitchen and Lao Er followed her and bent behind the stove with her and she asked him, lifting her eyebrows:

"Is it not They?"

And he said, "Who but They?"

Long after the food had been eaten and the children quieted and under this roof all were sheltered somehow and asleep, Jade and her husband talked together.

"It means our land lost and our cities taken," Jade said.

"It means that we may all die," he said. He could not bear to think of Jade's body dead and he leaned over her and enfolded her.

They lay without passion, for all their hearts were swelling not with love toward each other but with hate for what they could foresee and with rage because there was nothing they could do to prevent it.

"Why is it that we have not what all others in the world have?" Jade cried into the night. "Why have we not guns and flying ships and battlements?"

"They have been nothing but toys to us," Lao Er answered. "They are of no worth to people like us who love only to live."

And then Jade did not answer and she thought sadly how sweet life was to her now when she was sure that she was with child. To live and to bear children, to enjoy each day as it came, seeing new life grow and to bring more life into being, this was good, and what folly to destroy that which took life to make!

"But if all the world is playing with such evil toys we must learn how to play with them, too," she said at last.

"Still it is folly," he said stoutly.

Long into the night they lay awake thinking of what they must do. They fell asleep at last without knowing.

. . . In the morning there was no thought of work. By the time everyone was so much as fed half the morning was gone, and the rest of the hours they stayed listening to what Wu Lien and the eldest daughter had to tell and even old Wu Sao kept muttering as she wiped her eyes, "It was too much noise—there was such a noise."

Now at last Ling Sao understood what had happened in the city. It was no such small thing as one shop falling. Wherever the silver eggs had dropped and burst, all around fell into dust.

"And the people?" Ling Tan asked.

"Into pieces," Wu Lien replied, "as though they, too, were made of clay. Here an arm, there a head, there a piece of a foot, a leg, entrails, a heart, blood and ends of bone."

Then there was silence. Each looked at the other, but none could fully believe who had not seen.

"But why?" Jade cried for them all.

"Who knows?" Wu Lien said. "The sky is over us all."

His wife was weeping again and so were Orchid and Pan-siao and down Wu Sao's old cheeks were running tears and none could give comfort, for none could say from where death had now come. Death they all knew, for each knew his end, but a kind death, a gentle death stealing like a dream upon the old or like healing upon the sick, leaving the body whole and a thing to be tended and cared for and laid in its bed and honored in the grave. But this new death was monstrous, a destruction beyond the mind of man.

In silence each rose and went at last to his task, the women

73

to preparing the food and caring for the children, and Ling Tan and his sons to the field. Only Wu Lien sat alone and apart, for of fields he knew nothing, nor of plow nor beasts. He was a merchant and when he had no wares he was idle. But this idleness was worse than any he had ever known for he saw no end to it.

. . . Now Lao Er and Jade had made their own meeting place under the big drooping willow that stood on the far side of the pond. They had found it that day by chance when Lao Er had seen Jade before the tea house, and they went back to it again and again. From morning until night they had no moment when they could meet, these two who loved each other. In the house there were always others in every room except their sleeping room, and they were ashamed to go to that room in the day, for these others would have thought it shameful, and if it had been heard of in the village there would have been laughter because they could not wait for the night. So that day Lao Er had seen the deep shadows under thè great old willow and he saw how the branches hung down their strands like a curtain and so now he bade Jade come here sometimes and wait for him, and they talked or they only sat in each other's presence, looking at each other and smiling, or he put out his hand to take hers, and so their day was not so long.

This day when Lao Er went out with his father to work he nodded to Jade and she knew that when it was midday she must go and wait for him under the willow. This she did and she came there before him and sat on the mossy ground to wait for him. It was very still, and the only sound was of a frog leaping into the pool because she was there, that and the steady long drone of a cicada, rising and then falling into a hot whisper and then into silence. It was hard to believe that the world in this valley was not as it had always been, and yet she knew it was not. By the strange chance of the book that her husband had bought for her Jade was able to understand how peace was lost

74

among men, and what men did to each other then. Lust and fighting and killing were what they did in war and even to torture and the eating of human flesh, and all those wild and beastlike things that men do when peace is lost.

"How shall we be saved from this?" she thought, "and how shall we save our child?"

And then she thought of the young man at the tea house that day who had asked the people if they were able to burn their houses and their harvests so that the enemy would not profit by them and how she of all had stood up and said "We are able!"

"But then I had not my child in my belly," she thought.

And she sat and mused on this and wondered that now life itself seemed precious above all else because she was a woman and she was creating new life. What she was made to do must be finished and done and she must put it above all else.

At this moment Lao Er parted the long green fronds of the willow and took his seat beside her and wiped the sweat off his brown body and his face.

"I have been wondering at the change in me," she said, "and how I think of nothing except the life of our child."

"But if it were not so," he said, "there would be an end to all of us. While I worked I thought and now I know what I must do. We will not stay here. We will go away where the enemy cannot reach us, and you shall fulfill your time there."

"Leave your father's house?" she cried. "But what will he say to it?"

"I shall not tell him until I have found an answer to what he will say," Lao Er replied.

He took her hand and held it a while, thinking how sweet it was to have her gentle as she had been ever since she knew she was to have the child. And she sat clinging to his hand and thinking how sweet it was when she had her task to do to know that he would watch over her and make her safe while she did it. The old wilful restlessness had gone out of her for the time.

"Whatever you think I should do I will do it," she said.

"And I will do it with you," he said.

It was enough for them for the moment. He rose and went back to his work and she went back to the loom which she was learning. Waste it was, perhaps, to learn it, if she were going away, but still some time it might be useful to her to know how to make cloth.

"Where were you?" Ling Sao asked when she came in.

"I went out to meet my husband," Jade replied calmly and let the mother wonder why she was not ashamed to say it, and so she too went back to work.

. . . Now it happened that the next time the flying ships came back Ling Tan himself was in the city. In their ignorance it is true that he and his sons and even Wu Lien thought the ships were finished when they came and went and that they would come no more, and so did many people in the city think so, and they began building and mending and making what they could out of their ruins. Not one of them thought that the evil would come again any more than an earthquake would return the next day or a thunder storm or any other evil sent by heaven. Thus Ling Tan that morning had told his sons to work without him because he was going into the city to see what was to be seen. He went alone, that two need not leave work, but when he had left his house he heard behind him footsteps running in the dust, and turning, he saw his youngest son.

"Now, then!" Ling Tan cried.

"Father, let me come with you," the lad panted.

"Why should you come?" Ling Tan asked. "I have not heard that it is a feast day."

His son circled his toe in the dust, and stared down at the mark.

"I want to come," he said sullenly.

76

Ling Tan looked at him and weighed whether he would make a quarrel with this half-grown man. The day was so bright and good that he decided he would not, for he hated quarreling even in evil days, and always went on one side of a quarrel if he could. "Come then, curse you," he said, and laughed, and his son lifted his head, and they set forth, father and son, over the cobbled roads, walking easily on their sandaled feet. The day before had been gray and though there was no rain the clouds had hung almost to the roofs of temples and pagodas. But today the air was like autumn instead of mid-summer and soon Ling Tan and his third son could no more keep down their hearts than a bubble can be kept under water. Their hearts would rise and be gay under such a blue sky and in the midst of such good harvests everywhere as they saw promised.

When they entered at the south city gate at first there was nothing to tell them what had happened except the grave looks of the people who came and went. Now this city was a place famous for the gaiety of its people. It was an old city but for centuries it had been the place where rulers lived, kings and emperors and all those who can be idle and eat well and spend the people's money and so give it back to them again freely. Laughter and music were to be heard anywhere night and day and there were beautiful young women to be had for the rich and even good enough ones for the poor, and upon the lake there were pleasure boats of carved wood and there were great temples and several fine pagodas. These were the old things.

Since the revolution there had been no more kings and emperors but still there were rulers and these too built fine new palaces and houses of a new sort where water came out of the walls and fire lay waiting to burn at a touch in the lamps and they took the people's money too and gave it back to them freely in feasting and pleasure, and so there were still gaiety and good living and great new shops opened themselves everywhere and there were things now to be bought in this city which a few years ago had not been seen nor even heard about. Common fellows who pulled rikshas or carried loads on their shoulders could now buy self-burning lights to hold in their hands at night instead of candles in paper lanterns, and no winds could put these lights out. Such things kept the people merry, for who knew what new thing tomorrow would bring before their eyes? And all knew that these good things came from across the sea, and so the people admired those foreigners who made such things and thought them good men and to be admired. But this was before the flying ships came over the city.

Today Ling Tan heard men say sullenly on the street and in a tea shop where he stopped to refresh himself and his son, that they had rather do without all other good things from abroad if they were to have such evils as this, that their city was to be ruined.

"Where is the ruin?" he asked the waiter, and then he was amazed because the waiter burst into loud weeping.

"I had a little house of earth and straw leaning against a rich man's house on the Street of the North Gate Bridge," he said, "and his house and mine are gone, and I do not know who is dead in his house but all in mine are gone, and I would have been with them had I not been here, and I wish I were with them! I had two little sons, born in two years."

Ling Tan gave him an extra coin for comfort and then he and his son went toward that street to see for themselves. When he reached the place nothing he had heard could have made him ready for what he now saw. A score of men working for a hundred days together could not have done what here was done in the space of a breath drawn in and out again. He stood gazing, for the street was full of bricks and mortar and beams and dust, and upon these rough heaps mourning people dug with their hands and with pieces of iron and a few with hoes, and even as he watched a great wail went up from a woman who saw her husband's foot show out from between the ruins others had uncovered.

"Would I not know his foot anywhere!" she wept, and it was all she could know, poor soul, for when they dug still further, there was no more of him than this and a bit of leg.

Staring at what he saw with his heart beating in his bosom until his body shook, Ling Tan suddenly heard a violent retch and turning he saw his son vomiting.

"It is too much to bear," Ling Tan said, "and I do not blame you. Have it up, my son, for if it goes down it will poison you." So he waited while the lad had up all he had eaten, and then he led him away to the tea shop again to wash his mouth and to take into his emptiness a little hot tea. He saw that the proud boy was ashamed of his weakness and he was gentle with him and said:

"It is no shame to be sick at such sights as these. A man if he is honorable ought to be sickened and angry. Only wild beasts cannot know shame at what has been done here to innocent people."

And they both sat very heavy and silent and Ling Tan the worse because he could not keep from asking why this destruction had come about and what was its meaning. Even as he sat wondering and asking himself there came into the tea shop a young man, and he was one of the students who were everywhere these days among the people, and when he saw twenty men or so in the shop he climbed on a bench and began to talk to them.

"You who love our country," he said, "listen to me. Yesterday the enemy flew over the city and dropped the bombs which destroyed houses and shops and killed men and women and children. The war has begun. We must be prepared for it. We must fight against the enemy. We must resist until we are dead and then our sons must resist after us. Listen, brave men! The enemy is succeeding at first but they shall not succeed at last. They have taken our land one hundred miles deep, but we must not let

79

them take the second hundred miles. If they take it in spite of us then we must hold the next hundred miles. Fight! Fight!"

Now when Ling Tan's son heard these brave words he cried out, "Good!" and so did other young men. But Ling Tan looked at his empty hands.

"How shall I fight?" he called out.

That young man had already stepped down and was gone on his way and there was none to answer him, for all were as empty-handed as he.

And then as though to mock these empty hands suddenly out of the east there came the sound that these people now knew as well as they knew the beat of their own hearts.

"The ships—the flying ships—" men gasped, and before Ling Tan could stir, the room was empty and there were left only he and his son and the waiter.

"You, sir, had better hide yourself," the waiter said.

"Where can I hide from such evil as this?" Ling Tan shouted. "And why do you not hide?"

"I have no need to hide," the waiter replied, "since I have lost everything except myself."

And while the hateful roar came close the waiter went about the empty shop wiping off the tables and pouring the tea out of the bowls the men had left half full, and setting the benches straight. Nearer the din came until when Ling Tan tried to speak to his son he could not hear his own voice. He had been about to speak because his son's face was fixed in horror, and he wanted to tell him that he was not to be afraid for no man can die until his right end comes. But since his voice was lost he put out his hand and laid it on the boy's arm, and so they sat until the waiter came and by motions told them to creep under the table at least, for then the falling tiles would not hurt them. So they crept under the table and crouched there while the waiter came and went about the room, making it neat and ready for the return of those who had gone, and Ling Tan wondered

80

that he could do this, when at any instant the roof might fall and cover him and all the tables with its ruin. And he knew that in spite of all he himself was afraid and he heartily wished himself at home again.

For now they heard great thunders of noise and having heard and seen the thing that burst in his neighbor's field Ling Tan knew what was happening. He hid his face not only because he felt his own end near but because he knew that with every burst some died. His eardrums swelled and quivered as he listened and his eyeballs swelled and the breath would not come out of his bosom. He looked at his son and the lad crouched with his head between his legs and his knees pressed against his ears and his arms wrapped about himself.

So they endured instant by instant and the evil passed over their heads at last and went on and after what seemed like half the day there was silence again until they heard a new noise and now it was fire.

"Come," Ling Tan cried to his son, "let us get to our home and out of this place."

So he crawled out, and with his son's hand in his they went out. And yet, when Ling Tan thought of going, how could he leave a fire blazing and remember the screaming of people caught in the ruins, and the weeping of those who saw their homes burned and those they loved dead?

"No, we must see what can be done," he told his son. And so against all he knew of old wisdom which bade him leave distress to take care of itself lest he be held responsible for any life saved or lost, he led the way to the fire. Yet what could any mortal do against such ruin? A few men had buckets and poured out water, but the flames laughed and leaped at them, and so at last in their despair the people only stood and gazed into the flames and the fire went on until it reached a wide new road, and there grumbling and hissing, it died at last to smoke and then to ashes. Those new roads had caused the people grief enough when they were made, for the new rulers after the revolution had planned them so that they were straight and wide, and if there were homes in the way, then homes must be razed, and if there were shops then shops must go down and even temples. That was ruin, too, and the people complained bitterly, and they were helpless then as now, having no guns in their hands. Yet today they were glad, for the wide road stopped the fire, and they knew this ruin was worse than the other for it was done by the enemy.

Ling Tan went quietly away at last and his son with him. Never had they been more glad for fields and earth than now. Ling Tan said not a word, and so his son did not speak, but the younger behind the elder they walked the long way home. It was evening when they reached the village and as they went down its single street men called to Ling Tan to know what he had seen. Then he stopped and told them and they gathered there in the narrow cobbled road and listened to him. Not a word was said while he spoke, nor for a while after he had finished. Then an old man spoke, and he was the oldest man in the village, ninety when the new year came around again, and he said:

"The old ways were best, the old days, when we stayed in our own country and the foreigners stayed in theirs. There are those who say the foreigners are good, but I say this evil that has now come upon us comes from them and it is greater than all their good. I wish that we had never seen a foreign thing and that they had stayed where the gods put them, across the seas from us. The seas are not without their meaning, and the foreigners have broken the will of the gods when they crossed them."

They heard him out because he was so old and then in sadness each man went into his own house. In Ling Tan's house that night it was as though one of their own had died, there was such mourning and sighing. At last Ling Tan saw that he must take some sort of authority over these women and children, and over the men younger than he and so he told them to be silent, and to listen to what he was about to say.

They sat all of them together, and for once the men and women were not separate, because they all craved to be together. They were in the court where the table was. There had been food but little eaten, for who could eat? Around them sky and field were calm with summer and the night was hot and still. But none thought of anything except the evil that had fallen on them all and through no fault of their own.

Ling Tan looked around on these who were his, and his heart was soft in him as he saw their eyes all turned to him. "What can I do to save them?" he thought. From other troubles he could have saved them, from famine and flood, from sickness even perhaps, and from poverty and from the evils of usury and of cruel magistrates and all those evils that are common to man. But what could he do now?

"I cannot save you," he said aloud, "for I cannot save myself in this new trouble that has come upon us. Today I saw with my own eyes what you, Wu Lien, told us about before. Now I know that what has been and today was, will be again tomorrow and we have nothing but our bare flesh against these foreign weapons. The gods made us human beings of soft and easily wounded flesh, for they dreamed us good and not evil. Had they been able to see what men would do to each other, they would have given us shells such as turtles have, into which we could have drawn our heads and our soft parts. But we were not made so, and the gods made us and we cannot change ourselves. We can only bear what is come and live on if we can, and die if we must."

So he spoke, and he looked at each face that looked back at him. Then he began again, "You, my two elder sons, are men, and you, Wu Lien, are older than they. If you have anything to say, then say it."

His two sons looked at Wu Lien to speak first, and so Wu Lien coughed and said:

"Certainly I have no way to save myself, and I can only ask your forgiveness that I have had to come here to your house and to bring my household with me. I am a man who only knows how to do business with others, but in this hour who is there with whom I can trade? In times of war such men as we must live as they can and where they can and hope for peace."

Then Lao Ta said, "There are two things which can be done when fire comes down out of heaven, one is to escape it by running away from it, and the other is to let it come down and bear it. In this, my father, I say I will do what you do."

"But I," said the second son, "I will escape it."

This Ling Tan heard and he finished what he had to say:

"If I were a man with no land, I would go also. If I were a young man even, perhaps I would go. I will say nothing to any who go. But as for me, I stay here where I was born and where I have lived. Whatever comes, whether the whole city falls or not, whether the nation falls as some said today on the streets that it must fall, here I will stay. Let those who will, stay with me, and those who would go, let them go."

Then his second son felt himself reproached and he cried out:

"You blame me, my father!"

"I do not blame you," Ling Tan replied, making his voice gentle. "No, more, I think it well that you go. If all who stay here die, then there will be you to carry on our name somewhere else and I only bid you come back to see whether we are alive or dead after the war is ended, and if we are dead then to burn incense to our names and claim the land."

"I promise that," the second son said.

In all this no woman spoke, for it was not a time for a woman's voice, but each saw what her place was and prepared to take it. When they parted again, then each wife told her own husband what she thought. Wu Lien's wife praised him for

84

saying nothing and saying it so well, for she was pleased enough to stay here in the house where she had been born and she felt safe so long as she was not in the city, and Jade praised her husband because he had spoken so firmly. Only Orchid sighed and said she wished that she and her children could go away to some place where the flying ships could not come.

But her husband said to her, "If all the people in the east go to the west, will it not be to give the land here to the enemy? No, my father is right—we must stay by the land."

"Well, at least Jade will be gone," Orchid said. She did not like Jade because she would not gossip much or talk with her but when she had a little time she went and sat in her room and read her book. And she was jealous now that Jade had conceived, because until now she had been the only son's wife to have children in this house and her secret hope had been that Jade would be barren. "Women who like to read are always barren," she had often said and always thought, and now Jade had proved her wrong.

As for Ling Sao, she praised her husband heartily for staying where he belonged, in his own house and on his own land.

"Who would not have come here if we had gone away?" she said, "and maybe an enemy no further than our own village. Yes, and that woman and her stinking husband, your third cousin who is always picking at characters like a cock at grains of corn, they would be glad to come into our big good house, pretending to take care of it for us, and I had rather have robbers any day whom I could curse and have the law on instead of my kin that I must always speak well to and never say what I truly think however hateful they are."

As for the third son, what he thought no one asked and he said nothing. When he thought of what he had seen in the city his food came up again into his mouth, but not from fear so much as anger. He plotted in himself in wild young ways how he might take revenge upon the enemy, and he lay awake at

85

night weeping and biting his nails because he felt himself helpless and too young. But no one knew it. The younger daughter thought nothing at all because she did not know what to think, since she understood so little of what had been said and no one remembered her much more than the dog, to whom they were kind enough too, but without heed.

The next day the flying ships came back again and the day after that, and again on the next day and the next, and every day they came back and the city was scourged by death and by fire. But Ling Tan did not go there again, nor did any of his house. They stayed where they were and tended their crops and put by their food for the winter as they did in every other year. The only change they would allow the enemy was that when the ships came over their heads now they left the field and hid themselves in the bamboos. For one day a flying ship had dipped low like a swallow over a pool, and had cut the head clean from a farmer who stood staring at it. Then it went on again as though what it had done was play.

V

WHEN all could see that now death was to come every day except when it rained, then those who lived inside the city walls did two things. They filled the temples and prayed the gods for rain until they dared pray no more lest there be a flood, and then they went out of the city to find rooms in small country inns or a corner in a farmer's house or they slept on the gravelands or somewhere under a tree. Never had Ling Tan seen such piteous sights as he now saw, women and little children and old people with all they could save tied up in bundles they carried and most of them on foot, for only a few of the rich could ride these days. He had seen people come down from the North in times of famine, but they were the poor and the farming people whom the land had failed for a little while, but it could not fail them every year and they always went back to it.

These now were rich and poor together and they did not know if ever they could go back. Sometimes he felt more sorry for the rich than the poor because the rich were so helpless and delicate and knew little of where to find food. All their lives food had been served to them by others and they did not need to ask where it was found or how it was made, and the poor did better than the rich in these days, used as they were to too little always. And best of all those bold poor did who risked their lives to stay in the city and to go into the emptied houses of the rich and take what they liked from them.

87

These people poured like a flooding river out from the city over the countryside. And the stream of people from the city was joined by a greater stream from the east. For as the enemy toward the east took the land foot by foot people fell back from before them and joined themselves to others like them and the great river of moving people began to flow inland toward the west, not knowing where they went and sure only of death if they stayed.

At first Ling Tan let his house be open to these people, and the women spent themselves in cooking for them and feeding them and crying out in pity for their sufferings. There were the wounded and the little children too who could go no further and must be left behind, and these had to be put with those willing to take them, and many died. But this was what saved Ling Tan, that none of these people thought his house was far enough from the enemy as they gained the land foot by foot. They were restless until they had pushed on beyond river and lake and mountain, into the inlands behind the high mountains where the enemy dared not go lest they be cut off.

Now here was the chance for Lao Er to go, too, and so he and Jade waited until there came by those with whom they wished to share travel, those who were not old or sick or burdened with too many little children. Day after day they waited to find whom they wanted and one day there came by a party of forty or more young men and women. The women had feet as free as men, which had never been bound, and Jade liked them as soon as she saw them. Their hair was cut short like hers and in their little bundles they all had books.

"We are students of a certain school," they told her, "and our eyes are on the mountains a thousand miles from here where our teachers are gone already and there in caves we will go on with our learning and when this war is over we will come back ready to shape the peace well."

Not one of these men and women talked of wasting himself

in war, and this pleased Ling Tan very much. They stopped at his house not for a night, but only at a midday to ask for tea to drink with the bread they had with them, and so he heard them talk and he praised them:

"Those who have no learning have only their bodies and they are the ones who ought to fight if there must be fighting. But you who have wisdom stored in your skulls, you have a treasure which ought not to be spilled like blood, and it ought to be kept for the day when we must have wisdom to tell us how we ought to live. In times like these wisdom is useless because nothing can save us except the chance that we are saved. But when the folly of war is ended, then we must have wisdom."

And in the shade of the willows outside his gate, for the court was too small for so large a crowd, Ling Tan put many questions to these young men and even to the women, for to his amazement one answered as well as the other, and after a while he forgot whether it was man or woman who answered him. And from them he found out for the first time what had happened at the coast and why the enemy had attacked them at all, and long was their talk together.

This Ling Tan was a man who though he lived as his ancestors had in this valley was still acute enough. Life, he always told his sons, did not change. Men ate with different tools in different times, but food was food. They slept upon different beds, but sleep was the same. So now he believed that it was only men's times that were changed and not men. When he inquired therefore of these young men and women he asked what weapons the enemy had rather than what the enemy was. When he heard that the enemy envied his nation the land, he understood at once the whole war and its cause.

"Land," he said looking about on the many young faces and filling his water pipe as he spoke, "land is at the bottom of what men want. If one has too much land and the other too little, there will be wars, for from land come food and shelter, and if land is too little food is poor and shelter small, and when this is so, then man's mind and his heart are kept small too."

They listened to him with respect but unbelieving, for to them Ling Tan was only an old farmer who could not read or write and what did he know of all that they learned in books? But since they had not yet lost all the courtesy taught them by their parents, they made haste to seem to agree with him.

"It is true, old father," they said, not believing him in their hearts.

But he was content with them whether they believed him or not, and so when his second son came to him in the middle of the afternoon and told him that he and Jade wanted to go with these young men and women who were all strong on their feet and full of courage he thought it over for a short space and then as his habit was before he decided anything he went and talked with his wife.

Now she had never liked it that her second son and Jade wanted to leave this house, and she spoke out her discontent now while she washed the clothes at the edge of the pond where Ling Tan found her. She had a pair of his old blue trousers in her hand, folded on a smooth stone and full of water, and she beat the garment with her stick to drive out the dirt with the water and while she talked she went on beating.

"I do not see why Jade should go off like this," she said. "Who will look after her when her time comes and why should our grandchild be born somewhere out in a field like a wild hare? If our son wants to go, he will go, but I say she should stay here and have our grandchild decently."

Then Ling Tan answered her by grave words. "It may be better that we have very few young women in our house, and the fewer the better, and Jade is too beautiful for what may lie ahead of us." For he was troubled by a thing he had heard, and one young man had taken him aside and told him in private what had happened to some women at the hands of the enemy. So now he was eager to have the women out of his house, all except his wife who was brown and wrinkled enough for no man to see what he saw in her face, the girl she had once been.

She let her stick rest a moment to look at him.

"What do you say now when you talk?" she asked. "Is there any place safer for a young wife than her husband's home, and can any eye be sharper than mine on her? When he goes I will not let her foot stir beyond the door. I tell you it is he who makes her able to disobey me and he encourages her to her own way, so that I do not tell half of what I would tell her if he were not here. Let him go and I will say at once that her foot is not to go beyond the gate until his enters it again."

"There may come times when strange feet will enter our gate," Ling Tan said.

She went to beating again. "I fear no man," she said loudly. "Let a strange man's foot touch the threshold and see whether I or the dog is at him first!"

"Nevertheless, a woman should go with her man," Ling Tan argued, "and who will look to our son if his wife does not go with him?"

"No one would say you are right quicker than I," she replied, "if Jade were not carrying in her your own grandchild, and her duty to you comes first."

"I think it does not," he said gently, and went away before she could argue him into doing what he did not want to do. And she, knowing why he went, could only beat the trousers, and she did this without thinking what she was doing until when she lifted them up they were beaten to holes and then she called aloud to the gods to see what she had done and how it was no fault of hers but of these times that set one's mind awry.

As for Ling Tan he went into his house and told his son quietly that he had better go and take Jade with him, for he knew from what the young men had told him that the second hundred miles of land had been lost to the enemy and within the third hundred miles this house stood.

"But send me a word somehow when the child is born," he said, "and if it is a boy send me a red cord in the envelope and if it is a girl let it be a blue one." He wished now that he had let his son read and write so that he could have had a letter that he could take to his third cousin and ask him to read it to him. But who would have dreamed it would ever be well for a son to leave his father's house?

"I will do better than that," Lao Er replied proudly. "Jade can write enough to tell you."

Ling Tan was astonished enough at this, and he cried out, "Can she, then? But the matchmaker did not tell us!"

"Doubtless she thought it no added value to her," Lao Er said, and grinned.

"I would never have said either that it was needful for a woman to read and write," Ling Tan said, "but it only proves how strange our times are that it can be so." And he sat in the court smoking and thinking while his second son went in to tell Jade they were going.

Now Jade herself had been the one to say first that these young men and women were the ones to walk with, and so she had already tied into two bundles the few things they must have if they went. There she sat on the bed's edge waiting for Lao Er and she lifted her great eyes at him when he came in.

"Are we to go?" she asked.

"Yes," he said. Then he sat down beside her and put his arm on her shoulder. "Now that we go, I wonder if it is not too hard for you," he said tenderly. "I wish I could carry the child for you."

"One of these days you shall," she replied.

She rose as she spoke, and he saw that she had even shod herself for the long walk, for she had tied over her cloth shoes a pair of straw sandals such as he wore in the field, and she had put on her strongest plainest blue garments, such as country women wear, coat and trousers and not the long robe, that was her best and therefore made after the city fashion.

"I am ready," she said and took up her bundle. But he lingered. "I never thought a child of mine would be born anywhere except where I was born," he said, sadly.

"He will find a place of his own to be born in," she said.

"Yes, but we must mark the place," he said. "It is very meaningful to a man where he is born, and we must remember whether it is among mountains or in a valley or in a town, and whether it is night or day and if there is water near by, and whether the sky is clear or dark, and what the province is and how the people there speak, so that we can tell him everything."

"Oh," she said restlessly, "let us go, if we are to go!"

But still he lingered. "It seems to me I can remember the very moment I was born in this house," he said. "I seem to remember such darkness as I have never since known, and then light that was like a pain so that I cried out. And then I felt arms beneath me."

"Will you come with me or not?" she cried. "I hate to say I go then not go."

He heard the fear in her voice of a woman seeking safety for her young, and he rose and they went out and bowed to his father together and to the elder brother and they called farewell to all the others. But the mother they could not find anywhere, and since the young men and women were anxious to be gone and at another place for night they could only leave without seeing her.

"Tell my mother we searched for her everywhere," Lao Er said. "Tell her it is bad luck that we cannot find her before we go."

"I will," his father said. He would not tell his son what he now felt to see him go out of this house to a place unknown

93

and the time of his return unknown and perhaps never, for who could say what would happen before they met again and whether or not they would meet? He followed his son and Jade out of the gate and stood on the threshing floor to see them go, and with him were all his house except his son's mother. It was an afternoon like any other in midsummer, hot and quiet and the sky blue except for the piles of silver thunder clouds resting upon the green mountains. Still none could say whether or not the clouds would do more than lie there. Sometimes they made a storm and sometimes they did not.

And Ling Tan, feeling all around him seem so the same, as though there were no war, wondered if it were not folly indeed to let his good young son leave the safety of this house and with him his young wife, now precious to them all for what she carried in her, and he wondered whether or not these young men had spoken the truth in all they had said. It did not seem true to him now that less than a hundred miles away the armies of the enemy marched toward this place. A bird sang in a peach tree near his door where the peaches had but just finished their ripening, and his grain stood motionless under the hot sun. Its greenness was changing to a paler green and it would not be many days before the paleness turned to yellow.

When he cut the rice he would miss sorely enough this strong son, and now it seemed to him that this second son of his had good in him which none of the others had. He was quicker than the eldest and sharper in his thoughts and he laughed more wisely and kept his laughter for what was funny and did not waste it on courtesy and placating as his eldest sometimes did, and beside him the third son was fit for nothing except to herd the buffalo. And in spite of all Ling Sao said, Ling Tan knew that Jade was the best of the young women in his house. He looked at her now and for the second time since she had come here he spoke to her directly for he was a man of dignity and he obeyed the customs between the generations. The first time he spoke had been when she came as a bride and he must greet her, and now this time he bade her farewell.

"Do your duty, child," he said. "Remember that he is my son and his child my grandchild, and that all rests on you. Where the woman is faithful no evil can befall. The woman is the root and the man the tree. The tree grows only as high as the root is strong."

She did not answer, but she let her lovely mouth, always straight and grave, move a little in a smile. Whether or not she believed what he said, that smile did not tell him.

And so he let them go, and he stood looking after them a long time, as long as he could see them, until their two figures were lost among the crowd.

When he came in he saw smoke rising out of the kitchen and he went and looked behind the stove and there sat his wife, feeding grass into its belly.

"Where were you?" he cried. "We looked for you everywhere."

"I would not come to see him go," she said. "If he must go let me not see it."

"But you have been weeping," he said, staring at her. Her eyes were red and down her brown cheeks her tears had left a silvery skin as they dried.

"I have not," she said. "The smoke makes my eyes red."

He let her say this, seeing the tears well up into her eyes again, and he stood there helpless before her. It had always been that if she wept, who wept so seldom, he felt himself turned to stone and not able to move.

. . . Out of a house it seemed strange that two could be so missed as Ling Tan and his wife now missed their second son and Jade. There were all these others left and the same number of children ran about the court and teased the chickens and ducks and pulled the dog's tail until he howled with misery, and it was easier for all to sleep for Wu Lien and the eldest daughter and their children slept in the empty room, and they could put

95

the old woman who was Wu Lien's mother in the third son's bed, and him out in the court on a bamboo couch, and yet they missed those two. Some sort of strength had left the house with their going, and the eldest son without his younger brother seemed too gentle and docile and he agreed too quickly with what his father and mother said, and Ling Tan felt that in the time of trouble this docile man would do what he was told well enough but would not know what to do if there were no one there to tell him, and Ling Tan felt the care was all his. Now he saw that his second son was a man of his own mind, though so young, just as Jade, though wilful, was a woman who knew what to do next without asking.

Even Ling Sao missed Jade more than she would say and yet because she was a just woman she laughed with shame after a few days and told her husband so.

"I would have said that only peace could be here after that Jade went, and I will not say I want her back again, if it were not for our son. But still I do grow weary with Orchid who does nothing if I do not tell her, and with our elder daughter who cries at me like a sheep from morning until night, 'M-ma, what shall I do next?' I tell her to look and see whether the floor is clean and whether the court needs sprinkling for dust or is there fuel enough for the next meal, or are the clothes to be washed or do the drying fish need turning, or if there is nothing else, then slice carrots to salt down for the winter but no, then she says, 'Which comes first, M-ma?'"

Ling Tan's little eyes twinkled at his wife as she sat combing out her long hair before she slept. "She is your own daughter," he said, "and she still asks you what she is to do because you always told her. Jade, now, she did not grow up at your side, and so she is used to seeing with her own eyes and not yours."

"Is this my fault?" she asked, and held the comb, ready to be grieved. For these two were so close after all the years that she could not bear a word from him if he thought her wrong. To hear anyone else curse her and curse her mother and call her father a turtle did not touch her anywhere. She would only laugh or grow angry and curse back the bigger mouthful. But let her husband say she should have done other than she did, and though she would try to muster up her anger to flout him with, still she never could, and his words, though only two or three, would sink into her heart like a dagger, and she would carry it in her for days. So Ling Tan had learned never to speak to her to say she was wrong unless he must and he let many a small thing pass, knowing how warm and impetuous this woman of his was and how eagerly she secretly wished to do what he liked, though she would have denied she was so, and would have said what she so loved to say, that she feared no man, and not him either.

"You are the best mother in the province," he said, "and where is there one like you beyond the seas? I would not have you a cool thin soul. I like you hot and gusty and I like your quick tongue even when it is turned on me."

He laughed as he spoke, and she grew red with pleasure and began to comb her hair again, and to hide her pleasure she tried to be surly while she smiled.

"You old turnip," she said, and searched for something she could do for him. "Come here, old man, and let me see that spot on your cheek and see if you are to have a boil after all these years."

He came near to her and bent over her to humor her, knowing very well why she wanted to touch him and to do something for him.

"It is only where a flea bit me," he said.

"Do not tell me what it is," she said, "I can see for myself."

She felt it and saw that it was nothing and so she gave him a small blow on his bare shoulder because she loved him so well.

"And can you not catch a flea any more, and must you be bitten like a child, you bone?" she said.

97

They both laughed then, and he thought to himself that if this woman died before he did, even then he would not marry another, for after her any would be like a carrot dried without salt.

"Do you know why you do not like Jade?" he asked, to tease her.

"I know all I want to know," she said, beginning to comb her hair again, and making her eyes mischievous.

"You do not know this," he said. "It is because she is so much like you."

"That Jade!" she cried, trying to be angry. But secretly in her heart she was pleased for Jade was beautiful and she knew against her wish that the girl was no ordinary one.

"Both of you are stubborn wilful women and it is the only sort I like," he said. He put his hand on her neck and she felt it there as she had felt it when they were both young. But because she was long past forty she knew that to another it would have seemed shameful that two middle-aged people should be like two young ones, and so she tossed her head and pulled away and he knew what she was thinking and laughed and when she saw his brown face above her and his white teeth she forgot that he was the father of her children, the man she had lived with all these years, and she put her arms around his waist and held him hard against her and felt his heart against her cheek, beating so steadily and so strong that all her blood ran to the measure of that beat.

"Ought we not to understand our son and Jade?" he asked. "They are like us."

"I always did say our second son was more like you than any of the others," she answered. Then she let him go and went on binding up her hair, and so the moment was over, and both of them the better for it.

Yet as day followed day, they grew used to the two gone, and the rent in the house was mended and the work went on.

But Ling Tan moved his third son up and let him work in the fields with him instead of herding the buffalo and in his place he hired a small lad for a penny a day to sit on the beast's back on the days it was not needed for work.

As for Orchid, she was happier with Jade gone, for now there was no one to reproach her for too little work done, and no one to have smooth hair when hers was rough because she had not had time to comb it or thought she had not. Hers was easily the highest place among the younger women now that Jade was not there to do everything better than she did.

But Pansiao was sorry Jade was gone, for in the last few weeks Jade had taken a while in the evening to teach her to read a few characters. To the others it had seemed nothing more than a game but Jade knew what it was to the silent young girl who moved in such accustomed ways through the house that they all forgot her easily. Only Jade had seen how seldom the child spoke and to how few, for she, too, had been a silent child in her own father's household and one of many in the women's courts. Her father had been richer than most men, an owner of land he rented as well as farmed, and he had a concubine and so Jade grew up among two women's children and they numbered seventeen in all. Among so many she was alone and she was always drawn to the silent rather than to the talkative. In this household where both Ling Tan and Ling Sao spoke freely and Lao Er talked easily and Orchid talked as easily as she breathed and the third son was away all day she saw the quiet gentle girl and wondered if she were lonely. And so out of this wonder one day, not knowing what else to say to the child, she had asked:

"Would you like to learn a few characters? Then you could read my book instead of sitting alone."

"Oh, I am not able," Pansiao had answered quickly. "How can I remember the letters when I forget what my mother tells me so easily?"

"It is easy to remember the characters because they tell you

99

something you want to know," Jade said, and so she persuaded Pansiao and it was true that the young girl did remember and Jade had never to say a character's name twice, for every character spoke for itself to her.

Now that was over again, and Jade was gone, and Pansiao could only go over and over the characters she knew, until one day in her great hunger to know what others said, she drew near to one of the women students who passed by so often and asked her for a letter or two, and by this means she learned to read a little. Then one day a kind student gave her a book out of the few she carried.

"Take care of it," she said, "for in these times books are dearer than food."

Pansiao thanked her and took the book, and though she could not read enough yet to know what it said, it stood to her a goal to be reached some day, and she went through the book with a bit of charcoal and marked every character that she knew. But they were not near enough together to speak to her.

... As for Ling Tan, his only wonder was how quickly they all grew used to what was now their daily life. Day after day the flying ships came over, and they grew used to them, having said that they would stay where they were, though the enemy took the very city itself. Half of the city went away and then another third of what was left until only those stayed who had nowhere to go, or they were those who had no money at all, or those who said it made no difference to them who ruled the city so long as there was peace in it and they waited for any peace that was an end to war and these flying ships. Some end was near, all knew, for mile by mile the enemy armies drew closer and city after city fell into their grasp. There was no news of what happened in those cities because those who fled first knew nothing and after a city fell and the enemy had the land, there was only silence. None knew whether the enemy was cruel or good, and all waited.

Ling Tan waited, too, but while he waited the work had to

be done, and he could not always be running into the bamboos because there were flying ships above his head, and yet he did not want to risk his head and stay alone in the fields and tempt the enemy above to see him there. So he went into the village tea shop one evening at a time when most men are glad to leave their wives awhile and sit together in peace without the noise of scolding women, and of crying children being put to bed, and at such a time he rose and spoke in the tea shop and said:

"My elder brothers, you and I are laboring men. War or no war, we must bring food out of the earth, and how can we do it sitting idle in a bamboo grove for a long while every day in the best part of the day when we are not yet tired?"

"You do not curse idleness more than we do," a voice called out and a murmuring went over the crowd.

"Yes, but what will you say we ought to do?" another asked. "I saw a man shot beneath a flying ship, and he was dead and there is no idleness so great as death."

This made them laugh wryly, and Ling Tan laughed too and went on.

"What I say is we ought none of us to go into the bamboos. Let us all stay in the fields and work and pretend we do not see the flying ships and if there are many of us they will decide it is not worth their while to take the time to cut off head by head and so they will go on."

There was a clamor to agree with this, and thereafter Ling Tan and all his fellows worked in the fields without looking up when the flying ships went over them. They did only this one thing, they stopped every day about mid-morning and tied branches on their hats, so that looking down from above a man in a flying ship would see only green, for their big hats hid the blue of their trousers and the brown of their bare backs as they worked.

This village and the farms about it were now like an island in the steadily moving stream of people. Those who could go out of the city had gone, but every day brought fresh hundreds of fleeing people and how Ling Tan knew the enemy steadily came nearer was from asking these people where they came from, and day by day it was from places nearer and nearer to him, and at last cities that he knew, and this was how he knew that the armies of the enemy were winning the victory.

"Do our armies not oppose them?" he always asked, and the answer was more often rueful than not.

"Our men retreat to save themselves for a greater battle somewhere," one man after another said, but none knew where.

And that this great battle would be beyond his land Ling Tan soon came to see, for none of these people were willing to stop here but had their eyes fixed on a far distant place, and he began to make himself and his house ready for the time when over them all the enemy would rule and under this rule they must somehow live.

Was the enemy good or evil? He could not discover, for there were more tales than he could fit together. There was Wu Lien in his own house who said that such East-Ocean merchants as he had once dealt with on the coast where he went to buy his goods were always courteous and kind. And yet there was the tale he heard of a great crowd of people fleeing from that same coast and they were not on foot but in a train, and though they flew white flags for mercy and innocence, upon them the flying ships let down their death so that hundreds were wounded and dead. How could there be anything but evil in such an enemy?

These things he pondered hour upon hour as he worked under the green branches tied to his hat and as the flying ships came and went over his head.

"I will do my own work as I always have," he thought, and it seemed to him the greatest thing that a man could do in these days was to live and keep alive his own. . . . So the summer passed into autumn, and the harvests that year were all they had promised. The rice was heavier in the head than Ling Tan had seen it in ten years and the harvest so great that everywhere in that rich valley the people were hard-pressed to reap it. They could think of nothing but the harvest, and when those soldiers came to them who were to defend the city sometime, and asked for straw for beds, or they asked for help in digging trenches about the city, the farmers were surly and they said, "We are very weary of all who are soldiers, who earn nothing, and who feed from us. Do your work yourselves, for we have our own work to do."

When Ling Tan heard soldiers so answered, he was pleased, for he too despised all who took part in war. And yet he had cause one day to heed, at least for a moment, what one of those soldiers said, for when the man was thus repulsed, he began suddenly to weep, and he looked around on the half-harvested grain, and upon the healthy busy people and he said, "If we are not able to defend this land, we dare not dream what will happen to you, for with our own eyes we have seen the sufferings of our countrymen on the coastlands taken by the enemy."

But still the others gave this man no heed, and the harvest waited, and the soldiers went away again.

Now while the grain was to be cut and threshed Ling Tan pressed everyone in his house into the work except Wu Lien who could not learn, it seemed, how to hold a scythe. But the elder daughter remembered from her girlhood here, and she gave a great laugh for they were all happy with the harvest, and she said:

"Let my man stay in the house then and help with the children and I will go out to the fields as I used to do," and so she did, and it was a pleasure to her to feel the stalks so smooth and firm in her grasp and she still cut as well as any man and was proud of herself.

But this thing was for a day or two a trouble in the house, for when she came that night she found Wu Lien very peevish, and when she inquired into the reason for his ill temper he sent her into their room and came in after her.

"Are you my wife or are you the old man's daughter?" he asked her. "Am I to do your work? The next thing I will be asked to suckle the children."

She gave one of her big laughs at this, for Wu Lien was so fat that he was ashamed sometimes to go bare above his waist even in summer, because men laughed and said he was made like a woman, and there was always a man somewhere to tell of a strange sight he had seen of a man who could suckle a child. Now the moment Wu Lien spoke thus to his wife he wished he had not, and in his peevishness when she laughed he struck her across the mouth so that her mouth bled, and worse than that, her teeth cut the back of his hand.

"Bite me, will you!" he shouted and he was so unjust that she who was nearly always humble suddenly went angry as he had never seen her, and she was bold because she was in her father's house and she bawled at him as loudly as she could:

"Who feeds you if it is not my father, and why should I not harvest a little food to help him?"

With that she went at him with all her ten nails, and he went backward before her, never having seen her like this, and with the blood still dripping from her mouth she clawed at him. Upon them Ling Sao opened the door, hearing the noise of their voices, and she sprang between them and pulled her daughter away.

"You shame me!" she shouted. "When did I ever teach you to behave so to the man who is your husband? Wu Lien, she is not my daughter and if you do not want her any more I cannot blame you. I have cheated you with a wife not worthy of you."

So Ling Sao soothed the astonished man and scolded her daughter and she brought him out of the room and put a fan in his hand and poured out a bowl of tea for him and she told Pansiao to take the children away from him. Then she went back into the room where her daughter was, who was now washing her mouth and binding up her hair, and the mother made her tell what had happened and when she heard she could not keep from laughing a little, now that Wu Lien was not here.

"I take your side," she told her daughter, "for a more helpless man than yours I never did see, though a mild temper, and that is something to be glad for, too. Yet he is a city man and out of the city he is like a cat in a pond, but for that you cannot blame him. He fed you well and was good to you when he had a house, and the day will come when he has one again, and a woman must put up with the man she gets, and who can tell what he is beforehand? You must remember that it is very hard for him to be in this house and it shames him, so you must make much of him and do not belittle him. There are worse than yours."

So she taught her daughter and sent her out at last to ask her husband's pardon which he gave to her gravely as though none of it had anything to do with him.

But to her husband Ling Sao told the whole story, relishing it as she went, and these two laughed together in the night over the city man who was their son-in-law, and they were proud of their daughter for laying her nails into his fat white cheeks, so that there were five red scratches on each. They did not hate Wu Lien at all, but here out of his place he made something for them to laugh at and it was a pleasure to find something for laughter these days.

Nevertheless Ling Tan knew that at bottom nothing must come between a man and his wife and so he forbade his elder daughter to come into the fields any more and thus Wu Lien was placated and Ling Sao gave him some mutton fat to put on his scratches and after seven days or so they healed. But until they did, he stayed inside the court.

The rice was harvested and all day long up and down the valley there was the sound of the flails beating out the grain upon the threshing floors. Grain fell upon the beaten earth and the oxen and the buffalo trod it out under stones they pulled

105

over it and if a farmer had no beasts he pulled the stone himself, and the women winnowed the grain in the light winds of coming autumn.

And every day except when it rained the flying ships came from the eastern hills and flew to the city. There were few days of rain.

"We have prayed the gods so long for clear skies for harvest that now they send them anyhow because it is the ninth month," the old man moaned who was ninety years old, and then he said, "and who can blame the gods if they do not know what to do? What can a man know to pray for these days, if sun brings the enemy and if rain spoils the harvest?"

This Ling Tan heard him say one day when the old man came out to see the harvest, though he himself was long past working on it. And Ling Tan answered stubbornly:

"I will pray for what I always have prayed when the harvest is ripe—sun to shine, so that I can thresh my grain and put it into its bins for our winter food."

"It is true it is well to pray for what is known to be good," the old man agreed.

But no farmer with so much land as Ling Tan had could store all his grain and some of it had to be sold. Besides, the people left in the city wanted food, too, and there were those who dug holes underground so that they would have a place safe from fire and destruction for their winter's food. Then against his will Ling Tan had to go to the city to sell some of his harvest, and now he missed his second son the more, for he could send no one else and he had to go himself.

He waited therefore until a good rainy day and, putting on his coat of reed leaves laid upon each other so that the water ran off him as it runs from the feathers of a duck, he went to the city rice shops to sell his grain. It took him twice as long since he must walk through mud, but still his life was worth it and he took the time. It was a sad day. Since he had seen it last the

106

ruins in the city had grown greatly worse and all the rich and those who make a city a merry place were gone, and those who were left were doleful to look at.

And yet there was something very brave about the city too, and those who were still there did not complain or talk of flight. When Ling Tan went to the great rice markets, though half of them were boarded up, still the merchants made their bargains with him, and they said nothing except that they would be there whatever happened, for people had to eat and what would they eat if not rice? And when Ling Tan asked for a higher price than he had ever asked they gave it to him, and so there was that good to the evil times. He went home pleased with the pocket full of silver which they had put down on his promise to bring them his rice.

Yet any news he heard was not good, and the worst of all was that at last even the white foreigners were leaving the city. Now Ling Tan knew none of these foreigners, but he had lived through evil times before, though all lighter far than these, and he knew that when the foreigners left the city it was as though rats leave a ship. So when he heard here and there that foreigners were going he knew the worst of something was near.

"They will not all go," Wu Lien said that night when he told him. "There are always two or three or ten who stay because they have no homes elsewhere but the others go and it is bad news always, for they have ways of finding out what happens anywhere in the world. When we know nothing those foreigners know."

"What is this magic?" Orchid asked.

"They catch news from the air and they run words along wires," Wu Lien replied, and Orchid listened with her mouth wide.

"I hope I never see a foreigner," she cried, "for if I did I would be so afraid I should die before him."

But Wu Lien scorned this ignorance. "I had them in my shop

two or three times," he said. "They came to buy some foreign things, and they paid their money like any one else and they were two-legged as we are and they had all their features, and only their color and their smell were strange."

"Could they speak?" Orchid asked.

"Yes, but brokenly as children do," Wu Lien said, tolerant of her woman's ignorance.

"Still I would rather never see them," Orchid said.

"Well, you need not," Wu Lien answered. Then he turned to Ling Tan. "Whatever is to come, it is better if it comes quickly. I have it in my mind that once the city falls, if it must fall, at least there will not be these flying ships, and I can go back and begin my shop again."

Ling Tan did not say what he had in his mind, which was that many had their shops now and why did he not go back? He knew that there are men of little body courage and men of much and if Wu Lien were one born with small body courage, this was not a thing that could be discerned in a man until danger struck him.

"It will not be long now," he said courteously. "So stay here until it comes."

In those days to all who passed his house Ling Tan said, "I have a son and his wife in those parts to which you go, a tall young man, and you will know him because his eyes are very bright and black, and his wife is nearly as tall as he and she carries a child soon to be born. When you see them tell them we still live and all is as it was with us."

Many were the people who promised Ling Tan to look for two such as his son and son's wife, and Ling Tan wished that one would come back from there to bring him word from those two, but not one came back.

... The tenth month of that year came, and whether the tenth month or the ninth month were better to live in, who could say? The white geese went across the fields as ever they did in the autumn to find the grain left from the harvest, and the sky was blue above, and on the hillsides the long grass turned ruddy and dry ready for the scythe, and Ling Tan and all who could from his house went out to cut the grass for winter. All went except Wu Lien again, who could not hold a scythe, and Ling Tan told his eldest daughter to stay at home and take her mother's place, for Ling Sao was as good with a scythe as he was. Day after day they worked together on the grassy hillsides, cutting and then binding together the great bundles of long grass, and they carried them down at evening hidden each of them under his bundle except for two legs and piled the grass against the house. Food they had and now fuel, and Ling Tan thought, "Whatever comes, I can feed my house."

On the tenth day of the tenth month they took a rest, for it was a feast day, and on that day a few students came into the countryside, but only a few, and Ling Tan was amazed, for year after year on this day the students used to come as thick as locusts into the country, and on village streets and in village tea shops they used to preach to the people what they ought to do, and how they ought all to learn to read and how they ought to wash themselves every day and they ought to kill flies and mosquitoes and when one had smallpox others ought not to go near him. "Shall we leave the sick to die then?" Ling Sao once asked, when she heard this. The country people listened and laughed at all the students told them and believed them or did not believe, because the students were young and what they learned was what had not been tried by fathers and sons. But on the tenth of the tenth of this year, few were the students who came, and to the Ling village indeed came only two young men, and what they preached was not what they had preached in other years.

They were thin young men, yellow from reading books, and their hair was cut long and they wore foreign spectacles and blue students' coats and trousers, and they seemed in haste to be gone.

"You men of the village," they said, "our elder brothers, hear what we tell you. The enemy approaches and you ought all to know what will happen when they come here. Do not expect peace, for there will be none. They will rule over you and make you slaves, they will weaken you with opium and take from you all that you have. Where they have been they have looted houses and robbed the stores of food and they have violated many women."

Now Ling Tan had wandered into the street since he was idle, and the day being fine, and the air very cool he had gone toward the tea house to see if there were wandering actors as there always were on feast days in other years. But there were none, and only the two pale young men, so he sat down to listen to them and there were others there and among them his third cousin and his wife and their only son, who had loved Jade.

"Soldiers always do these things," Ling Tan called out to all when the young men said this, "and as for opium, in my grandfather's time the magistrates of our own city compelled men to plant opium, too, for the tax they could take from it."

This angered the young men and they said, "It is worse when the enemy does these things to us."

Then Ling Tan's third cousin called out of the crowd. "I saw an enemy once long ago and he had hair and eyes like ours and a skin, too, of our color, and except that he was short and bandy in the legs, he was more like us than not, and if he had been able to speak as we do, he would have done well enough for one of us, and much better than the white foreigners who have the devil's own look upon them."

For some reason that none could understand, this talk angered the two young men still more and they looked at each other.

"What use is it to waste our breath on such louts as these?" one asked the other. "They do not know what it is to love their country. If they can eat and sleep it is enough for them and they do not care who rules them."

Now it was the village men's turn to be angry and Ling Tan was the first.

"We have not been so well served by our own rulers," he shouted. "They have taxed us and eaten our flesh, too, and what difference is it to a man whether he is eaten by tigers or lions if he is eaten?"

And so saying he stooped and took up a clod of earth and threw it at the young men and when the others saw it they did the same thing and, thus pelted, the young men ran away as fast as they could and that was the last that Ling Tan saw of students for many days and months, and so passed that feast day.

In the evening Ling Sao killed a fowl for their meal to mark the day and drained off the blood and thickened it for a pudding and the children ate it too freely and two of them were sick in the night and the next morning Ling Tan was glad that it was a usual day and that he could work instead of doing nothing.

But he thought a good deal of what the young men had accused him, that he did not love his country. Those were the days when he plowed the land again for winter wheat, and as he plowed he looked at the dark folds of earth. "Do I not love this earth?" he thought. "And is this earth not my country? The young have left the land and gone to save themselves as my son and Jade have, but I love my country too well to leave it. Though I die I will stay with it, and can a man love his country better than this?" But to no one could he say what he meant for even his wife was not able to understand such thoughts. There were things she knew and he could speak to her of them, but not of these deep thoughts he had now and again. He thought them and valued them and kept them inside himself and he never forgot what he had thought.

On every rainy day Ling Tan carried a load of his rice into

the city according to his promise, and one day his two sons went with him to carry the more, and they heard in the city, breath from breath, the ill news that the enemy had vanquished all and now were marching straight upon this region, and they heard it first from the merchants in the rice shop where they went to sell.

These rice merchants were six brothers whose father and uncles had had the rice shop before them, and they were grave good men whose word must be taken.

"I do not know who will eat this rice," the eldest said as he measured Ling Tan's rice, "for it may be the enemy will be here before we can sell it. We are vanquished upon the coast and we ought all now to know our fate. Our rulers have gone and the capital that was here has been moved inland."

In the shop that day all was confusion for these brothers had decided they ought not all to stay in one place in duty to their ancestors, lest the six of them die together and there be none to carry on the name. Two therefore were chosen by lot to go west and two more by lot to go south and only two, the youngest and the eldest, were to stay. The shop was full of bundles and packages and anxious women and crying children and the brothers were troubled for who knew whether or not they could ever meet again? None knew his fate in such times as these, and Ling Tan and his sons stood waiting while their rice was measured and to have their money put in their hands, and all the time they stood they watched and into their hearts came more fear than they had yet had. What indeed was this enemy and what would befall those who stayed behind and was it better to stay or to flee?

Not one word did they say until their rice was all measured and the money in their hands that day, and then Ling Tan asked:

"When must we expect this enemy?"

"In less than a month if they are not somehow hindered," the eldest merchant replied.

"And do our rulers nowhere hinder their coming?" Ling Tan asked.

"The enemy has guns that we have not," the merchant replied. "While we have been building all these new schools everywhere and making new roads the enemy has been making great guns and ships on sea and in the air and what have we to fight them with except our bare bodies?"

Ling Tan did not answer, but he led his sons home through the chill air of the late year and pondered all the way what the merchant had told him. Yes, their ancients had taught them that no good man would be a soldier and that the warlike man was the least of men and not to be respected, and so they had all believed.

"And so I do believe still," Ling Tan thought to himself. "It is better to live than to die, and peace is better than war, and though there are some who deny this as robbers do, the truth remains what it is."

But that day he began to look to the strength of his gate and to the fastening of its hinges, and he mended the holes in his wall, and he closed a small window in the kitchen that gave to the outside, and he made up his mind that if the enemy came, he would put all his family inside the gate and he would be the only one to show himself if one must come to the gate. He had a deep new fear of the unknown that was to come, and never were days so precious as these few days before the enemy drew near. He counted every hour of them as a man might count the last hours of his life, and saw more clearly than ever before the beauty of the hills and the dearness of his land. Even the faces of those in the house were more dear to him than they had ever been and he bought Pansiao a new coat of blue silk, and for Ling Sao ten feet of fine white cotton such as their own loom could not weave, and to his sons he gave ten silver dollars apiece and to each of his grandchildren he gave a silver coin, and to his eldest daughter some good linen cloth for herself. None of them knew what to make of these presents out of time, but he wanted them to feel his goodwill toward them and toward all in these last days of peace.

"I can do this for you now," he said when they looked surprised, "and I cannot say whether or not I shall always be able to give you such tokens."

They took the gifts gladly and yet they felt uneasy too, and as if somehow Ling Tan felt himself about to die.

"Are you well?" his wife asked him anxiously in the night. "It seems to me you do not eat so heartily as once you did and I feel a difference in you."

"I am not changed," he said, gravely, "I shall never change. The man I am now I shall be until I die, and I will not die soon."

But he said this so strangely that she stared at him and made ready to say something and then shut her mouth. She knew that he was a man who knew what he did and why he did it, and before such a man a woman may keep silence and know that it will be well with her.

VI

EARLY in the eleventh month the enemy was near the city.
When the day was still, if Ling Tan lifted his head as he
worked in a field he could hear like distant moaning the
sound of battle. Now and again a deep roar broke out of the
east, and none knew what it was until some coming back from
the city one day said that it was the huge foreign guns the enemy
had.

The stream of those who fled had ceased. All who could
go were gone, and there remained only those who knew that
whatever happened they must stay. Ling Tan made himself
busy all day with the winter's work, and at night he sat long to
make straw sandals from the strong rice straw. There was one
light snow, and under it the winter wheat grew green, but the
snow was soon gone, and day measured off day and now each
day brought its own bad news.

On the seventh day of that month the last of the rulers went
away. There was an army left in the city to fight the enemy when
it came but what army would be brave when its rulers were
gone? The people groaned when they heard of it, and all around
the city for twenty miles the villagers armed themselves with
knives and ancient swords their fathers had left them and their
pitchforks and old guns they had bought long ago in thieves'
markets to use in times when the bandits were bad. First they
made ready to defend themselves against their own retreating

armies, for well they knew that soldiers in retreat whatever their flag will take what they see, because they know that they will not pass that way again and what they do will be blamed on others. Ling Tan armed himself with an old broad-sword his great-grandfather had. It had lain at the bottom of a pigskin trunk for two lifetimes, but now Ling Tan brought it out and his wife polished it with ashes and he swung it a few times and found it could be used like a scythe, and he hung it on a nail near his gate ready to use. Thus half a month passed, and all knew that any day might be the last that they were free, and they learned to measure the time of the enemy's coming by the daily growing clearness of the sounds of battle. Those roars of great guns were so near now that sometimes the dishes on the table jumped and the children cried.

In the last few days, the worst news that Ling Tan had heard came from the villagers nearest the city. For Ling Tan and his kin were lucky in this one thing, that their village was something more than three miles from the city. Within two and three miles the defending soldiers had burned the villages to prevent the enemy from plunder. Now bands of farmers and their families came by, their goods on their backs, and their small children swinging in baskets from carrying poles, as though it were a famine year, and they were hastening inland. When Ling Tan asked them why, they said:

"Our houses and our harvest are burned. Our land now is only scorched earth and why should we stay to be killed by the enemy?" And they hastened on their way.

That day, with the noise of battle loud in his ears, Ling Tan went out and looked on his land. Should he, too, scorch his earth? But where would he go with his household and among them so many women and little children and who would feed them if he burned his harvests of rice and grass? Deepest of all his unwillingness was the wish not to leave his land.

"If I could roll up the land and take it with me," he told his wife in the night, "then I could go. But my land goes deep under the skin of the earth and it goes down through the bowels of the earth, and I will not give it up. I will stay here, whoever comes, and keep this land mine."

"Then I will stay with you," Ling Sao said.

Days passed and with the rulers gone the people held themselves the more steadfast knowing that they and they alone were left to stand against the enemy and upon each man himself now depended what would happen. So it had happened again and again in other times, for rulers anywhere are always the first to fly, and the people must stay behind to be steadfast. And the noise of the battle grew more strong, hour by hour.

On the tenth day of that month like wind blowing through the countryside it was known that in three days the enemy would come. Now though Ling Tan was lucky in that his land was on the farther side of the city, and so the enemy would not come first to him and then to the city but would march on the city from another side, yet he was unlucky in this, too, for the defending army broke and ran without law and order, seizing all as they ran, and they streamed through villages, wild and frightened men, anxious only to be away from there, and their leaders being gone already they did not care how they disgraced themselves before the enemy so that they saved themselves.

Against these Ling Tan must now lock his gate and though there were those who beat on it he had made it so strong that in their dire haste it did not pay them to wait to break it in. When they found this gate did not open readily they went on and fell upon some other place and so his house was safe. But the ruin they left in the village and in all the villages in that direction was shameful to see and plenty there were who cried out that the enemy could not be worse than this, and there were even some who said plainly that they wished the enemy would come in and rule, that at least then there might be order. For now the robbers and bandits began to spring up everywhere like evil weeds. When a man sold some of his harvest and had a little money, these roving homeless men heard of it as though they smelled it, and they came down in the night and took what they wanted. To all other sorrows, there was added this ancient sorrow.

Wu Lien was one who wished for order at any cost. After the last of the defeated armies had passed he came out and walked up and down the street of the village and groaned to see every little shop emptied of what it had and the bakery cleaned of its last loaf and all gone without a penny in anyone's hand.

"Let no one say that there can be worse than what our own have done to us," he said, and when he was back in the house he said, "as soon as the enemy has occupied the city I shall go and open my shop again for I believe we shall be better rather than worse with their coming."

"If you are right, when they come, then I will say you are and take their rule for mine, too," Ling Tan answered. For while the soldiers had fled past his house he had climbed up on a corner of roof where he could be hidden and yet look down, and he was so angered by what he saw and by their wild ruthless looks that it was all he could do to hold on and not fall upon them, even though he knew that when a man becomes a soldier he ceases to be a man and goes back to the beast he once was in some other life.

But at last there was an end even to these retreating men. In that silent time between the retreat of the defending army and the coming of the enemy Ling Tan called the villagers together in the tea house and there they took counsel as to how the enemy was to be met. They knew the time was short.

"Surely they will see that we are a defenseless village," Ling Tan said, "and even an enemy will not fall upon those who have made themselves willing for their coming. Let us therefore think how to meet our conquerors courteously, not to welcome them falsely but to tell them that we are men of reason who can accept what has come in their life."

To this all were agreed, and then some asked, "When and from what place will this enemy come and on what road shall we meet them?" and others asked, "How should we meet them?" For not one of these men had ever seen a foreign conqueror before and though they all hoped for good and each told the others the good things he had heard of foreigners, they did not know what should be said to them or what the behavior ought to be of those who were vanquished by them.

Then the ninety-year-old said out of his long wisdom, "What ways do we know but our own? Let us do as we would do to any new gentry coming to our village."

Because of his great age all listened to him as he spoke, and they agreed that what he said was best. So it was planned that when they heard the enemy draw near they would go out in a body from the village, and that this oldest man should go first, and after him the others, and that tea should be prepared here and small cakes and fruits, and thus in decency and honor the conquest would take place. And as they planned there were some who said aloud that they hoped for order and peace at least, and that it would not be hard for the conquerors to be a little better than some of their own magistrates had been to them.

All having been decided, the inn keeper was called to the front of the tea house and it was told him to have tea and small cakes ready for the next few days and he said he would make some of his own small sesame cakes, and so they parted to wait.

In those next days while they waited there were those who went to the city and bought small enemy flags of paper for the people to hold in their hands when they went out to welcome the enemy, and to comfort themselves the villagers told each other that in the city they had heard, too, that foreigners were always better than their own people and in foreign countries there were more law and order than there were here and so in hope and fear all waited for the day of the enemy's coming.

... Thus dawned the thirteenth day of the eleventh month. On the morning of that day when he rose Ling Tan knew what day it was. All sound of battle had ceased. The air was as still as it had been in the years before the enemy ever came to the coast. A quiet wintry morning it was and the first heavy hoar frost was white on the land. He had risen early, for he slept badly now every night, and alone he went to his gate and looked over his whitened fields. The winter wheat was green under the white and he thought, "Shall I cut that wheat or will there be another in my place?" Upon the thatched roofs of the village the frost was beginning to melt from the smoke slowly curling upward as women lighted their fires, and without answering his own question he went into his house where Ling Sao had lit her fire, too.

He went to her in the kitchen where so often in their life he had found her and there she was behind the stove.

"This is the day we dread," he said.

"I know it," she answered. She lifted her eyes to his face and he saw they were steadfast.

"I fear no man," she said.

The old words came out of her with new meaning and he felt it.

"Nor will I fear," he said quietly.

In silence he washed himself and rinsed his mouth and in silence one after another of the household came out and took his place at the table. Even the children who on other days cried and laughed and quarreled and made commotion today were silent, too.

When all had eaten Ling Tan spoke to them as the head of the house. "By the stillness over the land I know that the battle is over. Our army has retreated and perhaps even by this time the enemy has taken the city. But here we must all stay within the walls of our own house. None of you is to go out without

120

telling me and especially no woman or any child is to go out for any reason. I myself will work only where I can see all roads and if I see a stranger coming I alone will speak, and none of you is to show his face except my eldest son and he only if he sees me distressed, and especially no woman is to show her face for any cause."

Each bowed his head after he had spoken and so within those walls the long silent day began. The women went to their work and Wu Lien withdrew to his room and each son went to his task of winter work of weaving sandals and twisting ropes, but Ling Tan sat smoking his pipe. His mind did not move, and after a while he perceived that the reason was that he was listening, listening, and yet he could hear nothing. He waited a long time and at last it seemed to him that he must know what was happening and what the full meaning of this great silence was, and so at mid-morning he opened his gate a little. The frost was gone from his fields and the sun was warm. The dog, which he had thrust out of the gate so that it would warn him if any stranger came near, leaped fawning at his feet and whined for food. Not another living creature was to be seen. Each man had shut himself behind his own doors as Ling Tan had and from the city none came or went. As far as eye could reach the roads stretched empty.

He came out of his gate then, and stood a while, his pipe in his hand. He looked toward the city but he could see no sign of any great fire. The high city wall circled those who lived inside, and there was no sign to read of what they were suffering. But there was no sign of suffering either. And as he stood there others who had opened their gates a little saw him and slowly one or two and then others came out of their houses and five or six until cautiously there were twelve or thirteen men in the street looking at one another. They moved toward Ling Tan.

"Have any of you heard anything?" he asked.

"Nothing," they said, and others shook their heads.

"Ought we not to discover something?" Ling Tan's third cousin's son asked.

"How can we?" Ling Tan asked. "Are you brave enough to go to the city and see what there is? You are the only one here without a wife and children and children's children he must think of."

"I will go," the young man said. "I am not afraid," and he shook back a lock of long black hair that hung over his eyes.

"Ask your father first," Ling Tan said. "I will not have your going put on me if any harm comes to you."

"My father lets me suit myself," the young man said wilfully, and to prove it he went off as he was that very moment, and the rest of them stood and looked after him as his one person moved along the empty road to the city.

"I am glad he is not my son," one said and all agreed with him.

Then because there was nothing else to say, they parted and each man went back to his own house and locked his gate again, and so did Ling Tan and thus noon came and afternoon. In all those hours the silence held except for a few times when a distant gun roared out.

By mid-afternoon Ling Sao was weary and the children who had been so quiet and good all day could be good no longer and they grew fretful and whined to go out of the courtyard to play, and Wu Lien who had heard from Ling Sao of the cousin's going to the city began to want to go out of the gate and Ling Tan was afraid for him to go, because he looked a rich man and an enemy seeing him might think there were food and goods in the house that such a man came from.

"If there are many days like this, our walls will burst apart from within," Ling Sao said, and so Ling Tan opened his gate a little and by now there had been other houses like his, and out in the street a few boys were playing and some of the gates were ajar, and a shop or two open. When he saw how peaceful all was, he called into his house:

"Let any who will come out on the threshing floor but no further than I can bid them back quickly if there is need to lock the gate."

They came gladly and looked around and everyone was astonished to see that all was the same.

"I swear I thought to see the very color of the ground changed," Orchid said laughing.

Ling Tan looked carefully everywhere himself and saw no one strange and nothing new and since after a while the afternoon was quiet he thought he would go to his cousin's house and see if there had been anything heard of his cousin's son. He walked down the street, and from the few open gates men called to him, and one or two laughed and said:

"If this is the way the enemy attacks us we can bear it!" and one said, "they leave us to ourselves, this enemy!"

Ling Tan agreed, meaning nothing, and went on to his cousin's house. There he found his cousin's wife all in a stir because her son was not yet home, and she had supper hot and she hated to waste the fuel to keep it so, and yet if he did not come there was nothing to do but wait. She seemed not afraid of any ill so much as of the waste of her fuel, and so Ling Tan told her to calm herself, because perhaps her son chose to come back by night. His cousin himself had eaten and sat picking his teeth and reading an old newspaper he had by him.

"It says here the enemy have sent down writings from their flying ships telling us all not to be afraid, because they bring only peace and order," his third cousin said.

"If it is true then they are good," Ling Tan replied, "and certainly today has been peaceful enough."

Somehow the words gave him comfort, and as he let down his heart, suddenly he was tired and he yawned and remembered how badly he had slept. Now the day he had feared was over and they were all alive and he had seen not the shadow of an enemy and so he felt his heart loosen in his bosom.

"I think I can sleep," he told his cousin, "I will go home, but if your son comes let me know."

"I will," his cousin promised and rose a moment for courtesy while Ling Tan went out, but his eyes were still on what he read for he was a man who valued what was printed on a paper more than anything a living mouth could say.

It was twilight when Ling Tan next looked out of his gate. He had eaten, and all his house had eaten and the children were in their beds, and he himself was about to go but he said to Ling Sao he would look out once more before he slept. When he opened the gate he thought he heard a moan. He listened and then he knew it was a moan, and his heart trembled with fear. He was about to shut the gate and lock it fast, not knowing whether what he heard was spirit or human, when a voice cried out faintly:

"Cousin!"

He threw the gate open at that and shouted for Ling Sao to bring the lamp and she came as soon as he called and they went out and there on the ground lay his third cousin's son, that young man who had left so wilfully this morning to go to the city.

Ling Tan would not have known him except that the young man had what none other in the village had, a red satin short coat without sleeves which he wore every day because he loved it and he had bought it in an old clothes' shop in the city before the last new year. This red satin Ling Tan now saw, but its brightness was dulled.

"Oh, my mother, how he is bleeding!" Ling Sao cried, and she gave the lamp to Ling Tan and was about to turn the young man over but her husband stopped her.

"Do not touch him," he told her, "else his parents will say we made him worse. Hold the lamp and I will run to call them."

He gave her the lamp back again and ran down the shadowy street to his third cousin's house, and pounded with both hands

124

on their locked gate and the dog inside helped him by barking and soon he heard his cousin's wife's voice asking who was there.

"It is I, Ling Tan," he called back, "and your son has come back wounded, how we do not know, but he fell at our gate because it was the first gate he reached and there he lies. We have not touched him."

The woman gave a great scream and called her husband, and the man came staggering out of his sleep, wrapping his coat around him, and he opened the gate, for the woman had forgotten to open it in her distress, and they all ran down the street together, the dog behind them, to where Ling Sao stood holding the lamp. By now the noise had roused Ling Tan's sons, and there were others, too, who heard it and these came out of their houses, so that in a few minutes there was a crowd about the young man, but none touched him until his parents came. His father was frightened when he looked at him, but his mother bent and turned him over and thought him dead and then she screamed.

There the young man's impudent face lay, pale and quiet in the flickering lamplight.

"What has wounded you, my son?" his mother cried in his ear, but he did not hear. "Oh, his red satin coat is spoiled and he will mind that!" she moaned, and then she struck off with her hand the dog who had followed them and now smelled the flowing blood and pressed forward eager to taste it, and the father was angry with the dog and gave him a great kick.

"I, who feed you," he cried to the beast, "and you would drink my own son's blood!" And he cursed the beast.

But moaning and cursing did not bring the young man back and at last Ling Tan said:

"We ought to lift him to his bed and call a doctor to see how deep the wound is."

He said this gently and in the kindness of his heart but the mother turned on him and cursed him bitterly.

"Yes, but it was you who sent him to the city this morning—I heard of it! He would not have gone alone, and he went out of the house without thinking of such a thing, but then you said—"

Ling Tan burst out to defend himself then, and he looked around at his neighbors and sons and called upon them to witness for him.

"Did I not tell my cousin's son I would not say he was to go and did I ask him if he went of his own will?"

"You did," they cried in his defense, and so the woman was silenced.

But Ling Tan forgave her, knowing it was fear made her angry, and he stooped and lifted the young man's head and bade his cousin take his feet, and the mother held his middle and so they carried the young man home and laid him on his bed and covered him. Yet where could they get a doctor? There might only be doctors in the city, if they had not fled, and who dared to go there, seeing how this young man had come back? None dared and they all went home except Ling Tan and he stayed by the young man's bed with his cousin and his wife.

Now Ling Tan believed this young man was not dead, but only wounded and faint from loss of blood, for if he felt the hands and feet cold, he felt the body warm where the heart was, and so he asked his cousin for a little hot wine and he poured it into the young man's mouth and though he heard no swallow, yet after a while when he looked the wine was gone, and so he poured more in and then that was gone. All the time he was doing this his cousin's wife was moaning and reproaching herself and all of them, and out of her came a bitterness that Ling Tan did not know was there.

"He has never been the same since you paid us to let your son have Jade," she mourned. "Ever since then he has not cared whether he lived or died, and we ought not to have listened to you, and you ought not to have asked it of us and tempted us with your silver. We are poorer than you and it is hard for us to refuse silver."

This made him angry, for in times past he had done much for this cousin of his who read books instead of earning his own food, and many a winter Ling Tan had sent one of his sons here with a bundle of straw for fuel or a measure full of rice or a cabbage or two, and now he set down the wine cup on the table and he said:

"Curse me if I ever give anything to anybody again, for it seems to me that the surest way to get hatred for myself is to feed the hungry and to lend to those poorer than I am! How it is you can be so surly with me because I give you something to help you, I will not ask or care."

This quarreling made his cousin anxious, for he did not ask where his food came from or his fuel, so long as he was left to his book, and so now he coaxed his wife, "Why do you anger a good man like this?" And he turned her anger on him, and she screamed at him that he was less than a man and she wished that she were a widow, and then she would sit and fan his grave dry night and day so that she could the sooner marry another and better man.

All this noise woke the young man from his faint, and in the midst of the fury he opened his eyes and spoke.

"Father!" he said.

They all stopped at the sound of that small voice from the bed, and the moment they saw him alive all the anger went out of them.

"Oh, my son, tell us how you were wounded!" his mother cried and she ran to his side.

The young man tried to tell her then but they had to bend to listen and to piece together his broken words and what they heard and put together was this, that he had been caught with others and stood against a wall and shot and left for dead. But he was not dead and in the night by crawling and moving he had crept into a street and there a rich Buddhist at this last moment escaping the city in a cart had taken pity on him and put him in the cart and left him near the village. But when the young man had crawled the distance to Ling Tan's house he lost his wits again and remembered nothing until now.

"Why should they kill you?" Ling Tan asked astonished.

"We ran," the young man gasped. "So fearsome were their soldiers I ran with the others—all who run are killed—"

The elders looked at each other and they were able to make nothing of this. Why should innocent men be killed because they were afraid?

At this moment the first light of dawn came into the small room and the young man moaned that his breast hurt him, and that was where the wound was. Yet when they touched him he screamed with pain and lost his wits again, and so they could only cover him and let him lie.

Thus it was when full dawn came and then Ling Tan knew that he ought to go back to his own house, and he told his cousin he would go and return later and so he left them.

That was a strange gray dawn, and made stranger by what Ling Tan now saw as he came toward his own house. For in the distance when he looked toward the city it seemed as though the gray land itself were moving. He stood still and stared, and then he saw that it was many people moving on foot out of the city gates toward his village. One instant he looked and then he went into his house and shut the gate and locked it.

"Where are you?" he shouted to Ling Sao, and at the sound of his voice she ran out. She had been combing her hair, and the great twist of it was between her teeth to hold it while she fastened the red cord that held it at her neck and so she was speechless.

In his terror Ling Tan pulled it out of her mouth.

128

"The enemy is coming," he gasped. "Bid all get up and put on their clothes and be ready for what is to come."

He himself ran out of the house and in doubt and yet not knowing what else to do except what they had planned, he roused the men of the village and bade the ninety-year-old to put on his best garments and his third cousin to put on his scholar's robes and he roused the inn-keeper of the tea house and told him to get his cauldrons boiling for tea and his cakes set out on the tables, and in a very few minutes they were all standing in the street, shivering with fear in the misty chill of that wintry morning. And for some reason which Ling Tan did not know himself the tears welled into his eyes at the sight of this handful of village men in their best clothes and the bent old man at their head and all with little enemy flags in their hands going out to meet the conquerors they had never seen. His heart misgave him and yet what could he do but go with them?

Down the road in the mists they could now see strange huge shapes.

"Let us go," he said, and he went slowly at the old man's side, and they went along the cobbled road of their village and beyond the last house to where the fields lay, and they held up their little flags.

But the strange huge shapes bore down upon them as though they were ants in the dust and to save themselves they had to step aside and let them pass. Now Ling Tan and his fellows saw these shapes were machines, and how could they speak welcome to machines? Ling Tan and his fellows could only stand aside, gaping and waiting, and the machines went through the village and on.

Then they asked each other, "Is this the enemy?" None had seen such machines before, grinding upon their own wheels as they went. But who could answer?

They waited a while longer in the cold cloud around them debating whether to return to their houses, when they heard the sound of tramping feet, and then they saw the dim shapes of walking men and these they knew were the real enemy. Now they gathered close together and in the road they stood waiting and when the leaders of the enemy drew near, they bowed to the enemy, and the old man took off his cap and the cold wind blew on his bare skull, and he began to speak the few words of welcome he had by heart and he lifted up his old piping voice,

"Friends and conquerors," he began, and then his heart misgave him and he stopped. The faces of those leaders were not good. They were fierce and savage faces, and upon them now were unnatural smiles.

When Ling Tan heard the old man fail he quickly took his place and stepped forward.

"Sirs," he said, "we are only farmers and a small merchant or two in a village and my cousin the scholar, and we are men of peace and reason, and we welcome law and order. Sirs, we have no weapons, but we have prepared a few cakes and some tea—"

At this point one of the enemy shouted out:

"Where is your inn?"

Ling Tan scarcely knew what this enemy said, so broken and guttural were the words.

"In the middle of our village street," he said, "and it is a poor village for we are poor men."

"Lead us there," the enemy said.

Ling Tan's heart misgave him more and he did not like the looks of the enemy as they came out of the mists and now close to him but what could he and the other villagers do except go on in front? Beside him the ninety-year-old hobbled as fast as he could, but it was not fast enough, for one of the enemy behind him prodded him in the back with a knife at the end of his gun and the old man cried out and then he began to sob with pain and surprise because no one in the village was ever hard with such an old man, and he turned to Ling Tan.

"I am hurt!" he cried, piteously.

130

Ling Tan turned to make protest to that enemy who had stuck the old man, but what he saw on the faces of those men behind him dried the spittle in his mouth and he went on, only putting his arm around the weeping old man until he came to his own door and then he thrust him in and told his son to go with him to care for him. So without these two they went on to the tea shop and there the keeper was ready with hot tea and cakes and his two sons had stayed to help him and the smiles were as thick as lard on their faces.

But the enemy swelled into the tea shop like an evil horde, and they sat down at the tables. By now Ling Tan and all the villagers knew that the outlook was not good with these men their conquerors and so he and his fellows stayed near the back door to the tea shop and waited while the keeper and his two sons poured tea. As soon as the tea was in the bowls a low roar went over the enemy and Ling Tan and his fellows could understand nothing of it, until that one spoke who could speak and that one said,

"Wine—we want wine, not tea!"

Ling Tan and his fellows looked at each other. Where could they find wine to feed so large a company of greedy men? Wine the villagers drank sometimes at the feast of the new year, or once or twice more when they went into the city after they had sold a good harvest, but there was no wine here.

"Alas, we have no wine," Ling Tan faltered, and he moved nearer to that back door.

This the enemy told the others, and the men looked darker than ever and muttered together and then that one spoke again, to Ling Tan:

"What women have you in this village?"

Now Ling Tan could not believe what he heard and for a moment he looked silly, thinking the man must have used one word for another.

"Women?" he repeated.

The man did not speak but he made an evil gesture toward himself and Ling Tan knew then that he did mean women, and now he looked at his fellows and he gasped out a lie to save them all.

"We will go and find women," he said, and then he and all his fellows ran out of that back gate and he stopped only long enough to tell the women in the kitchen of the inn,

"Run—run—hide yourselves—they look for women!" and then he ran to his own house and every man with him ran to his own house to save his own.

Inside his own gate Ling Tan drew the bar across and shouted to Ling Sao to get the household together, and he took down the old broadsword as he spoke and Ling Sao for once said nothing. She ran and called to her sons and daughters and their children, while Ling Tan stood and waited by the gate.

In a while he heard the sound of many feet come toward his gate, and he listened to this until it seemed he could not bear it, and then he opened the gate a little to see what went on outside. Well it would have been for him if he had borne his anxiety and kept the gate locked, for at that moment when he opened it there those faces were before his eyes, angry and full of fury, and under soldiers' caps he looked into eyes black and fierce with lust. They were like men drunk, their faces so red, and when they saw Ling Tan they plunged at him with a great shout. He stepped back and locked his gate at the same instant and the points of their guns struck into the wood. He heard his faithful dog, who had been barking and snarling at the enemy, yelp and then howl and then grow still.

"Our good old dog is gone," he groaned, but he could not help a beast now.

Well he knew there behind his gate that even its heavy wood could not hold and that he must prepare for the instant when they broke through, but he had this instant between. Now he thanked his fortune that he had seen war before this and that he knew how men in battle looked. He knew too how a man embattled is no longer himself but a creature with his mind gone and only the lowest part of his body left, and so his first thought was for the women in the house.

He ran back therefore into the house while the gate held and there he found all his household gathered in the main room, the women holding their children and the men's faces green.

"We are lost," his eldest son cried, but Ling Tan raised his hand for silence. Long ago he had made his plan for this hour.

"Every one of you is to go to that little back gate that has been locked all these years, and the vines hang over it so that it is not easily seen. Go out of that gate and scatter over the land through the bamboos and behind any hillock you can find. Let each man know where his own wife and children are, but pay no heed to others, and my third son is to look after his younger sister and his mother."

"I will stay by you," Ling Sao said.

"You cannot," he said, "I must climb the rafters and hide in the thatch."

"So will I," she said.

There was no time to deny her, and so he ran before them to the back wall and there he found the gate and he pulled aside the vines and wrenched off the rusty latch. It was such a narrow gate that he and Wu Lien saw at once Wu Lien's mother could never be pushed through it, and so he bade her stay until the last so that the others could be saved. Then he tried to push her through and Wu Lien pulled but it was true she was too fat and there was no way to do it without cutting her and that they could not, so Ling Tan pulled her back again and he told Wu Lien to leave and he would do his best for this old soul if Wu Lien would help the others. So Ling Tan saw them gone and over the sobbing old woman he let the vines hang, and he hoped for her safety but he could stay no longer to see to it, for she was not his own mother. The strong gate was

133

giving now, and he could tell it by the yelling triumph of the voices.

Back in the main room he climbed upon the table and swung up to the big beam above it and behind him Ling Sao came like an old cat, and he stooped and gave her his hand to pull her when she stuck and thus they reached the roof. Into that thick thatch which his forefathers had put over this house and which once in ten years or so each in his time mended and added to, he burrowed a hole above a side beam and he and Ling Sao clung there, suffocated with dust and straw, but still able to live.

Scarcely had they made themselves secure when the gate groaned and gave and he heard the noise of angry men surge into his court and then into the room above which he hid, but he could see nothing nor did he dare to move. Ling Sao clung to him and he to her, drawing their breaths only enough to live, and he prayed his forefathers to help him so that they would not cough or sneeze in the heavy dust. Lucky it was that the straw after all these years made a heavy mat woven together with cobwebs and with damp so that it held around them and the beam was beneath and yet they must not move lest dust or straw float down and tell where they were.

But it was only a moment that the men were in the room below, for when they saw it empty they howled and ran from one room to another of the eight rooms and the kitchen and Ling Tan and his wife heard their good dishes thrown down and broken and they heard their furniture broken and smashed, and they only trembled lest the house be set on fire and they burned with it.

They waited for this to happen next and Ling Tan planned how he would jump and pull his wife after him. But instead of the roar of flames they heard something else. It was a scream, which at first they thought was one of the two pigs, for it sounded like a pig stuck for butchering. Then they heard a word or two and a gurgle and a long moan, and they knew what it was. The enemy had found Wu Lien's old mother under the vines. Ling Tan moved to go down to her when he knew what it was, but his wife had her arms about him like a strong iron band.

"No," she said in the smallest whisper. "No! She is dead. You must remember us all. She was old. There are the young to think of."

And she held him and he knew she was right and he stayed.

So at last the wild enemy went away, but long after there was silence Ling Tan and his wife did not dare to move or to speak. They waited until their limbs were aching more than they could bear and until their lungs were choked and they must cough and spit out the dust, and their bodies were streaming with sweat, though it was a winter's day.

Then at last he whispered in her ear,

"I will go down because some of the children may come back and think us dead."

For herself she would not have allowed him to move but when he spoke of the children she let him, and she followed him, and down they crept again into what had been their good and ordered home.

It was ordered no more. They stood at last on the tiled floor of the main room and looked about them. There was nothing left whole, scarcely a chair and not the table even which now fell beneath their weight, nor the bamboo couch that the third son slept on, and they went from room to room, their two hands clasped together, and without one word of speech between them they saw the ruin of the house. When they had seen all, Ling Tan said:

"They have taken nothing but the rice. You see they wanted nothing we had and so in wantonness they broke to pieces what they did not want."

This the enemy had done, and they had torn garments and slashed the quilts on the beds and why they had not set fire to everything Ling Tan could not think except that in their wantonness they wished him to see ruins instead of only ashes.

"Oh, my good red pigskin boxes that I brought here as a bride!" Ling Sao moaned when she went into their sleeping room and saw them slashed and burst open. And among all the disorders of their ruined garments and burst boxes they saw a torn snarl of human hair and Ling Tan stooped.

"What is this?" he asked.

Then Ling Sao picked it up to see. "It is Jade's hair she cut off from her head that day," she said.

"Lucky it is not on her head now," Ling Tan groaned.

And yet they knew that worse than this was waiting them at the small back gate and so slowly they went toward it, dreading what their eyes must see,

"But we must be the first to see it," Ling Tan whispered. "We must not let any of the children come in first."

They crept through the ruined kitchen and out of the door and so to the small back court. There at their feet the old woman lay dead. It would have been enough had she been dead. But she was worse than dead. She was naked, and so wounded that they could see in a moment that in their fury those wild men had used her as they might have used a woman young and beautiful.

Now Ling Tan groaned for if this could happen to an aged soul, heavy with her years and half dazed in her wits, what of the young women in his house and what even of his own wife? He turned to Ling Sao, the blood all gone out of his face.

"The first thing I must think of is where to keep all of you who are women," he said. "Myself I can hide and the men can scatter themselves, but if the enemy is like this, what is to become of women?"

For once she could answer nothing, for she saw too that what had happened here might more easily have happened to her, and she could not speak a word to help him. She turned her eyes away in shame even before her own husband and she bent and picked up the garments the old woman had worn and put them over her nakedness. They could not lift her, the two of them, for the old dead one was too heavy, and three or four strong men would have to work together, and all they could do was to leave her where she was. And Ling Tan stepped beyond her and opened the gate a little and looked out. There was no one to be seen, and the sun shone down that day on the land as fair as it had ever done and he cursed Heaven in his heart that it could be so merciless. Then he told Ling Sao to come with him away from this old woman.

All the rest of the day they sat alone in their ruined house and they did not think of food or fire. They sat listening and waiting for the night when surely one of their sons would come back to tell them how the others were. Those in the village had fared as ill as they, they knew, but they dared not go and see. It was a time when each man ought to stay in his own house.

So night came on at last, at the end of this longest day that they had ever spent, and in the night the eldest and the youngest sons came creeping home. Sitting in darkness he heard the faint sound of their footsteps and then a noise of someone caught on a piece of furniture and then Ling Tan heard his eldest son's voice whisper:

"They are gone!"

"No, we are not," he said out of the darkness, and then he put out his hand and touched his son, and they found each other, still in darkness, for none dared to light the lamp.

"Where are the little children?" Ling Sao asked first, for all day long she had been thinking of those little grandchildren tortured perhaps and made playthings by such cruel men.

"All are in the city," the eldest son whispered and Ling Tan groaned out "In the city!" For it seemed to him the worst of all things that they should be there. But his son hastened to tell him how it came about.

137

"We took a long circle around the city," he said, "and we came to the little water gate, and there the people told us that though the city was full of death and grief, yet there was one safe place for women and for children. And, oh my father, by then we had heard enough to know that this enemy is worst of all against women, and we dared not bring ours back here, for what can our bare hands do to save them? This only safe place is inside the water gate, and there inside that gate you know the land is empty and quiet and they told us the enemy had not come to that place seeing there was nothing to be taken, so we waited until darkness came, hiding in groves and behind houses all day and fleeing if we saw an enemy come near, and then at darkness they opened the water gate and we crept through and we took our women and children to the place of safety. It is a foreign school, father, and there is a foreign woman there. I saw her close and she had a good face though she eats the foreign religion and not ours. But there is a high wall around the school and a great gate and when we knocked on it, the gate opened and the white woman looked out of it and when she saw our wives and little children, she opened the gate wide and took them in."

"Why did you not stay there, too?" Ling Tan asked.

"They have only room for women and children," his son replied.

"Are they truly safe there?"

"As safe as anywhere can be when devils are let loose," his son said sadly.

Now Ling Tan made up his mind what he must do.

"I have a command to put upon you," he told his sons. "If women are safe there, you must take your mother thither, too, now while the night is still dark."

The two young men looked at their mother wondering and she hung her head before them, ashamed because they were

SEP 1 4 2018

¹ f-- the first time in all their years she /vas silent.

happened to the old
ι word, until he had

ιy third brother can
fe I will come home
ιehow and we can if

ιds away while their
ing Sao came to this
her husband slept a
o how could they do
d, they clung to each
oing in any presence
in ot.   ust I leave you?"
"Yes, ̲   ̲ ̲   ̲   ̲ ɔn I would not have thought
could be at your age, ιɯ ̲ ̲   ny sons."

Wars he had seen and lustful soldiers among his own people, and yet never had he seen one who would have touched a woman of her years and place. That the enemy could do this told him more than anything that they were savages and wild men, beasts and animals. He held his wife's hand one moment more, and then he stepped back and called his eldest son.

"Take her, and do not let a harm befall her."

"I will not," his son said.

And so Ling Tan sent out of his house his own wife, and when she was gone he sat all night, not sleeping, but waiting until his son came back again. He wished a score of times that night that he had gone with his son; and yet what use would it have been? Two were better than three and he could not have left the third son alone, and four would have stepped twice as heavily as two.

139

"Find yourself a place to sleep," he told his third son, and the boy was still so young that he could clear a place upon the floor and sleep for weariness, and in spite of sorrow.

But Ling Tan could not. He sat in the ruin of his house and waited, and after a long time his eldest son came back safe and not having met the enemy.

"I put my mother into the gate myself," he said, "and the white woman took her in and said she would be safe if any can be safe."

Ling Tan sighed and did not answer. Now that his wife was safe, it seemed to him he was too tired to speak or move or sleep. But his eldest son dropped down where he was and slept a while, and Ling Tan sat on by his sleeping sons and did not know what time of night it was until he heard a cock crow.

"Does a cock still crow?" he thought and wondered that it could, and he sat on until the dawn broke and he saw the pale light fall upon his sons, sleeping in the ruins of his house.

VII

IN THE dimness of that night Ling Sao looked at the white
woman. The gate had shut behind her and her son was
gone. She was now locked in this strange place, with this
strange woman. The woman had hair as yellow as cat's fur, and
it did not lie smooth about her head as hair does, but it stood
out like lamb's wool. The eyes in this white face were pale yellow, too, or so they looked in the light from the lantern that the
woman held.

"Come with me and I will show you where your daughters
are," the woman said, and Ling Sao was frightened that she
could understand a foreigner.

"Is there magic put on me here that I can understand you?"
she said.

The white woman laughed a small laugh. "I have spent
twenty years in this city," she said, "and I study every day to
speak your language, so that I may tell you of the one true religion, and is it strange that you understand me?"

She led Ling Sao along a narrow brick wall, and on both sides
of the walk grass grew, and in the near distance were great trees
hanging down their branches. Never had Ling Sao been in such
a place as this. Then they came to a great house and into this
house the woman led Ling Sao, and into a hall which, though
long and wide, was full of people. A low light burned in the
ceiling and she could see upon the floor many people lying on
pallets.

141

"Women and children," the white woman said, "and your daughters and their children are there in that corner."

She picked her way between the sleepers and in a corner near a high table Ling Sao found Orchid and her two daughters and all their children. The children did not waken and at first Orchid too did not, but Pansiao was lying awake and sobbing, and when she saw her mother she sat up and put out both her hands and her face was all twisted as a child's is when it sees its mother.

"M-ma, have you come?" she whispered.

"Yes, I am here, my meat dumpling," Ling Sao said, and she sat down on the floor beside the young girl. Not since she was a small child had the girl heard herself so called, and it was the most comforting word Ling Sao could have spoken.

"And where is my father?" she whispered, her hand holding to her mother's.

"He is at home and so are your two brothers," Ling Sao whispered back. "Are you all unharmed here?"

"We are thus far," the girl replied, "but I could not eat I was so frightened and now I am faint."

"Lie down, then," Ling Sao said. "In the morning I will find you food."

"Oh, they feed us here," the girl replied, but she lay down, and now the elder daughter lifted up her head.

"Where is my husband's mother, M-ma?" she asked. "Did she not come with you?"

Now it is right for a wife to ask first after her husband's mother because she belongs to her husband's house, and after her marriage his mother must be more to her than her own, and Ling Sao knew the question was a proper one, and yet she wished for once her daughter had not done her duty, for how could she tell her what had happened to that poor witless old soul? She made up her mind to a good lie, and she said:

"She is so old she is safe at home." And then she asked, "Where is your children's father, child?"

142

"He led us here," her daughter replied, "and then he said he was going back to the shop. He said he was not afraid now that the city was fallen, for the next thing must be peace and he would leave us here until he saw what the pattern of the city was to be and how the outlook, and then he would take us home."

This whispering had begun to waken those who slept near and one woman after another sat up to see who the newcomer was and if she had any news. Now the woman who slept next to the elder daughter was a woman young and so exceedingly beautiful that Ling Sao did not like her looks the moment she put her eyes to her. No woman, she thought within herself, could look like this one and be a faithful wife and a good mother and all that a woman should be, and so to try her she said:

"Do we wake your child, good soul?"

"I have no child," the beautiful young woman said quietly.

"Are you here alone?" Ling Sao asked, to try her again.

"I am here with six others like me," the beautiful woman said.

By this Ling Sao knew that she was a courtesan and being herself a good woman she would speak to her no more and she stretched herself between that one and her own daughters, so that if there were any evil disease anywhere it must go over her before it reached her daughters and her grandchildren.

But at her side the beautiful woman still did not lie down.

"Good mother," she said, and Ling Sao wondered that she had so sweet a voice, "since you came in here after us, will you tell me how the city now is?"

"I did not come through the city," Ling Sao said shortly.

"Did you not?" the other said. "Are you from the country, good mother?"

"Yes," Ling Sao said again and more shortly still.

"Oh," the sweet voice sighed. "Then you do not know what

143

we have had in the city this day," and she bent her head upon her knees. "Oh, this day!" she sighed.

But before Ling Sao had time to ask her what she meant Orchid woke and saw Ling Sao and sat up, dazed with sleep.

"Are you here too, my mother?" she cried. "How did you come here and who takes care of the house, and what happened there after we left?"

She said this so loudly that others cried out to her to be quiet and little children woke and wept, and Ling Sao to show that she took the part of the public against her own silly daughter-in-law, shouted out more loudly still:

"Heaven look down on me that I have such an unmannerly wife for my eldest son, that she calls out in the middle of the night when she sees me and puts all of you to such trouble! Do not open your mouth again, silly child!"

So Orchid lay down again and after that there was some silence and all tried to get a little sleep after the sorrows of the day.

But Ling Sao had slept in only two beds in her life, the little narrow one where she slept in her father's house as a girl, and after that the wide bed where she slept with her husband, and she could not sleep now with a stranger on one side of her, and her own daughter breathing into her ear on the other, and from all over the great hall the sound of sighing sleepers and some who snored and some who moaned, and so she lay awake thinking of the day which had ended like this, and who knew how many more there must be like it before she could go home again, and what was her old man doing there without her? Many times in that midnight she thought that when dawn came she would dirty her face and tear her garments and make herself old and ugly and go home again, and yet when dawn came she could not do it, because whatever she did to herself, she could not be more old or ugly than Wu Sao had been.

So she rose early and helped her daughters to tend the little

144

children, and by that time all over the hall there were women stirring and little children crying and soon Ling Sao began to busy herself with others to help them. But the young woman at her side did not stir. She lay wrapped in a red silken quilt and slept or seemed to sleep and so did the others who slept around her.

"They are used to late sleep," Ling Sao thought with scorn in her thought. "They are the sort who sleep in the day because they do their work at night," and when her elder daughter and Orchid were awake she whispered to them who those young women were and that they must not speak to them or let their children speak to them, and to Pansiao she said, "If one of those strange women puts out her hand to you, do not let her touch you, and do not answer if one speaks to you. There are honest ones to talk to, and not those. Best it is if you stay with me, and speak to no strangers."

So she kept her own around her and out of the end of her eye she watched those sleepers.

When the sun was well up there were serving women who brought rice in great buckets and some salt fish and vegetables, and chopsticks and bowls and Ling Sao cried, "How can we eat when we have not money enough to pay for it?" For now she remembered that in their distress yesterday she had forgotten to ask her husband for money in her pocket, and to eat and not pay for it was shameful.

But the women who carried in the buckets laughed and told her to eat with the others, for there were those who gave the rice as a good deed to buy them into heaven. "Eat, good mother," they said, "for by eating you do a good deed yourself when you help our foreigner mistress into heaven."

"Is this why she comes here to help us?" Ling Sao said, wondering, and so she ate with the others and felt better after her belly was full.

Only when all were nearly finished did those seven sleepers

145

get up out of their beds at last and smooth back their perfumed hair and wash themselves in the basins that were on a table there with water in jars to fill the basins, and it could be told from the way these washed themselves what they were, for they made themselves clean beyond what any honest woman needs to do. Then they went together to get their rice and stood eating it apart from the others. These young women did not look at the others but among all the good and honest mothers and wives there was not one who did not look secretly to see what such women were, and who did not draw her child aside if one of them came near by chance.

So began this strange day, and it was not too evil, for outside of the great house full of women, so full that there must have been a hundred or more, not counting the children, there were fields of smooth short grass soft to the foot when it was walked. The grass was not green now, but still it was soft, and when the sun came warmer they all walked out with their children and then woman spoke to woman. And many spoke to Ling Sao, for she had a kind round face and bright eyes, and her black hair was mixed with gray, and she was the sort to whom all spoke easily and whom easily they called "good mother."

From one and then another she heard such things as had never gone into her ears before and the more she heard the more frightened she grew. For it seemed that though many in the city had hoped for the quick coming of the enemy, if the enemy must come, so that there could be peace, yet when that enemy did come it was with such madness, such cruelty, so fiercely and savagely, that all were dazed and put out of their minds. This was what she heard, that into this great rich city which was the center of the nation, the enemy had come like wild beasts, no, and worse, for beasts would have eaten men and women, and these killed only the men and took the women. Whether a woman was old or young was nothing. Young were taken first and then old.

146

"My sister's baby cried," one girl said, whose eyes were swollen nearly closed with weeping, "he was but five months old, and he was so hearty and strong and cried so loud, because they snatched him from her breast, and then the enemy who had hold of her was angry and strangled the little thing with her own garments, and she lay bound and not able even to cry out, and when he and thirty others were done with her she was dead, too."

"Did you see this?" Ling Sao whispered.

"No, but my father told me," the girl said. "I am not wed yet, and he brought me here early, but she was a married woman and who could have thought that she would have died like that?"

Yes, though all knew what any soldiers will do in their triumph when a city is taken, and all knew that young women must be hidden for a few days until there are calm and order again, and this certainly if women are beautiful, yet none had ever heard of such evil as had now come. Other soldiers had taken this city in other times, but none who were foreigners until these came in, and the people had been deceived and told that these foreigners were better than their own soldiers, and so not all had done as much for safety as they might have done in ordinary wars.

Many were the innocent and unknowing men who died, for these women told Ling Sao what they had seen with their own eyes, that if a man turned and ran when he saw the enemy he was shot where he ran and there fell thousands like that in one day. And if a man seemed at all a soldier or as though he had been a soldier, he was killed, and there fell more thousands like that in one day. And if any man was slow to move when he was given a piece of work, or if he was too young and not strong enough for a great burden on his back, or if he were an old man or a scholar who had never done hard work, then he too, was killed, and so fell yet more thousands in a day.

147

All through that morning Ling Sao heard these things so that by noon when the food was served again, even though the rice was dry and tenderly cooked, she could not eat it with ease, and by night when the supper was brought, though it was good rice and cabbage and the cabbage cooked with bean oil and nearly as well as she could have done it, she could eat nothing because of all she had heard, and that which had befallen Ling Tan and her, which had seemed so great and evil, now had shrunk into one small evil among others much greater. Many of the women who talked to her had seen those of their own blood killed before their eyes, or raped or beaten, and there were many who said nothing to any one because what they had suffered was beyond telling.

So when night came Ling Sao was dazed with sickness and weariness, and more than either of these, with the fear she had never known before. For what was ahead of them if the land was to be held by such an enemy as this, and what would they do with these rulers who were not men? Evil rulers all peoples knew and all had to suffer them sometimes, but these were more than evil. There was no human heart in them.

Thus night fell again, Ling Sao's second night out of her home, and it came to her with grief that she had scarcely thought of her husband all day, so busy had her ears been with what she heard. Yet now when she had seen her grandchildren in bed and one by one mothers were lying down beside children, she lay down, and there beside her again were the seven courtesans. It had been her plan in the morning when she rose that somehow during the day she would move her sleeping place and those of her children, but she had forgotten it and now she could not. She lay down silent, therefore, and she drew herself back from the young courtesan nearest at her side.

"Why are you here?" she asked that young woman somewhat angrily after a while. "Women like you ought not to be here."

That young woman smiled sadly. "Even we are women," she

said quietly in her pretty voice, "and we fear beasts, too." And she drew back also from Ling Sao, as though she knew what she was and would keep herself apart. She spoke no more to Ling Sao, but only to her companions who slept on the other side, and what they said Ling Sao could not understand, for they were from another city than this and they had their own language when they spoke together, though they spoke many languages since they must please many men, and they spoke even some foreign languages so that they could please the men who came in on foreign ships, and all this Ling Sao knew, because everybody knows such things.

"I suppose they are from Soochow," she thought, and only that she must prove herself right, she asked the young courtesan one more thing.

"Are you from Soochow?"

"Yes, we are," the courtesan said.

"Then why are you in this city?" Ling Sao asked. In her bosom she thought that if they had come here to profit from the soldiers, then why were they not outside these walls doing their work and so making the city safer for the good women who were wives and mothers?

"We were in Soochow when it fell," the young courtesan said, "and in our house there were twenty-three courtesans and of those there are only us left, and we are only seven. We escaped but not whole, and because we cannot forget what happened to us, we fled here, and then we could go no further for we had no more money. When we heard the white people could offer safety to women inside this wall, we came too, for we hate this enemy. Oh, they are not men—men we know, but not these!"

She turned her back then and they spoke no more but after a while Ling Sao heard her crying almost silently. Only an ear as close as Ling Sao's could hear it, so quiet was the weeping. And Ling Sao's warm heart moved after a while longer to ask

149

herself if she ought not somehow to comfort this creature who was still young and beautiful, and yet the strong dislike in her for such women kept her as she was. Ling Tan in all his life had never looked at a courtesan and she knew it, and yet as much as though he had she feared and disliked these women whom until now she had only heard of and never seen. And so she let the weeping go on until at last it was still and then in her great weariness she slept.

Deep in the middle of that night she woke, and then they were all wakened out of their sleep by the noise of thundering upon the gates and of shots of guns fired over the wall. They woke and every woman lay quaking in the darkness, fearful of what was to come. Soon they heard loud voices, the voices of men speaking a language they could not understand, and they knew that the enemy had come even to this gate.

Women rose then and in the darkness each put on any garment she had laid aside when she slept and each waited where she was, and not a word was spoken, and when a child cried, his cry was smothered somehow. Then after a while there was a light and into the hall there came that white woman, and she had a lantern in her hand and this she held high, so that the light fell over their faces.

"I have bad news," she said. "The enemy is at the gate. There are a hundred armed men there, and they say they will come in and I have no more power to keep them out. I have no arms, and I have only the power of my God and my country to hold them back. They do not fear my God, but they do fear a little my country, which is a great nation. Because of this they have not yet come in, and so I have been able to buy them with a price."

She looked out over their faces and they saw her narrow mouth quiver in her pale face. "It is such a price," she said, "that I am ashamed to tell you what it is and yet I must tell you that you may save yourselves. They say they will not come in if we give to them a few women who will go away with them, perhaps five or six, even—"

This she said, and was silent, and all of them were silent. Where were there women who would go with such men, even to save the others? None could speak.

That white woman waited, and there was the noise again, the shouting and the beating upon the gate. So the white woman went away and they sat there. Still no one spoke, but each woman said in her bosom, "It cannot be I—how can it be I?"

And after the space of about as long as one could have counted two hundred pennies, that white woman came back again and held up her lantern, and now she spoke in great haste:

"I cannot hold them back," she gasped. "They say that if I do not give them the women at once, then they will come in. Oh, my sisters!" She stopped a moment and looked down at them from the raised door where she stood. "Who am I to tell any woman she must go out of my gate for such a cause, and yet it comes into my mind that God may have prepared in this room those who—who would—would save the—the good women. I do not ask it—I only say, if there are such, if they feel they can do it—or perhaps it is better to—to—" She could not speak more, and in the strong yellow light of the lantern they saw her bite her lips, and in her hand the lantern trembled.

Then Ling Sao saw that which she was never to forget so long as she lived, a thing which until she died kept her heart soft and tender toward all women called evil. For at her side that beautiful young woman rose and smoothed back her hair and straightened her garments.

"Come, my little sisters," she said in the weariest and saddest voice, "come, get up and smooth your hair and put on your smiles again. We must go back to our work."

None spoke, while these others rose at the sound of her voice. None spoke while the seven stepped across the room between the pallets on the floor and moved toward the door.

Then that one who had called the others stopped before the white woman.

"We are ready," she said in her pretty voice.

"God give you blessing," that white woman said, "God take you into heaven for this!"

But the beautiful courtesan shook her head.

"Your God does not know us," she said, and quietly and with her body held very straight she led the way to the gate and the others followed her, and behind them the white woman lifted the lantern so that they might see the way.

In the room they had left there was darkness and not a woman spoke. But mothers lay down again beside their children, and Ling Sao beside hers, and now the place on the other side of her was empty. And she lay there, her heart crumbling inside her with pity and sorrow and tears came to her eyes and as soon as she wiped them away they came again.

There was no more noise at the gate then and the white woman did not come back, and the next dawn came as it always had and Ling Sao rose, and the day went on and not a woman there but thought of what had happened in the night, and yet not Ling Sao and not any other could speak a word of it. Each mother fed her children and tended to her little work, and it was a day of silence, and the white woman did not once come near them, and then night fell again.

VIII

In his shop alone Wu Lien worked. For the first three days of his return he did not go out on the street, but he opened the boards of the front, and he began to put in order the confusion he found inside, so far as he was able. And yet there was one thing he did before anything else. Before even he found food after he had put his wife and his children into the white woman's gates he took soot from the kitchen chimney and he mixed it with water and when he searched for a brush and could not find one in all the disorder of his goods, he tied a rag to a stick and dipped it into the inky water he had made and he wrote in large black letters upon the whitewashed outer walls of his shop these words.

"East-Ocean Goods Sold Here."

For the first time since the students had spoiled his shop he felt comforted. Where were those students now? There was not one to be seen. Those who had not fled were killed, doubtless. But he was alive, and he had opened his shop again and in a few days if all went well, he would bring back his wife and his children, and they would all be prosperous again.

"To love one's country," he thought, "is it to love one's country when one destroys honest goods in a shop? Is that the way for men of reason to behave toward each other?"

And it seemed to him that between him and those students he was the better patriot, because he was alive and he had

153

destroyed nothing and no one, and in a little while indeed he would be providing food and business again for others.

So although he had never done such a thing in his life before, now he took pleasure in cleaning the shop as far as he could with a wall fallen, and he thought that he might even put his house to rights somewhat before his wife came. He had not made up his mind when it would be well to bring her here, for he could not close his eyes to all the dead who lay on the streets, nor could he keep from hearing screams at night and sometimes even by day which told him that somewhere near a woman was suffering. But he never went out of his doors and he worked on and he thought, "These things are not my business," and he told himself that it was not his fault that soldiers were like this, and that whatever came he was a man of peace.

Nevertheless he thought after a while that before he brought his wife home he must have some sort of protective paper from the conquerors of the city which would prove that he was a good citizen and one able to perceive that not all times are alike, and that Heaven changes the rulers of a nation at its own will, and whatever Heaven sent he would take and go on with his business. Where to go for that paper and whom to ask for it he did not know.

Yet it was not too long after he had put up his sign that four enemy soldiers came by, one of them a small officer of some sort and the other his men, and they came in to find if he had any food to sell.

This much he made out from the officer's scanty speech, and the others could say nothing he understood. Fish was what the man wanted, salted fish, but all that Wu Lien had was some small fish put into little tin boxes and not salty but soaked in oil. These he brought out, and showed them to the man, and the man nodded that they would do.

"How much?" the officer asked, putting up his fingers.

Wu Lien was surprised and pleased that this question should

even be asked for he was used to soldiers who came in and took and went away without asking anything, and so he shrugged his fat shoulders and smiled and said, "Nothing—it is a gift."

Now it was the officer's turn to be surprised, and he smiled also, and his teeth were very white and clean. "Ah!" he said, "you do not hate us?"

Wu Lien smiled yet more, "I hate no one," he said.

The officer bowed, and he spoke to his soldiers, and immediately they also bowed. "You must take something for the goods," the officer said.

"I cannot," Wu Lien replied, "I bought them from your country and I return them to you." Then he too bowed.

At this the officer sat down on a small stool by the counter, and waved his hand toward the street.

"For all this—we are so sorry. Our soldiers, very brave—angry."

Wu Lien inclined his head. "We also have our soldiers and I know how soldiers are," he said. "But now—let us hope for peace. Only in peace can we do business."

And then, in simple words which the officer could understand, he told him how students had destroyed his goods, and then he said, "Of recent years in this city the times have been evil. It may be they will be better now."

"Oh, we promise!" the officer said, "if many are like you."

"There are many," Wu Lien said modestly. He now began to be encouraged and so he turned and chose from his newly ordered shelves some tins of sweet cakes, and he gave one to each soldier, and all were pleased.

"Forgive me that I have no tea," Wu Lien said, "but my household are not here, and I am alone."

"But why?" the officer inquired.

Wu Lien coughed behind his hand. "She is visiting her mother," he said, "but she will return in a few days."

The officer perfectly understood why Wu Lien did not have

155

his wife here, but he was pleased that he did not say so, and so he told him to fetch paper and a pen. Wu Lien hastened to find them in his own inner room, and the officer wrote some bold black letters that Wu Lien could not read, and then in letters that he could read he wrote his name and where he lived in this city, and then he gave the paper to Wu Lien.

"If any come here to trouble you, show them that paper," he said.

"How can I thank you?" Wu Lien answered. "What can I say except that whatever you want me to do I will do?"

"Good," the officer replied. Then he said, "And I will send you a sign from our headquarters to put at your door and a guard if that is not enough."

Wu Lien was glad to hear of the sign, but he trembled to think of a guard at his door, for whoever heard of a guard that did not eat more and drink more than ten usual men and who did not ask for the best chair and for whatever else came into his mind? So he made haste to say:

"For the seal all my thanks, even to ten thousand thousand, but I am too small a man for a guard. All that I have is not worth half his price. Let it be that I may come to you, and I beg that if you have need of an honest plain man, here I am, Wu Lien the merchant, and this was my father's shop before me, and with your kindness it will be my son's after me."

"Certainly," the officer said proudly. "We will do no harm to those who do not resist us,"

"Why should I resist kindness?" Wu Lien replied.

And so upon seeming mutual good will they parted. But after they were gone Wu Lien sat down and wiped his forehead, even though the day was cold. To his surprise his body under his garments was steaming with sweat, and now he knew that in his bowels he had been afraid of the enemy after all but that he would never be so afraid again, and with his relief sweat poured out. "I have only not to resist," he thought, "and certainly that is easy enough for a man like me."

He felt more cheered than he had in many months, and when in the afternoon of that same day a soldier brought to his door a box and in it folded an enemy flag and attached to it a piece of cloth with some letters on it, he felt as though he had won his own battle. He made haste to give the man some money, and when the man was gone he put up the sign upon the lintel of his door. Yet while he did this he heard a girl scream in the alley next to his house and he stopped a moment to listen and knew from the girl's babbling terror what was happening to her.

"That soldier," he thought, "that soldier who just now brought me this sign, can it be he?"

He listened until there was silence, and did not go near to see what the silence meant, for how could he accuse the one who had only a moment before done him kindness?

"Thus it is in war," he thought sadly and was a little distressed for a while, and he made himself some hot tea. Then while he sat drinking it he reasoned with himself and he thought with anger of the girl's father. "Why does he keep a young girl here in these days before peace is established?" he asked himself and he thought how wise he was to have arranged his own affairs so well.

And yet all was not so well as he thought. At sundown when it was time to put up the boards for night he looked up to take down the sign first. That sign was gone. He could not believe it for he had himself nailed it up, and yet it was gone and only a few rags of the enemy flag clung to the nails. He stared at it and grew afraid as he looked. Was there a student still alive and near him?

"An enemy has done this to me. I have an enemy near me," he thought, and he went in and put the bar against the boards and he hid himself in his lonely bed and could not sleep. "A guard," he thought, groaning, "it may be I must yet have a guard to keep me from my enemies."

. . . In his own house Ling Tan and his sons themselves made the coffin for Wu Lien's mother. These were days when every coffin maker and every carpenter must work day and night and there was not one for hire. Some of the wisest of the coffin makers, knowing how good wars are for their business, had for months ahead made coffins and stored them in their own houses and in temples and anywhere they could, preparing for what was to come. But even all of these coffins were not enough for so many dead as were now in and around that city. Many were buried without coffins and the enemy dug holes and shoveled the dead bodies into them and covered them shallowly so that hungry dogs clawed them up again. Lucky for all it was winter and not summer, or the stench of that city would have risen into the nostrils of the gods themselves.

So Ling Tan well knew that it was useless to hope to find a carpenter, and he and his sons took boards from the beds no longer slept in and two inner doors and they built the coffin and then with ropes and poles they lifted that great body and heaved it into the coffin and nailed the lid, and with the buffalo pulling on ropes and they all pushing they dragged the coffin into the fields and buried Wu Sao and made a high mound over her body so that they could point it out to Wu Lien if ever he came back, and could say to him:

"There she is, and we did all we could for her."

Then they went back into their house and they began to sort out the ruins and to mend what they could and make what they could, so that they could live. Thus it was with every house in that village for there was not one that had escaped without ruin except the house of Ling Tan's third cousin, which was so poor that the enemy had not even troubled to destroy its miserable furniture. The third cousin and his wife had escaped free, for when the enemy came they ran and sank themselves into a

158

great jar of ordure and the jar was nearly as deep as a man is tall, and wide enough around for five men. It stood at the edge of a field and its ordure was kept to enrich the land. Into this the third cousin and his wife leaped and only kept their noses out to breathe with, and they were safe, though still stinking even after many washings, so that the villagers laughed in the midst of their grief. Their son, too, had escaped, for he was in a faint when the enemy came in and his mother covered him with bundles of fuel behind the kitchen stove and so he was not found.

This house only out of all the village was as it had been, and the third cousin's wife was virtuous and said that it was because the gods saved them. Whether the young man would live or die, none yet knew, for he could not yet eat or speak, and if he came out of one faint he fell into another, and he bled again if he were moved, but at least he did not die, and one villager after another came and looked at him and said what he would do if it were his son, and his mother did everything that any said, and spared nothing, so there was hope that out of some one thing his life would yet be saved.

But except for this household, all the others were spoiled as Ling Tan's had been, and some had suffered worse than he, for they had not been so quick-witted to get their women away and hidden. Out of that village of less than a hundred souls, seven young girls were dead, and four women, and none knew how many were despoiled, for no man would tell if his own daughter or his wife had suffered. Among the dead, too, was that oldest man. He had laid himself down in his bed the very day the enemy had pricked him, and because it was so small a wound and the day so full of terror, none had given him great heed. In the evening when they went to him, they found him dead. And Ling Tan grieved for the old man as though he had been more than a distant kinsman in his village, and he thought sadly. "That prick went very deep. The old one knew the days

159

were gone of our happiness and freedom and so he did not wish to live."

When Ling Tan had seen his village and what it had endured, he and the other elders came together to decide how to put their women in safety and he told how he had his own women inside the white woman's gate and so they all said they would do the same thing, and thereafter whenever that gateman of the white woman heard the soft scratching of a willow branch on the gate he opened it and there were other women and more girls and the white woman took them in.

So at last in the village there were left only men and one or two grandmothers, and Ling Tan's third cousin's wife who could not go because of her son, and she said:

"There is always the jar of ordure, and what has been done once can be done again."

The only quarrel that came out of the jar of ordure was that her husband had a scholar's beard that he had raised with great trouble and only after years for he was not a hairy man, as men of learning are not, and yet every scholar wants his beard. So he had his little beard at last and try in every way he could, he could not now wash the stink out of his beard, and his wife who all these years had put up with the foul breath that came out of his belly complained that at least he could cut off his beard. But no, he could not smell himself and he would not cut it off, and this came to be a quarrel between them, and it made something for the villagers to laugh at and they were glad to have it, for there was little else. It is a sorry thing for men to be living alone in a village and every man missed his wife, and they teased the one man who had his wife left to him, and they said:

"Do you love your wife best or your beard, old head?" and in the morning they would guffaw and one would say, "ah, the old one still has his beard and so she would not have him again! Well, I had rather have my wife locked behind walls somewhere than in my bed and refusing!"

For this third cousin's wife had put her husband to shame by saying where she could be heard that she would not allow him her favor until he had cut off his little beard, and so that beard made jokes every morning for them all except the man who had it on his face.

Without going near the city himself Ling Tan contrived to send by any who took his wife or daughter there or his sister, some small thing to Ling Sao. The black hen laid a handful of eggs in spite of evil times and these he sent in a handkerchief, and he caught a fresh fish out of the pond and wrapped it in a dried lotus leaf with salt and sent it, or he picked two cabbages that a man could slip under his coat, and he longed that he could write to Ling Sao or that she could read, but all that he could do was to trust to another's ears and mouth.

"Tell her that we have cleaned the house and that we manage, though poorly without her," he told one, and he said, "tell her we buried the old dead woman and made the coffin ourselves," and he said, "tell her not to be impatient to come home, for we hear that now the city is despoiled the enemy comes into some village every day, though we do not fear, for all the women are gone out of ours."

Never had he thought he could miss anyone as he now missed Ling Sao, and yet it was not that he missed her as woman, but as though she were part of himself, and nothing was good in his mouth or to his hand because she was not there. He wondered somewhat that he did not miss her more, but no, his body was as quiet as though he were a eunuch, and he could not understand why this was so, since all his manhood years he had been used to what he wished. He put this to his eldest son one day when the youngest was out of hearing, and he said, not speaking for himself out of shame between the generations:

"Do you find yourself ill at ease with your children's mother so long gone, my son?"

And the young man answered, surprised at himself, indeed,

"No, I am not, and it is strange, too, but I take it thus, that we hear so many tales of lust and evil against women that the taste for any woman has gone out of us for awhile, and so I think it is with all men who are clean husbands and good men."

This Ling Tan had not thought of, and yet the more he thought of it the more he saw it might be true and he looked about him and he found that the men he knew were of two kinds, and some were like him and his son, and there were others who were stirred to greater lust because of all the evil that they heard, and so he knew that men are good or evil in their hearts, whatever others think they are, and such times show them out.

And yet there was another evil to fall upon Ling Tan, a new one, and if any had told him he would not have believed it until he saw it with his own eyes and it happened to his youngest son.

Now it was true that the city grew calmer as days passed and that it did was because from the horror of what was happening there went up a noise to heaven and spread over all the earth so that men and women in other countries heard it and cried out that such beastliness had never yet been known since the first man was made, and when the enemy perceived that all others knew what its own men did, a sort of shame fell on the enemy rulers, and so half-heartedly and in one way and another they let down commands that at least evil must be hidden and that not in the city streets could such things be done as would leak out and shame them before the world. Then the enemy began to come from the city and to spread among the villages, and one day Ling Tan looked up and there at his door stood four enemy soldiers. He was washing the rice for the evening meal, and his sons were at the loom, the younger one sorting out the threads. The loom alone in his house had not been destroyed, for it stood in a dark room where a lamp had to burn, and it looked like nothing useful, besides, to one who did not understand its shuttles and its ropes.

Ling Tan put down his basket and went to the door. Well he knew that it was no use to pretend he was not there, for he would only have his mended door broken in again. So he went and threw the door open, and the sunset light fell upon the hot faces of four young men. They shouted at him and first he thought they wanted food for he could not understand them, and so he stepped back and pointed to his rice to ask if that was what they wanted. With that they shouted more loudly and shook their heads in a fury and then they pointed at themselves and loosened their garments and he saw that what they wanted was women, and they were demanding that his women be given to them. He thanked his forefathers in his heart that every woman in his house was gone and so he said in his own language, since he knew no other:

"There are no women in my house."

But they in turn could understand nothing that he said and so they leaped in and pushed him aside and searched for themselves in every room and place and when they found no sign of women, except some women's garments left behind they grew fierce and bellowed at him, and still he could not understand what they said. But their anger he did understand.

"If there are no women here am I a god that I can make you one?" he asked them.

At that moment there was the sound of the loom again and with an evil yell these men ran toward the weaving room, and Ling Tan followed, fearful of what might happen in their fury when they found no women there. He stepped in behind the soldiers, and he saw their eyes seeking every corner. His eldest son sat high on the loom and now he stopped it, and stared down, and his third son dropped the loops of thread he held and stared, too.

When those furious soldiers saw that indeed there was no

163

woman their lust knew no bounds. It burst from them like wicked flames and now Ling Tan saw what he had never dreamed of seeing. He saw them lay hold upon his youngest son, that lad who had always been too beautiful for his own good, and now his beauty was his grief, for they took this boy and used him as a woman. And Ling Tan, his gorge rising and his vomit in his throat, could not bear it, and the eldest son could not, and they fell on the soldiers. Yet what could men unarmed do against four with weapons? Those four stopped and bound the father and his eldest son together with ropes they jerked from off the loom, and they bound them so that they must face the thing they did, and prodded them when they closed their eyes, and so the thing was done, and the beautiful boy lay like dead on the ground. Then, laughing, those soldiers went their way.

And Ling Tan and his sons said not a word. Slowly with great effort Ling Tan and his eldest son freed themselves, and the son gnawed the rope apart with his strong teeth, stronger and more whole than his father's, and when they were free, Ling Tan took the water he had prepared to cook the rice in, and washed his youngest son and put his clothes on him, and soothed him and helped him to rise, and the eldest son helped him. The lad was not dead, nor even wounded near to death, but he was like one dead, as though his heart had been stabbed, and his father was afraid he was out of his wits.

"My little son," he said, "you are living."

"I wish I were dead," the boy whispered.

"You must not wish for death," Ling Tan said, "for that is to be unfilial to your ancestors. No, my son, if you are alive it is because Heaven has said you are not yet to die."

But the boy seemed not to hear him. His skin was pale green in its color on his cheeks and his black eyes were like the eyes of the dead.

"I cannot stay here," he gasped.

164

"You shall not stay here," Ling Tan soothed him. "I have some money hidden in the wall where it was not found, and you shall take it and go anywhere you will. Ah, if we knew where your second brother is, and where Jade is with him!"

He was afraid of his son's dark dazed looks and in his heart he feared lest this wounded boy might join himself to other desperate men such as the bandits were and so he begged him:

"If you go to the hills, do not join the evil men who rob our own people. Seek out the good hill men who make war only on the enemy."

But the boy did not answer. He let his father put on his outer coat and he tried to eat some bread, and when he could not he took it in his hand tied into a square of cloth, and he took the money and put it in his belly band and then he stood, swaying as he rose, so that Ling Tan caught him.

"How can you walk?" Ling Tan asked him afraid.

"I can walk," the boy said, and he looked at his father with his dark dull eyes.

"Send me word somehow where you are," Ling Tan begged him. Now that the boy was ready to go he seemed so young, he looked so ill.

"I will," the boy said. He swayed again and then held fast to his father's shoulder. "Father," he cried, "father!"

His mouth quivered, and Ling Tan saw he was trying not to weep. He put his arms about his son. "Do not go until tomorrow," he begged. "Rest a night first," he begged him, "and I will make some hot thin rice for you to drink."

"I cannot rest," the boy said, "I must go."

He straightened himself and went toward the door, and by now it was dark except for the faint light of the moon and fainter stars. The night was still and cold, and he went out into it and with no backward look he struck out toward the hills, and Ling Tan and his eldest son stood watching him as long as eye could see.

"Is there anything worse that can happen to us?" Ling Tan whispered.

His son did not answer, and above them the night sky was as beautiful as it had ever been in time of peace.

"That sky," Ling Tan said suddenly, "will nothing change it?"

He looked up into it and Lao Ta was frightened, thinking that out of sorrow his father's reason was gone. "Come in, my father," he said gently. "The night is too cold."

He drew his father in and Ling Tan let himself be drawn and then Lao Ta barred the door fast.

"Can you eat if I cook the rice?" he asked his father.

"I feel tonight as if never could I eat again," Ling Tan answered.

"So I feel also," Lao Ta said.

They went each into his own room then but after a while Ling Tan got up and went into his son's room.

"I cannot close my eyes without seeing what I have seen," he told his son. "I cannot be alone."

"Come here and lie beside me," Lao Ta said, and the father came and lay down beside his son. Neither of them had taken off a garment for none now dared to take off at night when none knew what might happen in the long dark hours.

There they lay, two men left alone in this house that had been so full, and they did not speak, for each knew all the other knew. But they did not sleep. Together their minds followed the slender figure of the boy, limping lonely through the night and toward the hills.

IX

Now Wu Lien saw that if he were to have safety from his own enemies he must have his protection from the enemy who had the city in their power, and so after a day or two of terror and not daring to come out of his door, he made up his mind one night that he would seek out the officer who had been courteous to him and tell him all his troubles, and how he was no traitor at heart, but merely a man of business who had in his house more than his own mouth to feed.

So he waited until night came full and then, putting on his oldest clothes and taking no lantern, he went to the street and the number which the officer had affixed to the paper he had left with him, and there he knocked upon a closed door, wondering while he did so, because he knew this door. After some time the door was opened and by a soldier and Wu Lien's knees knocked together, because the soldier's face was so surly. But he calmed himself by remembering how often these men of the enemy looked surly, and he held out his paper and after looking at it awhile, the soldier pulled him in and motioned to him to wait while he went into the house.

This house Wu Lien knew when he saw it, for it had belonged to a famous rich man of the city, now run away from the war, and once two springs ago the ladies there had sent for Wu Lien to bring some of his foreign toys and small goods, to see if any pleased them. It had been that day a gay and noisy place, full of women and children and in the garden where he now stood there had been a traveling show of puppets, and everyone, even the servants and bondmaids, had been out in the sunshine to see and to laugh, and they had bade him wait until the game was over, and so he had stood and laughed, too, for the puppets were better than usual and the man who spoke for them more than commonly witty.

But now the garden was gray with winter and dark with night, and the house was silent. When the soldier came back he motioned that Wu Lien was to follow him and so Wu Lien went behind him into the house and there in the main room were three or four enemy officers drinking together, and they looked at him so sourly that for a moment he wished he had not come. Even the courteous officer looked at him coldly, and he thought fearfully that if these were such men as grew more cold the more they drank, he had come at an ill time. Nevertheless he was here, and in his own way he had a dogged courage when he was working for his own ends, and so he spoke to the one he knew.

"Sir, I am come upon business, and if I may speak plainly then I shall use less of your time."

"Speak, then," the officer said, but did not ask him to sit down.

When Wu Lien saw he was to be treated as a servant he did not like it, but he was a sensible man and he knew this was no time for pride so he swallowed it as fast as it came up, and went on. "I am a citizen of this city and I have the shop that you saw and I have long dealt in foreign goods, which for the most part have come from your honorable East-Ocean country. I desire nothing but peace so that I may go on with this business. Whoever is to rule let him rule, and I will say nothing so long as my business can be done. But there are those in this city who call me traitor because this is my heart, and they have it in their purpose to kill me, and so I am come to you who rule us now to ask if there is any way that I can be made safe."

This the officers heard and the one who understood told the

others what Wu Lien said, and they talked awhile together, Wu Lien understanding nothing of their foreign language, and at last the one he knew gave a short nod.

"You may be useful to us if you will," he said.

"Will I not be?" Wu Lien replied.

"We shall set up a people's government here," the officer said, "and it will be a government of those who will rule for us. What is your ability?"

"Alas, I am a man of small abilities," Wu Lien began, but the officer cut him short.

"Can you read? Can you write?"

"I? Certainly," he replied proudly. "And I am skilled at the abacus, and I know how to conduct a merchant's whole business. I am also a student of the Confucian classics, as my father was before me."

"That will be no use to us," the officer said. "Do you know English?"

"Alas that I do not," Wu Lien said, "I never thought it would be necessary to learn another language than my own, seeing that we are so numerous a people that though a man spoke to a stranger every hour of his life, he would die before he had spoken to every man in our nation."

"But are you swift with your brush in your own language?"

"Without boasting, I can say that I am," Wu Lien said with modesty.

The officers talked together again, and after a little while once more the one he knew said to him:

"You will move into this house at once. Your wage will be fixed according to your abilities. You will have a title, also to be shaped according to what you are able. Come here tomorrow."

Now as he heard this Wu Lien's head began to whirl around inside as though birds circled his brain.

"But I have a wife—my old mother—and two children," he said.

169

"They may all come here," the officer said. "Here they will be safe and you also. Rooms will be given them."

Such good fortune as this, to live safely in a city where none were safe, to have a wage when none knew where his food was to come from, to have his household with him, to know, above all, that he himself would not be stabbed or shot if he turned his back, all this fortune poured upon Wu Lien and he felt the joy that a man feels on a hot and thirsty summer's day when he finds a cool unknown spring on a steep mountain side.

"May I not bring my few things here at once?" he asked. "Most of my goods are ruined and what I can bring will take little room."

They talked together again, and then the officer nodded his short nod.

"You may come at once," he said.

"And tomorrow shall I bring my children and their mother?"

The officer gave a small smile. "Yes, you may," he said. Then he put up his hand to bid Wu Lien listen to what he said.

"You see how merciful we are to those who do not resist us!" he said in a loud voice such as priests use in temples when they speak to the worshipers who come on a feast day. "We seek nothing but peace and the good of all, and those who help us shall have their full reward."

"Yes, great one," Wu Lien muttered. He bowed three times, without thinking, as though the officer were a magistrate, and overcome with his fortune, he went quickly out of the room, stopping only at the gate to give a coin to the soldier there.

That night he spent in putting together his goods, and it was dawn almost when he went out and found a ricksha and piled his stuff into it and then sat himself on top of all. And so he entered into the gates of the enemy.

Great was his joy the next day when he put on his best garments and with a guard of two enemy soldiers he went toward that place where his wife was in the white woman's compound.

He only wished that he could hire a foreign motor vehicle instead of the old horse carriage he had found a few streets away. But even so he looked very well as the driver stopped his aged horse at the gate.

"Get down," he called to the driver from the seat where he sat. "Beat on the gate and tell them that Wu Lien has come for his household." And he sat himself back as an official does who has spoken to his servant.

But the driver shouted back at him, "I dare not leave this horse of mine. He has a failing that if he does not feel my pull on the bridle he sits down quickly on his tail like a dog to rest himself, and then I cannot get him up again with fewer than four men to help me lift him."

Wu Lien was still afraid of his guards and he dared not ask them to lift a horse nor could he do it himself, and so he could do nothing but get down and beat on the gate and when the little window in it opened and the gateman's old face peered out he had to say, as though he were his own servant:

"I am Wu Lien, and I am come for my household."

The gateman stared very hard at the two enemy soldiers, and he opened the gate enough to let Wu Lien through and shut it against the soldiers, who shouted and beat on the gate with their guns to come in. Then the gateman turned to Wu Lien.

"How is it you have these two with you?" he asked him gravely.

"I am a merchant," Wu Lien said, "and these two have been told off to protect me."

"To protect you!" the gateman repeated and laughed.

"I will guarantee them," Wu Lien said, with dignity.

"Still I cannot bring them in on my own body, seeing that they are the enemy," the gateman retorted. "I must first ask the white woman."

So Wu Lien had to stand there waiting until the man brought the white woman and then he had to explain as best he could to that woman why these two guards should be let in and the guards had not stopped their beating on the gate and roaring and Wu Lien was in a sweat and he heartily wished that he were not guarded at all.

But the white woman seemed not to hear any noise as she came near. She looked as cool and quiet as an image in a foreign temple, and she said to Wu Lien in her foreign voice that always made the words she spoke seem foreign:

"Are you not a traitor?"

By this time he was in such a sweat that he was peevish and so he said very peevishly:

"Lady, how do I know what you call traitor? In my own eyes I am only a man who wants to do his business as best he can, and I have my family to feed and I am the only one to do it."

But she said in the same cool voice, "Have you not seen what has taken place in this city?"

And he answered still peevishly, "What has happened has happened and it is only to be expected that foreign victors are worse than our own, and I say the sooner we forget such things, the sooner peace will come for us all."

Then this woman said, "I see you are a traitor and the sooner you have your household out of these walls, the better it is," and she turned to the gateman and told him to let the guards in. So the man opened the gate very unwillingly, and the guards burst in angry at the delay, but they were taken back somewhat when they saw this tall cold woman with her face white and her yellow hair.

"Be quiet," she told them, as sternly as though they were children. "Conduct yourselves decently and stay where you are."

And Wu Lien trembled to hear her, and thanked Heaven that the guards spoke no language except their own and so did not understand her. But her coldness they understood and her tones,

172

and they stood sheepish and angry before her and she turned to
Wu Lien:

"I cannot let you come further than the gatehouse with such
companions as these, and so I will bring your own to you here."

She left him and he watched her walking over the grass, her
long black foreign skirts brushing behind her. And there he
stood with these two surly guards and the truth was he was afraid
to be left with them lest they think the delay was his fault and
turn on him somehow, and he felt like a man who has against
his own will been given two wolves for pets, and he cannot
refuse them and yet he fears he will be eaten. And the gateman
stood there grinning and picking his teeth and watching the
three of them.

But in a few moments Wu Lien saw his wife coming and with
them her children and then Ling Sao. Now Orchid would gladly
have come too, but the white woman had forbidden it because
she was still young and pretty and she did not want the soldiers
to see her.

"I wish you well, mother," Wu Lien called to Ling Sao.

"And you also," she replied. She was surprised to see the soldiers and all that was on the edge of her tongue to say to Wu
Lien she held back in her amazement.

"Have you heard anything of my old man?" she only asked
him.

"No, I have not," Wu Lien replied. "I have heard nothing
since the day my children's mother came here, and I do not even
know how you are here."

"I came that night," Ling Sao said, and as she spoke she
reasoned that this man did not know of his mother's death and
she made up her mind that she would not tell him the worst
truth of it, but only so much as he must know.

"Since you have not seen my children's father, I must tell you,
and prepare yourself, son-in-law, for bad news. Your old mother
is no more. She was crushed under a beam when the enemy

173

came into our house and my old man buried her in the field in a coffin he made himself, and there is a mound over her, or so I am told by others who have come here since I have."

Wu Lien's wife at once put her sleeve to her eyes, for though by now she knew all, yet it was only decent to make a show of fresh weeping before her husband, and Wu Lien quickly wiped his eyes, too.

But the guards were growing weary by now and they prodded Wu Lien in the buttocks with the ends of their guns to signify to him that they were ready to return and so weeping had to be postponed and Wu Lien could not even thank Ling Sao as he ought for caring for his mother. And Ling Sao, though she would not be afraid, yet she bawled after him through the gate, "Is it safe for my daughter to go with you?"

Wu Lien, already settling his household in the carriage, and the two guards would have the two good seats, could only bawl back, "Yes, I am protected and so are all who belong to me!"

Then in haste he made off and Ling Sao was left there with the white woman of whom she was in hearty awe at all times and especially now because that woman looked at her with her yellow eyes and said:

"I am sorry for you, poor woman," and so saying she went away and then Ling Sao was left only with the gateman, and she asked him:

"Why does she pity me when there are others who have suffered much more?"

"Because," the gateman said, "your daughter's husband has gone over to be a running dog of the enemy."

"Is that why he had on his best wine red robe and his black velvet vest!" she cried.

And the gateman said, "That is why," and he grinned and began to pick his teeth again.

Upon this thought Ling Sao walked back into the hall where Orchid was and her daughter and her grandchildren, for it was

174

too cold a day to loiter out of doors. Rain had fallen and now it was changing to snow and she was glad of the warmth of the hall when she stepped into it. Yet she was very restless somehow because her elder daughter was gone and free, and she sat down and told everything to her little daughter and to Orchid, and the more they talked together the more these women longed to be free, too.

"I could eat my food down better if I saw that old man of mine," Ling Sao thought to herself, and she thought about her husband and her sons and she was sure they did not do well without her, for like all good women she had taught them to be helpless in the house without her, and she was very gloomy for awhile and in her mind she saw what was left of her house filthy, the work undone and the men eating their food cold and raw and anyhow, and she did not even know whether one of them had ever taken thought to see how she cooked the rice or how she braised the cabbage, not to consider fish or meat.

"Meat perhaps is not yet to be bought," she mused in herself, "but fish they can catch any day in the pond if they break the ice, if there is ice, but do they know enough even to take the entrails out, or if they do, then what to do next!"

And in truth there was restlessness all through that hall when the women heard that one of them had gone home and woman looked at woman and thought, "The times must be better," and they thought, each one, "It will be my turn next if my man has the wits for it." And so all were eager to be gone, and mothers lost their calm and slapped their children for small faults they overlooked on other days so that by evening half the children in the hall were crying, and Ling Sao cursed and wished she dared to go home alone by night, but she did not.

Nor were things bettered by a letter that came in a few days from Ling Sao's elder daughter boasting of the fine rooms she had that had been part of a rich man's house, and how her husband was given the greatest honor and how they lived better than they ever had and that all was peace for them, and then she said:

"As for me, I do think this enemy is better than we thought and certainly he has dealt well with my daughter and her husband and the city is now very safe and peaceful so far as we can see."

Well enough Ling Sao knew that her daughter could no more write such a letter than she could read it, and she had had to find a teacher in this school to read it to her, an unmarried female and the only true old virgin she had ever seen, for who knows what nuns in temples are? Now she supposed that Wu Lien had written the letter and she did not dream of doubting what it said, for she was one of those persons who need only to hear that a thing is written down on paper to believe it true.

But the old virgin one said, "I would not put too much faith in it. We still hear of many killed in the streets and of women violated."

This she said, her nose up, and Ling Sao smiled. What would such a one know of women violated, she thought, but did not speak, except to ask in curiosity:

"Are you a nun, then, lady?"

"Certainly I am not," that one replied as though she were angry. "I could have married many times, for matchmakers have sought me more times than I can remember, but I have preferred learning and books to all else."

"I have a son's wife like you," Ling Sao said, "but she is to have a child."

"Ah," the woman said, as though it was nothing to her and so it was not and Ling Sao went away, having thanked her for the reading.

Then to Orchid and her little daughter she told the good news in the letter and Orchid talked among the women and so the restlessness grew. Now none was more weary of the walls of this

176

place than Orchid was, for it was a place too peaceful for her, this gray building and the smooth spread of grass, still brown with winter, and no noise anywhere except twice a day the sound of hymn-singing in a small temple where they could go if they wished to hear the foreign religion. Orchid went once to see what they did but she could not understand what was said and the singing seemed in her ears like wailing and so she went no more. Then, too, the food they ate every day was the same and tasteless after a while, and she longed for something sweet in her mouth. In the village she was always running out at the sound of the little bell that the vendors of sweets strike to tell of their coming, and she bought barley sticks rolled in sesame seeds or she bought squares of sesame in dark sugar, and best of all she loved that kind of sweet called "cowhide" because it can be chewed so long, and she used to chew it half the day. Her children, too, were restless because they had no toys, and they cried for the small fragile toys they once had that vendors carry to village streets, little clay dogs and dolls, or windmills, or sugar men and women, or else they remembered that they once had kites and lanterns made like rabbits and fish and butterflies, and here they had nothing.

So when Orchid heard how well her sister-in-law did, she thought to herself:

"The city is at peace again and there is no reason why I cannot steal out of the gate some morning and see what there is in the shops. I might even go to visit my sister-in-law, and then if all seems well, I will send word by some one to my children's father, and we can come home again."

But she said nothing to anyone, for she was one of those soft stubborn women who pretending always to yield to others yet do what they like because they never tell anyone what they do. So one morning a few days later when her smallest child was asleep and the other playing, she made a yawn before Ling Sao's face and she lied to her, thus:

177

"I slept ill last night, and so I am going to my pallet for awhile if it will not trouble you to see to my two and the baby is asleep."

"Sleep if you like if there is nothing to do," Ling Sao replied a little sourly. Somewhere she herself had found a little cotton and a spinning spool and she was spinning white thread. But she was the sort of woman who finds work everywhere and if there is none she makes it, and she worked now with some show because she knew Orchid was not like her.

Orchid smiled and went her way into the building and she came out the other door and behind a wall she went to the gate and she knew beforehand that this was a time when the gateman barred the gate and went inside his little house to eat his meal. There was no one now to be seen and she drew the bar softly that he might not hear and she stepped into the street and pulled the gate after her, and if he looked out of his window it would seem that the gate was still closed. It seemed so good to be out that she felt herself a bird set free, and she had a little money in her bosom to spend, too, that she chanced to have there when she ran out of the house that day Ling Tan had told them to go. So she went happily down the street that morning, and there were few people about, for the hour was not yet noon, and it was a fair bright day, clear and cold and the air was strong as she breathed it in and out, and everything about her seemed at peace.

"How surprised my man's mother will be," she thought, "when I come back and tell her how peaceful the city is and how there is no reason why we should not go to our home! Nevertheless, I will not go further than the first shop, and then I will turn back."

So she went on a little further, never knowing that she was being watched by the enemy and had been since she left the gate. Now orders had come down from above that no open evil was to be done in the streets any more but what went on behind walls none knew, and as she passed a public watercloset for men, such as was to be found near any main street, she was suddenly fallen upon by five enemy soldiers who had been watching for a lonely woman to come by that they might draw her in. Such women were very rare now, for what woman would go out alone in these days? When they saw Orchid they thought she must be a courtesan, because she looked so gay, and indeed she had a soft round face, and her body was plump and soft, and her full mouth was red, and they held her fast, and gloated on her for a moment and quarreled for who should have her first.

Orchid was one of those women who live long when they are loved and cared for, but in trouble they die soon. Now as she looked into the black faces of these lust-filled men she was weak already. When one after another those men took their will on her, and no passer-by dared to come into that public place to save her when once they had stared in and seen five soldiers with their guns against the wall, then she was like a rabbit fallen upon by wolfish dogs, and she was helpless. She screamed and then they beat her, and one held his hand over her nose and mouth, and she struggled only a little and then her life went out as easily as a little rabbit's does, and the last man had to use her dead. When they were through with her they left her there and went away.

Then only did the few pitying passers-by dare to come in and they came in and covered that poor body, and wondered where she came from and they stared at her and wondered again who she was.

"She is a countrywoman," they said. "She has a village look, and see, her hair is bound on a silver pin such as our mothers used to use, and she wears a short coat and an old fashioned black silk skirt. She is from a village and she did not know how our times are in this city."

All these passers were men, for there was not a woman to be seen on the streets these days, and they did not know what to do with this body. None dared to take it home, because he might be accused of the death, and at last one head wiser than the others said:

"Let us take it to the white woman, for none will accuse her, and she can bury the body if no one comes for it."

So they called a ricksha and though the man was unwilling to pull such a load, still when he heard the white woman's name he hoped for an extra fee and he dragged the load the short way to the gate that Orchid a while before had opened with such pleasure. It was locked now and the gateman had finished his meal and was sitting on his little bench inside picking his teeth as he always did when he was idle, and he heard a scratching on the gate. He rose and opened it and when he saw Orchid he cried aloud:

"Why, this woman was one who sheltered here!"

"Why did you let her out?" the men groaned.

"I did not," the gateman swore, "I let no woman out." Then it began to come into his mind what had happened, and why the gate had been open when he had come out of his door. He had wondered if he had been forgetful and left it open, and he had barred it quickly, thinking he must be getting too old and he had been glad there was no one to see what he had forgotten.

"She must have stolen through when I was eating," he said now and he ran for the white woman, though first he shut the gate fast.

That white woman he found at her prayers, and she came fresh from her prayers and when she saw what had happened her pale face grew yet more stern.

"You did well to bring her here," she told them all, "for here she has been for many days and her husband's mother and sister and her two children are here now and I will send for her husband."

So they all went away content since she took on herself the

180

danger, and the ricksha puller was most content of all because of his fee.

When they were gone, that white woman told the gateman to call others to help him and to carry this poor creature now on the ground into the temple hall, and to lay her there on a long low table. She waited there while he went and until others came and lifted Orchid and carried her away. Then slowly and thoughtfully she went to find Ling Sao and with few words and yet gently enough she told her what had happened.

At first Ling Sao thought the white woman must have mixed Orchid in her mind with the many other women taking refuge in this house. "You are wrong, white woman," she said. "My son's wife lies asleep in her bed and I was thinking of going to call her, for her child is awake, and she has slept half the day."

With no change upon her always sad face the white woman said, "Come with me," and she took Ling Sao by the sleeve and led her into the hall of the temple, and there on the low table Ling Sao saw it was indeed Orchid, and she burst into wailing, though how this had come about she could not imagine.

"But I saw her not over two hours ago, fat and alive!" she wailed.

And then the white woman told her what they had surmised and again in her bare scanty words and Ling Sao could only listen.

"So it must have been," she wept, "and such a silly thing this pitiful fool could have done. She has always been secret and stubborn behind her smiles and softness, and by this she has met her death. Oh, send for my husband and my son somehow, for what to do now I cannot say alone!"

"I had thought you would want them," the white woman said, "and so I will send a messenger out by the water gate tonight when it is dark. Since this one is dead it is useless to risk a life for her by day."

And still without a tear or a change on her face she told a

181

temple servant to bring a cloth and cover Orchid and to keep watch of her through the day that was left until it was decided what was to be done. To Ling Sao's hearty weeping she gave no more heed than if it were a child crying, and at last Ling Sao sobbed:

"It is so piteous, and the two little children left with only me, and how shall I find a wife for my son again in such times as these? And yet, white woman, your eyes are dry!"

"I have seen too much sorrow," that white woman said in her pale clear voice. "I think nothing will ever make me weep again —or laugh." She lifted her yellow eyes and seemed to look off into something she saw that Ling Sao could not see. "I think my heart will not stir again until I come into my dear Lord's presence," she said.

Now it was Ling Sao who stopped weeping and because she was so astonished.

"But they told me you were never wed!" she cried.

"No, I am not, in the earthly way you mean," that white woman said, "but I have given myself to God, to the one true God, and one day He will take me to Him."

This she said and Ling Sao was so aghast at what she heard that her tears were dried for the time and she could only mutter, "*O-mi-to-fu,*" to protect herself from foreign magic.

"And you," the white woman said, bringing her pale eyes down upon Ling Sao and piercing her through with their light, "God wants you, too, dear soul. It may be that He has brought this sorrow upon you to soften your heart to bring you to Him." At this Ling Sao grew most heartily afraid and she began to back away from that white woman.

"You must tell him I cannot come," she said quickly. "I have my own husband and now these two children to look after and I am a woman full of cares and I never left my own house before this."

"In your own house too you can serve God," the white woman

said, and as she spoke she came toward her, and now Ling Sao was terrified and it seemed to her this white woman grew taller and taller by some magic and she towered white and tall and Ling Sao gave a great scream and ran out of the temple and across the grass and into the hall where the women and the children were, and there gasping and crying she told them all about Orchid and how the white woman's god had caused her to be killed.

In as little time as she took to tell it she had every woman frightened too, lest this foreign god would so kill them all, and there was such a panic that the serving women heard the noise and ran in and then that teacher who had never married, and it took all they could say to bring calm again and to tell the women what the white woman meant and even so they did not quite believe, and if it had not been that Orchid had fallen into such trouble when she went out of the gate, those women would have now run out together and they only begged that the white woman would not come near them at least until they could go home safely.

By the time all this had taken place it was near to nightfall, and she put the children to sleep and they slept, being still too young to know what it meant to have their mother dead. Beside them Ling Sao sat, weak from all the day had brought, nor had she eaten, and she waited to see if Ling Tan and their son would come. Half way between sunset and midnight she heard footsteps and she looked up and saw the door open and there stood the gateman motioning to her and she rose at once and picked her way among the sleepers. Outside in the cold darkness stood the two men she watched for, and never in all her life had she felt such comfort in her heart. She began to weep again and she turned from one to the other, sobbing and crying.

"Oh, my man—oh, what has befallen us? Oh my son—what shall I do for you?"

The white woman had herself met the two men and told

183

them what happened and at this moment she came again and at the sight of her Ling Sao's tears dried, but she was not afraid now that her husband was here and she could draw near to him.

"Come with me," the white woman said, and so they followed her into the room she prayed in, and where she read her sacred books, and they sat down as she asked them to do, and she told them that if they wished she would find a coffin for Orchid and for the time being bury her here.

"Then when better times come you may take her away and put her into your own ground," she said, "if that would make you happier."

They looked at each other, and Ling Tan spoke for the others. "There is no way now whereby we could get a coffin and a body out of the city and so we must do as you say and give you our thanks. Your mercy is beyond our understanding and it is not often found even around the four seas."

"There is no merit in me," the white woman said. "I do it in the name of the true God, whom I serve."

To this none made reply because none knew what she meant except that Ling Sao grew afraid again and now she made up her mind that she would go back this very night with Ling Tan. When he rose to go, she rose also.

"I go home with you," she said to him.

"Indeed, you shall not," he said. "The times are not calm yet, and I do not know what our life is to be with these victors we have to rule us."

"I go with you," she said stubbornly.

Now he knew his woman, and he knew the look on her round dark face and that nothing he could do would keep her here if she said she was going.

"Curse you for the stubborn daughter of a stubborn mother," he said, "and shall I be to blame if you fall into evil?"

"Whatever happens to me I will blame no one except myself," she said.

184

But he was still not ready to yield. "What of our little daughter?" he said. "Will you leave her here alone?"

For the moment Ling Sao was confounded, but the white woman spoke before she could.

"If you go," she said, "leave your daughter with me. We had in good times a girls' school here, but now the school is moved and all the pupils are a thousand miles up the river in free land. It happens that tomorrow others go on a foreign ship and guarded by two of my countrymen and their wives, and she will be safe and when you want her back you shall have her."

Those other three looked at each other and weighed what to do and again Ling Tan spoke for them all. "If the times were right it is not a thing we would think of doing, for we would take care of our own daughter and marry her to a good man, but who dares now to marry or to take into his house even for his own son a young girl? Let it be as you say—only tell us sometimes if she still lives."

"She will learn to write and tell you herself," the white woman said kindly enough, and to this the others said nothing. In the old days Ling Tan would have laughed at the thought of a daughter of his learning to read and write, but now in these times when families were divided in many places, he could see the use of such learning.

In all this the eldest son had said not one word, and they had almost forgotten him and now he suddenly spoke for the first time.

"I want to see once more that one who was my children's mother," he said in a whisper.

Now no one had told him the whole of how Orchid had died and he had not asked, and suddenly Ling Sao did not want him to know all.

"Let me go first, my son," she said, and she forgot to be afraid because now she was mother and this was her son.

"You may see her," that white woman said, and as though she

185

divined what was in Ling Sao's heart she said, "I washed her and put on her fresh garments and she lies at peace."

She led them as she spoke, taking the lamp from the table as she went, and Ling Sao followed, ashamed in her heart that she had been afraid of this woman because she was so kind, and while she had been telling her fear to others, this woman had been doing much for Orchid. She followed humbly and in silence and they all went into the temple hall where Orchid still was, and there the white woman lifted off the cover from Orchid's face and so her husband saw her. There was no wound on that sleeping face, and the soft full lips were closed and smiling and she looked as she had often looked at night in her husband's own bed, and as he looked the tears came up his throat and welled into his eyes and ran down his cheeks, and so did the tears come into the eyes of all except the white woman. She stood motionless and holding the cloth and at last Lao Ta turned away.

"Cover her," he said and the white woman covered her.

Then they went out and while Ling Sao turned into the hall to wake the children Ling Tan and his son stood out in the night waiting, and the father felt his son's sorrow and heard his smothered weeping and he drew him a little away from where the white woman stood waiting, too, and he said:

"Weep as long as there is weeping in your heart, my son, but remember that all weeping ceases at last. You are young and some day another mother will be found for your children."

"Do not speak of it yet," the son replied.

"No, I will not," Ling Tan said, "but let yourself remember it."

The young man did not answer, but the father knew that he had put something into him, not to lessen his proper mourning for his wife, yet to show him that his own life must go on for the sake of his family.

Inside the hall Ling Sao was dressing the children in all their garments and talking to Pansiao as she worked and telling her how she was to be left.

"You are not to be afraid," she said, "and if I was afraid this afternoon it was folly, for that white woman washed and dressed Orchid herself and now she says you are to leave this city and go to a safe place and to school and learn to read and write."

And she wondered, in spite of all she said, why the child was not afraid and she never dreamed the truth, that this young girl who worked so silently and never complaining in her house had longed ever since she knew how to long that she might go to just such a school.

"I will not be afraid, mother," Pansiao said.

"And write as soon as you learn," Ling Sao told her, "and we will have your third cousin read your writing."

"I will, mother," Pansiao said again, and she followed her mother to the door carrying the small child while Ling Sao carried the elder one, and they walked softly because of the sleepers.

When Ling Tan saw his daughter he, too, gave her commands for obedience and good behavior and then he turned to the white woman and committed his daughter to her in these words:

"To your mercy I give this worthless child of mine. It is a small gift and yet in her way she, too, is my flesh and blood, for in my house we have valued our daughters more than is done in some houses, and she is our last. If she is not obedient send her back and forgive us."

For the first time Ling Sao saw that white woman smile, and she reached out and took the young girl's hand.

"I think she will be obedient," she said.

So then with bows and thanks they parted, and Ling Tan took his younger grandchild and Lao Ta took his own elder son in his arms, and they stepped toward the gate. But Ling Sao's heart clung to her little daughter for a moment and she turned her head to see her once more and in the light of the lamp that the white woman held, she saw the girl's face upturned to the woman's. And Ling Sao heard that woman ask her daughter:

"Can you be happy with us?"

And she saw the young girl's face was full of purest joy and she heard her say, "I can be very happy."

As they went through the night together, hard as the road was to walk in the darkness and they dared not show a light lest the enemy see it and ask them where they went and why, yet Ling Sao found comfort in her belly because she was going home. In one part of her she knew there had been ruin in that home, for she had seen it with her own eyes, and yet she thought that her husband had mended more than he had, and so her heart expected to see the house as she had once made it and almost as it used to be before the enemy came. And Ling Tan had not thought to warn her of how it was, because he was so cast down by Orchid's death and by what he had not told his wife yet, that their third son had gone to the hills.

All that long way home he kept casting about in his own mind to know how much he must tell her of the boy's going and how much he could keep back. In his wavering between what he wanted to keep back and his long knowledge of her certain shrewdness which would smell out first that he was hiding something from her and second what he hid, by this and that he kept putting off until before he knew it there he was at his own house and it seemed to him that never had he made that journey from the city so fast, even though he had the sleeping child in his arms and it was night.

Ling Sao ran across the threshing floor and into her own gate and through the court into the house and she lit the bean-oil lamp which she knew stood in its own place on the table. There was a sort of table there but it was a board laid across two posts Ling Tan had driven into the earthen floor and when she saw this and saw all that the light showed her, she burst into a loud wail.

"Where is all I had?" she cried, staring around her. "Why,

188

where are our chairs and the long back table and did you never find the pewter candlesticks? Oh, I thought you said you had mended and put things to rights!"

And as she wailed her quick eyes searched for everything she had once owned and she marked its loss. "Where is my little pair of side tables I brought from my father's house—are they gone, too? Could you not find enough to put together again of the stools we had that were a pair?"

The two men had grown used to the room as it was, and they had half forgotten these other things because they were men and their daily work had not been to dust and clean and use the things she now mourned, which had been her pride to possess. They stood like idiots holding the children while she ran from room to room moaning and seeing this gone and that until she sat down and wept for everything, and the men had to lay the sleeping children down and comfort her, and they tried their best to comfort her each putting aside his own sorrow to do it.

"Oh, how can I keep house!" Ling Sao moaned, "and what have I to make me hold up my head among the other women? I used to have the best house, the best of everything, and now I have nothing!"

She did not know it, but she wept for more than this. She wept because she was weary and because her children were dead and scattered and because somehow she knew that the whole world in which they must live would never be the same as the old world she had lived in and loved. It seemed that once she had begun to weep nothing could comfort her and the two men gave over at last and the son went into his room and Ling Tan cursed and swore first that women could care so much for things of wood and pewter and pottery and then he cursed the war and that there was war at all.

"Curse all these men who come into the world to upset it with wars!" he shouted, "and curse them for spoiling our homes and fouling our women and making our life a thing of fear and emptiness! Curse such childish men that cannot have done with fights and quarrels in childhood but must still be children when they are grown and by their fights and quarrels ruin the lives of decent people such as we are! Curse all women who give birth to men who make war, and curse their grandmothers and all who are their kin!"

So he cursed himself hoarse and black in the face and then suddenly he too began to weep, knowing very well that sooner or later his wife would ask him where their third son was. When she saw him weep she came to reason and remembered she was a wife, and she wiped her eyes on her coat and came over to him and put her hand on his shoulder and said:

"Be quiet, old man. I know I have been a sour old woman to you, but I will be so no more. Here I am home again, and whatever happens I will not go away. You and I will stay together in our house—curse the enemy, but we will stay here!"

So he stopped his weeping and wiped his own eyes and she stood there as though she were listening. And then she lifted her head, still listening and asked what Ling Tan knew she would.

"Does our third son sleep so deeply he cannot hear his mother come home?"

Then he knew he could keep nothing from her, and that it was better that he told her all the truth. If indeed she was to stay here and if together they were to bear what must lie ahead, and whatever it was it could not be good, then their burden must be the same. And he told her heavily and with many breaks and sighs of that night when their third son had gone away, and she listened without a word or sound until it was finished. Then she asked no more.

"At least he lives," she said.

"At least he lives," Ling Tan said after her.

They went into their own room then, and lay down dressed as they were to sleep, and Ling Tan wondered wearily that after all these lonely nights he had no desire in him for this woman whom he knew he loved.

"It is more than weariness, though I am so weary," he thought. "I feel now as if that thing between man and woman must be made clean again somehow before a decent man can think of it."

To her he said, "These boards are hard after our big bed, but they cut the woven bottom into pieces and I have not found the rattan reeds to mend it."

But she only said, "What do I care for that bed or for the tables or the chairs and stools or anything any more?"

Then he knew that she was wounded to her depths at last and that she could be no more wounded than she was.

. . . And yet changeless were the skies above all their trouble, the sun shone the same, the moon rose and set, the stars were there, and clouds and rain, and the season passed as always from winter to early spring, and life went on, and even their life.

There was a day long enough after Orchid had died and the youngest girl had gone and Ling Sao had come home to ruin, when there passed through the village one who would not stay, and he left in Ling Tan's hand a letter. This letter Ling Tan opened and though he could not read it or know its full meaning until he took it to his third cousin, yet he knew its chief message. For when he unfolded the paper inside the envelope a braided cord of scarlet silk fell out into his hand and as soon as he saw it he gave a mighty shout and he ran into the house to find Ling Sao. She was in the kitchen behind the broken stove she had mended with mud, and he held the red cord up for her to see. At her cry the eldest son came out of his room where patiently he was feeding to his youngest child the pap that Ling Sao made of water and of rice she ground in their quern. And even he, his face still gray with sorrow, shouted out with joy.

There in this ruined house, in this village half destroyed and with no hope ahead, for the enemy ruled them as bitterly as ever, these three took heart because what this red cord told was that somewhere, and even where they did not know, but somewhere to Lao Er and to Jade a living son was born.

X

IN THE midst of all their trouble here was their joy, and the next day as soon as they had washed and eaten they went to his third cousin's house and Ling Tan drew his second son's letter out of his bosom and asked his cousin to read it.

Now a letter was no small thing in the village even in good times and there had been no letter here since the enemy came, and so it was not right to read it carelessly. First the cousin must wash his face and hands and rinse his mouth before he sat down, and his wife left the bedside of her son to come and listen and she told her neighbor and that neighbor another until by the time the cousin had read the letter to himself and mused over it awhile to be sure he had it, and was ready to read it aloud, there were some ten or twelve men gathered to hear it.

So at last all was ready and Ling Tan and his wife waited patiently, but this was not easy for by now that young man who had been wounded had begun to rot and the stench in the house was hard to bear, but still they bore it, so eager were they to have news of their son and grandson and even Jade. The cousin scraped his throat clear and spat and took a mouthful of tea and swallowed it and held the letter up and then looking sternly on all around because he was the only one who could read and all at this moment depended on him, he lifted his voice high and clear and began:

"Our father and mother, honored ones! We hope you are well

192

and that all is safe and as usual with you and to our elder brother and his household our respects and to all others our good wish and we hope all is well with them as usual."

Here Ling Sao wiped her eyes and cried out, "How little use their good wishes are!" but Ling Tan motioned to her to be still and the cousin went on:

"Since we left our good home and last saw your faces we have traveled well on to a thousand miles and we are now here where we paused for the birth of the child but we dare not stay for rumor is in every mouth that the enemy will press on. Yet if you, our honored father, can tell us how it is when the enemy comes and if it is not too bad, we may stay, because there is work to be had here and I, your lesser son, can pull a ricksha every day and make twice even what a teacher in a school used to make, because it is now the laborers who make high wages."

At this the cousin's wife bawled out to her husband, "I ever said learning was no use! See now, old man, if you had been strong enough to pull a ricksha what we might be doing, but no, your belly is full of ink, and I always swear that is why you smell so foul!"

The cousin could not bear this spoiling of his pride and he said, "But who would now read this letter to tell the news if it were not I?" He looked around at his fellows and they nodded to agree with him that he had the best of her there, and so he went on again:

"Your grandson was born on the last day of the thirteenth month, a little before his time because his mother had walked so far. But the child is well and strong and set your hearts free about him. When the times are good we will return with him and show him to you."

"When will that be?" Ling Sao asked.

But the cousin went on: "If the times are worse we will then go on to the upper river reaches and from there I will write again. If you send us a letter, send it to the care of one named

Liu, the eighth brother, in the shop on the corner of the two streets Fish Market and Needle." Here the cousin ended.

"Is that all?" Ling Tan asked.

"There is only his name and the farewell," the cousin replied.

Now that the letter was over and their minds free again they all smelled the stench once more and Ling Sao asked her cousin's wife how her son did, and at that the woman sighed and said he was already full of worms and the outlook was not good. She asked the company to come in and see what they thought and if there was any advice they had to give her, and so they all rose and went into the room where that young man lay, and there the stench was beyond bearing and they must hold their hands over their noses.

None could go close to the young man, now thin and yellow as though he had smoked opium for a lifetime, and they all sighed as the young man turned his dying eyes toward them and they made haste to go out again. Now the mother saw that none had any hope and she began to weep and while they went away she hid her face against the wall and wept. Nor would she be comforted when Ling Tan and his wife stayed to beg her not to weep at least until her son was truly dead, but she only sobbed:

"If I must weep I will weep, and he is as good as dead for his belly is full of maggots and next they will gnaw his heart, and what can I do?" And she refused comfort and so they left her.

As for the young man the little will he had clung to for living failed him when he heard her say this, and it was no more than an hour after that he turned his face to the wall and gave up his will and when next his mother went in to see him, all that was living in the body of her son were those maggots.

When Ling Tan heard of it he sighed and told his wife, "I think no good would have come from that young man, and doubtless he would have turned bandit with the other refuse, who rob us these days, and yet why should he die when there are other evil men alive? He had his life to live, too, and the enemy took it from him, and now day by day there is rising in me such a hatred for this enemy and for all men who bring war down on good and innocent people like us that I swear I cannot bear it if my hate does not come out of me somehow."

Ling Sao was afraid when she heard this, and she begged him, "Do not be full of hate for if you are your blood will turn to poison and you will fall ill, and then what have I left?"

And he knew she was right, and he promised to turn his mind to such things as the plowing of the ground for spring again and so he did, thankful that the land was here still, and that he could feel the soothing round of work that land demands of the seasons.

What he did not know was that from the moment of her son's death his third cousin's wife hated not the enemy but him, for she still believed that had their son wed Jade he would now be alive, and she would mutter through the night to her husband, "Had Jade been his wife, she would not have let him go to the city that day, no, and he would not have wanted to leave home at all because of her, or at least I would have had a grandson by now, and that child Jade has would have been ours and not Ling Tan's. It is by rights our grandchild and not Ling Tan's, before the gods, and he has robbed us in the worst way a man can rob another, for he has robbed us of our flesh and blood, and now we have no one to worship our bones when we are gone, and so he has cursed us forever."

Her husband twisted in the bed when he heard such words, for he knew that at bottom there was no reason in them and yet he was a man of peace and he did not want to bring her wrath down upon him, so he only sighed out that his head ached and he wished she would let him sleep, and with that she kicked him in the small of his back, and he was goaded beyond his own courage at this and he kicked her too, but a lesser kick, and he asked:

"Was I not his father and do I not sorrow? I sorrow more than you do because he was the only child you ever bore me, but I could have had a hundred sons in these years with all my wasted seed."

At this his wife was so full of fury that she rained her kicks on him with both feet, for what he said was true enough. She was barren from a fever that fell upon her after her only son was born, and with her evil temper she would not have allowed a concubine to her husband even had he had the money for one, which he never had. And though now he kicked back once or twice she was too much for him and so he rose at last and went and laid himself down on a bench in their one other room and wondered to himself why women were as they were and he envied monks and hermits and all those men who need not a woman, and dreamed an old dream of his that one day he would walk away and be a monk himself.

Yet even this little dream of his was now spoiled, for many temples were emptied of their priests these days and soldiers filled them and he feared soldiers as he feared his wife, and so he lay on that narrow bench and felt how evil his life was, and he a quiet man who asked only a little peace around him. But there was no peace now anywhere, and none for him either, in his small life.

. . . In her own house Ling Sao felt the emptiness too great. She had been used to every room full of her children and grandchildren and at night sleepers in every room and at meals the table crowded, and she herself busy and managing, and now here were only the men and the two little children. And even these little children were silent and full of fear of what they did not know, but they would not stir outside the house and there they would sit hand in hand, the elder like a little old man, and they were thin and yellow and shrank if any noise fell upon their ears.

As to their father, he who used to be so easy and cheerful now seldom spoke a word to anyone, for the truth was this eldest son of Ling Tan's was a man ill suited for these times. He was one who would have thrived in the good life they used to have and he would have grown into a quiet gentle older man, respected in the village for his wisdom, and the father of many children who would have loved him for his kindness, but in these times when nothing went well, he did not know what to do, and he fell into stillness so deep that it seemed almost witlessness sometimes. There was no hope of finding one to take Orchid's place yet, and if sometimes he wished there were such a one there were other times when he was glad there was not, for fear of more children and more trouble, and so he went on as dully in his ways as the water buffalo did, doing what he was told and plodding back and forth upon the land.

Ling Tan looked at him often and he thought, "There is one whose life is spoiled by war as surely as any other's has been," and then Ling Tan would fall into one of his deep rages that he had now-a-days against all men on the earth who make war. As he plowed back and forth across his fields he raged within, looking at the half-ruined houses of his village and his own house that he dared not mend lest it tempt the roaming soldiers of the enemy, and all about him in the valley the villages were so. And on the other side of the city, where he had not seen it but only heard, the land was itself ruined, scorched and barren, that good fertile land which centuries of peace had made rich for food. Never had their own little wars despoiled the land except through taxes made too high and the land urged to greater bearing. And yet even so for this fruitage there must be more ordure put in and more enrichment, and so the land still held its good.

Back and forth all through that spring while Ling Sao fretted in the house Ling Tan raged in his heart against the men who made wars, wherever they were, and he knew from hearsay that such men were in other countries too, and he thought of the foreigners on the other side of his land and wondered if they suffered as he was suffering, and he thought:

197

"We men of peace and sense, whether here on top of the earth or hanging downward from it on the other side, we ought to band together and forbid life to all who would make war. Yes, when we see a child like that we ought to keep him locked, if he will not be taught."

And the more he thought the more sure he was that only a certain kind of man made war, and if these men were somehow done away with, then there could be peace. Such were his thoughts these days, but what could he do, one man upon his land? And yet he said to himself, "Are there not others like me?"

This was a joyless spring, and one festival passed another and Ling Sao made no feasts, and none were made anywhere for how can a people rejoice when an enemy rules over them? The house was so silent that she grew full of fretfulness so that her very skin itched with it, and she would sit scratching herself in the evening because of her fretfulness. At last Ling Tan himself noticed it and he asked her one night in the third month of that luckless year:

"Why do you sit scratching yourself and rubbing your nose and jerking your arms like that?"

And she burst out with words as though a lid had been taken from a jar:

"Our house is like a grave and now I know we ought never to have let our second son and Jade go away from it. Our eldest son is helpless and what will these two poor children do if anything happens to you and me and we already old?"

He listened to this and marveled that for all their years together he could never know what would come out of this woman.

"Would you ask our second son and Jade to come back here?" he asked her gravely, "and shall we tell them to bring our grandchild back from free land to this land that is the enemy's?"

"It is not the enemy's so long as we live upon it," she told him. "That is where you are wrong, old man. It is not ours only if

198

we give up and go away and leave it. But that we will not do, and our sons should not either, because if we should die, how would the land be held?"

Now there was sense in what she said, and Ling Tan was too just to deny sense even to a woman when he heard it from her, and so he said:

"Speak on, old woman, and let me hear more," and he lit his pipe to keep him calm, though tobacco was precious these days and would be until he had his own small crop cut.

"What I say is that our son ought to come back here and live as he used to do," she said, "for we ought not to yield to the enemy. We are yielding when we let our sons go out and the enemy will think we are afraid if all the young men go out and only the old are left."

There was truth in this again and he smoked a while and then he said, "But the outlook is so ill. It is true that women are more safe these days than they were before the new year since courtesans are plentiful, they say, and the worst of the enemy soldiers have gone on, but there are other ills ahead."

"What ills?" she asked. Not once had she ever said again that she feared no man and never would as long as she lived, but what ill was worse than men?

"There are rumors that we farmers are to have bitter laws put on us," he said, "and how can we refuse to obey the enemy when we have no guns?"

"If there are such ills ahead our sons should be here to help us bear them," she told him, "and when you write the letter back to our second son, you tell him I said so."

"Hah," he said, and nothing more than that, but he sat a long time that night with the thought that his wife had put into his head. It was but a seed she dropped in that wilful half-childish way that women have, a truth she chanced upon not for itself but out of some simple wish she had doubtless to see her grandson. But his man's mind could take the seed and fertilize it with his thought and bring it up to fruit and so he did.

"If it be true that this enemy will spread over the land like an evil plague," he thought, "is it well that we all flee before it and let them have the land? Some flee because they dare not stay but there are those strong enough to stay and am I not one? She is wrong to say all my sons must be here, but she is right when she says this eldest son cannot live here alone, and he cannot. But my youngest son cannot be here for he will do better elsewhere, but is not my second son like me? If he is like me he ought to be here to hold the land with me. He and I and others like us, we must stay where we belong and hold as best we can what is ours and harry the enemy like fleas in a dog's tail so that the beast can make no headway for stopping to gnaw his rear."

He laughed silently at his own small joke and Ling Sao cried, "Why are you sitting there laughing to yourself like an old idiot in such days as these?"

"I am not ready to tell you yet," he said and would not tell her, but the seed had sprouted in his mind and was putting out its leaves.

Yet so evil was that spring that his courage might have failed him to call back his second son had not the summer brought its own disaster to his house, and this disaster was worse than the new taxes the enemy put down upon the land and worse than the laws they made about the price of rice or what they said a man must plant and all such tyranny as Ling Tan had never thought could be upon the earth. And this was the disaster. In that year so many people had been killed that to bury all was not possible, and to rid the streets of bodies, such as could not be buried were thrown into the canals and into the river and when the river rose with spring and swelled into the canals, those bodies were thrown up again or brought down from other cities and left upon the banks, and sickness came upon the people from all this rotting flesh, and among the poor it came from eating crabs that fed on

200

flesh, and so when the heat of summer came fluxes and fevers spread everywhere.

Where should it spread but to Ling Tan's house? There it fell upon the youngest and the weakest most heavily. All were ill for ten days and more, but those two grave little children went down first, and though the three grown ones tended them with all their care, and their own flux and vomit poured from them like water, so that even as the children died, Ling Sao had to turn aside to vomit while she held the little one to ease his dying. They died, those two, and with them died such hopes as Ling Tan did not know he had, and Ling Sao wept as she had never wept. These grandparents had been so troubled and distraught that they had let the children do as best they could day in and out, because all had to suffer now, and yet when the little creatures ceased living, the old ones felt their own lives gone.

"What have we left now?" Ling Sao moaned. "What is a house where no children are?"

As for the eldest son, the children's father, he did not weep or moan, but he crept about the house like his own shadow, and when the two little ones were buried and his parents better and his own flux stayed, one day he begged his parents to forgive him if he went away a while.

"But where will you go?" his mother cried.

"I do not know, except I must go," he said in his dull voice.

Then Ling Tan cast about and thought of somewhere his eldest son could go, at least so that they might have hope of seeing him again, and so he put his wits to work quickly and said:

"If you must go I wish you would turn to the hills and see if you can find your younger brother and tell us how he does. I always fear he went to the robbers and not to the good hill men. Find him and if he is with those wicked men, lead him to the good."

This, he said, would give the man a task and better a task he must do than to go out idle in despair, and at the same time to put to an end his secret doubt on his third son.

"Do you so command me?" the eldest son asked.

"I do," Ling Tan replied.

"Then I must obey," his son replied.

So within the next few days when Ling Sao had washed his clothes and had sewed into his coat some money Ling Tan had still, they watched him go, a bed quilt rolled upon his back and in his hand food for a day or two, and new sandals on his feet.

"How will you do all the work upon the land now?" Ling Sao asked her husband.

"I do not know," he said, "but I had not the heart to hold him."

"There is only one thing to do," she said, "Heaven has shown its will. You must write our second son and call him home."

Ling Tan turned to her then, a small smile on his face.

"Are you sure it is only Heaven's will, old woman? I did not hear you try to keep our eldest son."

But she replied, "Could it be my will to let the children die?" and there was no smile on her face.

The smile went from his face then and he said sadly, "Well I know that was not your will."

They watched their son go down the road and toward the hills until he too was lost and then they were alone indeed. Into the quiet house they went, and never had they been alone in it, because before Ling Tan's old parents died his own first sons were born, and so what was now had never been. In such quiet Ling Sao could not live and she kept begging him, "Will you not write that letter now? Why will you not write that letter today? It may take them a month and more to come."

"Wait," he told her, and on another day still, "wait."

And she had to wait until the thought was fully ripe in his own mind so that he was sure of its wisdom, and that day came. For the more he pondered this wickedness of war the more sure he was that it could only be overcome by such men as he, determined to live out their lives in spite of it, and his second son was more like him than any of the others and there must be one like him after him to go on living. For this war he saw would be no short struggle. This enemy would not easily let go its gains, and the war might go on to son's son and even after, and their strength must be that they could live, whatever came.

When Ling Tan had been seven days alone upon the land, such thoughts shaped in him to one strong end, and he told his wife the eighth morning when he rose:

"This day I send the letter to our second son."

Then she was overjoyed and she bustled herself about food and she said, "You must have an egg fresh to give you strength," and she took out of her basket her newest egg and broke it into a bowl and she made him drink it down now before he ate his morning meal and when he had eaten he went to his third cousin's house.

Now Ling Tan as he sat in his cousin's house telling him what to write to his second son well knew what a burden he took upon himself. Ling Sao saw only that now she was to have her son back and a little grandson she had never seen and the more precious because of the two who had died. If she were secretly uneasy she comforted herself by thinking that at least the worst of disorder was over, and the soldiers who had been most vile were checked or else sent on to new cities to conquer, and though the times were very bad if the people kept their heads low under the enemy perhaps they could live.

But Ling Tan saw further than she did and more clearly, and he knew his own temper and the temper of his second son, and that they were not men who could obey slavishly all that was commanded in these days. The outlook was not good for free men and he knew it, and so he made long pauses in the letter, thinking and rubbing his shorn head over what he ought to say to his son, and the cousin waited with the brush moist in his hand, and sometimes the brush dried before Ling Tan was ready, and then the cousin had to wet it again in his mouth until his mouth was full of ink he had rubbed from the inkstone onto the brush.

"Tell my son," Ling Tan said at last, "that he must understand he does not come back for peace, for there can be no peace. What has been was bad enough but what lies ahead may be worse. Who can tell? He and I must tighten our hearts to endure what can scarcely be endured."

This the cousin wrote down and waited and sucked his brush and after a while Ling Tan went on.

"Tell him that I and his mother are alone, that my other sons are gone to the hills, that my eldest son's wife and his two children are dead and our youngest daughter gone with the white woman. But he is not to come at risk only because we are alone. Tell him his mother wants him to come because the house is empty but I want him to come only if he feels as I feel, that, curse the enemy, I will hold this land as long as I live, and he with me, and when I die he is to hold it after me with his son until such time as the enemy leaves our country."

The cousin paused on this to say, "If this letter falls into the hands of the enemy will they not come to this village and destroy us all?"

"I will send this letter by no usual way but by a messenger until he reaches the border," Ling Tan said to give him courage to go on.

There were such men who came and went across the border from the free land into this enemy-taken country, and they made a business of coming and going, and they dressed themselves like beggars or farmers or old blind men who go about clanging their little bells and stopping to tell stories and sing songs among the people, and by such a one his son's letter had come to Ling Tan.

So the cousin went on doubtfully to write, and when the letter was finished he read it again to Ling Tan to make sure all had been said that he meant, and Ling Tan, struggling to discern the meaning in the flowery learned things the cousin put in extra, heard enough to make him know that his son would see what he meant. He knew, too, that his son would know the letter was written by this cousin who could never put his brush to paper without letting the learned useless words flow out of him, ancient sayings from the classics and lines of poetry and all such foolishness which the tongues of sensible men left to themselves never speak.

"He will see what is cousin and what is me," Ling Tan thought, "and I cannot offend the man because he loves to make his little show," and so the letter was finished and Ling Tan stayed to see it sealed and then he took the letter himself, because if he left it the cousin might think of other things to say and add them and confuse the whole beyond what it already was, for besides the learned words the cousin had put in all his own news, how his son had died and how the village was half ruined, and Ling Tan could only trust to his second son's shrewdness to pick out what was the real meaning of the letter.

With this letter wrapped up in a handkerchief and put safely away Ling Tan and his wife waited a few days until they were able to catch one coming and going, and to do this he went every day to the tea house and especially at night, for such men travelled by night and slept by day. On the fourth day he caught a young man who by his look signified what he did, and Ling Tan said to him in a low voice:

"If you are going to the border will you carry a letter to my son?"

The man nodded, and Ling Tan told him where he lived, and after nightfall he came to the house and Ling Tan brought him in and Ling Sao had a meal ready for him, and they ate together. While they ate the young man told of many things they had not known, how over the border in the free land a great army was gathering that would stand against the enemy like that wall which once emperors had built to the North, but this was a wall of living flesh to be two thousand miles long, and miles deep, sometimes ten but always one or two. And he told how in that free land there were schools and mines and mills and factories and though millions of people had fled there from land the enemy had taken, still they were determined to flee no further and they had taken their stand.

All this encouraged Ling Tan and though neither he nor Ling Sao felt a wish to go, for their own land was here and not there, he said, "I feel my heart take breath when you say these things, and when the day comes that the army drives forward I will be here and my son with me if he comes, and this piece of land will still be ours for we have never let it go."

Then he gave the letter to the young man and he tried to tell him how he would know Lao Er when he saw him, but Ling Sao stopped him.

"You do not know him as I do," she said, "for I carried him in my womb and he has a mole under his right eye, but very small so you must look for it and his eyes are bigger and blacker than another man's and his face is square like his father's, but his mouth is big like mine. His height is not above medium, but his shoulders are set square and the calves of his legs are round. On one great toe, that of the right foot, he has a deep cut, because when he was a child of twelve he stepped on a plowshare and I thought his toe was off, but I bound it on with a piece of my apron I tore off, a new apron it was, but I tore it, for was he not my son? And he had a boil once on his crown and it left a small bare place, but he keeps it covered with hair and you must look for it."

Ling Tan burst out laughing at this and said, "Do you think he will search our son like that, old woman? Give no heed to her, young man—she is like all women. Her sons are like no other men on earth. I say he is a strong young man good enough to

206

look at but not too good, and he is not our third son who is as pretty as a girl and I am glad he is not."

Ling Sao's face fell at that, and in the silence the young man rose and said he must be on his way.

"How long will it be before the letter is in my son's hand?" Ling Tan asked him.

"I cannot say," the young man replied. "If I am lucky it may be less than a month. But I am not always lucky."

So they told him farewell, and Ling Tan gave him some money and Ling Sao gave him a package of bread with meat steamed inside, and they both told him to come here and sleep whenever he came and went, and he thanked them and was gone without ever having told them his name. Nor had they asked, because in these times it was better not to know a man by his name, so that on being asked by the enemy one could say, "I do not even know his name."

With this letter gone, Ling Tan and his wife could only wait, and that year she alone helped Ling Tan on the land. The rice had been planted somehow in the early summer, and it was doing well, but they could not keep it so weedless as Ling Tan and his sons had in the other years, and the water buffalo had to go without its long days at grass for there was no one to take it to the low foothills for pasture, and yet as best they could these two, husband and wife, kept the land, and she let the house go and only cooked a meal quickly when they came in at night.

But they talked together much of how it would be when Jade and the little child were there and one day Ling Sao said they should have a hiding place into which they could put her, for never did she wish again to hide in the city with the white woman. They must have a place of their own to use if it were needful.

"But where?" Ling Tan asked. "Your thought is as good as an egg but go on and hatch the fowl."

"I will sit on it awhile," she said laughing.

So she thought and after a few days she said, "We could dig through the earthen floor of the kitchen behind the stove and then under the earthen wall of the house under the court yard. We have no time now for weaving and no place to sell the cloth if we did weave, and we could take the door frames and posts and beams from the weaving room and build a room under part of the court. Then we could cover the hole with a board and on that put straw."

He was so full of praise for this thought that she grew shy, while he praised her.

"It took no great thought," she said modestly.

"Yes, it did," he said, "and many a woman would have let her mind lie idle while she worked in the fields, but I have ever seen this difference between you and other women, that your mind cannot be idle, and I say I never know what is coming out of you. And so I never tire of you, old woman."

She covered her mouth with her hand while she smiled, for though usually she forgot the lack of two side front teeth which she had not had for many years, yet when her husband praised her she always remembered her gaps and covered her mouth until he forgot her again and she could know he did not see her when he looked at her.

That night those two began to dig their hole. It was a hot midsummer's night and the ground behind the stove was beaten into a rocky hardness by the many women who had crouched there, generation after generation, to feed their households. With all their sweating and work until they could work no more Ling Tan and his wife only dug down six or seven inches.

"The young ones will have to help us finish it," he said, panting and weary.

"But we can get it deep enough to hide in at least by the time they come," she said.

Thereafter day after day, they did not count their day's work complete until they had added a few inches to the hole. This hole became the great comfort of their lives while they waited for the coming of their son and grandson, and it gave them the hope of hiding not only themselves if it became a need, but the rice now growing in their fields.

For one day to Ling Tan's terror when he was working in his fields, he saw like an evil shadow upon the land a band of the enemy coming toward him from the city. He stood as they drew near, sure that his life was at an end, for among them were soldiers with guns, but no, when one began to speak he listened and perceived that they had not come to kill him. That enemy had a little book and a pen and he asked questions of Ling Tan, what his name was and how long he had lived here and how much land he had and how much rice he would have from the grain here standing. In his fear Ling Tan told more of the truth than he wished, but he made his harvest smaller by far than he knew he would have, because he was used to tax gatherers, and the enemy who questioned him knew no better and he put down what Ling Tan told him. Then he said in a loud voice:

"Farmer! This country now belongs to us who have conquered it and you must produce on your land as we say and the harvest is to come to us at the price we tell you it shall be. There is to be no more buying and selling as you wish, for we will establish law and order and all is to be done according to law."

Now Ling Tan was a good farmer and a shrewd man and he knew that prices must vary with each year, depending upon the weather and the harvest and the number of people buying and selling and how much is sent out to other parts and brought in from other parts, and never can it be said early what the price of rice or meat is to be. So he said, making his voice quiet and courteous:

"Sirs, how can it be decided thus early what the price of grain is to be? In our country Heaven decides such things."

Then that little enemy man puffed himself up and scowled and drew down his mouth and shouted at Ling Tan.

"We decide all now, farmer, and those who disobey us need their land no longer."

Ling Tan said no more, but he bent his head and fixed his eyes upon the rich dark earth on which he stood and he answered their questions and told them that he had one water buffalo and two pigs and eight chickens, a pond with fish and some ducks, and that in his household there were only himself and his old wife.

"Had you no children?" the man asked.

Then Ling Tan lifted his head and told his first full lie. "We are childless," he said.

This the little enemy man put down too, and then he pursed his mouth and said one more thing.

"Beginning with the first of the month there is to be control of all fish, and only we shall eat fish. You, farmer, if you catch a fish in your waters you must not eat it but bring it to us."

"But the pond is mine," Ling Tan said without thinking, for all the years of his life since he was a child he had drawn fish from this pond and fish was their chief meat.

"Nothing is yours!" the man bellowed. "Will you village men never learn that you are conquered?"

Ling Tan lifted his head again. He shut his lips over his teeth to save his life, but he looked that little man in the eyes. "No," his eyes said, "we will never learn that we are conquered," and "No" his lifted head said, and "No" the look of his whole being said before those men. But his voice did not speak, because he knew that living he could hold all his land, while dead he could hold only so much as he was buried in.

The little enemy man looked away and said in a loud voice, "Now you are registered, farmer, and you and your wife and your pigs and fowls and fish and buffalo and your land, all that is yours. Do as we tell you and you shall live in peace." Still Ling Tan did not speak, and he stood there with his head lifted up and his whole body still, while those men went away and he saw them stopping at every house and at every field where a man worked. Few were working this year compared to last for the young men were gone and some were dead, and the ones who worked were like him, those who believed that they must hold the land at whatever cost.

He would not go into the house as long as those enemy men were in sight. He took up his hoe again and went on with his work as though all else were nothing to him, but the heart with which he worked was sad. When they were gone from the valley to another place he looked around him and he saw that everywhere men were going toward the village and so he put his hoe on his shoulders and went too. There in the half-ruined tea house they gathered, between thirty and forty men, and each talked of what the enemy meant. Their rice was to be sold at a low price to the enemy, and they could eat no fish, even if one leaped into their hands from their own ponds.

"Such tyranny we have never known," they said, and there was little talk that day, for none knew what was ahead and there was no use in talk and anger until they knew.

"If we can bear it we must bear it," Ling Tan said at last, summing up their minds, "and if we cannot bear it we must find means not to bear it. But the land comes first."

To this they all agreed and they parted. They were of one mind and there was not a traitor among them.

Going toward his house for his noon meal Ling Tan thought to himself that he was glad his second son was coming, for how could he endure through these times alone? The men in the village looked to him as their leader yet how would he know to lead them if what lay ahead could not be borne? They needed a leader young and strong and able to think what to do in these times which were so different from any he had known.

At the table in the quiet empty court yard he and his wife ate together, now that there were only the two of them, and he told her what had befallen them. And when she had heard she rolled up her sleeves and bade him go to a village bigger than theirs and see if he could buy as much salt as he could.

"But why, old woman?" he asked amazed.

"Those pigs must die," she said, "and half of the fowls will die, and you shall have salt fish to eat if you cannot eat fresh."

"They will kill us if they find out," he cried. But she twisted her face at him. "Can we help it if a sickness carries off our beasts?" she asked. "I will go through the village and tell the women that all beasts are to be sick, and do you tell it as you go to buy salt, and the word will fly from mouth to mouth, among those who have not already thought of it, and be sure every quick-witted soul will think of it anyway."

He grinned and said no more, and he did go and buy salt, but it was too scarce to buy all in one place and he had to go to several. Then stealthily and by night, they killed and dried and salted their fowls and their pigs. But they left the sow until she littered and Ling Tan let her into the room where the loom used to be so that the piglets would not be seen.

"They at least are not registered," he thought.

For days thereafter they worked and whenever Ling Sao saw anyone like an enemy coming she hid the meats in the hole behind the stove that was daily getting deeper. And never had Ling Tan eaten so much meat as he did that summer, for there were the small parts that could not be easily salted and the blood to make puddings. And so it was done throughout that whole region, and the village dogs grew fat on entrails and offal. The only trouble was the scarceness of salt. Then suddenly salt came in from sources they did not know, but it was brought somehow by unknown hands into the villages and left at shops and people took it and were glad and did not ask whence it came. They knew it came from the hills.

The summer was long that year while Ling Tan and his wife waited for their son and grandson, and yet there was the hole to dig. Every day they looked down the roads and at night they woke and listened and thus the days followed on each other. Most of all was Ling Tan harassed with little enemy men coming to the village, sometimes with soldiers and sometimes without, to tell him what he must do and what he must not do, and to smell out his crops and sometimes only to stare and see. Now that he could draw his breath in their presence he was able to see that though all were evil not all were equal in their evil, and he learned to hear them and to hold himself in silence.

"I will wait until my son comes," he always thought. "I will do nothing but keep silence until my son comes."

Sometimes the enemy came even to the house, but Ling Sao had learned to be wary, and she had hiding places for meat and rice, and if the hole was not big enough she thrust what was left up into the thatch of the darker rooms where if dust fell it would not be seen. She sat there seeming a dull and silent old woman who stared at the strangers and did not stop her spindle while she twisted her white cotton thread, and if they spoke and she saw their lips move she pretended she was deaf and pointed to her ears and shook her head, and so they let her alone. She took care not to brush her hair smooth or wash her face clean these days and the sun made her brown skin nearly black and she let it.

"The uglier I am the safer I am," she thought, and she took heart that the hole was now big enough to hide Jade and the child at least.

Thus passed the summer and then the heat broke, and then they thought that any day surely their son would come, and Ling Tan only hoped he would come in time for harvest.

"Yet we must hide him too from the enemy," he said, "for the enemy compels the young men to labor for them, and our son must not be lost to us," and so they devised ways of constant watchfulness and how they would tell their son he must learn to work by night and sleep by day, and they would watch.

At last one night the hour came for which they had waited.

Nearly at midnight they were waked from their sleep and they ran into the court. There was a low knocking at the gate, and Ling Tan leaped toward it and was about to throw the gate open, certain of who was there, but his wife who held the lamp, called, "Wait. I must first put out the light, so that if it is not they we will have time to escape, and if it is they none will see them coming."

He was struck again with her quick wits, and so he waited while she put out the little lamp, and then he threw open the gate. In the dim starlight they saw two figures.

"Father!"

It was their second son's voice, and Ling Tan and his wife heard it, and then how they pulled those two in! They led them to the kitchen through the darkness for in the kitchen there was no window and then they closed the door and Ling Sao lit the lamp again and so they saw each other. There they were, Lao Er and Jade, but they looked like two men, for Jade had her hair cut off short and she wore men's garments and her feet were bare and thrust into men's straw sandals, and her face was so thin and brown that even one who had known her could have passed her on the road and thought her a farmer. But Ling Sao was famished and starving for the child.

"Where is my grandson?" she cried. "Where is my little meat dumpling?"

Then Jade smiling took the load from her back, and there cleverly hidden under a basket was that little boy for whom Ling Sao had been waiting. She thought of no one and of nothing else as she took him in her arms, her face all trembling and broken with weeping, and she unwrapped him and looked at him all over.

"He is exactly as I thought he would be," she whispered, and she lifted him and held him against her shoulder and rocked him back and forth. "Oh, how it eases me," she whispered. "Oh, how I am comforted to hold him like this!"

And the others stood about her, saying nothing, but tears were in their eyes because of the agony of her joy, for such joy is made up partly of sorrow and none can know that deep joy who has not had sorrow first. As for Jade, when she saw it she was for the first time willing for all the danger through which she had carried the child. She had not wanted to come back, but to go forward further to the West, and she and Lao Er had argued bitterly as to whether they ought to obey the letter which had come to their hands through many another. For that young man who had first taken it from Ling Tan was shot by an enemy gun and he had died. But all that he carried he gave to another before he breathed his end, not only Ling Tan's letter but other letters and first of all the secret messages that were his real duty, the messages between those who ruled the free lands and those who were in the hills, and thus by one way and another Ling Tan's letter had reached his son.

When they had read it, Jade had shaken her head. "We who are young, we ought to go on and not go back," she said. "We left that place because of the child and shall we take him there now?"

But Lao Er said, "When we left, my elder brother was at home and my father had two sons besides me, and we could think first of our own. But now those sons are gone, and the old ones are alone, and will our son care for us in our time if now we leave my parents? We cannot expect good in our time if now we do evil."

So at last she had been willing and they began their journey. Yet every step she took had been unwilling, and now for the first time she felt herself knit to this family of her husband, for she perceived that not unto one is a child born, but to all who go before him in the house. And so she did not, as some women would have done, put out her arms jealously to the child. She let Ling Sao have her fill of him and she stood there enjoying this worship of the child whom she worshiped.

As for that little boy, he had seen so many strange faces since he was born that he was afraid of none, and surely none had looked down on him so kindly as this wrinkled brown face. Since he had slept most of the day on his mother's back and was full of mother's milk besides, for Jade had taken care to nurse him well before they reached the house so that he would not fret the first moment, he was very gay and smiling. When Ling Sao set him on her knee at last and told Ling Tan to hold the light so that she could see, the child laughed and pulled the button on her coat and then she laughed, still weeping, and between laughter and tears she could not speak and Ling Tan thought she would choke. He grew frightened and gave the lamp to his son to hold and cried out to her:

"Guard your heart, my old woman! It has broken away from its anchor in you and you will lose your wits in a moment more. Too much joy is as bad as too much sorrow."

He took the child from her as he spoke, and bade Jade pour a little tea out of the pot for her husband's mother, and Jade did, and Ling Sao drank it and wiped her eyes and so brought her heart back again to its place. Only then would Ling Tan give the child back to her, and the truth was he, too, liked this little grandson in his arms, for the child's body was firm and hard and his thighs were fat and strong, and his little breast broad and his shoulders square.

"This is no usual child," he said to his son. "Look at his face, how square it is, and he has a square mouth."

Then he saw his son look proudly at Jade and she as proudly at him, and he took pleasure in their mutual pride.

"What can the enemy do to us when our family goes on like this?" he exclaimed, and indeed this sturdy boy of the generation to come after them put heart into them all and the house came to life again with him.

So at last they were able to bestir themselves. Ling Sao got up, the child across her hip, and how good it was to feel him there, and Jade helped her and she heated food, and Ling Tan sat down and lit his pipe and told his son to sit down and tell them all that had happened since they met. Thus over food and tea, and the two women sat with the men and Ling Sao still held the child and laughed silently at all he did while the talk went on, they made known to each other something at least of what had come to all since they last met.

There was only one moment's small cloud over their joy, for Ling Sao as she had always done for her own children and for her grandchildren chewed some rice soft and leaned to put it into the little boy's mouth, but Jade spoke against it.

"I beg you not to be angry with me, mother," she said, "but do not put food from your mouth into the child's."

She said this softly and prettily but still she said it, and Ling Sao was astonished, first that she should speak so to one older, and then that there could be any harm in feeding a little child soft chewed rice.

"Why, I fed my sons so," she said with anger, "and it did no harm to them, I swear."

"But it is not thought good now," Jade said bravely. "I bought a little book in that upper river city that told of how to care for children, and this it spoke against, that food should be put from one mouth to another."

"Am I foul then?" Ling Sao said with more anger still.

"No, you are not," Jade said pleadingly. "But, mother, I myself do not do this, and I beg you let us keep this little child the best we know."

To this Ling Sao made no answer, and the men at first said nothing either, for this was not their quarrel.

"You had better take your child," Ling Sao said to Jade. "Doubtless I pollute him when I hold him."

"Oh, mother!" Jade said pleading with her. "For you I brought him home at all."

"Cool your anger," Ling Tan said suddenly to his wife. "Shall

217

we quarrel this night of all nights and over the child who is the center of all our hearts?"

So Ling Sao let her anger cool but she never forgot what Jade said, and ever after she did not do that thing. Now as the others talked she sat brooding in herself about the book that Jade said she had and she thought with scorn, "Are children then to be reared and fed out of books? Did I ever have a book to feed my children and did I ever lose a son?"

But she kept these thoughts in herself and the innocent child was still precious to her, and after a while she forgot the matter in hearing the tale of all that her son and Jade had done, and in what they told of the free land.

When each knew all it was nearly dawn, and Ling Tan took his son and Jade and showed them the hole behind the stove.

"There you must hide if the enemy comes," he told them. "You are not registered and they do not know you are alive." And he told them how he had lied and said that he and his wife were childless.

"I am glad of that," his son said, "for we came through the hills and with those in the hills we made our plans, and it is better if my name is nowhere."

Ling Tan did not understand what he meant. But by now he was too weary and his mind too full of all he had heard to hear more, and he thought, "I will leave this until tomorrow to ask." So they went to bed at last, though Ling Sao would have been glad to sit and hold the little boy all night and let him sleep in her arms, if Ling Tan had allowed, but he said:

"You must have your sleep too, old woman, and I shall not rest if you are not sleeping."

So in the deep blackness before dawn they parted, and when Ling Tan lay down on his bed, though he was weary it was a good weariness, and all that his son had said was strong and full of hope and it had given him hope, too. For the first time since the enemy had come he turned toward his wife with his old

218

self come back in him, and he felt clean again because of hope ahead and so he renewed himself with her and then he slept.

In their old room Lao Er and Jade lay side by side, too tired to sleep. The way home had been twice as hard as the going, because then they had gone toward freedom and now they came back to what they knew could not be freedom, and perhaps never in their time would they be free again.

"We must learn to live free within ourselves," Lao Er said.

But he did not want to talk much tonight, even with Jade. He had seen death and trouble enough over all the land that he and Jade traveled, night after night, for they walked or rode by night and hid by day, once they had left the free land, and everywhere helped by the people in the hills, so that by now Lao Er knew those men and women and they him, and indeed they had been sorry to let him go.

But he told them that he must come home because his parents were alone and he promised to plan with them and see how he could help them. Yet now that he was here he knew that what the enemy had done in this city and the laws they made were worse than had been elsewhere.

"Then I must work the more," he thought, "I must be more clever, keep my wits more sharp, be ready to die and yet sure I will not die."

And he praised his parents that they had had the sense to dig the hole and he said to Jade before he slept, "We must work on that hole and dig it deep and strengthen it with posts and beams under the court and make it like a secret fortress. It must shelter more than us and hide more than our goods."

"I will make it my work," Jade said.

"And it shall be my first work," Lao Er said. "Then as soon as we have it done, I will let the people in the hills know and then we will see what we can hatch between us."

Jade slept at last, the child asleep already at her breast. But still Lao Er could not sleep. He heard again and again what his father had told him of the taking of the city and all that had been pillaged and burned and looted and what had befallen women, and the blood fevered in his veins and he grew so angry lying there in the night that he swore to himself that the rest of his life he would give to war against the enemy, and he would teach his children after him to carry on the war. Only then could he sleep.

. . . Not in one night could all be told, and the next day Ling Tan told his son all that he had forgotten. What made his son more angry than all else put together was when he heard that Wu Lien had gone over to the enemy.

"Such men are traitors and when we push the enemy into the sea, be sure that men like Wu Lien will go with them or be killed if they do not."

"I had not thought of the man as a traitor," Ling Tan said, considering. "It is more to his kind to be thinking only of himself and his profits, and he is the sort of man who smells out profits as a dog does a hare, and he follows as heedlessly."

But his son would not allow this for an excuse. "Any man who thinks first of himself now is a traitor," he said, and Ling Tan did not answer. He thought to himself, more humbly than usual, for he was not by nature a humble man, that perhaps the young must be right these days, since certainly he did not know what to do except to stay by any way he could upon the land.

Thus in humility he listened to his son rather than commanded him and then Lao Er said:

"Father, the first work to be done is the finishing of the hole and since I ought not to go out into the fields anyway until I see what the outlook is, then I will work at that hole and make a strong good room under the court where we can live if we must or where we can hide others."

"What others?" Ling Tan asked surprised.

"We must ally ourselves to those in the hills," Lao Er said, "and it may be that sometimes we must hide them."

To this Ling Tan said not a word, and how could he when now two of his sons were in the hills?

So when they had eaten he went out alone to the land until such a time as Ling Sao could bear to leave the child, and his son went to work on the hole and Jade worked, too, as long as Ling Sao held the child, and worked as much as she dared without spoiling her milk for the child if she grew too weary.

"My legs are strong enough," she said laughing, "for I have learned almost to walk in my sleep, but now my arms must take their turn."

This Jade had in these hard months grown almost as strong as a man and her slender body was hard and all the softness of her face was gone. Anywhere she might have passed for a young man if one did not take notice of her little bosom, which for all its smallness yet nourished the child well. What she ate seemed to go to the child and not to her, and Ling Sao rejoiced in this and she said:

"I wish that poor Orchid could see this, for she was so fat and yet when she had a child to nurse all she ate so heartily went to herself, and her big round breasts that you would have said were full of milk were empty and only fat."

"She would have hated me the more," Jade said sadly. "Oh, if she saw me reading a book and nursing my child at the same time how angry she would be!"

But Ling Sao was grave about the book. "Are you sure you do well to read a book when you nurse the child?" she asked. "It seems to me a danger to do two such opposite things when you are a woman."

But Jade only smiled. "Look at me when the child eats again," she said.

And Ling Sao did look and while Jade read and held the child to nurse, the milk flowed out of her so rich and full that the child had to gulp to take it in, and out of the other breast it flowed, too, there was so much. Ling Sao could say no more, and she could forgive Jade anything because she had so much milk for the child.

In the morning how beautiful the child was, and how sweet his flesh smelled to her! She could do no work nor anything except sit and hold him and gaze at him and smell him and laugh at him, and her eyes were dazed with pleasure and she heard nothing anybody said and cared not whether a dish were washed or the floor swept or whether there was anything for the next meal.

"Leave your mother alone," Ling Tan told his son, "and tell Jade to indulge her and let her hold the child to her heart's wish. It will heal her for everything."

They did as he told them, and now and again they looked at her and she did not see them. She was murmuring to the child, laughing because he wet her so often, and she carried him into the courtyard for the sun to fall upon him, and she rubbed oil into his little arms and legs, and once she cried out and they hurried in and she said to them:

"Look at his back! I swear I never saw a child under a year so strong and able to sit alone! Look at this back of his!" And her eyes were full of tears.

So they laughed and went back to their digging, and in that one day of digging Lao Er and Jade made the hole deeper than Ling Tan and Ling Sao had made it in seven.

Out in the fields at his own work Ling Tan thought whether or not he could keep his son hid and how, for others in the village must know he was there, and after a while it seemed to him that it would be best to hide nothing from the village, who were after all of his own blood. So when he came in to eat at noon he told his son so, and the son agreed with him, and that night after the day's work was finished Ling Tan took his son to the tea shop openly with him. When all greetings had been given and taken, he rose and said:

"This son of mine has seen many things which if you are will-

222

ing he will tell you, not because he has any merit in seeing them, but to hear will give you heart."

They clapped their hands on the table at this and so Lao Er stood up and in his clear and quiet voice without any pride or bombast he told his kinsmen how he had traveled westward to a city a thousand miles away until his father's letter found him and he turned back again, and how everywhere the people were of one mind that the enemy must be resisted, openly where the land was free and secretly where the land was lost, but always resisted.

"There are only two kinds of men who are not of this will," he said, "and they are the ones who think of their own profit first and the others are the weak and the evil, the ones who can be bought with opium and with drugs, who are less than nothing anyway and now dangerous only because they can be spies on others. These are the traitors."

"Good!" they shouted back to him, and they looked at each other and nodded that he was right, and Lao Er looked about on these brown dark faces that he had known all his life, and his heart rose in him.

"Uncles and cousins," he said, "we must join ourselves to those in the free land who make war on the enemy, and how shall we join? Only by working in secret with the nine thousand men in the hills."

Now when he said this he well knew that he invited those men of his blood to be ready to die, for if the enemy knew that the hill men had anything to do with a village their anger knew no reason and they burned that village down.

But man by man in that room held up his thumb and his forefinger to signify that he agreed to what Lao Er said, and of them all there was only the third cousin who hesitated, and then out of shame he too put up his thumb and finger. Yet no one blamed him for this, knowing that learning makes a man weak and a learned man can never be so brave as one unlettered. Lao Er waited until every hand was up and then he said:

"What does this mean? It means that we must hide our rice and wheat harvests and give to the enemy the least we can to save our lives. It means that where we had cotton fields our land now will not grow cotton. It means that as often as can be done an enemy or a few enemies suddenly die from unseen guns."

To this they all listened with uttermost silence.

"But we have no guns," a voice now said.

"I know where to get guns," Lao Er said, "and every man shall have his gun."

A great sigh went over those men like a wind of joy and they murmured and said aloud,

"If we have guns what can we not do! It is our bare hands that have kept us back, or having nothing but pitchforks and old swords, when the enemy has such weapons as we have never seen."

As for Ling Tan he sat ready to burst with pride in his son and he thought, "The wisest thing I ever did was to call this son home."

When they were in his house again he said so to Lao Er and he said, "I only wish you had not gone away at all."

But his son said, "No, I am glad I went and saw the free land and the people there, so that I know what they are, and I know that they and we together will push this enemy into the sea if we are steadfast. Yet I well know their way of fighting in the free land and ours here must be different. They can fight openly but we secretly. Ours is a harder war than theirs, for we live in the midst of the enemy, and we have nowhere to go."

Thereafter the people in that village waited for Lao Er to bring them guns, and he waited until he had finished the room under the court. But he worked no longer alone. Seeing how loyal the villagers were to each other, and how they were all the same clan, he chose a few to whom to tell of the room, and he called them to work with him, and then how quickly was that room finished! Four strong men working together hewed the clay out, and they set up poles and beams and door frames and they made another secret entrance. Lao Er dug all deeper than had been planned, because in the free land he had seen the shelters against the fighting ships and he went very deep, only praying not to find a river. In this he was lucky, for he found only a small stream which he drained off into the well through a tube he made from bamboos joined and their joints knocked through.

But now and again those diggers came upon strange things, an old bowl or two, some jars full of something now dust, a broken skeleton of a child long dead, and some bones of a man's leg, and deepest of all a small brass box all green which when they forced it open held a few jeweled pins and a pair of heavy gold earrings, such as none of them had ever seen.

"These belonged to our ancestors," Ling Tan said reverently, "and we are not worthy to touch them." He took them and he buried them again in the wall of the room, and left them there.

They made the secret room strong and deep and bigger than Ling Tan had ever thought it could be. They put beams across the top to keep earth from falling in and these beams were held up by pillars of brick they took from the walls of the loom room, for Ling Tan's house was not earth but brick, and when there was not enough brick, men from the village who had brick houses took down inner walls and by night they carried the brick into Ling Tan's house. So in less than two months after Lao Er came home that secret room was finished.

Now Lao Er said, "We have a place to put our guns."

The morning of the day after the secret room was finished he left the house before dawn, food in his hand and two pairs of extra sandals tied to his belt, and he went toward the hills.

XI

IN THAT year when the rice harvest was ripe to be cut and while the grain stood yellow in the fields, the enemy sent men everywhere to see to the harvest and to make guess of what the yield would be and to command the farmers that rice was to be sold at a fixed price. The price was so low that it scarcely paid to sell the grain at all. Though Ling Tan and the men he knew took the commands in silence, as they had schooled themselves always to do, for anger was too dear if it gave the enemy a cause to kill one of them, yet their hatred of these small bandy-legged men who were the enemy grew until their skins were tight. For a farmer is a man who will bear much until it comes to the matter of his land and his harvest that he takes from it. The harvests are his life, and if they be taken from him what has he to show for his life?

With their heads bowed Ling Tan and his fellows stood sullen before the enemy, and when the enemy were gone they met together and planned how they would hide the grain. They cut their grain all together and quickly so that it was not possible for the enemy to be everywhere at once, and secretly they threshed at night behind the doors and the windows they covered with cloth to hide the one small light they threshed by, and such grain they hid. There were those who dug under their houses as Ling Tan had and made holes for the hiding of the grain and some had relatives living in villages in the hills, and these took loads away by night. And yet so evil were these times that many such loads were seized by the robbers and the bandits who hid themselves wherever the enemy was not, and robbed their own people. There were such men, even in these times.

In the daytime Ling Tan and his fellows threshed what was left in the open and on the threshing floors and the enemy wondered that so much standing grain could bring so little rice. That year the yield was only half what it had been the year before, and the farmers told the enemy that some years it was so with them that the straw grew very thick and strong but there was little grain in the heads, and could they help it if now Heaven had sent such a year?

Then what could the enemy do? If they believed the farmers lied and killed them who would till the land next year? They could only take the rice that was left. What made Ling Tan's gall come up in his throat bitter and hard to swallow was that the enemy not only took their rice at the price set, but they sold it again in the city at their own price after they had what they wanted for themselves, and the price they sold it for then was three and four times what they had paid the farmers, and in this way, too, did the enemy pillage the land and the people.

Now the law against fish was enforced, that in all the land only the enemy should have the right to eat fish, and Ling Tan caught no more fish in his pond by day, but he used a seine by night if he wanted fish. Every bone of a fish they ate must be hid and the scales and the fins and any offal must be buried, and they ate fish only at night behind their locked doors, and so did all the village. And yet a show must be kept too, and so once in a while a man walked into the city with a little fish in his hand to give to the enemy. Sometimes the enemy came out and ordered them to catch fish, and then only did Ling Tan and the others have to catch some good fish to save their lives.

Ducks and fowl of all kinds, and pigs and cows, all were taken by the enemy at their own price and meat grew so scarce that men did not think of meat any more. Ling Tan was glad he had killed his own meat early, and he kept his old water buffalo thin and tough so that even the enemy looking at that stringy frame did not ask its death yet.

It was after his son had gone to the hills that they came to bid him deliver his pigs and his fowl which they had registered. He saw them coming one morning, but now he was used to looking up from his work and seeing little bandy-legged men coming toward him. He gave no heed until he saw their feet before him and he could always tell the foot of an enemy because the great toe is forced apart from the others.

When he saw these feet he made his face stupid and his eyes dull and he let his mouth hang and slowly he rose and stared at them. And one who spoke to him shouted loudly:

"We have registered for you two pigs and some ducks and hens and it is required that you sell them to us."

"Pigs!" Ling Tan said stupidly, "I have no pigs."

"You have!" the little man bellowed. "It is written down here that you have two pigs."

"My pigs died," Ling Tan said.

"If you killed them you will be killed," the little man said severely.

"They died of sickness," Ling Tan said, "and I dared not bring their carcasses for fear you would say I killed them."

"Where are the bones?"

"The dog gnawed them and we cracked them and pounded them to meal and put them in the land," Ling Tan said.

Now Ling Tan had kept the eleven young pigs in the loom room until it was taken down, and then he had killed them all except two and Ling Sao had salted them. Only the two had he kept alive to breed more and these two he had driven far behind the village and tied them to stakes, and if they were found they were found.

The enemy was angry enough and yet what could they do? If

they took Ling Tan who would tend the land? So all they could do was to threaten him and say that if they found him lying it would go ill with him indeed and he listened as though he understood nothing and so they went away, complaining that the people of this country were so stupid that it made the lives of those who conquered them a burden.

When they were gone Ling Tan squatted down again and hidden under his wide bamboo hat he smiled and took a little comfort for the moment because even in a small way he had harassed the enemy. And thus did all the other men on the land, each as skilfully as he could but few were as skilful as Ling Tan.

But Ling Tan's eighth cousin, who had been the village butcher, as his father was before him, and his father's father very far back, could no longer live. The loss of all his business filled his belly and his grief was a load in him that would neither come up nor go down, and he could not eat. One day his neighbors saw the boards of his shop still not opened at noon, and since his wife had gone into refuge and his two sons had escaped to the hills, they knew he was alone. They called Ling Tan, therefore, and he opened the boards. There in the empty butchery Ling Tan found his eighth cousin hung by his own girdle from an iron meat hook. The man had cleaned his shop before he died and had cleaned himself and put on his blue coat and trousers freshly washed, and now he hung there, a good and decent man dead.

"This one, too, the devils have killed," Ling Tan said sorrowfully and he lifted his cousin down and the next night buried him. Even for the funeral his wife dared not come home and his sons came only because it was night.

All the life of Ling Tan's house now was shaped day by day to the sight of the little bandy-legged men coming down the road—"The devils," men called them now. Ling Sao in every waking moment of her life watched from door and window and she sat spinning or she worked near the house and when they came she went and told Jade and Jade took the child instantly and went

229

behind the stove and down the ladder and Ling Sao closed the hole and spread earth and straw over the wooden cover and no one could have dreamed what was there in the dark kitchen. When the men had gone Jade came out again and took up her work, but she never went outside the gate, nor did Ling Sao take the child out until night fell.

But the fame of the child leaked out and one by one all the women of the village came to see him and praise him. The third cousin's wife came too, and she praised him somewhat, but she could not praise him much because of her envy. When she saw that boy, how he was beyond any other child that she had ever seen, her belly knotted in the middle and for a day or two she could not eat and sleep. By some evil chance she saw him first when Jade was nursing him at her breast and the sight of the young mother and her full bosom and the greedy handsome boy turned her blood to gall. She could scarcely get out the words she must speak for even scanty courtesy, and she followed these words by other mournful ones.

"It is no good sign to have so fine a child as this," she said sadly. "It is always such children who die young. My son was like that when he was that age."

This Ling Sao could not bear and she burst out, "Why, cousin, how can you say so? I was with you when you gave birth to your son, and he came out so small and green that I swear I thought he would not draw breath and I dared not wash him but I rolled him up as he was in your man's old trousers and let him be until you could wash him. And do you not remember how he had the flux and stayed like a little starved cat until he was nearly three? Only when he was ten or eleven did I draw my own breath easily when I saw him."

But the cousin said angrily, "I think I can remember my own child better than you can, cousin, and you have always liked to help children to be born and you have helped so many you have mixed another with mine."

Then she could not forbear saying to Jade, "Yes, such a child mine was and he could have fathered this child of yours and ought to have if the will of the gods had been heeded, and we have been punished enough that it was not heeded, for had he wed you as he ought to have done, he would now be alive and this would be his son."

Now Jade was angry and she covered up her bosom and said proudly, "I am content with my life, though I grieve that you have lost your only son."

When at last the cousin went away Ling Sao and Jade were angry together for this child they loved, and it was a bond between them that they did not like this cousin's wife, and they agreed that she should not be allowed to take the child in her arms before he walked lest her venom poison him when she breathed upon him.

As for the cousin's wife she went home and cursed her husband that her son had not wed Jade and that this was not their grandchild and that their son had died and that they had no more children and that when they died they would be dead indeed with no son to live after them. She worked herself into such a misery and fury that the poor old scholar was crazed and went and beat his head against the outer wall of his own house, where Ling Tan happened to see him and ran to save him. When he found out what was the matter he laughed the laugh of a man who has no trouble with the women in his own house, and he took his cousin to the tea shop and let him tell his woe and ease himself over tea and small fried rice cakes. Then Ling Tan advised him to tell his woman next time she was so evil in her temper that he would take a concubine.

"But can I?" the poor scholar groaned. "I have not for months tried myself."

At this Ling Tan was angry indeed at his cousin's wife, and he said, "Can it be that she denies you everything?"

"I ask only for peace," the man said, mumbling in his scanty beard.

"But peace is not to be had for asking," Ling Tan answered back. "It must be sought and fought for and sometimes brought by force, in a house or a nation."

The old scholar sighed at this and looked humbly at his cousin.

"I am a man of learning," he said, "and how can I be as strong as a woman is? The strongest thing on earth is a woman, and our father Confucius spoke well when he said that a woman should not, by law, be allowed a will of her own, and I tell you, cousin, let us even be glad the enemy are men and not women, for when women conquer then men are lost indeed."

Ling Tan could scarcely hold back his laughter at this and he said, "Doubtless you are right, cousin, but I swear that if I were you I would beat that woman until she leaned against the wall to keep from falling."

"Would you?" the poor cousin murmured wistfully. "Oh, if you only would, cousin!"

"No—no," Ling Tan said, laughing more than ever, "not for you, cousin! Two things a man must do for himself, sleep with his own woman and beat her if she needs it."

He rose as he spoke and the cousin rose dolefully, too, and Ling Tan watching him walk slowly home shook his head and had no hope that by anything he had said he had given his cousin greater strength.

. . . So those autumn days went on until Ling Tan's fields were bare of grain and he had stored food enough to feed his house. He was beginning to wonder if any ill had happened to his second son when one night at midnight he heard a knock upon his door, and it was a knock he knew, because his son and he had agreed upon it when he went away. He rose, for his wife was asleep, and he went to the door and opened it a crack, ready to

232

shut it if he had been wrong. But when he opened it he heard his second son whisper:

"It is I, my father," and he let him in, and not him only for with him came two others. One by one in the darkness they spoke, and Ling Tan heard the voices of his two other sons.

"Oh, Heaven and earth are good," he whispered and he led them into the windowless kitchen and there he lit the lamp and saw before him, all alive and well, his three sons, and he knew as soon as he saw his third son, that he was not a robber.

"What more can I, who am a man, ask, than the sight of you three?" he said. Indeed they were a sight to make a man proud, for the months in the hills had changed those two, his eldest and his third son. Never had he seen them look so strong and sun-browned, so fearless in the eyes. That was the greatest change, that the two who had left his house sad and weakened by their grief, were now fearless and they had forgotten what their grief was. "You went to the good hillmen," he said to his third son.

"I am only with those who make war on the devils," his third son answered and then he said, "Tell my mother I am hungry and I want some of her good food before we leave."

"But must you leave soon?" Ling Tan asked.

"Before the darkness changes we must be at the foothills again," the eldest said.

"Even though we hide you?" Ling Tan asked.

"Yes, this time," the eldest said, and seemed to want to say no more. So the father led them down into the secret room, and each soon took off his back a load he carried there and when they were unrolled he saw that each had carried a dozen guns. There were such guns as he had never seen, short strong guns of a foreign sort. He took up one and looked at it.

"Where did you get these guns?" he asked.

The youngest son laughed. "We take them from the enemy," he said.

Then Ling Tan when he had admired the guns awhile re-

233

membered his last son was hungry and he put the gun down and went and waked Ling Sao. She rose and had the fire going in a few minutes and Lao Er waked Jade and she brought the child and there in that secret room they all gathered and ate the noodles and salt pork that Ling Sao soon had ready. They had a table there and benches and they dared to have the light, and as long as the two sons stayed they talked and told each other everything and Ling Sao could not have enough of looking at her sons. Ling Tan had warned her to mention no sorrowful thing and not to bring to their minds again anything that had happened of evil. Still she was a mother first and she could not forbear whispering to her eldest son as they were about to leave again:

"Son, have you found anyone yet to take to be the mother of more children to you?"

He smiled down at her but he did not shake his head.

"Is this a time to think of it?" he asked.

"It is always a time to think of more children," she said sturdily. "Who will take up the work after you if you have no sons?"

"Well, mother, perhaps you are right, and I must look and see what can be found," he said.

And the father laughed and said, "What would come to us all if the women did not keep us breeding?"

And Ling Sao emboldened by their laughter said loudly, "What would happen to you if you had no women would be that none of you would be born at all."

"No man can deny that, old woman," he said.

And she went on:

"And I shall not be satisfied until you, too, my little son, are wed, and I want grandsons from you all before I die."

"You are a woman never satisfied," Ling Tan exclaimed and in the laughter of all this the two went away and to the hills again. Ling Tan shut the door and barred it behind them, well content once more within his house.

234

But all through these weeks and months he had heard nothing of his elder daughter nor of Wu Lien. Then one day at about noon, when they had just eaten their food, and Ling Sao was dipping the bowls and chopsticks into water to wash them, there was a noise at the gate. By now when such a sound was heard at the gate Lao Er, if he were there, and Jade and the child went into the secret room before the bar was drawn and so they were about to do now. But Ling Sao heard her eldest daughter's voice at the gate and she called out joyfully.

"Wait, it is only my daughter and your sister!" and she was about to draw the bar from the gate when Lao Er seized her arm.

"Mother," he whispered, "you are not to say that we are here. Tell nothing, mother!"

With that he hastened to the secret room and he lifted the child out of Jade's arms and bade her make haste too, as though those who came were enemies. Ling Sao stood staring after him as though he had lost his wits.

"Well, this is a strange day when brothers and sisters must hide from each other," she told Ling Tan who had watched all this.

"All days are strange now," he said, quietly.

He rose and went to the gate as he spoke, for they could hear their eldest daughter bawling over the wall:

"Are my old ones sleeping or what? Here am I and my children and their father!"

He opened the gate and saw before his eyes Wu Lien and his household. It had been many a month since he had seen anything like these. He did not know how used his eyes had grown to the miserable, to people afraid and hungry and wounded and fleeing, until now he saw at his gate Wu Lien, fatter than he had ever been and his flesh the color and smoothness of mutton fat, and his daughter fat and about to have another child, and the two children fat and dressed in red silk coats, and they had

235

all come in rickshas. But what made him grave was the sight of two enemy soldiers behind them, and he made up his mind that he would not have these two in his court. So he closed the gate enough except for his own face to look through and he said in a cool voice:

"You are welcome, daughter's husband and daughter and little children, but I cannot let others into my house."

Wu Lien let his laugh roll out of him at this, and he said:

"You need not fear, my wife's father. These two only came to guard me."

"What guard do you need in my house?" Ling Tan asked. Though he would not have said he was afraid, yet the very sight of those low-browed enemy men with their drawn guns made his belly quiver and he wished he had not eaten his noon meal.

"It is a discourtesy to leave them outside the gate," Wu Lien urged.

"Whoever heard of being courteous to guards?" Ling Tan asked.

And he stood firm and would not open the gate and when Wu Lien saw how stubborn he was he yielded and turned to the guards and tried to laugh and say that the man was old and they must forgive him if he was afraid of them.

"I am not afraid of them," Ling Tan said in a loud voice. "But I will not have them in my house."

The upshot of it was that the women went into the house and Ling Tan brought out two stools and a bench and gave the bench to the guards and he sat on one stool and Wu Lien on the other and they stayed outside the gate, and since the day was warm for late autumn it was hardship to none and all pride was saved.

Now Ling Tan did not like what he saw of his daughter's husband and the more he looked at him the more he smelled out evil. He filled his pipe, and smoked it slowly, never taking his eyes from that fat round face before him.

236

"How is it you are so fat?" he asked.

"My business is good," Wu Lien replied in a small modest voice.

"How can your business be good when no one else has good business?" Ling Tan asked.

Wu Lien broke into a gentle sweat and took out a silk handkerchief and wiped himself, even the palms of his plump smooth hands, and always smiling, and with an eye to the guards, he leaned forward and spoke in a low voice. "You must know that what I do is done only for the best."

But Ling Tan said in a loud voice, "I do not know what you do."

Then Wu Lien wiped himself again and laughed and coughed and said, "Times are times and the wise man takes his time as he finds it and he bends himself to it as a sail to the wind. There is to be a government set up in the city and it is to be a government not of the enemy but of our people, of men like myself, who seeing that if for the time we must yield, then it is better to yield by compromise and to our own rather than to aliens. You see what I would say, my wife's father."

"I am a common man," Ling Tan said, taking his pipe out of his mouth. "I am so stupid I understand only when a thing is said to me and I hear it."

He stared at Wu Lien with his eyes wide open and Wu Lien gave up and smiled in silence, for he saw that Ling Tan was determined not to understand him.

"Where do you live now?" Ling Tan asked after a while.

"At the tenth house of the North Gate Street."

"That is a street of fine houses," Ling Tan said. "How can you live there?"

"I am told to live there," Wu Lien replied.

"And your shop?"

"It is open and I hire two clerks to keep it for me."

"What are your goods?"

"Cloth and foreign goods of all kinds."

"And you—what do you do?"

"I work for the new government," Wu Lien said calmly.

"Do they pay you?"

"I am well paid," Wu Lien replied.

"So you are content," Ling Tan said bitterly.

Wu Lien did not answer this but he leaned forward and making his voice soft he began to plead with Ling Tan.

"My wife's father, I am come here today to help you. Indeed I have no other wish. I warn you that the outlook is not good. Those who have friends are better off than those who have none. If you will do as I say, your life will be easier."

It was on the edge of Ling Tan's tongue to cut the man off and his hands twitched and longed to fly at that soft pale face, but Ling Tan was no child. He could hold back both tongue and hands when it paid him to do it, and so he sat looking as stupid as he could and smoking his pipe and listening.

"What must I do?" he asked.

"Do whatever is told you to do," Wu Lien said, "and I will manage for you here and there as I am able."

But Ling Tan paid no heed to his offer. "And what have you to do, son-in-law?" he asked.

"I am a controller of all incoming goods," Wu Lien said. "It is part of my task to see that the rice and wheat, opium and fish and salt are taken in at a place and then made ready to send out again or sold—"

"Opium!" Ling Tan shouted in a terrible voice.

Wu Lien went the color of mutton fat again. That word had slipped over his lips of his own accord, for he was used to handling opium as part of his every-day goods. Opium was brought down from the North, and of all the goods, it alone was not sent to the East-Ocean people. No, opium was kept here and scattered everywhere in cities and villages and by every wile and trick the enemy were teaching the people to use it. It had been an ancient evil here, driven out with great pain and suffering once, and now it was brought back again, and the people who yielded to it were many.

Wu Lien coughed behind his fat white hand. "I am not my own master," he said mildly.

But Ling Tan could endure no more. He spat on the ground twice and cursed. *"P'ei!"* he shouted at Wu Lien.

Wu Lien coughed again behind his hand and now his face grew very red with his coughing. He wished that for one moment Ling Tan would take his black eyes away from him, for he felt uneasy under this unchanging look. But Ling Tan did not move his eyes.

. . . Inside the gate Ling Sao questioned her daughter fiercely.

"But where do you get all this meat and rice to eat?"

"There is plenty of food," her daughter said innocently. "Rice we have in great bins and meat is brought to us, cows' meat and pigs' meat and fish and eggs and fowl."

"What I hear is that nobody has meat," Ling Sao said, "and the enemy comes searching the villages about and none of us has anything left. Ducks and hens, pigs and cows, all are taken, and that we have our old buffalo is only because it is so thin and old, and yet the enemy stares at it, too, and your father says one of these days it will go."

"If I had known I would have brought you some meat," the daughter said, "and next time I will bring it."

But Ling Sao gave no thanks for this. Instead she said sourly, "I do not like anyone of my blood to look so fat when others are lean. It is not well in a time of famine when all are starving for one to look fat."

"But I only eat what I am given," the daughter said.

"Who gives it to you?" Ling Sao asked.

"My husband."

Then Ling Sao searched her daughter to know if she were innocent or not.

239

"How is he able to do this?" she asked.

The daughter began to weep. "I know you cannot understand how good he is," she sobbed, "because he seems to yield for the time, you blame him. I told him it would be so. But he hates the enemy, too, and he says that each must resist in his own way and he says that he is able in a hundred ways to turn the advantage away from the enemy and to us, and he says what is the use of opposing what is already here? The enemy rules, and somehow we must live under that rule."

"But not grow too fat under it," Ling Sao said.

"We had better be fat than the enemy," the daughter said in sudden anger. "Is the enemy worsted when we refuse to eat?"

"If you can eat," Ling Sao said bitterly.

And Ling Sao looked at the two little fat children and to her own surprise she took no joy in them. She who could never see a child without wanting to cuddle it and smell its flesh looked at these two and did not want to touch them. Their flesh was not hers, she thought. They had eaten foreign food. But her daughter only saw that her mother looked at the children and she said proudly, "Have they not grown?"

"Yes," Ling Sao said. "They have grown."

And then she looked at her daughter between the eyes. "What will they think some day when our land is free again and their father's name is among the names of traitors?"

At this the daughter began to weep again and to wish that she had not come home.

"We came at great inconvenience," she sobbed, "and we came only to help you and to see if you were safe, and whatever you think of us we think as we ever did of you, and you will see some day that perhaps we can save even your lives."

Ling Sao rose. "If I had anything in the house to give you and your children for courtesy I would prepare it for you," she said, "but indeed we have nothing. We are not given plenty of meat and rice. What we have is only enough to keep us from starving. I cannot treat you courteously, therefore."

This was to say that she would talk no more, and her daughter knew it.

"How can you be so hard when there are only you two old people in the house and we are all you have!" she said.

"We can live," Ling Sao said proudly.

So Ling Tan outside the court saw the gate opened and his daughter and the children come out and Ling Sao made a small show of courtesy and she and Ling Tan stood there until Wu Lien and his household were gone, and there were no words said of their return.

When they were gone they barred the gate again and then Ling Sao shouted down the hole and the others came up. They talked a while of the visit and the more Lao Er heard the angrier he was. He made up his mind to creep into the city in one way or another, and see for himself what was there, and see whether indeed all had yielded to the enemy.

Jade, out of her reading of books, devised a beggar's garment for him and with red clay they made a wound on his face that twisted his mouth to one side and seemed to blind an eye and a few days after that Lao Er went into the city pretending he was a beggar. Avoiding the main streets, he came and went and said little and saw much. What he saw grieved him, for everywhere opium was being sold. The ruined houses he overlooked, and the hungry people, since war brings them everywhere. Yet they could scarcely be wholly overlooked in this city which had only so little while ago been beautiful and rich and full of pleasure. Now the streets were silent. Thousands upon thousands of those who had once walked there in full life were dead. Houses that had been homes were empty and burned. Shops were closed, except those like Wu Lien's which flourished on such times. But like a new and evil growth there were other shops, some hovels, some gaudy with paper and paint, some openly brothels and some not, but all selling opium. By such a hovel Lao Er paused and made as though he would go in and was waiting to get his courage, when a wretched man crawled by on a crutch, his right leg gone. He was yellow and dried and Lao Er could see that he had come to this place many times before. He laid hold of him and spoke to him as a stranger speaks.

"Does this place sell—that?" he asked and pointed to the sign.

The man nodded and Lao Er asked again, "But ought we to go in if the enemy sells it?"

The man looked at him. "What does it matter what happens to men like me?" he asked. "Nothing can give me back what I have had. The best of times and all the enemy gone will not give me back my leg, no, nor my good inn and my wife and my sons, and all that was once mine. I do not care even for victory. What can victory do for me?"

And Lao Er groaned and thought that such as this one were indeed the vanquished. He limped home by night and there he told what he had seen and how the markets had no food in them and how the marketmen told him the prices were scraping heaven because food was being sent out, and the people in the city were starving, but the enemy did not care, and for food they were giving the people cheap opium and so forgetfulness.

Now such mournfulness fell upon Ling Tan's house as they had not yet had, for Ling Tan knew from his own mother what opium could do and how a whole soul could be changed and made something else by it.

"What is our refuge from this?" he mourned. "We can hide from the flying ships and we can build up houses that are burned, but what can be done if our people forget what has befallen them?" And to Ling Tan this seemed the worst evil that the enemy had yet done to them.

XII

Now secret war is not open war, and of the two secret war is the harder to wage. As the winter passed, Ling Tan had to keep his face smooth and his eyes dull, and yet his mind had to be working and quick to spring to every advantage large and small. While his sons and those who were with them came and went by night and used the secret room as a fortress for their weapons, he had to seem to be an old farmer who knew nothing and saw nothing if the enemy came to inquire. And be sure they did come, for in the spring there began to be so many of the enemy found dead that a great anger rose among the enemy rulers. Guards were found shot upon the city wall, though the city gates were locked at night, and the wall was eighty feet high and how could any climb it?

Yet Ling Tan's youngest son, and others like him, climbed that wall somewhere many a night. He thrust his bare strong feet into the crevices of the great old bricks and into vines and into the roots of small trees, and thus in darkness pulling and feeling he scaled that wall and crept along the shadows of the crenellated edge until he came to an enemy guard somewhere and then he shot him. The next moment he was hiding in the vines again and there he clung until if there were noise and clamor it had died away and then he climbed down and went home and before dawn he was back in the hills.

And the enemy who came to the countryside to search for food and goods found themselves surrounded by innocent dull villagers, men and old women together, fearful and timid, and then suddenly these same people brought out guns and knives and fell upon them and there was not one left even to tell what village it was, and all the enemy in the city knew was that too many times those who went out did not come back. Yet the villagers were wise enough not to fall upon any who came too strong for them. No, wherever they were, they waited for a sign from one they chose to be their leader and if the sign was made they moved in swiftness and in silence.

In the secret room under Ling Tan's court there were strange weapons now, some guns new and bright and with foreign letters on them of the countries where they were made, and also some weapons so ancient that it was a marvel to think where they had first been made and where used. These came always from the men in the hills, many of whom in other times had been bandits and so had kept weapons they had from generation to generation of bandits under the many different warlords who had led them. Of all these weapons Ling Tan chose for himself a very strange old gun that had a wooden handle like a club at one end and at the other end it was set into iron, and the iron shaped into four tubes like the four fingers of a man's hand, and at the base of each tube was a hole for the fire to be set to the powder. So simple was this weapon that Ling Tan could use for a missile any piece of iron he found, the heads of nails or the fragments of hinges and such things, and with four small charges of powder and a little cotton, he could fire four times at once. The wound thus made was very grievous.

Now in his village Ling Tan was the man chosen to give the sign of death to the enemy and this he did whenever the enemy came, and he did not mistake the power of the villagers. Twice in the winter and once in the spring he gave the sign and each time they were able to kill all the enemy so that not once did any escape to give a bad report of the village and so they were safe.

The anger of enemy rulers rose very high when month after month their loss grew more severe, especially in the hill villages that were far from the city. How could they rule the countryside if they did not dare to go out to it, and yet how could they send an army everywhere to gather in the food and goods they took? At last in the middle of the summer the enemy in great rage began to burn all those villages where they found men of the hills. Ling Tan's village was not burned, for though at the very hour that the enemy searched it there were in the secret room some men of the hills, they did not find them, and so though they threatened they did not destroy.

But there were villages far in the hills where innocent people were burned in their houses by night and this for no cause except that the villages were in the hills and the enemy reasoned that there must be hillmen in them. And yet as mid-summer came on, Ling Tan's sons told him, from somewhere there came out piteous creatures even from the burned villages, a few men and women, to till the blackened earth that was still theirs.

Under such cruelty the temper of the people could not but change. In the old days when men had been free, the very faces of men and women had been open and free and laughter was ready and quick and voices were merry and there was loud cheerful talking and cursing in every house, and none had need to hide anything from anyone. But now the villages were silent, and the faces of the people in the whole countryside grew grim and hard, because of the hardships of their life under this enemy and the bitterness of their hatred which they could not vent except by secret killing. This secret anger and this constant search for ways to kill could not but change men's very hearts, and Ling Tan felt this change even in himself.

This enemy having always burned wood and wood only to cook their food, they knew no other fuel and so they cut down trees and they took out beams from people's houses and lifted gates from their hinges, and whenever there was a need for wood they went out and took it where they saw it.

And they felled with all other trees in that spring the great old willow tree near Ling Tan's house under which Lao Er and Jade had used to meet in the first year of their marriage. When Lao Er came and saw the huge beheaded stump he felt sorrow and he went back and said to Jade:

"They have cut down our tree, my heart."

And she said sadly, "Were there once such peaceful days that we could meet beneath a tree?"

Now there chanced to come to Ling Tan's village one day in the first month of the summer, a band of the enemy looking for wood. They were a band of some eight or nine men, but Ling Tan's sharp eye, veiled with pretended dullness, saw that there were only five with guns and the others had no weapons. The villagers came to their doors as they always did, and their old women or their old men stood ready inside to hand them their weapons if Ling Tan gave the sign. This day, after considering the enemy, Ling Tan did give the sign, and in one body the villagers sprang out and fell upon the enemy and killed them all except one who was wounded by Ling Tan's four-muzzled gun. He was able to crawl away into the bamboos at the south of Ling Tan's own house. Here Ling Tan followed him, and the man rose on his hands and knees like a dog, and he turned a beseeching face to Ling Tan and in language that Ling Tan could understand he begged for his life. He was a man near to Ling Tan's age and he said, gasping, "Let me live, I beg you, let me live! I have a wife and children. See, here they are!" He tried to find something in his bosom and could not.

But Ling Tan reached into the man's own belt and took out a short knife he carried and without waiting a moment or indeed taking thought more than he could have for a snake or a fox he thrust it into the man's belly. The man turned a dark sad look on him and died.

246

Then Ling Tan, who had killed an enemy three times before this, stood looking down on the man's face and he thought:

"He has not an evil face, this devil." He thought of what the man had told him, and the stain of his blood had not yet reached his bosom, and Ling Tan stooped and put his hand into the man's pocket and took out a small silk case. He opened it and there were the pictures of a pretty woman and four children between eight and fourteen years of age. Ling Tan stared at them for a while and thought how they would never see again the man to whom they belonged.

At this moment Ling Tan knew how changed he too was, for he could think about this and could look at these faces and feel no sorrow. There was neither sorrow nor joy in him. What he had done he had done and he did not wish it undone, and if the chance came to him he would take it again tomorrow.

He had once been so soft at heart that he did not want to see fowls killed and Ling Sao had always to wring their necks behind the house where he could not see. "I do not like to kill," he thought now, "and even today I would not kill for pleasure. But how is it I am able to kill at all?"

He went back to his house, pausing only to tell the villagers who were burying the dead that there was a dead body in the bamboos, for it was needful always to bury quickly lest these bodies be discovered. With the silk case in his hand he went into his house and put the case into his room. Yes, he was changed. Tonight he would eat as well as ever, and it would be nothing to him that because of him a man for whom a woman and children waited somewhere was now buried in the earth. There had been others, and the people in the village and he among them had often made jokes about these dead men and how they enriched the soil or poisoned it, and had wondered whether or not the same crops would come up next year. They were all changed. Before the enemy came it was never heard of that anyone was killed in this village, except perhaps a girl child too many and

247

then only when it was new born and had not drawn the breath of life. Now they killed the enemy like lice in winter coats and thought no more of it.

"When the devils are gone can we get our old selves back?" Ling Tan asked himself and could not answer. He began to think of each one in his house, and he thought of Ling Sao who with all the other men and women ran out with her spade and her hoe and dug the ground to bury the enemy in, and came back as though they had buried offal, and then went into the kitchen or took up the child. He thought of Jade who held a gun and fired it from a doorway as cleverly as her husband did, and then nursed her son, and what did that child drink into himself with her milk? But of them all, none were so changed as he and his three sons were. For Ling Tan knew that women are more able to kill and do hard deeds than men are. They shed their blood each month, and they pour it out when they give birth, and so they are not afraid of blood. But when a man's blood flows, he knows his life goes out with it, and so he is more squeamish than a woman is and to learn to shed blood easily moves him and stirs his being and changes him.

Thus it was with Ling Tan's eldest son. He had been a simple tender-hearted man, and at first when he had to kill he went against his nature, and then when he did kill his nature was changed. Now Ling Tan seeing his eldest son come and go from his house to the hills saw a man who had been laughing and child-like even when he had children of his own, grow into a man who laughed no more, but went about his daily work of death as easily as once he had tilled the land.

This eldest son laid a trap so well that none could tell there was a pit under the dust. He did the thing over and over on many roadsides, and he went to his traps night and morning. If an innocent man were there he pulled him out and let him go free but if it were an enemy he thrust his knife into him as easily as though he had caught a little fox in his trap. He would not waste a bullet on an enemy who had no gun, and he put his knife into him where the heart lay and then tossed the man into a thicket and laid the trap fresh again. Ling Tan saw this eldest son, one day when he was home and eating his food, get up quickly from the table and go out. There was a solitary enemy at the gate who had come to write something down on his little book, and the eldest son killed him and then came back to his meal.

"Do you not even wash your hands?" Ling Tan asked in a wonder. "Why should I?" his son answered simply, "I did not touch him—I only pushed him with my foot into the bamboo thicket."

In this same fearful simpleness he ate his food heartily and only when he had finished did he bury the enemy he had hidden in the thicket. But Ling Tan could not eat his own meal then with heartiness, not because any had been killed, but because of the change in his son.

"Can he change back?" Ling Tan asked himself. "When peace comes, will my son be gentle again as he once was?"

Yet nothing was so fearful to Ling Tan as the joy of his younger son in these days whenever he killed an enemy. This son, only now a young man, had come out of his dreaming silence, and he grew into a beauty more terrible with every day. He was far taller than most men are and his face was such that man and woman turned to look at it, and he went disguised except among his own because his was a face not to be forgotten. His brow was square and his eyebrows were black and clear, and his eyes shone with his will. His nose was straight and high and his lips still fresh as a child's and yet everything he had was bigger than another man had. He had known no women but they looked at him and yearned for him, though he turned his head away from them. For what the enemy had done to this son was to turn his being away from nature, and all that passion which he could have put into loving a woman he put now into one deep will, and it was the will to kill, and it became his joy to kill.

Now Ling Tan saw before his own eyes that this son had become the sort of man he feared and hated most, a man who loved to make war and found it his pleasure and his life. There was no way to hide this knowledge that the youngest son was full of zest for war and that he liked everything that had to do with war. The men in the hills knew it and he had easily risen to be a leader of a division of them and he, so much younger than them all, devised schemes and plans as though he were playing a game. He became a master of ambush and secret attack, and he was the boldest of all the hillmen of that region, and the enemy came to know when an attack was his rather than another's, because the plan was so masterly and the escape difficult, though who he was they did not know.

This youngest son did not often come home, either, but when he came it was always to tell of some success he had had, and he told of it, laughing and proud, and he grew vain of his success and his luck, and he came to believe that luck was his because he had some favor of Heaven. He would boast, "Heaven chose me to that work," or he said, "To that place Heaven led me" or he said "Heaven put power in my hand," until one day Ling Tan burst out, "Do not say Heaven this and Heaven that! I tell you what happens on earth now is not the will of Heaven. It is not Heaven's will that men kill each other, for Heaven created us. If we must kill, then let us not say it is Heaven who bids it." This he said as a father may speak to a son, and he was not pleased when he saw his handsome son lift his lip at him and sneer at him and say, "This is old doctrine and by such doctrine we are come to the place where we now are. We have lain dead with our ancestors instead of living in the world and while we slept others prepared weapons and came to attack us. We who are young know better!"

Now this was such impudence as Ling Tan could not bear and

he let fly his right hand and slapped his son full on his red mouth. "Talk to me like that!" he roared at him. "By the doctrines of our ancestors we have lived for thousands of years and longer than any people on this earth! By peace men live, but by war they die, and when men live the nation lives and when men die the nation dies!"

But Ling Tan did not know this son of his now. For the son stepped forward and raised his hand against his father, and he said in a bitter voice, "These are other times! You may not strike me! I can kill you as well as another!"

This Ling Tan heard with his own ears, and his hands fell limp at his side. He stared at that handsome angry face which he himself had begotten and at last he turned away and sat down and hid his own face with his hand.

"I think you can kill me," he whispered. "I think you can kill anyone now."

The young man did not answer but he did not change his proud and sullen look. He left the house and went away and Ling Tan did not see him for many days.

They were not good days for Ling Tan and the nights were sleepless and he thought to himself, "Is this not the end of our people when we become like other war-like people in the world?" And he wished that this younger son of his would die rather than live beyond this war.

"A man who kills because he loves to kill ought to die for the good of the people, though he is my own son," Ling Tan thought heavily. "Such men are always tyrants and we who are the people are ever at their mercy."

"I do feel our youngest son is dead," he told Ling Sao one night. "He is so changed that I feel that tender boy we had is now no more—he who retched with horror when he saw the dead, even!"

He had thought that she would not know what he meant and he was surprised when he heard her sigh into the darkness.

"Are we not all changed?" she asked.

"Are you changed?" he asked in his surprise.

"Am I not?" she replied. "Can I ever go back to the old ways? Even when I hold the child on my knee I do not forget what we have done and must do."

"Can we do differently?" he asked.

"No," she said.

He pondered a while and then he said, "And yet in these days we must remember that peace is good. The young cannot remember, and it is we who must remember and teach them again that peace is man's great food."

"If they can be taught anything except what they have now learned," she said sadly. "I wish it were not so easy to kill people! Our sons grow used to this swift and easy way of ending all. I sometimes think that if you and I oppose them, old man, they will kill us as easily, if they have no other enemy, or they will fall upon each other."

He could not answer this, but he lay sleepless long after that and so did she, for he did not hear her steady snore that always told him when she slept. And he made up his mind then that though he would oppress the enemy as bitterly as ever, he would not let it be his life. Each day, whatever he did, he would take a little time to remember what peace was, and what the life here in this house once had been.

And the more he remembered the more he knew that for him to kill a man was evil.

"Let others kill," he thought. "I will kill no more."

Thereafter he reasoned to himself that in his own way he served, because he kept alive in himself the knowledge that peace was right. Without excuse he gave no more the sign of death in his own village, and if any wondered, he let them wonder, and he made amends by putting poisons in his pond and killing all the fish so that the enemy gained nothing from it, and when the rice was ready for harvest, he threshed by night inside the court and hid more than half of what he had, and when that crop was reaped, what the enemy took was scarcely worth their fetching, and to their anger he gave only silence and he made silence his weapon.

. . . But Ling Tan's second son was not like the other two. He killed when he must, but not because it was the easiest thing as the eldest son did, nor because it was his pleasure as it was the third son's pleasure. This second son laid his schemes far and wide, and if in carrying them through he had to kill, he killed, but he thought of the end and not of the moment. And in this scheming no woman could have helped him more than Jade did.

"We ought to use Wu Lien as a gate into the enemy's fortress," she told Lao one day. "It is idle to be angry and hate such persons. They are not to be loved or hated, but only to be used. But how can we do it?"

"You speak wisely," Lao Er said.

At this moment they were in the secret room and they oiled and cleaned the weapons that were hid there, for word had come from the men in the hills that a sortie would be made some time within the next three days upon an enemy garrison in a certain town in the region, and the weapons here were to be ready.

"How can we seem friends with them again?" Jade mused. As she spoke she peered into the bright barrel of the gun she held. It was a new gun taken not long ago from some enemy and placed here with the others. She put a rod into it and moved it slowly up and down. Upon the beaten earth of the floor her son sat playing with some empty cartridges. They made good toys, safe and clean to bite upon. One little empty shell he loved especially because it was slender and fitted into his gums, and upon the brass were the marks of his first teeth. Jade watched where he dropped it, because when he was tired of it she planned to put it in a box she had of his first things, his little first shoes that she had made, with tiger faces on them, and his baby cap with Buddhas sewed upon it, and all those things that mothers love to keep.

Now though these two did not dream of it, Wu Lien knew of their hiding in the farmhouse. For he had ears and eyes in the village, and who could this be but that one who was jealous of Jade and her little son? The third cousin's wife knew, as all the village did, that Wu Lien and his wife had come to Ling Tan's house rich and well fed. And so one day she took some fresh fish she had caught and with the pretext that she must turn them over to the enemy since fish was forbidden for others to eat, she went to the house where Wu Lien lived. There she gave his name to the soldier at the gate and the soldier let her in, and with her fish still wrapped in lotus leaves she came easily into Wu Lien's very presence as his wife's kinswoman.

He greeted her with courtesy as he greeted all and bade her sit, and sent for his wife, and to these two the cousin's wife, pretending only old friendship, told of Ling Tan and his sons.

"Your brothers are well," she told Wu Lien's wife, "I saw the second one not many days ago."

"My second brother!" that one cried, "and is he here?"

"Yes, and Jade, too, and they have a fine child. Still I would not wish him mine, that child, for he is marked for an early death. Death sits on his eyebrows, I say whenever I look at him."

She sighed and cast up her eyes and marked the secret look that passed between Wu Lien and his wife. So she went on, "And your other two brothers are very well, cousin," she said, "and I see them sometimes when they come in from the hills."

"Do they live in the hills?" Ling Tan's eldest daughter cried.

"Yes, they live there now," the cousin's wife said. She meditated whether or not she ought to tell of the secret room under Ling Tan's house and how from that fortress the men went out to make their secret attacks. But after she had thought a minute

254

she decided against it. "I ought not to tell everything at once," she thought. "I had better keep something in my belly for the future, lest I need it."

So she smiled, and then she sighed and said, "You have heard doubtless that my own son died. Yes, the enemy struck him and he was lost. Now I have no one. He was doing no evil, either. He had only come to the city to look and see what went on, and he had no weapon in his hand. I always said that if your father had not put the notion into his belly he would never have come. Yes, when I see Jade I know that all our evil came from the day your father bought Jade from my son. Because we are poor we lost all. But that is what it is to be so poor." She wiped her eyes, and Wu Lien coughed and tried to comfort her.

"Is your son's father well?" he asked.

"How can he be well when we have not enough to eat?" the cousin's wife replied. Then an idea came up out of her vitals into that witless brain of hers. She turned to Wu Lien, her eyes suddenly dry.

"Wu Lien, you are a kind good man," she said. "I never look into that smooth face of yours without seeing goodness there. A man does not grow so fat as you unless he has an easy heart and a liver without gall in it. Can you not find my old man a worthless little piece of work here in these walls that would pay us something?"

She looked about her as she spoke and thought how fine it would be to live here in this safe place. There were easy chairs to sit on and the beds were as good doubtless, and the food plenty, and who cared what rulers paid for them?

"But will my father let him come?" Wu Lien's wife asked. "He is angry with us, and will he not be angry if his cousin follows us here?"

Now nothing made the cousin's wife more vexed than this. By rights her husband should have had more power in the village than Ling Tan, for he was older, but no one remembered

255

that he was, and Ling Tan had easily taken his place as the head over his cousin, who was a small weak man with a piping voice and the little goat's beard that quivered as he talked.

"Your father ought not to tell us what to do," the cousin's wife said. "And my man always thinks as I do, and what I think is that we must first get food, for who will feed us if we do not feed ourselves?" It was running off her tongue to tell these two that Ling Tan had half his grain in secret stores and that he had told them all to kill their pigs and fowls and salt them down, but she hesitated, for she had done this, too, and then what would she say if it were found out?

But Wu Lien had been thinking while she spoke and now he said, "It will be best if we help you in the village. That is to say, come here sometimes and we will give you food and a little money and whatever you need, and then you can give us the news. We always like to hear how you do, and my wife's father and her mother and all her brothers."

This he said innocently but what was behind it was plain enough, and the cousin's wife saw it and smiled. Soon she rose and said she must be going. Wu Lien put his hand in his bosom and brought out some money and gave it to her, and said, "Take this for your trouble in bringing the fish, and next time, eat the fish yourself. If anyone condemns you, then I will speak for you to those higher than I." She bowed herself double in thanks and Wu Lien waved his hand to wave her courtesy away.

"I have a little power," he said modestly, "and where can I use it better than for old friends?"

And his wife looked at him proudly and thought what a noble figure was his in the wine-red robe of satin he wore, and she said earnestly to the cousin's wife, "Cousin, do us yet one more kindness. When you can, speak for my children's father to my parents. They do not give him his due. They cannot see his wisdom in seeming to agree here, and—"

But Wu Lien put up his hand for silence. "I do agree," he said

256

loudly. "I believe that what Heaven brings to pass is best, if we can see it so."

"What wisdom that is!" the cousin's wife cried. "Be sure I will speak all good for you whenever I can. It is what I say myself—it is only folly to deny what is here, and I tell my old man that every day."

So she bowed herself away and went out. In the city streets she bought a few things she wanted, a needle and some inches of cloth for shoes, and a small piece of meat, though she had to walk far to find even these, and the prices she paid made her all but put her money back again. Yet she did spend it, for she walked far and passed many empty shops, and a doleful man who waited on her at last said, "Buy or not as you will, woman. You will not find better anywhere. We are all ruined together here."

But she was smelling the meat. "What is this meat?" she asked. "Is it dog meat? If it is I will not eat it. I can kill my own dog."

"If it is not dog it is ass," he said. "They keep all other meat for themselves."

She considered a while, holding the meat in her hand, and then she took it. It was meat, whatever it was, and she did not want to kill her own dog.

But as she went homeward through the barren silent streets and saw the ruin everywhere, and how the half-starved people crept along from door to door, and how few were the rickshas even, since so many men had been killed and those left were too weak to pull a load, she grew frightened, and she thought, "Certainly we must make some sort of use of Wu Lien in that good place. We must get our fingers into fat, too, my old man and me. What use is it if we starve?"

And she walked homeward, sure that she would do whatever Wu Lien asked and she determined to keep her ears close to Ling Tan's door, for in that house the center of the village was.

"I shall tell that man of mine what we must do," she thought, and she planned how she would feed him well tonight and then even perhaps grant him some of her favor when they went to bed. Then when he was well content she would tell him how their fortunes could be made.

This she did, and the poor man was too innocent to know why that night he had one good after another given him, and only after he had partaken of all did he see why she was so unusual in her temper. Then when he had heard, he groaned and said:

"I ought to have known that you had made up your mind to something," and he felt he was between two grindstones, the one his wife and the other his deep fear of Ling Tan, and something more than fear, too, for he respected the man who was his younger cousin. In his heart he thought Ling Tan more powerful than Wu Lien sitting in the midst of enemies, and he told his wife, "If Ling Tan or his sons should find out that you and I had betrayed them, do you think our lives would not end at that moment? Why, those men kill as easily as they breathe nowadays, and if they saw us their enemies, down we would go with all the rest!"

At this his wife reviled him and she said, "Of all the men on earth you are least like a man, and why am I tied to you? Will you do what I say or not?"

"But what do you say?" he urged, trembling at her side.

"We are Ling Tan's enemies," she said, "and I have always hated him."

"But I do not," he muttered, "he has been good to us, and fed us often and when he had the loom he gave us all his short pieces, or nearly all, such as he did not need in his own house, and once a year he gave me enough for a robe, too, or a coat. It is hard for me to forget all this."

"It is not hard for me to forget it," his wife said. "Do you think this meant anything to him? He likes to give us his short pieces and his small gifts of food. It makes him bigger in his own eyes. Do people give anything away unless it makes them better to themselves? Shall we thank him for his own pride?"

Thus she twisted the poor wretch at her side and he listened and groaned and shut his eyes and tried to sleep, and she pulled him awake again until in his weariness he cried:

"Oh, do what you will, for you will do it anyway, and I am no stronger than another man that I should defy a woman!"

Thus Ling Tan's cousin and his wife became ears and eyes in the village for Wu Lien, though the cousin was always unwilling and kept as much as he could to himself. Yet how could he keep all? That woman had her ways of torture, and to keep peace in his house and himself from misery, bit by bit he yielded to her the news he heard when Ling Tan called the men together to tell them what they must do, and faithfully the woman went to Wu Lien and told him, and took her reward. But Wu Lien never told the things she told him, and he kept them only for his own knowledge.

Then Jade, not knowing, planned how it could come about that through Wu Lien a gate might be found into the enemy. She made up her mind one day that she herself would carry food into the city and sell it if she could at Wu Lien's door. She told no one what she did, for this young woman could be as cool and bold as any robber. She chose a day when her husband was in the hills, and waited until her child was sleeping and then she put on a wig of gray hair, which she had from a wandering troupe of actors that she and Lao Er had met when they went west, and Lao Er had bought it for her so that she might hide her youth and beauty with it. Now she put it on and smeared her face with dye, and lifted up her lip with putty and dyed that, and blacked her teeth and put a false hump on her back, and old shoes to hide her young feet. She slipped out of the little back door while Ling Sao slept and went to a secret field behind the bamboos where Ling Tan raised some winter cabbage out of the eye of the enemy, and there she plucked a basket full. He was

259

working on the front land and did not see her. Then winding her way among the grave lands, she went toward the city.

She knew where Wu Lien was and to that gate she went, but she could not have had a better key, though she did not know it, than a basket of fresh cabbages. For the markets had no green things in them and the very soldier at the gate let his mouth water at her cabbages, and she did not need to use even the name of Wu Lien.

"Go to the kitchen, old woman," he said, in broken words, "the cook will pay you."

"Where is the kitchen?" she lisped as though her teeth were bad and she made her voice cracked. For it was one of Jade's ways that she could make herself seem anyone she chose. When she was dressed like an old woman, she took on, scarcely knowing that she did, all an old woman's ways. She could have deceived Lao Er himself had he not seen her in this guise and in many another, too, so that he used to be amazed at all her different ways.

"Come with me," the soldier said. He led her through many courts, she limping behind him and snuffling through her nose, and seeing nothing except the two feet on the ground before her, and so they came to the kitchen.

There the soldier shouted to the cook, "Here is an old woman with a basket full of something better than gold, and all I ask is a taste of the dish when it is done!"

He laughed and went away, and there Jade was at the kitchen door. A cross fat cook came out, and it was not an enemy but a man from some kitchen of an inn or eating place now ruined. He lifted the towel from her cabbages and cursed beneath his breath, but she could not hear what he said.

"Two pieces of silver," he said aloud.

She shook her head. "You know what cabbages cost now," she told him.

"Three, then," he said carelessly. "It is not my cursed money that buys them and I have no time to argue. There is to be a great feast here. A feast again, they tell me—they are always feasting, and where can I get food to make a feast? Have you any meat, woman? Can you get any pork? Fish I have—fish—fish—but what is a feast without pork, or even a duck?"

She stared at him steadfastly. Was this man a traitor?

"If I bring you two ducks, will you pay me ten silver pieces for them?" she asked.

"Bring them and see," he said.

He took the silver out of his belt to give her for the cabbages, and she asked him, "What day is this feast?"

"Two days from now," he said, and then the bitterness leaked out of him. "A year ago two days they had their first great victory over us. So they tell me to make a mighty feast, and all the heads will gather together to eat it."

She leaned toward him. "You are one of us," she whispered.

That fat cook looked quickly round the court. Behind him the kitchen was empty, but still he did not answer her.

"What a place of power is yours," she whispered. "By accident you can put anything you like into their food! How many cooks are there?"

"Three," he said.

"Three!" she said after him. "Are three enough for a great feast? Ought you not to ask for help at such a time? There should be ten cooks. Are you to do all, or does a restaurant come in?"

"They trust no one from outside," he said. "They guard themselves."

"Ah," she said.

He lifted the cabbages out. "Will you bring the ducks tomor row?" he asked.

"I will," she said, "at this same hour."

"The money will be ready when you come," he said.

He showed her a back gate, and she went through it and so into the empty streets again.

Now Jade had put the thought of poison into the cook's mind as she might have cast a seed into the ground, though beyond it she herself had no clear thought. But as she went through these ruined streets, she stopped here and there as though to rest and she talked in small quiet places with men and women who whispered to her the fearful evil in which they now lived. In one such place where she stopped, a peddler of old clothes had newly opened his shop again, and she went in to pretend that she looked for a coat, and she asked him how his business did, and the tears came to his eyes and he said, "Can anything be well with me again? I have lost my only son and my three daughters are worse than lost."

"How did you lose your son?" she asked.

"Will you believe me if I tell you?" he said. "Yet this is the truth. He was only fourteen years old, because he was the youngest of our children. The gods gave us nothing but daughters until the last, and he was the best. When the enemy passed this door one day he liked the bright show of so many guns and uniforms and he gave them a salute—a child's trick it was, to show himself clever. But the moment he did it, one of the enemy stepped out of their ranks and shot him here at my door and I stood beside him and caught him as he fell dead."

"Can this be?" Jade asked sadly.

"It can be, for it was," the man sighed.

Jade went on, and she stopped next at a half-burned house. There were many such in the city where the people lived as best they could in what was left of their homes. She sat down on the doorstep to rest, and the aged woman in that house came out to ask if she would have a drink of well water, for they had no tea, and Jade said she would only rest. But the old woman saw her looking at the ruins, and she made her voice low and said:

"Do not seem to notice too much, for who knows who watches

us? We are more lucky than the many who had all burned to ashes around them, or those who died in the ashes of their houses."

"But how did it come about with you?" Jade asked. "Were there bombs that fell on you?"

To this the old woman shook her head.

"No, we passed through that safely," she said. "But afterwards the enemy sent their soldiers to live in our houses, and they did not care how they let fire start in our houses, and when a house caught fire they moved on to another, and my house was one of those. A soldier went to sleep smoking in that inner room, and when the bed caught fire he got up and walked out and let it burn and went elsewhere and said nothing, and we who were crowded to the other side of the house away from the enemy as far as we could go, we did not know until it was too late. So were many houses burned." The old woman paused and shivered. "Oh, how they laugh when our houses burn!" she said.

Jade could not speak nor answer lest she say too much and one hear her. She sat a few minutes more, her head hanging down, and then she rose and went away.

Yet her rage was not full until she lifted her eyes and saw pasted upon the walls of a main street she chanced to enter a great sheet of paper, and on it were false pictures of the enemy smiling and holding out in their hands cakes and fruits to a group of kneeling vanquished, old men and young, and women and little children, who looked up at them thankfully. On this sheet were written in large letters these words: "The People Welcome Their Good Neighbor, Who Gives Them Food, Peace, Safety."

When she had read these words Jade's anger brimmed over and she went back to a certain shop she had passed, and there she asked for an ancient and well-known drug. The man behind the counter himself was as old and dried as a root. He smiled a melancholy smile as he measured out the white powder.

"There are many who buy this medicine these days," he said, "and they are nearly all women."

"Do they buy it for themselves, too?" Jade asked to deceive him.

"The women buy it for themselves, be sure," the man said quietly, and though he looked at her very closely he asked her nothing. He measured out the stuff and he sold it cheap, and Jade put it in her bosom and went homeward.

Only that night did she tell those in her husband's house what she planned, and tell she must, for she needed two ducks, and in spite of all Ling Tan had some ducks that he kept secretly for breeding. Without a word he rose and he went to where those ducks roosted and pulled down two and killed them, and Ling Sao and Jade cleaned them and plucked them and rubbed the poison into their flesh and inwards and then hung them for the night. The great power of that poison was that it was as tasteless as flour, or nearly so.

The next morning Jade took those ducks into the city and gave them to the fat cook. She said nothing until she was paid, and then she said in a low voice, "Make your sauce rich for the ducks and put in extra oils and wine. Our ducks feed on wild food these days, and sometimes the flesh is tainted."

He made his little eyes wide at this and stared at her. She stared back at him full and strong and suddenly he saw she was no old woman, and he opened his mouth, but he shut it again and nodded. Then he locked the little back gate behind her and she went home by the shortest way.

Whether or not what she did bore its fruit, how could Jade know? The news of that which happened in the city did not easily come into a little village. She waited, and she thought, "If I succeed in this, I will do it again and again. It will be my way of making war on the devils." At last news did leak back after a long time, and it came through the third cousin's wife. She said one day innocently that her man had seen Wu Lien on the street and he was as thin as an old goat because he had nearly died and some of the enemy had died after a feast they had eaten.

Hardly could Ling Sao keep her eyes straight when she heard this, and she was glad that none other was there to hear it that day. For Jade had taken the child down into the secret room when the woman came as she did very often. But Ling Sao must know more and she pretended surprise, and asked:

"How many died and who were they?"

The cousin, wanting to make herself as knowing as she could, said solemnly, "They were all very big heads, and five of them died and all were sick. Wu Lien told my man that more than twenty were sick. Of them all he was the farthest from death, for he had eaten little of the meat." She pursed her lips and wagged her head and went on in a whisper. "They blamed the cooks, but how could they tell which it was? Besides their usual cooks, they had in several from outside to help, and when they went to look for the ones who came in from outside, they had all fled."

"Was there no meat left for the cooks to eat, and did they not fall ill?" Ling Sao asked.

"Those enemy heads were so eager for meat that they chewed up the very bones," the cousin replied.

"Ah," Ling Sao said. "Who does not know how the enemy loves meat!"

And indeed that enemy did love meat, for next to women and then wine what they always asked for was meat. Ling Tan had heard from his sons in the hills that there they had seen the enemy fall upon a rare fat buffalo as it grazed, and they cut the flesh from it living and ate it raw. Never had any seen or heard of this before, and whenever it was told those who heard it cried out, "Can these be men?" So it was easily to be believed that of ducks even the bones were eaten.

That night when Ling Sao told them all that Wu Lien had

eaten the poison too, they listened in silence and her second son said, "I wish he had eaten more and ended himself."

This Ling Sao knew was wrong for him to say, and though she was proud enough that she and Jade had used poison against the enemy, which is woman's weapon, she said, "Still, he is your sister's husband."

Since she was his mother he turned his back on her, but Jade said for him in her quiet voice, "In these days, mother, there is a stronger duty than the duty to sister or brother. You must not speak against him."

To this neither Ling Tan nor Ling Sao answered. Many things were said in their house now which they did not answer, for they knew these times were not their times, and the future belonged not to them but to those who carried the struggle after them.

But in the night in her bed Ling Sao wept a little, and she said to Ling Tan, "I doubt that anything can ever be the same again, even though peace comes."

And Ling Tan said steadily, "Nothing can be the same and we old ones must know it. And the sign of the great change is this, that the young have cut themselves off from the old. They must cut themselves off even from us so that they may be free for their duty which is to drive out the enemy. Do not many in these days swear against their parents?"

"Yes, and it is an evil thing," Ling Sao said passionately. "For where is the earth under our feet if the very children we bring to life deny what they owe us?"

"We cannot say it is an evil thing," Ling Tan told her. "We old ones, we must see that they do this to declare their freedom for the new that lies ahead."

But Ling Sao could not see this. All that she could see was that nothing was left to anyone if the old could no longer look to the young for obedience. Where was the order in life if this were to be?

But Ling Tan could see further than she. Though what he saw was as dim as a mist because he was not a man of learning, he understood now that when his sons no longer obeyed him, it was not because they hated him. It was because they must be free of all that was past, that they might be ready for what was now and to come. His sons had gone beyond him.

... "Do you hate me?" Jade whispered to her husband. Now that she had succeeded in what she had planned, she was afraid.

"How can I hate you?" Lao Er replied.

She looked down at herself, and twisted her mouth into the least of a smile. She was naked, for she had just bathed herself.

"I see no beauty in me," she said, and crossed her arms upon her bosom. "I am so thin, my flesh is so hard. Today when I was washing clothes I looked in the water and my face was dark and not like a woman's face."

She snatched up her garment as she spoke and wrapped it around herself.

Lao Er sat at the table in their room, drinking a little tea before he slept.

"You do not look as you did when I married you, it is true," he said.

She threw him a look over her shoulder and drew on her cotton trousers. "Would you have married me then if I looked as I do now?"

"Doubtless I would not," he said, beginning to smile. "But I myself was not then the same man that I am now, and what pleased me then would not please me now."

She saw his smile and her heart lightened and she made her face mischievous at him, "Now that I look at you," she said, "I see that you too are not so handsome as you were. How black the sun has burned you!"

"I am very black," he agreed.

"And your hair is the color of rusty iron," she said.

"It is," he agreed again.

267

She seized a small mirror that stood on the table. "Still, what does it matter how a man looks?" she asked him.

"If it does not matter to you, it does not matter," he said, laughing.

She stared at herself in the mirror and made her mouth pretty. "Shall I ever wear paint and powder again and put earrings in my ears?" she asked.

"Who knows?" he said.

"You never did give me those earrings," she said.

"You chose the book," he said.

But she still looked at herself. "Perhaps I was wrong," she said.

"Then some day I will buy you the earrings," he said, and now he was laughing heartily. Between them was rising that sweet warmth that nothing could chill. So close they were, these two, that in weariness and danger and in all the evil of the present world still they could give themselves up to the love there was between them, and return to it, and it was there always.

And yet this night a little later he thought Jade hung back from him somewhat.

"Now what?" he asked her, and stayed himself to find out what was in her mind to hold her body back.

Then she hid her head under his arm in the old way she always did when she grew shy before him, and he had to pull her out and then she faltered, looking every way except into his face, "Are you sure that you do not think me less a woman—because of what I did?"

"Of which thing you did?" he asked. "You are always doing something!"

"The poison," she whispered. "Sometimes when I wake up and think I did that—I hate myself."

"But they were the devils," he said.

"I know," she said. "But I mean—will there come a day when you will look at me—perhaps long after peace comes—and you will say to your heart, 'She could put poison into food,' and then think me less a woman than you like?"

At this moment it seemed to Lao Er that at last he had the true knowledge of Jade. She could be so full of courage, so seemingly strong, and yet now he knew hers was a shrinking tender heart, and he loved her more for this than for all her bravery. But he knew what would please her best and so he said it.

"What you did was brave. I wonder that a woman can be so brave as you."

Then he took his place of command over her. "Now you have proved yourself," he said, "and it is enough. There are many who can kill the devils and you have a greater duty."

What could he say to make her know he loved her and would love her while he lived? What could he say to make her know that what he loved in her was not a woman, any woman, not woman even, but the creature that only she was?

He cast about and all the time his love grew and rose and was too big for words again. He held her hard, his hands upon her arms, and searched out every little line of face and hair and eyes and mouth and her two nostrils. If her face had a fault it was that those nostrils were the shadow of a shade too wide, and yet for him they were not, for they matched the fullness of her mouth and the liquid length of her eyes set shallow on her face like two dark leaves.

"It is time we had another child," he said. "I want children out of you, and many children and if you would please me, make them all yourself—over and over again you and only you!"

XIII

WU LIEN was writing while the enemy told him what to write. He held his camel's hair brush erect between his thumb and two fingers, and his third and fourth fingers were poised like the legs of a cricket. When he had finished writing the enemy would take the copy and print it out many times in large letters and paste the papers on the walls of houses and temples.

The room where he now sat with one of the enemy was full of fine foreign furniture which had been robbed from the houses of many people, and especially from white people in the city. There were three pianos, among other things, and on the floor carpets of blue and gold. These were waiting to be put into boxes and sent away to enemy houses across the ocean. But now in the midst of such luxury Wu Lien sat in perfect silence while the enemy read to him carefully and slowly what he should write. At every letter or two the enemy asked, "Have you written as I told you?"

"I have written," Wu Lien always said mildly.

"Write on, then," the enemy said.

So Wu Lien wrote on. At the top of his page in bold black letters were these words. "Star of Salvation! The New Order in East Asia!" Beneath were these words he had written in smaller letters. "Fellow Citizens! We have suffered the oppression and enchainment of the white peoples for more than a hundred years.

Within this period of more than a century, although we have resisted earnestly, and have sought opportunities to cast off this yoke and to escape from bondage to the white race, yet there has been no result!"

Here the enemy paused. "Is this not true, you Chinaman?" he cried. He was a small angry-faced man, and because he was more than usually short he kept himself fierce. When he was alone he brushed up his eyebrows with a small toothbrush he hid in his pocket, and he was never seen without his uniform which was that of a captain in the enemy army, though his sole task was the composing of public papers to be pasted on walls. These papers he signed with three words, Great People's Association. They were supposed to come not from the enemy but from the government they had made for the conquered people.

Wu Lien looked up as though surprised, and held his brush, "Is not what true, sir?" he inquired in his soft placating voice.

"What you have written, fool!" the little enemy shouted.

Wu Lien excused himself. "I have not heeded it," he said, "and you must forgive me, for my head is still giddy from the poisoning and I cannot think."

It was true he was still very pale. Nevertheless, he did not wish that he had not been poisoned, for because of it he had proved his seeming faithfulness to his masters. Had he alone come from the feast sound when all others were ill, how could he have escaped their suspicions? Never had he seen men so suspicious as these enemies. They knew that everywhere about them were those who wished them dead, and Wu Lien walked on a rope above a pit.

The little man glared at him. Then he said in a loud voice, "Write on!"

So Wu Lien wrote on. "Why has this been so? It is because the country has been too weak, deficient in power, lacking in strength."

The little enemy rolled these words out of his mouth like

thunder, but Wu Lien's mild pallid face did not change. He wrote, murmuring the words to guide his brush as he used to murmur the names of the goods he sold in his shop.

"But now," the little enemy roared, "to our great fortune, we have the opportunity afforded by the present turn of events to use the strength of a friendly nation, and thus to attain our long cherished desire and gain revenge upon the white race! After this we can be a completely free people! But our friend Nippon, although she has put forth this great effort on our behalf and has made this great sacrifice, nevertheless asks nothing in return, only that we establish the New Order in East Asia!"

The little enemy puffed up his breast and twisted his short and scanty mustache and coughed. Wu Lien looked at him and waited. In his mind he was thinking, "How is it that these little wild men can grow such scanty hair? I always thought savages were hairy."

"Write on!" the little enemy said.

"I write," Wu Lien replied gently.

"This New Order," the enemy shouted, and now he rose to his feet because he was so pleased with what he had composed. "This New Order, whose objective is not only our temporary salvation but also in truth our eternal redemption! So from this time forth we shall certainly attain our lasting freedom! Fellow citizens, the New Order in East Asia is truly the Star of Salvation for our four hundred million people!"

At this point the enemy was overcome with himself, "Banzai! Banzai!" he bellowed.

Wu Lien looked up again. "Do I put that down, too?"

But the enemy was not pleased at his coolness.

"Say Banzai to these noble words!" he shouted.

"Banzai," Wu Lien said in his soft voice and wrote it down. "And is that the end?"

The enemy stared at him furiously. Something was wrong with this man but he did not know what. "You are not to write

Banzai," he shouted. "Have you no wits? This is a people's document!"

Wu Lien crossed out "Banzai." "With what name shall I sign it, sir?" he asked. And he held the paper up and blew on it as he spoke.

"The Great People's Association," the enemy replied.

Wu Lien wrote down the letters of this association which did not exist.

"This is to be put in the usual places?" he inquired, rising to his feet with the paper in his hand.

"It is to be put everywhere!" the enemy shouted.

Wu Lien bowed and went out, his cloth shoes noiseless on the carpeted floors. Once outside he gave his orders with correctness and dignity to those beneath him, and then feeling faint he went toward his own rooms. There his wife waited for him. Ever since the poisoning she had been alarmed, though like Wu Lien she was glad that he had been poisoned a little, lest he might have suffered more had he not been. Now she had some chicken broth ready for him, with a sort of moss brewed in it which was known for its healing power in the intestines. When she saw him come she poured a bowl and gave it to him with both hands, and being a good wife she did not speak until he had drunk it down. Then she said, "Do we do well to continue in a place where your life is in such danger?"

"Is there any place where my life is not in danger?" he answered her. "In these times one chooses to live in the den of the tiger or the lion. There is no other place."

He closed his eyes as he spoke and lay back in his chair and she left him.

. . . Outside this compound in a few hours there were men busy with long brushes full of flour paste. They were putting on walls large sheets of paper bearing the words which Wu Lien had written. Everywhere they went a small crowd went with them, seeming to read the words. But few truly read. Most of them were hungry people who hoped for a chance to dip a bowl into the mixture of flour and water and then hide behind a wall and drink it down. Flour these days was scarce and dear and after the enemy had taken what they wanted there was little left for the people. As for those men who pasted the sheets, they seemed not to see how quickly their paste was gone, and when they went back for more there was always the excuse that they had pasted in many places. If there were too many sheets left to make this true, then they gave the sheets away, and people burned them for fuel. But still there must be enough put up to deceive the enemy.

Now in one place that day it chanced that Ling Tan's third cousin was one who saw that something was being put on a wall. When he saw the letters he must go to see what they were, partly because he was made so, and partly because he liked the little show he made when in the midst of an ignorant crowd who did not know one letter from another, he could read aloud what the letters said. So today he moved to the front of the crowd and he put on his brass-rimmed spectacles and began to read aloud in his largest voice and very slowly those words which Wu Lien had written down. At the sight of such learning all the crowd fell into silence from curiosity and respect and they listened until he came to the end. Then he took off his spectacles.

All that crowd was still more silent when they knew what the words said, and so was the cousin silent. None could say what was in his heart, nor did any dare to laugh. These people who had once been free, who on these very streets, when they were their own, had laughed and cursed and spoken out their angers and their hatreds as easily as their praises of all, gods and men, now had learned to keep silence and to drift in bitter silence from one place to another. So they did now and this third cousin went away too, and he wished he had not read the words because they made more cause for vengeance, and he wanted only to forget all.

274

This man, Ling Tan's third cousin, had in recent days found his comfort, for now daily he turned to opium. He went at this moment to the poor small place where what he bought was cheap. It was on another street toward the south, and he crossed three streets and entered a low mean door that stood open night and day. A thin yellow girl with crossed eyes came toward him and motioned him to an empty bed of boards spread with straw. He went and lay down, and he put his head upon the wooden pillow and waited while she mixed the dregs of opium and put it into the bowl of the pipe and lit it, and thrust the stem of the pipe between his lips and he breathed the sweet smoke deeply in and he closed his eyes. Oh, the calm of this, he thought, the lonely calm! It did not matter who ruled outside, for none ruled him here. His body lay like dead and his soul could wander far from it and all its ills. He was free.

How had it come about? This man caught between the grindstones of his life was nevertheless a little better than he need be, and therefore he was miserable. Afraid of his wife, he had gone back and forth with her messages to Wu Lien. They were small messages, often useless, such as that she had that day seen some men whom she was sure were hillmen and they had gone toward the west. But sometimes she sent word that Ling Tan's sons had come and were in hiding in their father's house. Small or large, her husband had to carry her messages because of the money Wu Lien gave for them, and often the man meditated whether or not he could twist these messages and put north for south or forget to mention Ling Tan's sons, but his courage was at first too weak. He did not know in what large affairs these messages were links and he feared being caught and tortured as the enemy now tortured, gouging men's eyes and pulling out the ends of their entrails, and cutting off their ears and noses or right hands and all those cruelties which now the people took as things that might happen to anyone any day.

"The New Order!" he now murmured as he began to sink to sleep.

The thin girl bent over him. "What do you say?" she asked him.

But he was already gone and he could not answer. In three hours she would wake him as she always did and he would pay her a small coin and go away. Still drowsy, he would go to Wu Lien and tell him whatever he remembered and Wu Lien would give him two coins, and one he would take and one he would keep hidden for another day here. At first he had been frightened lest surely some day he would be found out. But he had now passed fear of any kind and all he wanted was enough money to come back, and his greatest hope was a little more money so that he might go to a place where he could buy real opium, and not the scrapings and the ashes of pipes from houses better than this one. Nor was he alone here or anywhere. The people crowded into these opium houses, because they saw no hope of freedom to come in their lifetime. They longed for the old years back, and of that there was no hope.

In the village none noticed what had befallen the third cousin, for none heeded one whom they thought only a silly old man. Ling Tan saw him grow more dry and yellow, but so did they all, since food was now dear and scarce, and great floods this year had spoiled the crops. And yet Ling Tan could not curse Heaven for flood as he always did in other years. Hungry though he often was, and though he knew he risked his life by hiding food for his house, yet he was glad when the rains fell, because this year the enemy would pay the loss.

"Heaven helps earth, after all," he said.

All that happened in Ling Tan's house the third cousin's wife knew, or guessed, and she sent word on it to Wu Lien, but of what he learned Wu Lien still told nothing. He sat in his place in that enemy palace and did his work and his words were few. To the enemy he seemed a mild man who would do anything he was told, and they paid him well. This money Wu Lien saved as he did his knowledge, and without knowing what he would do with it. He did not give it to anyone nor did he do good with it, nor did he spend it for himself or for his family more than was needful. His children grew within these walls and they played with enemy children and learned their language, and he let this be also, and he did not send them out to school. His wife he loved moderately and in his own way, and he comforted her when she mourned that she never saw her parents, and he told her that when times were better they would all understand each other again.

But within himself Wu Lien kept all that he knew, and he was careful never to let anything in his manner or his voice or his look betray that he had any special knowledge. Yet he did have, for to him came ten or twelve men and women who told him news of every kind and were his ears and eyes everywhere. Thus he learned fully how evil the enemy was and how they continued to burn villages and to pillage the land as they had the city, and he learned what the hillmen did, and before Ling Tan knew it he knew what Ling Tan's sons did. He was stuffed with knowledge he seemed never to use.

This Wu Lien was a man of his own loyalties. If ever this city was taken from the conquerors, he would turn again to his own. But while the conquerors were here, in his way he worked hard for what he thought was right for his own people, and he comforted himself always by thinking that at some time he would be able to do one great thing to show how right he was. Meanwhile he did small things that were right. Since that money he paid his ears and eyes was enemy money and he must show some return for it, he did write down long reports of small things and gave them to the enemy. But of Ling Tan's village he wrote nothing, not so much as its name, nor did he tell what the hillmen did except in some far distant place where he knew Ling Tan's sons were not, and in all ways he spared his wife's blood, not only for her sake, but because Ling Tan had buried his old mother, and had given her shelter in the earth in a day when many had no such shelter.

All this time the city had been like an island in the middle of the sea. There were no messages from the outer world. None here knew what the people in the free lands were doing, and people often asked each other, "Is there any hope that our own armies will come back?" For of all those who had complained of their own soldiers there was now not one who did not think of them with longing and as good men, so evil was this enemy and so cruel these East-Ocean soldiers who took what they wanted from miserable shops and gave worthless money long since not honored. Sometimes they gave foreign money and more often they gave nothing, and they took the women they wanted, even though the city was full of courtesans who had gathered here from everywhere around, because here were the great men among the enemy and their many soldiers.

But even among the enemy Wu Lien had a friend, a good man. He was no warrior but a man who made pictures and sent them away, and this man went out every day to see what he could see for his pictures, and he sought for good and he found much evil. With his own eyes he saw his fellows seize young women and foul even old ones, and he saw the wine-filled soldiers of his own people do their filthy deeds in daylight before the eyes of decent people who would have been killed had they lifted a voice to cry out, and indeed he saw them die. He grew so weary with such wickedness that one day he spoke to Wu Lien when they were alone and he said:

"I have no chance to talk elsewhere, but to you at least I can say that I hate what we have done to your people, and I am ashamed, and I wish our Emperor could know, but he cannot, for none would dare to tell him. Yet why do I say the Emperor? Even our people at home would never believe if they were told the cruel things their sons and husbands and fathers and brothers do here."

Wu Lien listened and answered well, and after that a sort of friendship grew up, Wu Lien saying little and the man saying much, and from this one Wu Lien first heard that not only in this nation of his was there war but in other nations, too, and perhaps in the whole world.

"How can you find out so much?" Wu Lien asked. And then the man took him to his own room and showed him a small black box, a thing of which Wu Lien had heard but had never seen. The man turned a peg and then another and out of the box came a voice, very low.

"Listen!" the man said.

So Wu Lien listened and out of that box the voice told of vast happenings and for the first time Wu Lien heard for himself that nation had declared war on nation, and in the great western cities the bombs were falling even as they had fallen on this city. What were the small things Wu Lien knew from his little spies when such things were happening as this?

"Where can I buy one of these boxes?" he asked the man.

"I will get you one," the man said.

And then they talked and Wu Lien heard for the first time how great was this war. The man told him that here they were a part of a whole, and that some day there would not be a single country outside the war, and he sighed as he said it.

"My fellows rejoice at this," he told Wu Lien. "They see a chance to grow powerful and rich, each man for himself. But I have no wish for such things. I should like to go home to my town which is a quiet place by the sea and there live with my wife and children and old parents. I ask no more."

"It is enough," Wu Lien agreed.

"And too much, it seems, to get now-a-days," the man said sadly.

This was how Wu Lien himself came to have such a box for

279

his own, for not long after his enemy friend gave it to him. Wu Lien kept it in his room and thereafter in his every empty moment, far into the night, he kept the voice alive and he listened. Most of the time there was nothing, nonsense or strange music or idle words, but now and again truth came out of the box. Then he took it in greedily, and he heard how the peoples abroad suffered and how what befell them was the same as had come here, and he heard the anger of nations and the fury of rulers. When it was over, he went to bed dazed with what he heard and trembling with the size of the times.

"Evil—evil," he muttered, "it is all evil."

"What is wrong with you now?" his wife asked him one night. "It is that soup you drank. I thought it had a smell."

He only groaned, for how could he tell a woman that the world was being destroyed? He grew closer than ever in his being, for now he knew that peace was so far off that by the time it came men might have forgotten it as they forget a dream long past and the young could not even dream of peace because they had not seen it since they were born.

It happened one day that as he was listening to his box, and it grew to be a thing he did more and more often, Ling Tan's old third cousin came in to give his news and he saw Wu Lien listening, and he asked what it was. Wu Lien told him, and then full of what he had just heard he could not forbear saying to the cousin that the whole world was at war. When the cousin asked him how he knew, he showed him how this box did its work, and what peg to turn, and which to subdue, so that the voice would come out. At this moment nothing came out except music, but there it was, a pleasant noise, and from it an evil thought came into the cousin's mind.

This cousin was not altogether the fool he looked, but he had been in his life so badgered and oppressed first by his mother and then by his wife, and his love of learning among men who had no learning had so set him apart that he had never had his own will and his wits out and at work. But now opium had done for him what he had not been able to do for himself. Since he had begun to smoke opium and to hide it, he felt himself desperate and in such danger anyway that more danger or less was nothing, so long only as he could get his opium every day. This man who had never been able to put his head out of his quilt at night to see what a rat did in his room, now without changing his meek outer looks grew daily more brazen within. He stole what he could from counters in shops and sold it, and he took his wife's good clothes and pawned them, and when she cried out that she had been robbed he kept his face as it ever was, and no one could have pretended better surprise. Every thing he had went for opium. Many a day he lied to his wife and said that Wu Lien had given him nothing because he had spent all that Wu Lien had given him. And he took to smoking before he went to Wu Lien to give him courage to make up lies for news, and after he left he smoked again because he had two coins in his pocket, and his daring grew with his hunger.

Today, as he listened to the box, it came to him that what a thing it would be if he had such a box and he could set it up in a secret room and listen to it, and there in a tea shop take people's money to hear what he knew and from that money he could do as he liked. This notion which would never have entered into his skull had his brain been his own, so full of danger to his life it was, now seemed to him a thing possible and easy to do because of his false courage. He sat on and on that day, pretending to listen to the box and he learned every-thing about it with twice his usual quickness to learn anything, and still he sat on. At last Wu Lien was called away.

"I do not like to leave you here," Wu Lien said to him as he went. "It is against the enemy law for any of our people to listen to this box, and I am safe only because I live within these walls. But if any know that you listen here alone, there may be trouble for both of us."

"Only let me finish this that I hear now and I will go," the cousin begged him.

Wu Lien was willing for this and he went away. As soon as he had gone that cousin took the box and unwound its wires from a metal pole that ran through the room for support to the roof, and he put the box under his wide scholar's robe and tied the wires to his belly band and he walked out of the room as coolly as he had come in. By that time everyone knew him and let him come and go as he liked. Well he knew he would never dare to come back and face Wu Lien again, but he did not care. He had the way to make money enough for what he wanted.

And yet now the thing was done he must have an accomplice here in the city, and who could it be? He could not take the box home for he must still deceive his wife and let her think he came and went to the city to Wu Lien and she must not know how much money he had. He knew no one, and so what could he do? Yet his unnatural brain could think of this too, and he thought of the thin yellow girl who stirred his opium. She always wanted money, and he would give her some of what he earned. He would not teach her how to turn the pegs but he would only give her something to keep the box safe for him.

To that usual place he went then, and when she bent over his pipe to light it he said to her in a low voice.

"Would you like to make more money than you do now?"

"How can I?" she asked cautiously. "Do you want to keep me?"

"No—no, I have one woman too many already," he said quickly.

"What then?" she asked.

"Let me smoke only a little," he begged her, "only enough to stop my hunger but not enough to make me sleep, and then lead me where none can hear us and I will tell you."

So she did, and when he woke fully to himself he was in a room he had never seen before, a poor room, with only a board bed and a broken table and two benches in it. But it was clean and there was a bamboo bird cage in the small window, and in the cage a plump small yellow bird. The singing of this bird was the first thing he heard when he came to himself. For a moment he thought it was his box, but he put his hand to his belly and felt it hard and square under his robes and the corners bit into his belly.

Then he came to himself wholly and there was the thin girl and she was shaking him.

"Wake—wake," she called in his ear. "It is long past midnight."

He woke then, and asked where he was, and she said this was her own room and it was in the court behind the opium den where she worked. He brought out the box from his belly when he had all this clearly in his mind, and he told her his plan. She listened, her face as narrow as the palm of a hand. It grew more narrow as she understood and saw what the thing might mean.

"You have had a thought for once, you old book-fool," she said, "and luck has brought you to me. You may keep the box here in my room, and it is safe. No one comes here whom I do not bring."

By now the man was clear in his head and with far more than his usual clearness. He set the box under the bed where it was hidden and he put the wire into the wall where the light was and then he looked for a metal pole, but there was none. For a while he was distraught and then they found a hole in the plaster, for this was not an old house but one built quick and new and inside the wall were rods of steel, and to one of these he wrapped the wire. Then carefully turning the pegs he waited and power filled the box and the voice came out.

"The news today from the free land," that voice said, and then it went on and told of enemy bombings and how the people hid themselves in the caves of the hills, and then the voice said, "but we are not alone. Today in the western countries, too, the people hide themselves in the pits of the earth, and the same enemy oppresses all. We do not yield—"

The cousin heard a strange noise. He looked up and there was that thin girl with her hands at her throat as though she would choke herself.

The cousin turned off the box and cried out. "What is the matter with you?"

"Do they still resist?" she whispered. "I thought no one resisted any more, anywhere!"

"Everything this box says is true," the cousin said proudly.

"Then fortune is in our hands," the girl said, "for what this voice says is what men long to hear."

For a few days the cousin told a hundred lies to his wife. He told her that Wu Lien said he was to come at night and no more by day, and since he brought back double the money he had before and said Wu Lien gave it to him because he came by night, she believed him for awhile. But the cousin was lost from that day when his hand was first full of money. He smoked no longer the dregs and ashes but he went to a fine place where the pure black sticky stuff was put into his bowl and now he fell into such dreams as he had never had before. The day came soon when he did not go home and then another day passed and another and then being afraid the thought came to him, "Why should I ever go home any more? Why should I be scolded and be set upon by a woman when I can be free?"

And he wondered that he had not thought of this earlier, and from that day on he stayed in the city, sleeping all day and rising by night to tell the news he heard out of the box, and no one knew who he was, not even the thin girl, for he told his name to none, and to her he was only the old opium-smoker who owned the box. As for the cousin, he did not see from day's end to day's end a face he knew, and at last he was truly free.

Thus Heaven used this man, too, worthless as he was. In

that whole city there were few voices that came from outside to tell these people, beleaguered by the enemy, what went on in a world still free, and the news of the box leaked secretly from mouth to ear, and all knew that in the free land their people still fought the enemy and held them back. There came to be a password among the people of that city and it was the word "Resist." "Do we resist?" one man asked another secretly. "We resist!" was the secret answer. And now courage began to live again where it had died.

. . . Since nothing was clearly known in city and countryside, since all knowledge was forbidden the people and they were told nothing from above, everything came to be whispered and everything guessed and hoped. When man met man the first question asked secretly was what he had heard. "Is our army holding the free land?" each asked each, and they asked, "is there reason for more hope?"

It could not be long therefore before mouth to ear everyone knew there was news to be heard in the city, though none knew it was from the old man who was Ling Tan's cousin.

In the village Ling Tan's second son heard first, because he made it his business to be the one who came and went between the hillmen and those who resisted the enemy in the city and nearby. First he heard in the silent way men now had learned to talk, their eyes wandering, their lips scarcely moving, that half the world was at war now and that what they suffered here was only part of it.

Why was this news so comforting to them? Yet it did comfort everyone who heard it to know that they were a part of a whole, that their trouble was part of a greater trouble and they did not suffer alone and neglected. Eagerly men named the countries that were with them and against the enemy and they cursed the countries that were for the enemy and counted these as against themselves. Men who had never heard the names of Germans and Italians and Frenchmen, who scarcely knew there was Canada or Brazil, who had never seen an American or an Englishman, now divided these all into friends and enemies, measuring them by whether they were for or against their own enemy. It was somehow easier to eat their own miserable food when they knew there were others in the world who had no better.

Such news Lao Er carried to his father on the very day he heard it. He had gone into the city in disguise that day to sell some vegetables and to hear what there was to hear. He had soon sold all he had, for food was snatched at these days and a farmer's baskets emptied as soon as he had passed the enemy guard at the city gate, who searched all who came and went. Then Lao Er had turned aside into a tea shop to hear what was said. He sat at a small table in a dark corner to hide his disguise. He was not so clever as Jade and it was easier for him to forget and to show his stout young legs or throw back the sleeves from his young arms and thus deny the gray beard he wore fastened into his nose with wires, and yet he dared not go without disguise lest the enemy seize him for hard labor. For the enemy everywhere pressed all young men into labor and even the old, sometimes. Not many days since he had heard of an old farmer he knew, who had come to the city to sell his radishes and who, going homeward, had been caught by enemy soldiers moving a great foreign gun along the streets. They had forced him to pull the heaviest part of that gun, and when he was slow with age and terror, they broke his right arm so that the bone stuck from the flesh, and then with laughter they had forced him on.

Remembering this, Lao Er took the more care today, and so he chose his seat far back and listening with his sharp ears that by now had learned to pick out the words he wanted, he heard two old men talking of news. After a while he took up his courage and went to those two men and said:

"Sirs, I am only a farmer, but the times are evil and if you have any good news, let me hear it and take it to my village so that we can bear a little longer what we have to bear."

Those men were unwilling to say much but at last they did say that it might be one day that others would fight with them and against a greater enemy, and that in the common peace they too would share, and so throw off their present yoke. To this Lao Er listened and this is what he carried home.

When they gathered to eat their evening meal he said, "In the city mouth to ear it is whispered that this war spreads over half the world, and there are others like us who are oppressed, and though some weak have yielded, strong ones still resist as we do."

Ling Tan held his chopsticks half way to his mouth, and the two women looked up from the child. "Are they the same devils we have here?" Ling Tan asked.

"Not the East-Ocean devils, but the same in heart," Lao Er said.

"And there, too, the people resist!" his father cried.

"So I heard," Lao Er replied, "but I heard no more."

"It is enough," Ling Tan said.

Now Ling Tan took such heart as he was still pondering what his son had heard, that it seemed to him that he could go on forever against anything. He went out into the autumn night and looked at the sky and he felt the earth under his feet and for the first time in his life he thought, "This valley is not the world but only a part of the world, and there are others like me whose faces I have never seen."

It was deepest comfort to him. He was no longer alone. Elsewhere there were men such as he who loved peace and longed for good.

"If I could know them," he thought. "If I could see them!"

Then it came to him that their tongue would not be his, and how could they speak together?

"But we would not need speech," he thought, "if what we wish is the same, there would be understanding between us."

And then he fell to thinking of those who lived on the under side of his land, and he thought, "They, too—perhaps a man and his house not like me and mine, and yet like us if what they suffer is what I suffer." And he imagined a man there beneath his feet on the other side of the world struggling against such an enemy as he himself had, and he seemed to feel a circling power sweep around the world and sweep him and that man together.

He remembered that Jade had told him once that there were only one moon and one sun for all. He had been surprised and unbelieving when he had first heard this, but now it came to him that it might be true as she said, that at night the people on the other side of the world had the sun and by day they had the moon, and thus heaven was shared by all.

"So ought we to share the earth," he thought.

These thoughts he told no one, for they were scarcely thoughts so much as the movings of his spirit, and yet he took comfort in them because for so long he had had no such thoughts. His whole mind had been taken up with the misery the enemy put upon them and with how to live and save themselves and how to hide their food and how to manage not to be caught and killed. There had been no room in him for larger things, and even though everything was still the same with him and evil had not abated one whit, and ahead there was no hope, yet he was taken out of this little valley and he was set into the world, and he felt it.

XIV

MEANWHILE the whole village had to wonder where Ling Tan's third cousin was and why he did not come home. Be sure his wife blamed Ling Tan for it somehow, and she came to his house every day and wept and besought him to find out whether or not her husband were dead. In his heart he more than half guessed that his old cousin had of his own will decided not to come home any more, but how could he tell a woman so? He could only listen to her and scratch his head and think what he could do to find the old scholar in a city where men disappeared every day and there was nowhere to ask questions.

The cousin's wife was more than half afraid that her husband had fallen by an enemy's hand in coming and going to Wu Lien. She did not dare to go therefore to Wu Lien herself, nor did she dare to tell Ling Tan that she and her husband were ears for Wu Lien. So she begged Ling Tan to go or to send one of his sons to Wu Lien to see what he could do to speak for her husband to those now above him.

"My man was your senior," she said, "and all the laws of the family compel you to bestir yourself for him."

This was true and Ling Tan took counsel with his second son, and his son said, "I will go, for I have long wanted to see Wu Lien and to talk with him and know if any use could be made of him."

"I am afraid for you to go," his father said and his mother wanted to forbid him, but this could no longer be done. Lao Er and Jade now did as they pleased, though always with courtesy.

So it came about that one day in the ninth month of that autumn Lao Er went boldly to Wu Lien's house as he was, for once without disguise. He safely presented himself there as Wu Lien's brother-in-law, and he was let into the enemy gate and then led into Wu Lien's house. There in a room he was told to wait and while he waited he stared around him in astonishment at what he saw.

"How rich this is!" he thought, wondering at the carpet on the floor and the satin-covered chairs and all such things as he had never seen. Yet what were these to Wu Lien himself when he came in wearing a brocaded satin gown and on his hair fragrant oil and on his fat forefinger a gold ring.

Lao Er smiled at him coldly. "Well, brother-in-law," he said. "How fine you are!"

"I am very well," Wu Lien replied in his same smooth way, and he overlooked all inward meanings as he had long since learned to do. He made courteous inquiry of his wife's family and then he waited to see what was wanted of him.

So Lao Er told him how the old cousin had disappeared and what a burden the wife was and asked him if anything could be done. At this Wu Lien smiled, and rising he opened a door suddenly to see if any were listening and when no one was there he came back and in a small whisper he told Lao Er the whole truth of how the third cousin and his wife had been his ears in the village and how one day the cousin had come in and seen the foreign box and had stolen it.

"I have my ears in the city, too," Wu Lien said smiling, "and after these listened a while they found the old man," and he told Lao Er everything of where the old cousin was and how he did.

290

Lao Er could not but admire the cleverness of this man who now had risen so high with the enemy that they trusted him wholly and yet he did not belong to them, but kept his own ears everywhere.

"I thought you were against us," he told Wu Lien, "and there was a time when I wished you dead."

"I am against no one," Wu Lien said, smiling his peaceful smile.

"Are you for us?" Lao Er asked.

"As far as it is sensible at such a time," Wu Lien said.

And then he told Lao Er where he could find the old cousin and he said, "At this hour he will be dead in opium. Go late to the inner room of the Willow Tea House and there he will be."

And then he asked Lao Er to wait until he called his household in, and he did, and Lao Er saw his sister and by now she was delivered of her third child, a fat little girl, and they all looked so fat and fed that Lao Er could scarcely believe what he saw.

"Are you as well as you look?" he asked his sister, and she laughed and said she was. Then she looked grave and said that she only wished she could see her parents sometimes, and she would be content.

"But you," Lao Er said to Wu Lien, "are you content?"

But Wu Lien only said, "Who in this world is all content?" and he smiled his steady smile.

And there were the children prattling half in the enemy tongue and half in their own. After Lao Er had looked at all, he went away feeling very strange that these, too, could be of his own blood.

He did not go straight to the Willow Tea House, for he thought he must first bring his father and he went home by the quiet inner streets he knew. When he reached home he told his father secretly what Wu Lien had said and Ling Tan thought he had never heard so strange a tale. But when he heard that his third cousin and the cousin's wife had been ears for Wu Lien, he grew very grave and silent and he sat a long time pulling at his lip and thinking what this news meant and wondering how much Wu Lien knew and whether it were safe for him to know. He asked close questions of his son, and his son could only answer:

"Whether the man is true or false I cannot tell. It may be he is true only to himself. If that is so, we are more safe, because he will not tell the enemy too much, so that on the day when they are driven out, he can say he played the traitor honestly and so save himself."

"But does he know of our secret room?" Ling Tan asked.

"Who can tell?" his son replied, "and how dare we ask him?"

"If he knows, our lives lie in his hand," Ling Tan said, and he cursed that cousin's wife, and for a while he thought he would find and take her by the throat and choke the truth out of her. And then more wisdom came to him, for how would the woman know what the man had told?

"It will be better if I tell her nothing," he thought. "Then her fear of what I know or do not know will give me power over her, and if my cousin is dead I am bound to care for her and I must have some power over her."

So Ling Tan put the woman aside for the time, though had he hated her before, how well he hated her now! Still, she was nothing but a woman, and at last he threw her out of his thoughts and to his son he said:

"I will go with you tomorrow myself to hear my cousin."

The next day, late toward evening, telling Ling Sao no more than that he had business in the city, Ling Tan and his second son walked through the city gates and toward the Willow Tea House. On every street they saw change in the city. Everywhere the enemy advertised their wares, of medicine and courtesans and sometimes he thought drugs and courtesans were all they had to sell. "Benevolent Pills," and "University Eyewash"—such medicines, the enemy said, could cure all ills. And then there were the numberless houses for opium and for brothels. Upon the streets there were opening new shops with little enemy keepers, and on the streets he saw enemy wives and children, and he thought for the first time how strange it was that these small fierce wild men had wives and children, too. It troubled him, because in their way women and children were more dangerous than the soldiers, for soldiers easily keep hate alive, but could hate persist when enemy families came and made their homes?

In these days there was one very great evil in the tea houses of the city, and it was here as in others. The decent men waiters were gone and in their places were bold young women. As Ling Tan chose his seat one of these women came up to him to see what he wanted. At first he would not speak to her, for her look was too evil for a good man. Then his son whispered to him that it was like this everywhere, and he said aloud:

"Do you tell her, then, to bring us only tea."

The woman smiled scornfully and went away and brought back two bowls and a pot of tea at a price which made Ling Tan all but cry out, and he could scarcely drink it.

"If I had a way to save the stuff I would," he told his son.

At this the woman lifted her thin shoulders and turned down her painted mouth and she said:

"If it frightens you, old man, what would you say to this?"

She took out of her bosom a small silver box and in it was a white powder.

"It is three hundred silver dollars an ounce," she said proudly, "but a dollar a day will buy you pleasure and end your care."

She put it before them half-secretly, but Ling Tan pretended within not to see it nor to understand what she said, and after a moment she put the box back in her bosom.

"It is a devil drug," Lao Er whispered when she had gone again. "Worse, it is said, than opium!"

"I do not know," Ling Tan said. "For me it is not," and he sat looking about him, as though he were too stupid to understand what he saw, though very well he understood what that evil powder was. Who did not know it? Even the children in the city streets were tempted with it, hidden in sweets the enemy made, and once any had tasted it the hunger for it was fire in the veins. Yet Ling Tan put the knowledge away now. It was only one more of the monstrous evils of these times, and he drank his tea as best he could and what made the tea most bitter to him was that the one who had brought it was no foreign devil but a woman of his own people, spoiled forever by the enemy.

The room in which they sat had once been very fine, but now it was not, for the enemy had torn the paintings from the walls, and the wood had been stripped from the walls, and fire had blackened the painted beams of the roof. What was left were the walls and the floors and there were enough common tables and benches. Ling Tan and his son sat in a back corner looking about them. In the old days they would never have come to so fine a tea shop, for there would not have been another farmer in such a place, but war had brought all men to the same poverty and they looked no worse than others around them. So they drank their tea, being careful not to drink beyond the price they had paid, and at last watching those around them they saw one man and another and another rise quietly, and they rose too and with about ten others they entered a small inner room, and waited. In that room there was no window, and it must once have been a kitchen, for there were the ruins of a brick cooking stove, but nothing else except some benches and a chair set a little apart.

Ling Tan and his son hid themselves among the other men, for Ling Tan had told his son:

"Whether or not I will make myself known to my cousin I do not know. I will judge when I see him."

In a little while an inner door, made very narrow, opened, and by the light of a candle set on a ledge of the wall, Ling Tan, scarcely believing what he saw did see his old cousin come in. But how changed the man was in this short time! He had bought himself, doubtless from some pawnshop, a dirty satin robe of plum color and a pair of big horn spectacles to set on his nose. The robe was too wide for him, because he had grown dried and yellow, and now Ling Tan knew the moment he looked at him that his cousin had turned to opium, for so his own mother had looked in her time. He leaned to his son and whispered:

"I know where he has found his courage!" And he made a sign of opium smoking and his son nodded.

But they said no more and the cousin did not see them. He walked in, swaying his robes as any old scholar loves to do, and he sat down on his chair as though he were the teacher and all these his pupils, and he gave his greeting and pulled his little beard and in a low solemn voice he began to speak.

"You who hear me," he said, "today there is good news and bad from the outside. Evil is the news of our capital in the inlands, for there the enemy flying ships labor to do their worst before the year ends and our people are exhausted and their homes are in flames. But our great leader is dauntless and though he shares the sorrow of the people, he says all must resist until the end."

Here a murmur went over the crowd, and a voice called:

"But does he say how we shall resist? Is our army growing strong?"

"Doubtless that I shall be told another day," the cousin said, and he went on, rolling his eyes and making his voice a big whisper. "As for the news from across the seas, it is also good and bad. Still we have no clear aid and our friends are still not our friends. They send us money for food and medicines for our wounds, but to the enemy they send oil and fuel for the flying ships which destroy us. In the west the western enemy destroys also the great cities of the Ying country. Night after night the Ying country people must hide in the earth and their palaces are destroyed over their heads and the dead mount up to the sky."

All listened and wondered where this old man learned such things and yet they took it as truth and they waited for what was next to come. Then the old man coughed and he said, "The most evil news I have kept until now. There is to be set up here in this very city a puppet who will rule for the enemy but in the name of our own people, and we are all to obey him, and to pretend that he is our choice. Who is he? He is that Three Drops of Water King. Has he the spirit to defend us? He weeps easily, but the day will come when all the pebbles from western mountains cannot fill the seas of his regret."

At this a great mutter rose from those who listened. The old cousin nodded and said, "A very great evil, and tomorrow at this same hour I shall have more to tell you."

When he had thus told all he knew the old cousin took a small bowl out of his bosom and he rose and set the bowl on the chair and he stood with his back to it and them, to avoid shame, and those listening knew that it was time for them to go out and let others take their place and so each man went forward and put a few pennies in the bowl or what he was able, and so did Ling Tan for himself and his son.

Then they went out and home, and Ling Tan could not marvel enough at what he had seen and heard and he laughed at his cousin and cursed him, too, for an old rascal.

"How he stopped like a story teller at the point to make men want more and come back tomorrow!" he said. "Still, he looked happier than ever I saw him, and let him be. We will tell no one what we know. Heaven uses the useless."

Thus having put aside the matter of his old cousin, Ling Tan fell to thinking of what he had heard told, how in this city there was to be set up a puppet, a man well-known among their own people. His gorge rose at that weak and handsome man who had so betrayed his nation, and for a long time he did not speak. Was it betrayal or had the man a trick in his mind?

"Who knows the heart of any man now?" Ling Tan thought.

All around them as they walked was the wide good country-side, the land still good though many villages were ruined and many were blackened with fire. The people were scattered, so that where once this road would have been busy with farmers going to sell in the city, with donkeys carrying bags of rice crossed upon their back, and peddlers coming from the city to sell in the villages, and people riding on wheelbarrows, now there were almost none. A rare sight now was a farmer with full baskets of food. But the land was here and what it had done once could be done again, if the land too were not betrayed. He looked down at the brown dust of the road where his sandalled feet went and he said to his son:

"We who are on the land, we must not betray it. Let those above betray us, if they are so evil, but let us not betray the land."

His son did not know out of what thoughts his father spoke but he could see they were grave, and so he said heartily, "Be sure we will not."

. . . The next morning when the cousin's wife came to inquire Ling Tan told her a lie and made his face calm and stern while he told it.

"Woman," he said, "what you feared is true. Your man is dead and you will never see him again, and you must count yourself a widow."

With that she fell into loud weeping.

"How did he die?" she screamed, "and where are his pieces?"

"Do not ask me," Ling Tan said, "for I will never tell you. As for his body, there is no way to find it."

297

She was silenced and for the first time in her life he saw her overcome with true misery and fear. After a while she went home to mourn and to consider her plight, for what is more evil for a woman than to be alone and have no man in her house? She feared lest Ling Tan knew she had been ears and eyes for Wu Lien, and feared the more because he did not tell her if he knew, and now her life was in the palm of his hand. At the end of two days she was humbled to the core of her heart and she went to him and made herself low before him and said:

"I have now no one in this world but you, and I can only look to you."

Then he replied to her coldly, "Be sure I shall always see that you are fed so long as I have food."

And Ling Tan and his son kept their secret, and Ling Tan did not tell even his wife. The burden of the extra woman he took and counted it one more thing that he did against the enemy because it left his third cousin free.

But Lao Er told Jade everything, and he told her this, too, and without fear, because he and Jade were one, and he trusted her as he trusted himself. It was like Jade to laugh at the old cousin but to be very grave at the news of the puppet. She was silent a long time when she heard this most evil news, and she said, "Such men as this puppet are our worst and our true enemies, for they have betrayed themselves and us in them. The enemy from outside is a disease but the puppets are our own weakness, and how shall we fight the disease if we are weak?"

"Those of us who are strong must only be more strong," Lao Er said.

At this she lifted her head.

"You have said a true thing," she told him, and from that day on these two were yet more steadfast against the enemy.

XV

WHETHER or not the hillmen and young and old men everywhere could have held firm against the enemy year in and year out, who can tell? But certainly it was true that now they were determined to hold and never to yield when they knew that their war was fought elsewhere in the world. They could wage no great battles and what they did mounted small enough if one compared the enemy killed to the enemy left alive. Yet what they did was not small, for day by day they were learning to live in resistance to the enemy, and this is a greater thing than to die in resistance.

But Ling Tan's soul was often wearied with the difficulty of his days and with the steady evil force of the enemy who abated nothing of their greed and their oppression. It was the oppression of evil little men who work for themselves, and because they have a petty power they wield it to make themselves as rich as they can. Thus again when the harvest came this year Ling Tan had to sell his rice at the enemy's fixed price, and again the enemy sold it elsewhere at great profit. Again Ling Tan had to eat meat secretly and twice his pig was discovered, once most unluckily when his sow had just farrowed and all were taken and Ling Tan dared not lift his voice and say they were his to the petty men who took them. He had doggedly to find another pig and again to try for his own meat. And there were many taxes, taxes on the land and on opium, on seed and on harvest, and on all that was sold, so that Ling Tan looked back on his old taxes with wonder that he ever complained of what had been in those days. Added to all the oppression was the gnawing constant anger that these were foreigners who oppressed him and his land and they were men who had no right to be here. It seemed to him that even the bandits were less hateful than the devils, only because they were not foreigners.

For besides all else, there were those wild-hearted men who cared only for themselves and still robbed and pillaged where they could, staying far from the enemy, and yet coming down by night upon any man rumored to have more than another, however little, so that honest men had to hide what they had not only from the enemy but from the evil of their own kind.

In the midst of this Jade went on with bearing her second child and Lao Er went on with his work between city and hill. He took his life in his hands often, but such danger must be, and day after day that autumn Jade bade him farewell in the night and each knew that this might be the time when they parted never to meet, and yet neither said so.

"Care for yourself first," she always told him.

"I will," he always promised her, and yet they both knew that he could not. Had he cared for himself first he would not have done the work he did.

Now what Lao Er did was to come and go between the guerrillas in and about the city who were farmers by day and those men in the hills, so that upon a plan they could meet and strike together. And he was no common courier, for to each he brought news and all depended upon him. He was clever in passing through the enemy, sometimes a vendor, sometimes a beggar, sometimes an old man, but never himself and all these disguises Jade devised for him at home. When he was in the hills he often met with his two brothers, and between them and the ones at home he was a messenger, too, and more than a messenger because he kept them patient with each other.

For there had come a rift between Ling Tan and his two sons in the hills, ever since he had made up his mind that he would not kill another man as long as he lived, even an enemy.

"What would it be if all of us made such a rule for ourselves?" the youngest son asked angrily when Lao Er told him this. "Shall we allow the enemy to kill us and we not kill them? My father is growing too old for the good of all."

This youngest son now wore a uniform such as soldiers wear and his mind was altogether on war and death. He still could not read a letter and for him books were evil and learning was evil and all was evil except the simple force in his right arm when it lifted a sword or shot a gun. He lived in these days in a temple in the hills, which he had made into a fortress, and with two hundred and fifty young men under him, he went out from there again and again to strike small garrisons of enemies and little companies sent out to sortie and to search for food. He had a circle of spies through that country so closely woven that he knew within an hour when an enemy band was within striking distance of him, and nothing would stay him when he knew.

Every look of the slender boy whom once the enemy had ravaged had now gone from him. He had grown still taller than he was then and his body had put on flesh and bone and muscle and his skin was golden, and his eyes were like a tiger's, always restless and always fierce, and that he had not twenty wives was not his fault. Those women whom he and his men sometimes rescued and women who wanted him to stay and eat and rest in their houses and any woman with her womanhood yet alive in her could not let him pass her without making some sort of sign to him. The virtuous women did not know they did this, but still they did, and women who had no virtue were shameless and knew what they did.

What this young man had suffered had delayed his natural manhood, but still he was a man, and in this nineteenth year of his age he now felt returning to his blood his natural desires.

301

But by now so many women had invited him that he was scornful of them all, and though he learned to sleep here and there with a woman, he had never seen one whom he considered worthy of him. In his own mind he had a faint picture of what this one would be and he wanted someone who was more than a mere bedfellow.

Yet where was such a woman to be found?

There were days when his need for this woman grew keen, and then he let his temper out here and there and his men feared him greatly and nothing assuaged him unless by chance there happened to be an attack that day on the enemy. Only if he could be lucky and could himself kill some of the enemy, was he good humored again for awhile. But this could not always happen and there were whole days and many days when no such chance came, and then his temper was very hard to bear.

One day toward the end of the eleventh month of that year when Lao Er came to make his usual journey to the hills to bring news that he had heard from outside, his younger brother's aide asked him to step aside into a room in that temple. It was a room where few came now, because it belonged to Kwan-yin, the Goddess of Mercy, whom only women worship, and now there were no women who came to this temple. Lao Er went with the man and there beneath that high goddess, the man told the trouble they suffered from their captain's temper.

"I would not mind it for myself," the man said, "for I know now that his heart is not evil, but only his temper, and I have learned how to jump to save myself. When he lifts his foot I jump high, when he lifts his hand to pick up a stone or his sword, I stoop low."

"Is my brother as evil-tempered as this?" Lao Er asked.

"On days," the man said patiently, "and we forgive it, for what he needs, sir, is a woman of his own. Therefore I was chosen by lot from these two hundred and fifty men to beg your father to find this son a good wife somewhere who will calm him and make him a whole man, and so we will all be better."

Lao Er could scarcely keep his face from laughter, but he promised the man he would do this. Then he said:

"But I have no thought of what sort of wife my brother needs."

The man looked grave at this. "It is no easy task to choose a wife for such a man as he," he said. "She must be strong in body, for he is strong, and she must have a temper able to bear his temper, and yet it must not be like his. When he is hot she must be cool, and when he is dark she must be light, and when he is wilful she must be full of reason."

"There are few women as wise as that," Lao Er said, and he thought of Jade, and even Jade was not so wise.

"I know it," the man said sadly.

They stood silent a moment, each thinking of the difficulties, and then the man said, "Here is a strange thing, but that captain of mine comes here often and stares at this goddess and frowns at her."

"Does he?" Lao Er asked.

"We have seen him," the man said, "and it is what put it into our minds first that he wants a wife."

"Well, I will speak to my father," Lao Er said, "and I will tell him all you have told me, and then we will see what the future brings."

The man bowed and went away and Lao Er was alone. He went up to that goddess and looked at her closely for the first time in his life. He had never been a worshipper in temples, and his father was not, for men left such things to women. But Ling Sao had always been too busy to go more than once a year and she had not had the need that some women have because she had sons enough. So Lao Er had never been taken to the temple often as a child and even when he did go with his mother, she had not worshipped the goddess who gives sons to women since

303

she was fertile, but she had worshipped the god who gives riches and fertility to the land.

Now he stood alone in front of this goddess. Her little feet were upon the coils of a gilded dragon and she was shaped in such smooth grace from clay and gilt and paint that as he looked at her it seemed to him that she had a sort of life because she was so beautiful. Somehow that ancient idol-maker, being a man, had put into this goddess the thing that makes a woman female to a man. Though he had made a goddess, he had secretly and with great cunning made a woman too, and it could be seen in the tender curve of her proud lips, and in the corners of her long knowing eyes, and in the fullness of her limbs hidden beneath her robes and yet not hidden, and in her bosom covered and yet plain. The more Lao Er looked at the goddess the more he felt the woman.

At this moment who should come in but his own youngest brother, and he said very peevishly, "I have looked for you everywhere and only chanced to hear from my aide that you are here. What are you doing?"

Lao Er pointed with his chin to the goddess. "I never saw her close before," he said.

"Clay," his brother said, "clay and paint, like any other woman," and in his youth he looked very scornfully at the goddess.

"There is something more than that here," Lao Er said cunningly to draw his brother further. "The man who made this goddess loved her."

His brother came before the goddess then and frowned up at her.

"There are no such women," he said at last.

"Have you seen all the women there are?" Lao Er asked with a small smile.

"I have never seen one like this," his brother said.

"Were there one, would you want her for your wife?" Lao Er

said laughing. "Come, I will make a bargain with you—if such a woman comes will you take her to be your wife?"

As he spoke he turned to look at his brother and there he surprised upon his brother's face so moved a look, all mixed with a struggle for anger and scorn, that he roared his laughter.

"I want no wife," Lao San said. "What would I do with her when I go out to fight?"

"Leave her at home where she belongs," Lao Er said.

"Yes, and have her cry and whine and beg me not to go!"

"This goddess would not cry and whine," Lao Er said looking at her again.

"I do not like a joke," Lao San said angrily.

"Wait and see if it is a joke," his elder brother said.

Then he knew that he had said enough, so he drew his brother away from the room and they talked no more except of war.

But the next night when he was in his home again, he told his father what the man had said about his younger brother. Ling Sao and Jade were there and they all heard, and the father said:

"Though you made a joke of it, nevertheless there is something here that is very grave." And he told them how he had been troubled because his youngest son had learned to love war and killing and how such men would not allow peace to come in the world anywhere, and from them war always sprang as fire will spring from secret tinder. "So troubled have I been," he said, looking around on them all, "that I have told myself I would not grieve on the day when one came to tell me that my third son is dead, for such men must all die in the same way they have made others die." He paused and went on. "And I have seen these men like my son, and they are always evil with women and they do not make good husbands and they are not good fathers." He paused again, and then went on again. "And yet this man is my son and I do not forget it."

"But where can we find a woman like Kwan-yin who is a

305

goddess?" Ling Sao said. This youngest son of hers was now so far away from all she knew and understood, that she could not be surprised and she was only dismayed. "I never saw a woman who was like a goddess," she said.

"There are none, doubtless," Jade said, "but if we can find the one he thinks is one, it will do as well." She looked at her husband and laughed and he met her laughter with smiling eyes, but the mother would not laugh at such a serious thing as a wife for any of her sons.

"A woman of any kind is scarce enough now," she said, "and I see no young woman hereabouts who has not been fouled by the enemy, and I know my son would not have one of those, however cheap she can be had."

"He would not," Ling Tan said sternly.

"Then we must find one somehow in the free land," Jade said, and though they all saw this was a clever wish, how could they make it come about?

Now for many months and nearly a year they had heard nothing from Pansiao.

And Ling Sao fretted in herself because she could not go to her daughter or see to her marriage or bring her home. "It is very well for her to be safe now but what will be the end of it?" she said. "She cannot go on forever in caves learning to read and write. What of her betrothal and what of her woman's life?"

"You must be content that in these times she is beyond the reach of the enemy," Ling Tan told her when he found out why she was pettish and restless one day. "Do you forget Orchid?"

At that Ling Sao kept quiet and said no more, but she longed for her daughter and puzzled how to get her married safely though she was so far away. She planned how she could get a letter to someone there to see if a good marriage could not be made somehow for her daughter. If a woman were not married she had better die, for why should she live?

Now with her mind always running on marriage for her chil-

306

dren, because this she knew was her duty and she often thought that she could not end her own life in peace until it was done, Ling Sao suddenly thought of her younger daughter and she said:

"If we could write to Pansiao we could ask her to see what she can find for her brother there in the free lands. A school is full of virgins and she knows her brother, and what could be better than this? And it would do her good to think of marriage and to speak for her brother. It would set her mind on such things and make her more ready for her own time and we must arrange that too."

At first they could only think of Pansiao as a small quiet creature sitting at the loom, and how could she do such a large thing as this? Besides, they did not know where to send such a letter. More than once Ling Sao had told her husband that he ought to go to that white woman and get the name of the school where Pansiao was and the name of the place. He always said he would go, but he had put it off in the many troubles he had, knowing the girl was safe, at least. Now Ling Sao turned on him and cried:

"I have said and said that you ought to go to that white woman and find out where she has put Pansiao. It is a sorry thing when I do not know where my own child is!"

"Do not heat yourself, old woman," he told her, "I will go to-morrow."

So he did, winding his way over the country to the old water gate and he went into the city and through the empty land about those high walls where the white woman lived. The gate was locked when he stood before it, and he beat upon it, and none came and he waited a long time, hearing nothing but the thickest silence. Then he took up a stone and beat without stop until the gate opened. There was that old gateman, but now very fearful and downcast, and he opened the gate only enough to let his own face through the crack.

"What do you want now?" he asked Ling Tan, for he knew him when he saw him.

"I must speak with the white woman," Ling Tan said, and he felt in his girdle for a coin he had put there lest he need it.

But that gateman said, "Can money buy your way to her now? Have you not heard?"

"What?" Ling Tan asked.

"She is dead," the gateman told him.

Ling Tan could only gape, and the gateman opened the gate further and came out, and he sat down on the high stone threshold. And he sighed and took off his felt cap and scratched his head and put his cap on again. "Yes, and she died of her own will," he said sadly, "and it was I who found her. I went into the chapel to open the windows early one morning as I am paid to do on a worship day. There she was, dead before the altar. Oh, her blood! She had cut her wrists and the blood was flowing down the aisle. The stain is there forever. With all their washing it is still there."

"But why—" Ling Tan faltered. "She was safe—she had food—"

The gateman wiped his eyes with the end of his coat. "Is it not enough? But not for her—she left a letter, they said. I cannot read. Besides, she wrote it in her own tongue and only our old virgin can read that. She wrote it to those in her home on the other side of the sea. She said, 'I have failed.' "

"Failed!" Ling Tan said, not understanding. "Failed where?"

"Who knows her meaning?" the gateman replied sadly. "But so she wrote."

Ling Tan stayed silent awhile, sitting on his heels to rest himself, and what he felt was half pity at the white woman's end and half distress for himself, for now how would he find where his daughter was? So he told his distress to the gateman and that one said:

"I will fetch our old virgin, and she knows what I do not. Come in and ask her."

So Ling Tan went inside the gate and waited while the gate-man went away. Soon there came out a thin, half-old woman with spectacles on her nose as though she were a scholar like a man. When she heard what Ling Tan wanted she said:

"That school is in the caves of a great mountain in free land, and all are safe and well, and another white woman is at their head. You need not worry."

"Still, I would like to send my daughter a letter," Ling Tan said. "Will you write down the name of that place?"

So the woman tore a white piece of paper from a book she had under her arm, and watching he marvelled that she could write as easily as though she were a man, and she gave the paper to him and went away again.

"Is there only this old virgin in this great place?" Ling Tan asked, folding the paper into his girdle.

"Only she, and a few women servants," the gateman answered. "And it would make your eyes run tears if you knew how many years that white woman worked and spent herself to raise these houses and gather pupils from the provinces. I swear those pupils came here from all the directions under heaven. This was once a very famous school."

"Here, too, is the work of the devils," Ling Tan said looking at the wide wasted gardens and the hollow buildings, and went away.

When he was come home he told them what had happened and they all listened and Ling Sao was sorry that she had seemed less grateful to that white woman than she might have been.

"If I could have known that she would kill her own body I would have been better," she said half sorrowfully. She sighed and took her earpick out of her knot of hair and scratched her ears a while, wishing she had been more kind. "Poor foreign heart," she said at last, "I wonder why she came so far from home to do her good deeds? Now she cannot even be buried in

309

her own earth." And then she said, "It is not well when women study too much and do not marry. What can they be then but nuns? Let us write to Pansiao and hasten all our marriages."

"Write to her," Ling Tan said to Jade, "and tell her what the business is, and tell her what we want her to do, and that her mother and her father bid her do it."

Then he said a thing which never in the old days could he have said, "And tell her that her brother needs someone like that goddess. A common woman will not do for him. Write it down according to your own mind, child, for you know such things well enough, what with all your reading and story-making and your disguises and what not. I often think you should have been one of these actresses that we used to see in the foreign pictures before the city fell."

He went red as he so spoke, for it was not natural to any man to say so much to his son's wife and on such a matter. Then he rose and with all his dignity he left the room, and behind his back Lao Er and Jade looked at each other again with secret laughter. How these two loved each other in their laughter!

But Jade did write that letter out of all she was and knew, and she wrote it out of her own love for her husband, and she wrote it out of her knowledge of his young brother, and so she wrote, "And do not choose a fool only because she has a pretty face. Some day he might kill a woman like that out of anger at her witlessness. He has a quick right arm now. He does not dream any more. Kwan-yin is no fool."

When she had finished she read it to her husband and he said to tease her: "Why, you have written so well that I am ready to love that goddess myself, and you should be jealous!"

She dropped her lids at that and fluttered them once or twice and then leaned over to him and put out her red tongue.

"There is no such woman," she said pouting at him.

And he laughed again with pleasure in her.

XVI

IN HER own small part of the cave Pansiao sat with her back
to the others and read the letter which Jade had written.
She read it easily and yet it was so new to her to be able
to read that she still read with pride in what she did.

Two thousand miles away Jade had written the letter, and it
had come here through the air and over the land and water,
and carried by many hands, and the miracle was that there were
those who did their duty thus in the midst of war and fires and
flood. Here by the time the letter reached Pansiao it was winter
again, and the caves were chill and the water stood in drops on
the rocks and would have frozen had there not been a fire
burning in the middle of the cave on the rocky floor. A hole
through the rock roof led the smoke up, but the draught from
the door when it was opened led the smoke often away from
the hole, and there was the smell of smoke everywhere. But
Pansiao did not notice this. In the kitchen of her home if the
wind blew from the northwest as it often did in winter the
smoke came back from the chimney. So it had done since the
time of her ancestors, and knowing that Heaven sent the winds
they had always borne the smoke.

She folded the letter slowly when she had read it and put
each fold in its place. The paper was thin and fragile but all
paper was hard now to come by and very precious and no one

would have thought of throwing away paper. And how great was the duty this paper put upon her!

"How can I find a wife for my brother, and this brother among the others?" she thought.

For Pansiao of all her father's family was able to separate one from the other and she knew better than her mother did the inward secret differences between them. In those long days when she had sat at her loom there had been little to put in her mind, and once the pattern she wove was clear, what else had she had to think about except that house which was all she knew? Therefore she had dwelled upon each of the family, and especially upon her brothers, for she had always sighed that she was a daughter instead of a son. From the moment she had been born even in Ling Tan's house she had known that walls are close around a woman but the gate is open to a man. Yet here she was, made free by the chance of war, and the only one in her family to be living in free land, beyond the reach even of the flying ships of the enemy. Was there one among her fellows who would give up such freedom?

She put the letter in her bosom and she turned about. In the cave were twelve others who had their beds there with her. They were all there, for it was an hour when each could do as she liked, and some read and some talked and there was laughter and pleasure. But which one of these twelve could be a wife to that brother of hers? Some were pretty, some were plain; careless and careful, small and tall, there was not one whom she could see as her brother's wife. Yet these were the ones she knew best, and if she could not choose among them how could she choose among the nearly hundred others whom she did not know except that she saw their faces when they learned their lessons together or when they ate together in the central cave? It was a very heavy task that her father had put upon her. A goddess! She had seen no goddess here.

A clangor rose through the rocks and they rose in a confusion, crying out and screaming with laughter and pushing each other and in pretty disorder they ran out of the cave along a wide ledge of rock and into another cave where their teachers waited for them. There the whole hundred and twelve assembled. There were not seats for them and they sat on straw mats on the floor, such as Buddhist priests use to keep their knees from the dampness of the tiles when they pray. Pansiao looked at every face and saw no goddess, and that day it was hard to listen to her teacher.

For days whatever she did, coming and going, she thought of what she had to do. She dared not write she could not obey her father, and yet dared not write she could. After much worry and doubt, it came to her that she was wrong to think of the girl and she ought to think of her brother first. Let her remember all she knew about him and when she was full of memory so that he seemed living and with her again, she would look at the girls once more and see if one seemed his.

So thereafter whenever she had a little chance, and sometimes in hours when she sat before her teachers, she thought about her brother, and he came back to her, that tall slender boy with the beautiful face. She knew things about him which none other in her father's house knew, for she was the only one younger than he, and upon her he had wreaked small vengeances sometimes and his secret cruelties when they were children. If their father had reproached him for anything he did and he could not answer, being son, then she had learned afterwards to keep away from him, for without warning he would seize the soft skin on her under-arm between his thumb and finger and twist it, and then his beautiful face would lower at her.

"But what did I do?" she had wailed at him, and never did he answer.

"He was a child then," she thought now in her soft heart. And yet she thought, "Still, he must not have a wife too gentle—

313

not someone like me. I would not want such a husband," she thought.

And there had been the times when he fell into dark silence, and the elders did not notice, for it is right for the young to be silent before the elders, but she knew. Then when she had spoken to him as a sister may speak to a brother he would not answer, or he spat at her, and then if she asked him, "Why are you angry?" still he would not speak to her.

"She must be able to laugh," Pansiao thought now, "and she must not be like me because if anyone is sad near me, then I am sad."

And yet there were times when he had been only kind and good, and when he had taken half a day to make her a small flute from a willow branch, pulling the wood so skilfully from the bark that the pipe was left whole, and then so delicately shaping the mouthpiece that she could pipe a melody on the flute. He would do this for her, wanting nothing in return and only pleased with her pleasure. On such good days they had talked together as neither talked with any other, they being nearer in their age than any other two, and in such talk she had learned how he longed to leave his father's house and go out to places he had never seen.

"But what would you do in strange places?" she had always asked, "and when night came where would you sleep and who would give you food?"

"I do not care where I sleep," he would say, "and as for food, I can beg or steal!"

"Steal!" she had whispered. "You would not steal?"

"I would if I liked," he had said wilfully.

But even now she could not tell whether he said that to make himself big before her, or whether that was his nature.

"She must be very clever," she thought, "wise enough to tell whether or not he is lying, for I could never tell."

And of course she must be beautiful, for all know it is evil for a woman to have a husband more beautiful than she, and the more beautiful the man is the more beautiful the woman must be.

Did she love her brother or hate him when she thought thus of him? Some of both, she thought, for he was both lovable and hateful. Perhaps any woman, even the one sought, would love and hate him, and she must be one in whom these two did not quarrel, so that when hate came love was not killed by it, and when love waxed, hate stayed for self-defense.

This was as far as Pansiao could think, and in her own way she had come near enough to this, that the woman must be stronger than her brother was or else she was not strong enough.

But when she saw this clear she looked again among the hundred and twelve, and not one of them was she.

. . . Yet at this moment there was coming nearer hour by hour to the mountains a woman of whom Pansiao had never heard. This woman had come many thousands of miles from a foreign country to this country of her own which she did not remember. Years ago she had been taken away by her father, and there alone with her father, for her mother was dead, she had grown to womanhood. She was not nineteen and she had quarreled with her father, that is, as far as he would allow a quarrel. He did not wish her to leave her school and her home abroad where they had lived so many years in safety and return at such an hour to the country they had left many years before.

He himself had never wished to return, because leaving his country was mingled in his memory with the sorrow of the death of his beautiful young wife on her first childbed. She had been of a Mohammedan family, and the strain of early Arab blood had given the arch to her brows, and a high delicacy to her nose, a dark luster to her eyes, and height beyond what is usual for a woman. He had loved her for the differences, and then had lost her in an hour, and all that was left was the small, strong crying girl. He had named the child Mayli for

315

her mother and then had taken willingly a post abroad which he had steadfastly refused for two years because his young wife had not wished to leave her home in her own province. Now she would never leave the city where she was born, for she lay buried outside its walls with her ancestors and he wanted to flee from it as quickly as he could, nor could he bear even to think of return. He had by now lived abroad so long that he knew he would die there. Only his bones would be sent back to lie beside his wife. When she died, he had taken her faith so that when he died, he might be buried beside her.

"But I cannot stay here safe and be happy when the East-Ocean people are taking our country," Mayli now told her father in that foreign country.

She spoke her own language badly, but she had recently determined to speak it. This, her father observed, was only one of the many signs of her purpose to return to her own country. She had also stopped wearing the foreign dress to which she was used and now wore only the long narrow robes of the modern Chinese women. He had said nothing while these changes were taking place, but he saw them all.

One morning at the breakfast table he had dipped his delicate aging fingers in a silver bowl of water before answering her. They were finishing breakfast together and there were no servants in the room for the moment.

"I cannot imagine what you think you will do if you go back," he said in English. "They need men, engineers and military experts, but scarcely a young woman who has not yet finished her education."

She looked like her mother, he thought, and yet he was glad that something, perhaps this foreign country, had given her a look that to him made her wholly different from that one he had buried long ago, and yet who had remained alive in him, so that although he had often thought he ought to marry and have sons he had never been able to come to it. It was not as necessary in this country as it would have been in his own.

"I will find something," Mayli said firmly.

Her big black eyes flashed at him in a way he knew only too well, and he said no more. It would be a waste of his life force to argue with her and he had given it up when she was fourteen. Since then she had done exactly as she liked. There were times in the night when he, Wei Ming-ying, first secretary to the Chinese ambassador in this foreign capital, had lain awake half through the night because of his failure to make his daughter possible for a man to marry. So far as he could observe, in nothing was she fit to be a wife. He shuddered to think of his future son-in-law one day turning bitter reproach upon him.

"I swear I cannot help it," he often muttered to that man in his imagination. "I did my best. She early became too strong for me. I could not waste my life in useless struggle. Besides, I have had to support her and pay for her education. I have had no time for anything else."

And yet no such son-in-law had appeared. Young men had fallen in love with Mayli, but she herself had refused them, and her father had had nothing to do with it.

"Then you are going," Mr. Wei now said, sighing. He lifted his mild brown eyes in one last appeal. "What of me, left alone in a foreign country?"

Mayli laughed too loudly for a Chinese girl. "That you are alone is only your own fault, father," she said, and rose from her chair as she spoke. "Are there not at least three ladies who long to comfort you?" She could not remember her mother, and so she did not spare her father from her teasing. He was a very handsome man and his natural courtliness led him often to go further than he knew. A strain of malice in her took pleasure in the discomfiture of those ladies whom he thus innocently deceived.

"At least tell me when you leave," he murmured hastily. She knew so much more always than she ought to know!

It was only a matter of weeks before she was actually on her way across the ocean. There had been no trouble in finding a place when the Chinese Embassy knew she wanted it. The only trickery her father had practiced in the matter was to keep from her that he had allowed nothing to be offered her in a danger zone. He wished if possible that she be put in a mission school as a teacher, so that her surroundings would be the strictest and most old fashioned. Luckily a girls' school in the caves of the high western range of mountains in inner China had seemed romantic to her, and in her own opinion she was able to teach anything.

Thus she came one cold clear morning to Pansiao's school. The ice was crusted on the small rickety airplane that had brought her here. That it had been ready to bring her at all was another arrangement her father had made in the capital of that foreign country far away. It had seemed simple enough to her. When she stepped off the ship a pilot was waiting for her. When he had escorted her from the landing field up the mountain to the caves he told her that he had orders to be ready to take her back whenever she liked, and he gave her his secret address.

"I do not go back," she said haughtily.

"Nevertheless, take it, so that I may have done my duty," the pilot said hastily. He was terrified of this tall and wilful young woman who knew every moment what she would and would not do, and he was glad to be rid of her. Suppose she had wanted to fly the plane herself, then what would he have done? But she did not propose it. She had sat motionless and in silence, the west wind blowing her short black hair from her face. Midway she ate heartily of a large package of bread and meat and fruit that she had brought with her and did not offer to share it with him, so he ate his cold rice and fish.

Nevertheless at this moment of parting she opened a bag of

foreign leather that she carried in her hand and took out a sum of money three times the amount he had hoped for and gave it to him. So he liked her better when he left her than he had at any time. He bowed and went down the mountain on foot as he had come up, though she had ridden in a mountain chair of bamboo, and he hoped he would never see her again.

Mayli was full of pleasure at the room that was given her in a cave, with one window toward the south. The openings of the caves were boarded and had doors and windows in them, and the outlook from her little window was wild beyond her imagination. The bare mountains rolled on like great waves of solemn music, thundering in their silence.

She had thrown the window open, although it was a day of piercing cold, and now she stretched out her arms in a gesture that seemed false and was not.

"Mine!" she murmured. "It is all mine. Mountains, I come home to you!"

She stood a moment, then remembered that she was very hungry and that the old servant who had led her to the room from the gate had told her the classes would be out in a few minutes. But first she must go to the office to see the foreign principal who was now teaching, and after that there would be food. She turned and examined herself in a small thin mirror which stood on the table. She brushed up her strong black hair, wiped her face with a wet towel, and then powdered and rouged it a little. Her lips also she made red but to the exact shade that suited her. Her gown she left as it was. It was a robe of dark red foreign wool and the warmest she had.

She went through a winding dark passage and back to the point where the servant had told her was the office. Without shyness she opened the door and went in. At the table sat a stern, large white woman whose look was nevertheless not unkind, though more than usually plain.

"Are you Miss Freem?"

319

Miss Freem thought it was a foreigner who spoke and she looked up astonished. She was the only foreigner in hundreds of miles and none of her girls were able to put more than four foreign words together. But the moment she looked up she knew who this was.

"I won't like this woman," Mayli thought.

"If I am not careful, I shall have trouble with this bold-looking girl," Miss Freem thought.

In this mood their life together began.

. . . In the main cave where the girls ate their meals, Pansiao looking up saw the new teacher with love instant in her heart. The new teacher had come in with the foreign principal to whom Pansiao had never yet dared to say a word, and she was talking to the foreigner as easily as though she had lived with her in childhood. Pansiao put down her chopsticks and stared.

Whispering rippled over the crowd of girls, "It is the new teacher—the new teacher." They rose as they always did when the principal entered and remained standing until she sat down. But as for Pansiao, she rose only for the new teacher. They were all staring at her now, at her color, at her height, at her ease, at her quick foreign movements and at the foreign stuff of her gown. Yet she was one of them, for her hair was black and her skin, though fair, was still their skin. Pansiao was dazed with her beauty. Under the bare board table her small chilblained hands were clasped together. She felt the sweet hot love from nowhere rush into her bosom.

And then with simplicity that could only be in one so simple as she, Pansiao thought, "Heaven has sent me one for my brother!"

This was a strange return. Mayli, rising in the mornings from her bed, looked from her window over the wild and tempestuous country. Mountains tossed together as far as eye could reach. All that was human was contained in one village, clinging to a creviced valley, a village at this distance so small that the palm of a hand might have held it.

From this outer vastness she turned to a pattern of days within so minutely planned, so empty of present meaning that she wanted to tear it apart like a cobweb in which she had been caught. "In these great times in our country," she thought with waxing anger, "to teach these girls exactly as though they lived in some small American town!" Impatience came to be her constant mood. Thus one morning coming early to the class room she found Pansiao, bent over a book, murmuring to herself, her little face twisted with effort.

"What do you study, child?" Mayli asked carelessly. She had not yet learned to know one of these faces from another, but she thought, surely this is one of the smallest girls in the school.

Pansiao had of her own intent come to this room early. Here in a little while her adored would teach her the mystery of numbers. If she came early she might be the first to see her. But she had barely hoped for such fortune as this, to be alone with her. Meanwhile she must learn her English, which Miss Freem taught. Now with this beautiful face over her, this voice asking her the question, she was speechless. She could only hold up the book.

" 'Paul Revere's Ride'!" Mayli said with scorn. "I cannot believe it!" She took the book. "Yes, it is so! You have to memorize this?"

Pansiao nodded. "It is very difficult," she murmured. She was confounded when her beloved threw the book down on the floor.

"What trash—what nonsense," Mayli cried out. " 'Paul Revere's Ride'—when every day our own guerrillas fight like heroes!"

Pansiao stooped to pick up the book, understanding nothing of this fiery English. But Mayli forbade it. She put her not too small foot on the book and stamped on it. Then she stooped and picked up the book and strode from the room.

Behind her Pansiao trembled. "Now I have made her angry,"

she whispered. Her heart caught in her breast and she wanted to weep. "Of all things I wish not to make her angry," she thought, and was bewildered by her ignorance.

But Mayli went straight to Miss Freem's office and without knocking entered. Miss Freem was reading her Bible for the morning, but Mayli gave no attention to that. Upon the Bible she put the book she had taken from Pansiao. The floors of the caves were damp and the imprint of her own foot was still upon "Paul Revere's Ride." Miss Freem sat back and looked at her. Within a month she and Mayli had quarrelled at least ten times. Both of them were frank and fearless on opposite sides of every question.

"See this!" Mayli said without respect for Miss Freem's position. "I found one of the girls learning this thing by heart!"

Miss Freem straightened her spectacles and bent to see what it was. "That is the lesson assigned for English today," she said. "They have been learning it for a fortnight and today the whole is to be finished."

"Why have they had such a stupid assignment?" Mayli demanded. "In these days, in these times, in a war infinitely greater than any that has ever been fought for freedom, here in her own country, why should a Chinese girl learn by heart 'Paul Revere's Ride'?"

Miss Freem was now shocked and somewhat frightened. There were times when she wondered if this girl had her right mind.

"But it is in the curriculum," she said firmly.

Mayli shouted laughter. Then she told herself she would be reasonable. "Listen, Miss Freem, do we have to go by an American grade-school curriculum, here in these mountains? Think, Miss Freem, where we are! We are two thousand miles in the interior of China, in caves, hiding from the bombs of the invaders. We have a handful of Chinese girls here educating them for who knows what? But not for this!"

322

She seized the book and tore it in half and threw the pieces in the waste basket beside the desk.

Miss Freem did not move. Long ago as a little girl her father had warned her about her temper. "If you are not careful, Ellen," he had said, "some day you will kill someone. You must ask God to keep you from sin."

All her life since then she had been frightened, because she knew that what he had said was true, and every day she had asked God to help her to control her temper. That was why she kept always on her table the very Bible her father had given her. When she felt the hot thick rush of rage to her head she reached out her hand and put it on the Bible. She did so now, her hand pressing its pages, seeking for help. When she felt she could speak she did so, her voice rough and choked.

"I am the principal of this school. I decide what the pupils are to learn."

"I am a fool," Mayli thought. She sat down on the chair opposite Miss Freem and leaned on the table, her beautiful impetuous face much too near Miss Freem's. How could she know that nothing frightened and repelled Miss Freem so much as too pretty a face, a face like this one?

"See, Miss Freem," Mayli began, "I am only saying—do not rob us of our own greatness! This is our fight for freedom— you had yours! We ought to be teaching our girls our own poems, our own songs. Why do we always sing hymns? We ought to sing the songs of our own people, the new songs— Can't you see how wrong it seems to me to come home in the midst of this"—she swept a long powerful arm toward the window, full of craggy mountains—"and singing—what? Oh, well, 'Abide with Me,' and—and 'From Greenland's Icy Mountains—'" She began to laugh loudly. "Can you see what I mean, Miss Freem?"

Miss Freem rose to get away from that strong, too beautiful face. There was passion in it of some sort and she was terrified of passion. "I think of this place as a refuge," she said solemnly, "God has made us a refuge."

"We want no refuge!" Mayli cried. "We are in the midst of war!"

She rose, and between the two women there mounted every barrier, though neither spoke. Then Mayli turned and left the room and Miss Freem stooped and picked the torn book from the wastepaper basket. Books were precious and this one could be mended.

But Mayli was tramping in full fury back to the classroom. "I cannot stay here," she muttered. "I will not be paid to stay here. I must get out."

She had forgotten the girl she had left in the classroom and she burst in, frowning and muttering to herself. Then she saw the girl sitting there exactly as she had left her, but her face was pale and her brown eyes frightened.

"What is the matter?" Mayli asked.

"I have made you angry," Pansiao whispered. The tears filled her eyes. "I, who would have died before I made you angry with me!" Her adoration shone like a candle through her tears. She put out a timid hand and took the edge of Mayli's robe.

"Why, you are only a child," Mayli said. "How did they let you come so far from home?"

"I am nearly sixteen," Pansiao said. "That is not to be a child. I worked on the loom for three years. Then the enemy came and my father sent me out."

And in her simple way she told Mayli the story of her home and near what city it was and she told even of her sister's husband, Wu Lien, who had gone over to the enemy and lived in a rich house in the city where the enemy had showed themselves so evil. Before she was finished other girls came in and so Mayli said, "I must hear this for my mother was born in that city. Come to my room, child, this evening, before you sleep."

Pansiao nodded, worshipping. She went through that day in a daze. Once or twice Mayli caught her eyes and smiled at her. Then Pansiao stopped breathing without knowing she did, until she was almost faint.

"How can that child have suffered so much?" Mayli thought. What Pansiao had told her remained with her all day. She forgot that she had quarreled with Miss Freem again and spoke so pleasantly to her in passing that Miss Freem thought God had answered her prayer and had given Mayli a change of heart, and she let the day pass, thankful for peace. As soon as God showed her what to do she would do it. "O God," she prayed silently that night at her bedside, "show me a way to get rid of this girl!"

. . . In the evening Mayli awaited her visitor with eagerness. She always read every paper she could find, she listened nightly on the forbidden radio which she had brought with her from abroad, escaping search because she traveled with a diplomatic passport, but the story that Pansiao had told her was one she had not yet known. When she heard a delicate cough at her door, she called, "Enter!" The door opened and she saw Pansiao and she smiled one of her lavish rich smiles, and welcomed the child.

"Sit here," she said, pulling a stool to the brazier full of charcoal. "It is so cold. And see, I am going to give you a sweet I brought all the way across the sea. I have been saving it for a special hour, and I think this is the hour."

Then Pansiao felt herself placed on a cushioned stool by the fire, a fire such as she never saw elsewhere, and then she found in her hand a sweet square of some sort of brown sugar.

"It comes from a tree far away," Mayli told her. "Taste it—it is good."

She tasted it, licking it with the end of her tongue, and Mayli laughed. "Your tongue looks like a kitten's little tongue," she said.

Then Pansiao laughed too. Mayli's voice seemed to come

325

from a long way off. She was so dizzy with happiness, so drunk with love, that there seemed to be a cloud about Mayli's head.

"You do look like Kwan-yin," she murmured.

Mayli opened her big eyes. "I? Ah, you do not know me! How my father would laugh! Why, child, I have a very bad temper. I am very fierce!"

"I cannot believe it," Pansiao whispered. She had forgotten the sugar she held in her hand. She gazed at the lovely face now ruddy in the light of the coals.

"I beg you," she said faintly, her love giving her strength. "Oh, I pray you—will you marry my brother?"

Now of all the things which Mayli might have heard from this young girl, here was the last she could have expected. She dropped her pretty lower jaw and stared at her.

"Do I hear what you say or not?" she asked.

Pansiao put down the sugar and dropped on her knees. "My third brother," she faltered. "At home he is the captain among the hillmen. He looks for one like you. And my father wrote me a letter bidding me find a wife for my brother in the free lands, because there is no woman fit for him where the enemy is. But I could find no one—there was no one fit for him here, before you came."

Then trembling with her boldness she brought out of her bosom Jade's letter. She had put it in her pocket when she came tonight, thinking that if her own words failed her the written words would speak for her.

Still unbelieving, Mayli took the letter and read it and while she read Pansiao rose and dusted off her knees and nibbled her sugar and watched Mayli's face. First there was laughter and then there was surprise, and then gravity crept about the beautiful full red mouth and hung upon the edge of the straight black lashes.

These lashes she lifted when she had read the letter. Then

326

she folded the letter and gave it back to Pansiao without speaking.

"Where else in the world could this happen?" she thought to herself. "Who could believe it who had not seen it? What shall I say to this child?"

Pansiao put the sugar down again and waited.

"It is a good letter," Mayli said. "The writing is very clear and the style is simple. Does your brother write as well?"

"He?" Pansiao repeated. "He does not read or write."

"You see," Mayli said simply, "it would be difficult for me to marry a man who did not read or write."

"Oh, he is very clever," Pansiao cried. "He has not learned only because he saw no good in it. Nobody reads or writes in our village except one old cousin, and he is a fool."

She examined Mayli's face anxiously. "If you wished him to learn he would learn. If you taught him he would learn very quickly!"

Mayli said gently, "Could I marry a man I have never seen?"

"Who has seen the man she is to wed?" Pansiao asked in wonder.

"It is another world," Mayli thought. "And yet, is it not mine? If I had not been taken from it young, so I would have answered."

"Tell me all about your brother," she said aloud. She had not the least thought of the man and what the child had said was absurd and only to be laughed at, and yet this was her world and here was her country.

Then Pansiao did tell her all that she remembered of her third brother from his boyhood, and even until now, and she was honorable and told of his evil tempers and his cruelties. At them Mayli only laughed. Then Pansiao told of his brave deeds and Mayli grew grave as she listened. It was a long time before Pansiao was finished, so long that over the red coals there had come a covering of soft gray ash, and the night was half over and neither of them knew it. They were far from here, each in her own way living another life and seeing a strong wilful bold young man, ignorant but powerful.

"That is my brother," Pansiao said at last.

"You have made him very clear," Mayli said.

She saw Pansiao looking at her and hoping for more answer than this, and she shook her head.

"Dear child," she said. "It is all strange to me and like a story out of a book. Now you must go to bed. The good Miss Freem will find you away, perhaps, and if you are here, how angry she will be!"

She touched the young girl's cheek and rose and led her to the door, and Pansiao could only beseech her with her eyes, for she felt her tongue forbidden.

"Good night," Mayli said. "I shall dream dreams tonight!"

When Pansiao had gone everything was changed to Mayli. Until now this room had been hers, a part of the country from which she had come. She had made it foreign, with here and there a cushion, a small unframed picture, a photograph of her father's home. Now it was no longer her room. It had become a cave in a rocky cliff upon a mountainside in occupied country. A young guerrilla captain stood here, a strong shadow, a powerful ghost, a presence she could not drive out. She sat down again by the gray coals and thought of him and of all she had heard about him.

"A pity," she thought, "a shame that a man like that has had no chance!" She thought about him again. "Would he be the braver if he could read? Would he be any bolder against the enemy?" She remembered the morning and laughed small laughter. "Perhaps Paul Revere was an ignorant man too," she thought.

Then she rose and shook herself to cast off the spell of this man she had never seen. "I must not be romantic," she thought.

Thus determined she went to her window and opened it and

stood there for a long time. The moon was high and poured its light over the barren peaks. They were gray and fierce. Not a tree could be seen upon them, and the shadows they cast upon each other were black. It was a landscape like none other in the world for beauty, but it took a strong heart to look at it and not be afraid. She was not afraid. She stared at it, motionless for almost an hour.

"I must not be a fool," she thought, and went to bed.

XVII

S
HE avoided Pansiao for days and often, when by chance she
met the young girl's waiting eyes, she smiled quickly and
turned her head away. What those eyes asked was impossible.

And yet upon that which was impossible certain powers
worked. There was the power of the mountains, and she felt
their wild power day and night, urging her away from the docile
pattern of the days.

"I was never meant to be a school teacher," she thought
passionately. "I never can sing hymns!"

Yet what was she meant to be? She had now come to ask herself that constantly. What could a woman do alone? She played
with her imagination. What if she sent for that pilot who had
brought her here and told him to take her—anywhere?

But where could she go? To her mother's family? They were
scattered, the city occupied by the enemy. No, alone she could
do nothing. She must ally herself. Ally herself with what? With
an army, perhaps. There were the armies in the northwest.
Women fought there beside men. But she did not want to fight
as one of many. She was too proud for that. She wanted a place
of power, or where she could create power. She thought of a
certain woman known all over the world, a woman of her own
race, educated abroad as she had been, a rich, beautiful wilful
woman, who had married a warlord—a man such as she could

imagine this brother was of whom Pansiao had told her. That woman had taken a raw strong ignorant man and as his wife she had shaped him into a ruler whose name the whole world knew now. Could not she do the same?

. . . "I shall have to do something," Miss Freem thought day after day, staring at her through thick spectacles. "I feel as if this girl were turning into a tiger. O God, please let me find a way to get rid of her!"

. . . Alone in her room at night Mayli turned the radio to the voice. It came between two and three every night, that voice from the heart of her country, telling of victory and of hard-held losses. In the midst of the days patterned like a cage about her, she waited for the night. When she had heard the voice she always turned to the mountains, and however bitter the cold she opened the windows and stood there, and the mountains did their work.

"I must get out of this place," she thought.

. . . But it was Miss Freem who set her free.

"God gave me strength," Miss Freem said to the other teachers when it was done. "I had been praying for weeks that He would rid me of this burden. But I had not been shown the way. Then one day I heard her with my own ears. She was urging the girls to run away, these dear girls, committed to my care and keeping! I happened to go by her classroom, where she was supposed to be teaching American history, and she was saying, 'It is despicable that we stay here in these caves studying what other nations have done. We ought all to be out and fighting our own war. Come—if I go, who will go with me?' That is what I heard. I opened the door and God gave me strength. 'Miss Wei,' I said, 'Miss Wei, I consider that your contract is broken.'"

The docile teachers murmured their horror. Most of them had once been Miss Freem's pupils and they knew how she felt.

Mayli, hearing later through some of them how God had

331

helped Miss Freem, laughed her too loud laugh. "Does she know how God used her for me? He used her to set me free!"

She scornfully demanded of Miss Freem her full salary and bade the gateman call a mountain messenger and when he had gone she sent him with a telegram to the nearest city. That telegram called the pilot to take her away. She went away without seeing Pansiao again.

As for Pansiao, when she found her goddess gone she wept secretly and long. Where was that goddess, and had she made her go, because she had besought her to be the wife of so human a creature as her third brother? Who could say? There was none to answer.

. . . Mayli settled herself in the small narrow seat of the plane.

"I go back to the coast," she told the pilot.

They had met in a village at the foot of the mountains. He was there this morning when her sedan was let down before the inn, and he came forward, smiling because he was afraid of her, his old cap in his hand and his blue cotton uniform more faded even than it had been. He was not surprised when a few days before this one he had her message telling him to be here on a certain day. He had not thought when he left her that such a young woman would stay long in the mountains.

"I shall be ready in half an hour," had been her only greeting.

Then she went into the inn, and after she had told the innkeeper that his was the filthiest inn in the two halves of the world and after she had eaten a bowl of noodles, she came out again, her fur robe wrapped around her, and she stepped into the plane.

She twisted in her seat for one last look at the mountains as they soared upward. Then she set her face toward the sea, and her mind she put on what she wanted to do. She had never let Pansiao know what she thought as she had listened to her tell of her father and his house, and when Pansiao pressed her

332

with shy questions, she had only laughed. To anyone she would have said that it was folly to think of an ignorant man she had never seen. And yet what Pansiao had told her had nevertheless directed her thoughts and her imagination. Now with the whole world to choose from and no one knowing where she was, she felt as free as a wind-cloud. Never had she had such whole freedom. The man with her was nothing to her. He was part of the machine. She did not once speak to him, and when he looked at her he saw her face set toward the sky, motionless and gazing ahead.

But out of the freedom her mind was shaping its plan. Why should she not go and see for herself if that brother were as handsome as Pansiao had said he was? For Pansiao with a woman's cunning had told her again and again of her brother's great beauty. Tall, she had said, "much taller than you are," she had said, and his eyes were long and the black so black and the white so white that whomever he looked upon felt the god in him. So she had said.

Now Mayli was one of those women who had never seen a man she thought her own equal. She was scornful of men and yet she was passionate, and since she had been a child of thirteen she had dreamed of a man whom she could not flout as she flouted every one who came near her and her own father too. Learning in a man she did not value, and by now it even added something to this man of whom she had been told that he could not read and write. If without learning he had such power, what would he be when he had learning too? She imagined him her dragon, stronger than she was and yet dependent on her for learning. She wanted him untamed and untameable, and yet she wanted a way to shape him. It would be sweet to have her own power over a wild and powerful man, a man such as she had never seen in palaces and cities and seats of government where suave smooth men gather together.

So through all the long day, high above the earth, she plotted how she would get near enough to this man to see him and know whether or not he was anything like the one of whom she dreamed but whom she had never seen.

It was not too hard. She could see a way very clear if she cared to take it. Pansiao had told her of her elder sister's husband, who was working with the enemy in the city, and his name Wu Lien. From the coast she could write to the puppet ruler in that city of her mother's birth, and ask merely that she be allowed to come there with his safeguard so that she might visit her mother's birthplace and her grave. The puppet had been her father's friend once, and she had known him in the days when the country was free and there had been no puppets. A rebel always, not from strength but from weakness, because he had never been given as much as he wanted, this man, now a puppet, had quarrelled with his own government and had spent years abroad, an exile, though with some faint honor, because he had strength of family and wealth to support him. Mayli had seen him more than once in her father's house, for there the man went as he went to many places to make secret complaint of what went on at home and how he was never listened to and how he had been put aside, and in his way he plotted weakly in foreign capitals and among any whom he thought had any power. Nor could her father put him wholly aside, for the man was his townsman and they had been schoolmates in childhood. When the enemy came conquering, who should be a better puppet than this discontented man?

And yet so eager would he be to justify himself in the eyes of those who had once been his friends, that if Mayli wrote him asking him to safeguard her while she went to her mother's home in that now captured city, he would give it and urge her to come and stay at his house, and he would show her fawning honor, so that he could prove to the enemy what friends he had, and how the daughter of an honored man came to seek his protection. Well she knew how angry her father would be, but had she ever told him anything she wanted to do if she knew he would not like it?

Thus her plan shaped itself more and more clear. Yes, and after she was in the puppet's house, she could easily have him find for her that brother-in-law Wu Lien, and go into the countryside to the burial ground, since she knew from Pansiao where Ling Tan's house was and his village. She could go and see for herself all in that house and perhaps the one whom she most wanted to see. All was plain before her, and she would follow it without telling anyone. If she found the man what Pansiao had said, why, then, who could tell what would happen? If the man was only a hind, she had but to go away again and call it adventure and pleasure. She took no risk on herself, whatever came about.

Thus she planned. They came down and spent the night at a small town on the border, at an inn dirty as all inns are dirty, and she was bitten by bedbugs besides. This made her angry and she told the innkeeper so before she left in the morning. The innkeeper only grinned, but his wife was not so kind and she cursed the tall foreign-looking girl and said:

"Be sure it is not you I am sorry for but the bedbugs! If they drank your black blood, you have poisoned them. And whoever heard of good honest folk who have no bedbugs and no lice? When such small creatures leave a house luck goes with them."

"You are an ignorant fool," Mayli said, "and the enemy is welcome to such as you. What good is it to our country to have such old images as you?"

In the end the pilot besought her to come away and the innkeeper held his hand over his wife's mouth and so the men parted the two women. And the pilot made the more haste that day so that he could be rid of his charge before night and so brought her to the coast.

Mayli did as she planned and sent by telegraph her message to the puppet. Within a few hours there was his message back again, as she knew it would be, begging her to come and saying that he would prepare a special place for her on the train and that she would be met with his own car. He himself would give her protection and he signed his name plain and openly as the ruler of the land. She smiled sidewise when she saw this, remembering his weak face.

She waited for two days, seeming only a handsome and proud young woman who had money in her hand. She came and went alone and bought herself some new garments and some fine pearls and if she saw anything hateful about this coastal city she did not say so to any of the strangers about her. But she saw, nevertheless, much that was very hateful. There were ruins in many parts and the city was crowded with the beggared and the homeless, not only from her own people but from other parts of the world as well. She saw hungry white faces, the faces of Jews driven out and desperate, and seeking shelter here in this sad place. Half the world was homeless and ruined. But this great and rich city had belonged to her people and why need it have fallen? Alone and knowing no one and refusing the friendly looks of all who wished to know who she was, she brooded on what she saw, and all her passion gathered into anger against the enemy.

In such mood she took the train and found the place prepared for her, and like an angry princess who will not tell the cause of her anger, she went to the city which had been her mother's childhood home, and by night was there.

. . . "I am very lonely," the puppet ruler said, and she knew he wondered whether he could lean still closer toward her and touch her hand. She had grown into a woman since he had seen her last. She looked at him and he knew he could not touch her. He drew back and set his cup down on the table.

"Naturally you are lonely," she said calmly. "What you have done has cut you off."

They spoke in the English which both knew equally well.

"But you understand me?" His handsome, weak face besought her understanding. "I am not a traitor. I am a realist. If we recognize the truth, that these East-Ocean people have conquered half our country, the only hope for our future is to work with them. Besides, what I am doing is thoroughly Chinese. History tells us again and again that we have always seemed to yield to our conquerors, but actually we have ruled and our conquerors have died."

"But in those times we were stronger than our conquerors," she said. "Are we now?"

She did not say what she thought, that among the company of high enemy officials with whom she had dined she had been terrified by the dark concentrated power in their faces and by the weak and placating good nature in this puppet's face.

He did not answer. Someone had come into the room, and he turned in instant peevishness, because he had given command that he was not to be disturbed while he was alone with his guest. But when he saw who it was he held back his fretfulness.

"Ah, Wu Lien," he said, and to Mayli he said, "this is my secretary, a man very faithful to me, who understands me."

So that brother-in-law had risen as high as this among the enemy, and so it was all even easier than she had planned!

Wu Lien bowed, without looking directly at the handsome woman. He was trained in courtesy by his father, who had been used to selling his goods to rich ladies. Then he said to his master:

"Sir, I grieve to disturb you, but there is bad news."

The puppet rose at once and they went out and Mayli sat alone thinking of this Wu Lien.

When her host came back, his face was disturbed. "I must excuse myself," he said. "A frightful thing has happened. A band of men has swept down from the hills and killed the garrison stationed at the foothills. There is not one left."

"But will you be blamed for it?" Mayli asked him.

"Naturally, somewhat," he replied. "They know I cannot help such savagery from my own people, and yet I feel its effects."

Wu Lien had followed him in, and now he turned, wanting to have her gone.

"Take my guest to her rooms," he said.

Wu Lien bowed and waited for Mayli to follow him.

"Good night," the puppet said, "tomorrow we will find something to amuse you."

"Do not trouble yourself," she said. "I can amuse myself."

When she was alone with Wu Lien she said, "Is it possible to go about the city tomorrow?"

"With escort, it can be done," Wu Lien replied.

"And outside the city—may one go?"

"With escort," he replied again.

She paused. "Need it be soldiers?"

His face was as smooth as a stone.

"You understand," she said, "it is hard for me to have—enemy soldiers. This city was my mother's birthplace and mine."

Thus she tried him, but that face did not change. "I hope to go and visit my mother's grave," she said, "for I am her only child."

He would understand the necessity before Heaven of this, she thought.

He nodded. "I will see whether I cannot go with you myself," he said. "Then we can leave the guards at least at a distance."

All she had said was true. Her mother's grave was in the burial place of her religion, but where she did not know. Yet it seemed to her that if she heard the name of the village she would know it.

"How shall I thank you?" she murmured.

"I need no thanks," he said bowing.

"But I will find a way to thank you," she said, and smiled.

Thus they parted, for they were now at the door of her room and she went in. They were rich and comfortable rooms and it

338

was like her that she could enjoy them, though they belonged to the enemy, and she slept well.

. . . When one has a plan, is it not easy to follow it? She went out the next day, and her host understood too her wish to visit her mother's grave and he was eager to help her remember the name of the village, and Wu Lien was called in. When he heard that for which he was wanted he said:

"Let me send for my wife, for she grew up in this countryside and her family still lives here, and she knows the names of villages better than I do."

So without effort Mayli saw Wu Lien's wife come in, and she knew at once that this was a sister to Pansiao, for the two looked alike, except that the elder had a face more stupid and less pretty than Pansiao had. When Wu Lien's wife heard what was wanted she thought a while and she said:

"That burial ground must be to the west of my father's village and I know it well, for it is the only Mohammedan burial place in these parts."

Then she turned to her husband. "And why should I not go with you today and take the children and we could stop at my father's house and while you went on with this one I could ease myself of my long wish to see them and know how they are?"

Thus simply was the thing done, by Heaven's will.

XVIII

Now on that day Ling Tan sat on a bench on his threshing floor and mended the yoke of his buffalo. The beast had become like his own father to him because he had so many times saved it from the enemy. They had looked at it often and weighed it for meat, and each time Ling Tan had told the enemy how aged it was and showed them how its bones almost pierced its dark hide, and he bade them look at the sores on its back. Ling Tan rubbed these sores secretly with lime to keep them raw, though when he did he begged the beast's pardon.

"It is to save your life," he always said into its hairy ear, and though the buffalo moaned he bore it at Ling Tan's hands.

But this morning as Ling Tan was plowing the yoke broke, and so he had sat down to mend it. He was weary because he had been sleepless most of the night. There had been two days and nights full of danger. His eldest son had come to warn him six or seven days ago that there was to be an attack on a village in the foothills which was the village nearest here, and the enemy garrison there was to be wiped out. This had been done three times before and the enemy had made the garrison stronger each time until now it was a very bold thing to attack them, and it was to be asked whether or not the hillmen could win.

They had won, and at this very moment Ling Tan's two sons lay sleeping in his house, weary with what they had been through, and the third son had a small wound, too, in his arm, so that he had to hold it bent and bound against his breast.

Thus, although on this morning Ling Tan looked only a peaceful old farmer, he was very uneasy and he watched all who came and went near him. He was afraid lest his two sons be found, and this the more since his wilful third son said he could not sleep in the secret room because the air was heavy and so he slept boldly in another room. If any one came to the gate and he had to hasten to the kitchen to gain the secret place, he would be seen. But what word of his father did that third son ever obey now?

"What will I do with him if this war ever stops?" Ling Tan thought again and thus thinking he sat frowning over his work. "How will my house hold this third son of mine in times of peace, when there is no use for such heroes?" he asked himself once more and could not answer.

At this moment his eyes, lifted often to search the road, fell upon Wu Lien and his daughter coming near with their children. When they saw him they came down out of the horse carriage in which they were riding and drew near on foot. By now Wu Lien had risen to such a place that he was no longer afraid of the enemy guard and so he bade them wait by the carriage and they did. But when they had come near enough Ling Tan saw that they had a stranger with them, a woman young and tall and so foreign in her looks to any woman he had ever seen that he took her to be one of the enemy women, and he was little pleased.

He did not rise as they came near but called from where he sat, not stopping his work, "Are you come?"

"We are," Wu Lien said, pleasantly, "and we hope we find you all in health."

"We are as well as we can be, in such times," Ling Tan grunted. He had no wish to show himself a friend of Wu Lien's and yet he knew it was folly to seem his enemy.

"Here we are, my father, and here are the children," his

daughter said. "And this is a friend who visits those above us, and she is come to look for her mother's grave in the Mohammedan burial ground."

At this Ling Tan knew that here was no enemy woman, and so he rose and said to Mayli, "I thought you were an enemy, because you look foreign, but if you are a Mohammedan, that is why you have your look."

She smiled and made a courteous answer, "I trouble you by coming."

"No, you do not," he said, but he was troubled because his sons were hidden in his house. He thought to himself that it was like Wu Lien to choose this day of all others to come here and he wondered too if Wu Lien had some secret knowledge and he was afraid he had. He tried to think of some quick way whereby he could go in the house before them and warn his sons. If there had been no guest he could have done it, but how could he show himself so ill mannered as that now? For his eye could see that this was no ordinary woman who stood here. She was a woman of great place somewhere.

Now while he hesitated, trying what to think, he saw to his fright that third son of his come to the gate and he was pulling at his girdle to loosen his trousers ready to make his water outside as all men do to spare the filth inside the house.

"Hold yourself!" Ling Tan roared. "There is a strange woman here!"

But that third son was outside the gate already and his sudden look of shame was so strong and Ling Tan's dismay so great that Mayli laughed, as no woman less free than she would have done, but what did she not dare? And so the first moment Ling Tan's third son put his eyes on her she was laughing and the sunlight fell on her and he saw her like this, her hair shining black and her cheeks red and her lips red and her teeth white and her head thrown back in laughter, and he was struck as though a sword had fallen across his heart. By now how shamed

342

he was! He hung down his head like a sulky boy and frowned and turned and ran into the house.

"Was that not my third brother?" Wu Lien's wife called out. Then Ling Tan did what he would never have dreamed he could. He fell on his knees before Wu Lien because he knew their lives were in his hand and he put his forehead in the dust and well Wu Lien knew why he did. He made haste to raise Ling Tan up and he looked at his wife and said, "I did not see anyone."

By this Ling Tan knew that Wu Lien promised he would not betray his sons, and he stood before him, his heart changing to him in this moment, and he said, humbly:

"Never will I judge again. Let only Heaven judge!"

Now he could dare to ask them to come into his house, and he made haste to invite them, and they all came in and he called his wife and told her to set out tea.

Before her eyes Mayli saw this family gather before her of whom Pansiao had told her, and she learned to know them every one. She listened to them and looked at them, smiling and silent, and she saw Jade come out, heavy now with child, and Mayli liked her, because Jade was not shy, and she liked them all. Only the two hidden did not come out.

But Ling Tan had shut the gate and now they were all locked in the court and safe and so he said to his second son:

"Tell your two brothers to come out. There are none here except friends."

At this the eldest son came, a shy and quiet man, plain of face as Mayli saw. But that third one would not come out. He sat inside the room where he had been sleeping and he cursed himself that he had been so loutish and such a fool as to rush out like any common man who wakes out of his sleep with a need, and then at that moment to see a woman such as he had seen! He was prouder than ever for he had grown used to himself as one above his fellows now and he thought himself shamed, because she had laughed at him. He sat there on his bed glowering and frowning and biting his red lips. When his second brother came to call him he did not answer but he picked up the wooden pillow from the bed and threw it at him, and the second brother had to stoop and shut the door quickly to save himself.

"My third brother will not come," he told his father, laughing.

"Why, what now?" the mother shouted. "When I have not had my three sons together all these months, will he not come?"

And she bounced off her bench and rushed in and took her son by his ear and led him out, he protesting and hanging back and yet he always obeyed his mother better than he did his father. But he pulled her hand off at the door.

"Let me go," he muttered, "I am not a child."

"You bone!" she said laughing.

But here they were now in the court and to save his own blood Lao San could not keep from looking full at Mayli and she looked at him.

And he thought, "I never dreamed to see a woman like this."

And she thought, "He is exactly what Pansiao said he was."

"I must go on," she told Wu Lien hastily, and Wu Lien rose at her voice. And then each pulled their eyes away from the other. He turned to his wife. "Stay here, mother of my children, and when we come back be ready for us."

She rose when he thus commanded her, and Mayli rose, too, then, and with a small smile and movement of her head she took her farewell of them for a little while, and they all watched her wrap her cloak about herself and they stood for courtesy while she went, and Ling Tan and Ling Sao went to the door with her.

Now when Ling Tan came back to his seat, he soon saw that his third son wanted to speak with him, for the young man jerked his head to the inner room and he strode into that inner room and the father followed him, his bowl of tea in his hand. It was the room where Lao San had been sleeping and now he

344

sat on the bed again and put his hands on his knees and leaned forward while his father sat on a bench.

"What now?" Ling Tan asked. He wondered to see his son's face so red and hot and to see him frowning so heavily.

"That woman," Lao San muttered through his teeth.

"What woman?"

"The one in the cloak—" Lao San said. He flung his hand out and toward the gate.

"Well, what of her?" Ling Tan asked. He prepared himself to hear his son say that she was a spy and ought not to have been let in, and indeed he had some such secret fears himself, but he had been so overcome with Wu Lien's kindness that he had let himself forget wisdom.

"Get her for my wife," Lao San said.

Now Ling Tan was the most saving and careful of men, and in this house it was a cause for mourning if so much as a small dish were broken, but when he heard this, in his astonishment his hand opened itself and his good tea bowl, which he had had from his father, fell to the ground and was broken to useless pieces.

He was so vexed that his anger spurted out of him at his son. "See this!" he cried. He stooped to pick up the pieces but they were too many and too small. Even the best dish-mender could not put them together, and Ling Tan cursed his son heartily. "You bone!" he cried, "you big turnip!"

Now Ling Sao heard the noise and she came running in to see what was wrong, and she cried out in her turn at the sight of a good bowl gone, and then Ling Tan shouted at her. "This turtle to which you gave birth!"

"What now?" she shouted back, and made herself ready to take her son's part against the father, as she always did for any son. Only when there was a daughter in the wrong could Ling Tan hope for justice from her.

"He made me do this," Ling Tan said.

345

"What is a dish?" she answered him.

"It is not the cursed dish," he said. "It is this son of yours—he wants to swallow the sun and the moon. He has forgotten he is a man and a younger son. No, this one, he thinks he made heaven and earth!"

"You yourself are only an old bone," she said. "What are you talking about? I had rather get sense out of the ducks quacking. Whose son is he if he is not yours?"

By now both were angry and the eldest son and their daughter came in to cool their anger, and the daughter said:

"Since none but you knows why you are angry, father, we will keep silence until you can speak."

So they waited until he had his breath and his daughter brought him a fresh bowl of tea and his eldest son lit his pipe for him, but the youngest son only sat there and said nothing.

At last Ling Tan was near to himself again, and drawing on his pipe he said, while the smoke puffed out of his mouth:

"This thing who is my third son—he who will not marry any woman, now he says, 'get her for my wife.'" He swallowed smoke and coughed.

"What her?" Ling Sao asked and was amazed and overjoyed. Marriage talk was perfume in her nostrils and food in her belly, and especially if it were for this son.

"What her?" Ling Tan repeated. "Why, that foreigner in the cloak!"

Now they were stricken too. When Ling Tan said this none said one word, and in that silence Lao San stole a sulky look at one face and another from under his handsome brows, and the more he looked at them the angrier he grew. He flung up his head and leaped to his feet.

"Not one of you knows what I am," he said. "To you I am a child. I am no child. Mother, I have forgotten that I ever fed at your breast. Father, I do not eat your food. As for the others, who are you? I have no parents and no brothers and no sisters. I swear myself away from this house!"

He strode toward the door, but his mother ran and hung on his coat and twisted the tail of it in her strong hand.

"Where are you going?" she screamed. "What do you do?"

He jerked away, but so strong a hand did his mother have that his coat tore and he went on with his coat hanging from his bare shoulder.

"At least let me mend the rent!" she shrieked after him, but he would not stay.

"When you give me what I want I will come home again," he said over his shoulder, and he strode from the gate and into the full sunlight with all its danger to him. They ran to the gate after him and saw him walking swiftly down the road toward the hills.

Then Ling Tan sat down and put his head in his hands and groaned to his wife, "How is it such a one came out of your womb?"

"How was it you put such a one in me?" she cried back.

"Out of you or me he was not born," he said heavily. "He is born out of these times, and what will we do with him when these times are gone?"

And he sat trying to ease himself with great groans and yet feeling no easier, for he knew it was his duty as a father to see his son married, and his duty, too, to the generations before and after. But how could this marriage be made? Looking at it from all the four directions, east and west, south and north, he saw no way by which the thing could be done. How could he, a farmer and his son a farmer's son, make proposal for such a woman? His gall was not so big, nor his liver so bitter.

But Ling Sao thought her sons good enough for any woman, and after she had turned things over in herself awhile, she motioned to her daughter to come aside and so the daughter went into the kitchen with her and the mother said:

347

"You are there at the heart of affairs, and you can put out ears and hands and see what the outlook is. Find out whether the woman is wed already, and if she is not—well, a man is a man, and she could look very far and not find so much of a man to look at as my son!"

"She is a very learned woman," her daughter said doubtfully.

"What is learning in bed?" Ling Sao replied. "Who wants reading and writing there?"

At this the daughter blushed, for she had lived long enough in the city to grow more delicate than her mother, and so she did not answer either by words or laughter.

"At least I can talk with my children's father," she said.

Ling Sao leaned over to her and now she was very grave and she whispered, "Arrange this for your brother, child, and I swear I will forget everything that ever I had against you and your man. Whatever comes in the future, I will say your duty toward your parents is done, if you will do this one thing."

"What I can do I will do," her daughter said, but she was still doubtful.

Thus it was left and Ling Sao told her husband what she had done, but he shook his head and was full of dolefulness.

"Do what you can, you women," he said. "This is beyond a man. As for you, old woman, I know your power in mating two together—you could wed an eagle to a crow, I swear—but these are eagle and tiger and the one flies in heaven and the other walks on earth."

"Leave it in my hands," she said stoutly.

He sighed and gave it up to her.

. . . Now Lao San had not gone so straight as he pretended. Well he knew his father and mother and brother and sisters were all watching him and frightened by his temper, and so he made as if to go straight to the hills. But out of their sight he turned west and went toward the Mohammedan burial ground. When he came near he crept through the long new grass in the

348

noiseless way hillmen learn from hill tigers, and he parted the tufted grasses and peered from between them. There he saw the woman he now loved so suddenly and powerfully. She stood at her mother's grave, her head bowed, and her cloak wrapped about her, and he liked her the better that she did not kneel.

"She is very tall," he thought, and he liked her tall. He liked the eagle beauty of her face, and the smooth amber of her skin, and her long hands holding her cloak together.

He was not a simple man such as his eldest brother was and even the second brother was more simple than he. The blood of his ancestors had brought up in him something that was very old. Once in the long past there had been another like him who had battled against an emperor and had all but won. So now when he looked at the woman he wanted it was no simple lust that he felt. He wanted her in many ways to fill out his own being in its lacks, and he was pleased to think her learned and different from himself, and because he knew his own worth, he was not afraid to let her be in some ways better than himself and besides he felt that in some ways she was like him, and he felt her like him in his deepest parts.

Thus he stood steadfastly watching her and not once did she look up or see him there. But that pleased him, too. He was young enough to think, "I do not want her to see me again until I am at my best. I will get new garments and put them on and I will buckle on my sword, and have my hair cut and oiled."

So he stood, his eyes and mind full of her until she turned at last and with Wu Lien went toward Ling Tan's house again. Behind her the young man gazed at her until he could not see her, and then he let the grasses come together and he made his way to the hills.

... Now Lao Er and Jade had not been there to see all that had happened, for Jade, as soon as Wu Lien had gone, had plucked her husband's sleeve and led him down into the secret

349

room. There she turned on him a face brimming with triumph.

"Do you see?" she asked him.

"See what?" he asked, not having knowledge of what she meant so much as the mote in a sunbeam.

"Why, that is she!" Jade cried.

"What she?" he asked again.

"Oh, you bone!" she wailed, "oh, you lump of mud under my feet! Why has heaven made even the best of men in the shape of a fool? She is the goddess, your brother's goddess!"

His jaw fell down as he perceived her meaning. "But she is so high," he said, "how will she ever look down on one of us? And besides, what is she to the enemy?"

Jade looked grave then. "What indeed?" she said, "I had not thought of that. You are not such a fool."

Her woman's mind ran along the ground like a sniffing hound. "But I doubt she cares for the enemy," she said. "No woman thinks first of who rules and what is above, if she sees the man she wants at her side."

"He is not at her side," he said. "He is very far from her. And will he think her fit for him if she is with the enemy? Men are not like women there."

"Now you are wrong," she said. "Men think a woman so little worth, and they think themselves so strong, that it does not matter what their women are."

He laughed. "Are you and I to quarrel because of men and women?"

But Jade would not laugh. "No, but here is a thing," she said stubbornly.

"It is a thing which we cannot decide because a strange woman happens to look like a goddess in a temple," he said.

So after a while they came up again, and he helped her tenderly to mount the ladder that led upward, for she expected her second child any day. When they came up Lao San had gone and they found that while they had been talking underground, here on the top of the earth what they had been saying was not possible had already taken place.

"But how bring these two together?" Jade asked.

It was the question none could answer.

... But Mayli went straight to her own rooms when she returned to the puppet palace, and she took off her cloak and folded it very carefully and she washed herself and brushed her hair, and then she sat before a small table and looked at herself long in the mirror. The morning had made her bold heart strangely soft. There was the visit to her mother's grave, and her mind was stirred with things she could not remember, and yet she felt she did remember them. Her mother had died when she was born and yet this morning standing at that grave among the summer grasses, she felt she did remember a lovely face, wilful enough to say that she would not go with her husband, and yet so sweet that it made him glad to stay where she was. For her father had told her through her childhood of her mother, and she knew the love between them, and to her it had made love the best thing in the world to be had if it could be love like that.

Upon her softened heart was now imprinted a young man's face. Whatever he was, ignorant or not, he was brave and exceedingly beautiful and there was power in him and she could feel it, and were these three not enough? She had never seen them put together before in one man. And yet how would it be possible for her to become a part of that house? Ling Tan's house was more foreign to her than any foreigner's. She had not entered one like it in her life, and there she could not live.

"We would have to go away," she thought. "He would have to forsake them all and cleave only to me, and I would forsake all I have known and cleave only to him. Well, would we not then be equal? We could make our own world."

But where could such a world be made? She rose, most restless, and walked about the room as though she were on wings.

In the old times, now never to return, what she dreamed would have been impossible. There would have been no place for two like them to make a world. That old world was made and shaped, fixed and firm, and they would have been outcast had they not belonged to it. But now the old world was gone, old laws were broken, old customs dead. The young could do as they liked and tradition was no more.

"We could go into the free land," she thought, "anywhere we liked. Why should his power not be joined to mine? What I know I would tell him. What he knows he would tell me. Oh, how sick I am of learned, smooth men! How strong his hands were! He was wounded in battle. It was victory."

She remembered every look of his face and the proud way he walked, and all that was distasteful to her was the family from which he sprang. They were too humble for him.

"He ought to leave them," she thought. "Men like him are born by chance into lowly families. They belong to no one."

So she mused, and when she went down to meet her host at dinner he found her silent.

"Have I made you angry?" he urged her. He had had a morning full of suffering, for his rulers had not spared him. "Do not you be angry," he said, trying to laugh. "I need a little comfort. I have been told that I must catch the leader of those men who murdered the whole garrison yesterday. How can I do it?"

"How can you?" she repeated coldly. She saw within her heart that bold young face. "You cannot," she said.

. . . Thus its own way Heaven moves toward its end. Though Ling Tan and his wife were sleepless, and though Lao Er and Jade could see no way to bring their goddess down to earth, and though Wu Lien shook his head at what his wife told him and said the thing was impossible, and that her third brother must have drunk too much wine, and wisdom was to forget it all, yet Mayli alone, herself deciding nothing, but moving along the way of Heaven's will, went back to Ling Tan's house.

She waited for two days, and by then she knew that what she now felt she could not put aside. The only way to cure herself, if she could be cured, was to yield a little to her sudden love. Love she would not call it, for she was too shrewd not to see the folly in it. But at least she could go to Ling Tan's house, and she would make no pretext. She would ask for Jade and tell Jade that she knew Pansiao and see what came of it.

So in her too fearless way, she left the puppet's palace on the second day in the afternoon. As coolly as though there were no ruins anywhere made by the enemy and as though she saw nothing to make a young woman afraid, she hired an old horse carriage, and few there were, because by now the horses had been eaten for food, and she told the driver where she wanted to go and there she went.

Now Jade that day was not at work of any sort, for she moved too clumsily to be at ease. She was large with this child and she wondered that it could be so large, but so it was. She was sitting alone in the court with her two-year-old son when there came a strong knock at the gate. She listened and it came again. It was not the noise the enemy made with guns beating there. Ought she to open the gate? Ling Sao was in the fields that day with Ling Tan and Lao Er was away at his work. The father had told him to see whether or not his youngest brother had reached the hills safely, since he had left home in anger. So Jade being alone with the child made her voice cracked and old and she called out. "Who is there?"

"I!" Mayli called over the gate, and it was like her to forget to say her name and to think that all would know that I.

But Jade was quick and she did know it. So she rose and opened the gate.

"Oh," she said, and then made haste to be more courteous. "I swear I am too loutish—but I am so—I did not expect you—"

"Why should you?" Mayli said.

She came in and Jade shut the gate and barred it and Mayli

353

sat down. She looked so full of ease and calm that no one could have known how her heart twisted and beat inside her breast, and Jade did not know. And yet she told her husband afterward, "I knew it was no common day. I felt that I was being led along a road that had an end in some destiny."

Yet to another these would have seemed only two women talking. Jade poured tea, and took up her shy small son, and Mayli praised the boy, and drank the tea, and then she said, after such little talk:

"I could not speak as freely as I wished when I was here two days ago. I had my duty to my mother in my mind. But today I am come back to tell you that I know your husband's sister Pansiao, and I taught her for a while."

Here was news, and Jade could hardly take it to be true. But Mayli went on to tell her how it had been, and Jade hearing it thought now it had all come about as though by nature, and yet who could say that Heaven had not shaped it all?

"So when I came here," Mayli said, looking about the court, "I seemed to know what I saw. She had told me everything. The child was fond of me—how do I know why? But she chattered to me, and I was glad to hear her—I have been so long away in foreign lands and she told me of my own."

"Did she tell you of us all?" Jade asked. A thought of cunning had come into her mind, and she crept toward a certain knowledge as a cat creeps to a mouse.

"She told me of each one," Mayli said, "so when I saw you I knew your names."

Jade made herself very busy with her child, and lifted him upon her lap and smoothed his hair and seemed to see a mote of dust in the corner of his eye. "Did she show you a certain letter that I wrote her?" She asked this and she looked full into Mayli's eyes, and Mayli did not turn her head.

"I saw that letter," she said clearly, and still she did not look away.

354

The fearlessness in her made Jade fearless too. Indeed they were not different, these women, except in where they had spent their lives and how.

"He loved you when he first saw you," she said.

"Some men are so," Mayli said, and tried to smile, and wondered at how stiff her lips were.

"He is not like any other man," Jade said. She put the child down, "I must speak when Heaven bids me speak. What shall I tell him?"

Now both were caught together as though one wave swept them upward to its crest. Mayli gazed into Jade's long eyes and thought how beautiful they were, and Jade gazed into Mayli's black eyes and thought how clear they were and how brave, and each admired what the other was as lesser women cannot admire others.

"How tall you are," Jade said. "You are taller than I am."

"I am too tall," Mayli said, smiling at her.

"He likes women tall," Jade said, and then she put out her hand and touched Mayli's hand with the tips of her fingers. "What shall I tell him?" she asked again, very softly.

Beneath that strong and gentle touch Mayli moved and she turned her head away.

Then she put her hand into her bosom and took out a small piece of bright folded silk and she shook it out, and Jade saw the flag of the free people—blue and red, the sun upon it white and pure. None could have that flag here for fear of death if the enemy found it, but some had it and hid it.

"Oh," Jade whispered, "the free flag! You are as bold as this!"

But Mayli put it in Jade's hands.

"Tell him I go to the free lands," she said to Jade. "Tell him that I go to Kunming."

XIX

A<small>FTER</small> Mayli had gone Jade sat for a long time idle. She watched the child at her feet and felt the child stirring in her body and though she was glad for both, she knew she was wistful with envy of that free tall woman. In her bosom was the folded flag.

"If my man and I had stayed in the free lands," she thought, "could we together not have done great things? But he chose to return into this bondage."

And she thought how close her life was in these walls and how little time she had for anything except the work in the house and the care of her son, and how she had no time to read books any more, nor any money to buy a new book, though there were no new books. Such books as were to be bought were only lies written by the enemy. Everywhere it could now be seen that the people, taught from their ancestors to revere the very paper on which letters were printed, now burned such paper for enemy lies, and their reverence for learning was nearly gone.

"All that I do is to sit here and bear children," she thought half sadly, and in her bosom the free flag seemed to burn.

When the others came home at noon, she had their meal hot and ready, and she had done well with the poor stuff they had to eat now-a-days, with little salt and less oil. Though she had her great news to tell, Lao Er could see that a secret cloud hid Jade's heart from all and he made up his mind to wait until he could be alone with her and could ask her why there was this cloud.

Meanwhile here was the news, and she told it with pleasure and while they ate they talked between themselves and turned it over and over to get all its light upon now and the future. And they looked at the flag Jade had, and they gloated on it, and yet dared not keep it here.

"Take it to the secret room," Ling Tan told his second son. "If ever that room is found, we must die, anyway."

So Lao Er took the flag and hid it, and he came back, and by now Ling Sao had had time to think of a thing she did not like.

"Did she mean my son was to go after her?" Ling Sao asked with some anger. "But what is that for a daughter-in-law? I never heard of a man going to find a woman. The woman must come to him."

"Be sure that woman will never be a daughter-in-law," Ling Tan said. He took his bowl from his face and chewed as he talked. He was hungry and though there were times in these days when he would have sold his right thumb for a piece of good meat such as he used to buy any day when he went to the city to sell his grain and his vegetables, still this food was better than none, for Jade was a clever cook.

"How can any woman be my son's wife and not be my daughter-in-law?" Ling Sao asked, ready to oppose him.

"If he weds her, you will see, old woman," he said, and grinned and put his bowl to his face again and supped down the noodles and wild clover that made their dinner.

"Then she is not a woman," she said coldly, "and I doubt we have a grandchild out of her. I ever say let a woman take to running around on such big feet as she has, who has been to schools everywhere, and it is the end of the woman in her."

"She is woman enough to have our son swear he will have her and no other," Ling Tan said. "There must be something female in her somewhere."

357

"When did any young man ever know what he wanted?" Ling Sao said peevishly. "I wish she had never come into our gate. Some devil sent her, and he had our son here, when he ought not to have been here for once, and nothing good will come of it."

"Give over," Ling Tan told her. "You are only angry because you have not all your sons' wives where you can press your thumbs on them. I tell you, there are some who can fight in the free land, and there are others like us who can fight here on our own land, and well I can see our younger son is for the free land. Let him go where he wills, then, as long as he fights the enemy."

This was a handful of words for Ling Tan to say, and whenever he spoke gravely there were none in his house who answered him. Even his wife remembered her duty when he took this place above her, though it was always hard for her to keep silence, and be sure that in one way or another she had her way somewhere else.

"As for you, my son," Ling Tan said to Lao Er, "take the message to your younger brother, and tell him that I have no way to follow this woman. I cannot leave my land for love or for anything. But his feet are loose and tied nowhere, and let him do what he likes. Only he is not to go away without sending us word that he does, and if he goes, he is not to stay long years and tell us nothing."

Lao Er bowed his head and so the meal was over, and he would have lingered until Jade had washed the dishes and to follow her into their room and there ask her why she seemed sad, but well he knew he could not do this in the daytime without his mother wanting to know why he did. So he could only smile at her secretly and asked her if she felt well, or was the child beginning to come, and when she shook her head at this, he said:

"I will not go to my brother until tomorrow, and today I work with my father to finish the wheat field."

She nodded and tried to smile, and so he left her. All that afternoon Jade was very quiet, and Ling Sao, who stayed to spin cotton thread on her spindle, let her be silent because she thought she was feeling the weight of the child in her. Cotton was hard to come by now, and Ling Sao saved any she could raise and they sold none of it, because they needed it for their own winter garments, and since another child was coming then there would be more winter garments to be made. She sat twisting her spindle and wetting thumb and finger in her mouth to make the thread smooth and firm, and now and again speaking to Jade and telling how it was when her self gave birth, and Jade listened and said little.

. . . In the field Ling Tan and his second son worked together. The times were somewhat better for farmers now than they had been, in this one way, that so many farmers had died or had gone to the free lands that there was not enough food for the enemy, and so less than they had the enemy took men off the land either for death or bitter labor. Yet Ling Tan kept his eyes on the road and whenever he saw the enemy, he would tell his son and Lao Er would go quickly into the house and take his wife and child down with him into that secret room until it was safe to come up again. For who could trust that enemy for anything except evil?

But the bitterness of the enemy's rule did not abate. Of what Ling Tan took from his land he had the good of less than one third, and his taxes were grievous. He could only curse in his heart because well he knew that even the high enemy did not get the good of these taxes, but the little enemies at the bottom, the petty men. For they all knew, mouth to ear, that never had such rapacious rulers put themselves over any people. There was nothing this enemy would not do for money, and if any wished to buy or sell or smuggle goods, it could be done if money enough was put first upon the palms of the enemy. The very guns the hillmen used nowadays, that came from foreign parts, were smuggled in by little enemy men who thought only of their own gain, and were traitors even to their kind. Up the river guns could be smuggled to the army in the free land, if money were given to the many outstretched enemy hands.

All these things Ling Tan knew as every one knew, and it was so much good news. Though men might gnash their teeth for the moment, such rottenness in the enemy everywhere meant that one day they would be rotten enough to be overthrown and to be cast into the sea.

"We wait the day," Ling Tan often said to his son. "We will hold the land against that day."

. . . "It is nothing," Jade said. She turned her head away from her husband and poured him a cup of hot water before he slept. There was not often tea in the pot now, and most of the time they drank hot water.

But he caught her wrists and took the teapot from her. "There is something," he said. "Do you think you can draw your breath differently and I not know it?"

"You must not watch me so," Jade said, and she tried to pull away from him, but she could not.

"I do not watch you," he said. "I know without watching you. When you change I know from within myself."

So coaxing her and commanding her and she biting her pretty lower lip and first laughing and then saying again it was nothing, and then putting her sleeve to her eyes to wipe her tears away, but angrily because she wept too easily now while she waited for the child, she yielded to him, and she said:

"It only came to me today—how I am no better than any farm woman, and if we had stayed in the free land, would we not have done something great, too? I could have been of more use—you and I together—"

"This is because you have seen that woman," he said.

"Is there any sin in her or me because she makes me want to do something greater than sit behind these walls and bear children?" she asked hotly and now she did pull away from him, and he let her.

"Is it so little to you that you bear my children?" he asked.

But now she would not answer and for a while he did not speak, either, first because he was somewhat hurt by her, and second because he had not the words ready. He had always to sort the feeling out of his mind and then to put it into words for her. The feeling was there, strong and stubborn, and he knew she was wrong, but how could he tell her so and make her feel as he did? This Jade was so mixed with large and small, and he must be sure to pluck the right part in her now. But he struggled against his own simplicity.

"Had I only been a learned man!" he murmured.

He could not have spoken better, for this touched her, and she was so made that she would not hear of fault in any that was hers.

"You are well enough," she said more kindly, and he knew that as far as he had stepped it was well, so he went on.

"To me, we do the bravest thing," he said, speaking slowly and with care for truth. "How easy it is to go to the free lands! How safe it is there! It is easy to get guns together and men and to fall upon here a garrison and then there again. It is the easiest way to risk life. And we all risk life these days if we hate the enemy. And then there is glory—to do as my younger brother does, is to get glory very easily. But who gives glory to us? We only stay and try to live as ever we have. But this is our way of making war—to stay, and to take no suffering as cause to leave. In this there is no glory."

He paused and considered. "It may be that some day we shall be given glory for this too," he said. "But I do not know. What does it matter if there is glory, so long as we hold the land?"

361

"Yet even the land belongs to the enemy if they rule here," she said sadly.

"The land belongs to those who till it," he said. "If the enemy put us off the land and sent their own kind to till and to sow and to reap, then—but then we would still fight."

She did not answer this and he went on. "You in your way, when you bear a child, you add another to hold the land. And can any other do this except women like you? We who are men, we can grow food, but can we make other men to take our places? It is you who do this, and what you do is the thing that must be done if our people are to live. If women do not bear children, can we live?"

She sat very still, hearing these words as he let them come from him one by one, as painfully as though he forged them.

"When you have our child," he said, "you hold our land through him."

That was all. He could say no more, and he was as weary as though he had fought a battle. He had fought a battle and he had won. She knew that he was right.

. . . Now in all this, who had given one thought to the eldest son? He stayed in the hills doing his simple duty, and he laid his traps here and there and caught an enemy or two a few times a month, but not so often as once he had. For the enemy had grown wary of traps, and he had to beat his brains to devise new ways of making traps. In his own way he was brave enough, for he came nearer and nearer to the city and laid his traps so close sometimes that others except the enemy were caught. But if he peered down into a pit some morning and found an honest farmer cursing at the bottom, or a beggar or a peddler, he always let him free, and he was forgiven when that one knew why the trap was made.

He went on with this work, but these days he carried in him a sulky heart, and he told no one why it was. The truth was that he felt himself neglected and overlooked and forgotten in all this matter of his youngest brother. He felt that it ought not to be that his younger brother had a wife before he did, and that his father and his mother had put aside their duty to him.

When his second brother came and told their younger brother what the woman had said, that one made great noise to get himself ready to go to the free land. From among his men all who wanted to go with him were to go, and every man who had not his family too heavy on him was eager for it. Him, too, his brother had called and he had been very lordly and he said:

"Do you want to go with me, my brother, to the free land? If you do, you may tell my parents I said you were to go, and I will see that nothing but good comes to you."

Now Lao Ta did not at all like this way of speaking. Lao San had not called him elder brother as he should, and how could he go beneath one younger than he? He wanted nothing to do with that woman or with what his brother did.

"Since what I do best is to lay my traps," he said, "what good can I be there, where there is no enemy?"

His younger brother pulled down his eyebrows at him. "Do you tell me I go because there is no enemy there?" he asked in ready anger.

Lao Ta made a meager smile. "I hear you go because a woman is there," he said. "Whether she is an enemy or not, I cannot tell."

"Would she go to the free land if she were?" Lao San asked him angrily.

Now Lao Er had told him of the token of the flag, though Ling Tan would not let him bring it here lest the enemy find it on his person, should he by chance be stopped, as any might be. But even to hear of it was to Lao San proof of her he loved.

"How do I know anything about her?" Lao Ta answered. "I am a stupid man."

Thus he refused his brother and he went away before Lao San could speak again and back to his work. But his anger smoldered in him and he did not go to his father's house for many weeks, and then he was angry because no one sent word to ask why he did not come.

"Who cares whether I live or die?" he thought. It seemed to him that the good part of his life was over, and he thought of his little dead children and of Orchid and what a wife she had been to him, always ready and warm and kind, and how lonely he was without such a woman any more.

Thus brooding, he grew longing and ready for a change and yet where could he find a woman to take Orchid's place?

"Be sure I will not ask my mother or my father to help me," he thought. "If they do not care for me enough to do their duty to me, shall I beseech them and shame myself?"

But he knew he was ready to begin a life for himself and he wanted a wife and children again, and so without knowing he searched, he did search. But where was there a woman for him in that countryside? There were no women except old or sick, or those who had been fouled by the enemy, and he would not have a courtesan.

Yet one day he happened to find a woman. She was such a woman as once he would not have dreamed of thinking fit for him, but when a man grows as ready as he was now, any woman seems fit, if she is clean and whole. This was how he found her. He had chanced to lay a trap on a new road where he had not put one before and he had dug it deep and had put boards across strong enough to hold stones, and yet so cleverly that one board leaned upon another and the least weight would pull them all down. This he did because he had heard that the enemy was sending tax gatherers into that region within a day or two. When he had finished the trap, as he always did he went and warned the people who lived near that road not to use it until the enemy had passed by, and they thanked him.

When he opened that trap the next day to see what lay in it, he found a sobbing woman. She had been there all night, and since none came by, none had heard her crying for help. He peered down in the pale dawn light and he saw she was no enemy.

"I will bring you up," he said, and he leaped down into the pit to help her up. Then he saw that though she was a woman no longer young, she had a soft pouting face and a childish mouth, and her eyes were red with weeping.

"I am so frightened that half my breath is gone," she wailed.

"It was an evil chance that led you this way," he said. "How could I know?"

He helped her as he spoke and pushing and pulling he got her up and on her feet, and she thanked him and put her clothes right. Then she said, wiping her face with the end of her blue cotton coat:

"Can you tell me where I am? I am a stranger, and my man was killed by the enemy and he told me I was to find his village if he died and his father and mother, and see if they would care for me."

Then she named a village of which he had never heard.

"I think you are far wrong," he said. "I never knew that village."

At that she began to weep again and she said, "How can I go on? I have spent my money and now what can I do? I hear that the enemy is very evil to women, and what if I fall into their hands?" Then she looked piteously at him and she said, "You are an honest good man, and I see it in your face."

At this he thought to himself, "Are not all women alike? Certainly this woman looks soft and kind. She is a widow, but is that her fault?"

And to her he said, "Have you had anything to eat?" When she said she had not he took her to the nearest inn, only stopping to lay his trap again, and there he bought some food for her and while she ate he sat thinking. He did not sit with her, for that would have been beneath him and discourtesy to her, but he

365

watched her from the ends of his eyes, as he sat himself elsewhere and he thought, "Has not Heaven sent her? She fell into
my trap."

When she had finished eating, therefore, he told her to follow
him. Then with much mustering of his courage, and he could
not have done it had she not been so piteous and so anxious to
please him for his kindness, he said to her:

"My own father's house is not far from here, and a day's walking will bring us to it and my mother is a good woman, so let
me take you there."

This he said to test her to see whether she would be willing.
And why would she not be willing, who had no roof to creep
under and no man to feed her? She said with great thankfulness:

"How can I refuse one into whose hand Heaven has put me?"

So without a word more he walked ahead of her toward his
father's house and she followed behind him, carrying her bundle
of goods tied into a coarse blue cloth.

For many miles he said nothing to her, and when he did not
speak she did not, but he heard her footsteps behind him in the
dust. And as he went he thought, "If it is well, I will speak again
before I reach my mother's. I must give a reason for bringing
home a woman."

So when they were within sight of the village, he gathered all
his courage together again and he turned and said to that woman,
though his mouth went dry so to speak for himself:

"I have lost my wife and my two children. You have lost your
husband. Are we not two parts? If we come together would we
not be a whole?"

By the time the woman was so weary and so anxious to find a
home for herself that she could scarcely have refused any man
and so she said, "If you will have me!"

Lao Ta nodded and without more talk he went on, and so they
came to his father's house.

Now there could scarcely have been a worse moment for them

to come than the one they had chanced upon. For early that morning Jade's child had begun to come, and her labor had gone through the whole day and the child for some reason clung to the womb and would not come out. Ling Sao was beside herself, and Lao Er was frantic, and all the women of the village had gathered there each to tell what she would do. All had been done and still the child would not be born, and Jade's courage was beginning to fail.

"This child is too big—" she whispered, and in her own heart she began to doubt whether or not she could bring it to birth.

So when at this moment Ling Sao beheld her eldest son come in with a strange woman, she had no time for what he wanted to say. Her temper was at its worst with what she had been through and the evil outlook ahead, yet the eldest son, being too simple to think of any except himself, blurted out as soon as he saw his mother:

"Mother, this woman is your new daughter-in-law."

"Do not speak of daughters-in-law to me," she cried. "I have eaten nothing but bitterness with them. Here is this Jade who cannot bear her child, and now what shall we do? There is nothing but bitterness in children and children's children, and I am never to have any peace."

Now this new woman had lived long enough to know what was best for herself, and the moment she came to the village she had liked it. Then she saw that this was a good farm and a fair farmhouse, and at her age how could she look for anything better? Her luck had put her in that trap and she must make the most of it, and thank the times for giving her a chance for a man as strong as this one, though he was ten years younger than she, at least. Well, then, she must try the more for him. So, weary as she was, she put down her bundle and smoothed back her hair, and she said in a soft and pleasant voice:

"I am too bold and I know my little worth, but still I have often delivered women of their children and it may be that I can be of use here. Else why did Heaven send me to a house I have never seen before, and did not Heaven put my feet on the wrong road for some purpose, so that I am miles from where I thought I was, and fell into your son's trap and could not climb out until he saved me?"

"Come with me," Ling Sao cried, not understanding any of this except what she needed. She took that woman by the wrist and pulled her to Jade's bedside, and she said to Jade, "Here is one sent by Heaven to help you, child, and let us all take heart."

Then that woman pushed up her sleeves and she smiled at Jade and she put up Jade's garments and she began to knead her belly and her loins. Whether a new face gave Jade courage, or whether the kneading eased her for a moment, it was sure she felt better and she took heart and tried again. And that woman had great patience and she coaxed Jade with her words, and kept on at her work, and all waited to see what would happen.

"The child has moved a little," Jade gasped at last, and fell into fresh agony. At this the woman thrust her hand and arm up into Jade's body and cried out:

"I feel a boy's head!"

At that all took new courage, and Ling Sao urged Jade that since it was a boy she must go on. Now the woman pulled gently with her hand and Jade pushed, and that unwilling child had nothing for it but to yield, though hardly. So after about two hours more, he was born. Then Ling Sao seized the child.

But the woman looked at Jade and cried, "There is another one."

And then she fell hard to work again and in a few moments more another child was born upon a great gush of Jade's bright blood.

"O Heaven's mercy!" Ling Sao cried, and reached out her arm for this second boy. And such boys they were that they both cried as lustily as though they had been born a week.

Who now could doubt that Heaven had sent this woman?

"You must eat and rest and calm yourself, and be sure I will thank you in any way you want," Ling Sao said.

She gave the children to those women who waited, and as proud as though she had done the thing herself, she went into the kitchen to make ready for Jade the red sugar melted into boiling water that would renew her strength, and she called her second son to take it in and tell Jade how well she had done.

But while she did this she thought secretly, "This woman—she is too old for my son, and yet how can I refuse her now? But how will it be to me to have so old a daughter-in-law?"

And when Lao Er had gone with the sugar drink, she called her husband to her to talk with him so that she could know how she was to behave to this woman, whether as daughter-in-law or as a stranger. Now Lao Ta had already told his father what he wanted and so Ling Tan was ready, and he knew his mind.

"Heaven plays us tricks these days," Ling Sao said, feeding the fire as she talked, to heat food for the woman. "I swear I could never think that I would get women like this out of the air for my sons. These are no proper times."

"Nevertheless, how can we refuse our eldest son now?" he asked her.

At this she saw that he was willing, and so she only put one barrier up. "If she is too old for childbearing then he cannot have her. What is the use of a woman in the house if she cannot have a child?"

"She has been useful today," he said.

"But today is not every day," she said. "Not once in the life time of a few is such a day as this."

And she would have her way, and so when she took food to the woman she asked her age in all courtesy as one must ask a stranger, and that woman said half sadly, "Well I know I am too old. I am thirty-six."

And Ling Sao thought to herself, though she liked the woman's honesty, that indeed it was very old, but still the

369

woman might bear three or four children in time if she were fertile. So she put another courteous question, and she said:

"Have you any children?"

At that the woman began to weep and she said, "I did have children, for I ever bore them easily, but I lost them all—five of them together in battle from the flying ships. Only I and my husband lived and then he lost himself, too, in a soldier's battle, for he was taken into the army. He was a cobbler by trade and his trade kept him out on the streets and he could not stay at home and hide, as some men can. When word came down from those above that from our district a thousand men must be sent to make the army in the free land, where we lived, he was easily taken, for he was strong and his legs were hearty from his long walking with his load. He did not come home for many days and I feared he had been taken. Somehow he sent me word of where he was, and then I went near to him. But I never saw him, for there were many thousand soldiers there, and before I found him I heard he was dead."

"What bitterness!" Ling Sao murmured and at that moment from pity she yielded to her eldest son, and took what Heaven had sent.

XX

THUS Ling Tan's house was full again, and with yet no
abatement of hardship from the enemy's rule, his life went
on. So far as he could see there was no hope of abatement.
He bore as all others did the cruelest taxes and the most unjust
greed and every spring as far ahead as he could see there was the
battle of opium to fight with the enemy. And in this battle the
enemy was now the victor. Opium in these days sold in the city
for twenty-one silver dollars for an ounce, and a dollar a day was
enough for a man, if he did not buy food, and more and more
were those who chose opium rather than food. Opium lamps
and pipes were sold openly on the streets, a thing never heard
of since ancient times, and the enemy put a tax on every lamp
and every pipe and prospered upon the weakness of those who
were desperate. But among the enemy opium was forbidden.
And there were few shops for cloth or silk, for the enemy took
all such goods, and all the factories for the making of silk were
in enemy hands, and flour belonged to the enemy still, and fish
and rice and cement.

Seeing how robbed the people were and how the enemy took
away to their own country all the goods in houses and shops,
and iron of every sort, even nails and locks and knives and
forks and hoes and spades, and any metal thing not hidden,
Ling Tan thought bitterly, many a day:

"The earth is the one thing they cannot take back to that

371

cursed country of theirs." And yet as though the earth itself rebelled, the harvests shrank to half what they had once been.

And again he said, "This enemy, they did not declare war, but they made war upon us. Now they declare peace, but they cannot make it."

And he hated them the more because he who all his life until now had been a proud and free man had to compel himself to silence before this enemy, and before the smallest and the weakest and the most evil of these little crooked-legged men he had to listen and to say nothing. This he could only do because there was the land and he was still faithful to it.

But there were times when his gorge rose in him and then he could not eat, and nothing made him better, not his wife's coaxing nor the sight of grandchildren, nor anything that he had.

"If I must meet that enemy one more time upon my land it will be too much," he told his wife, and she said nothing for once, because he could not be comforted. There was no comfort.

"If I had so much as a seed of hope," he said again, "if I saw an end, however far away, that one day we could rise up and push the enemy into the sea! But all we do is to endure, and can victory be won only by endurance?"

And again Ling Sao could answer nothing. These were the times that she dreaded, for when Ling Tan was downcast, the whole house was dark with his gloom, and even his sons could do nothing against it.

There came such a time in the late summer of that year and it was the darkest that Ling Tan had yet had, and it began on his birthday. In the old days Ling Tan's birthday was a holiday for all the village, and he invited his friends and gave a great feast. Year after year he had looked forward to this his sixtieth birthday, for the sixtieth is the best birthday a man can have, if he is a good man and if he has sons. Had the times been right, his sons would have gathered around him and there would have been days of rejoicing. He would have had new garments and there would have been many gifts given to him, and he would have given money to all his house and all would have been gaiety and good cheer.

But how could such a thing be now? His third son was far in the free land, and his eldest son in and out of the hills. Ling Tan saw his birthday coming near and they had not even so much as a piece of meat in the house and no money wherewith to buy it. All they had must be saved for the meager food that kept them living. Besides this, the summer had been long and hot, and now near the end of it Ling Tan felt weary and old and his life was too much for him.

"I do not take joy even in my land," he thought one day as he went out to see the rice and how thick it stood for harvest. "If the harvest is good it is a trouble to me, because it goes to feed the enemy. If it is scanty then I feel the land is angry somehow and I have not done well by it. A man can take no pleasure in anything so long as this wicked enemy crouches upon us like an evil beast."

He wondered, for the first time, if it were well that he had chosen to remain on the land, because he had to feed the enemy year after year, and this was a very bitter thing.

"If there were a little hope somewhere in the sky," he told his second son one day. "If we saw hope as large as a man's hand even, raised to help us, but there is none who will help us. Everywhere in the world men think only of themselves."

For by now even such men as he knew that none of the countries in the world had come forward to stand at their side or to give them aid in this desperate war, and he and all his fellows had heard that even in countries which called themselves friendly, men sold weapons and goods of war to the enemy for the price that they could get, and he and others like him were sore at heart because righteousness was not to be found any more among men. Each in his own way was like the other, and though some men did not make war as others did, if they sold their goods for profit to the war-makers, did it make them better because the weapon was not in their own hands, if they had made the weapon and sold it and so put it into the hands of those who used it upon the innocent? Well Ling Tan knew all this, and he was weary of waiting for help. There was no help, and slowly hope went out of him, as the fifth year of war wore on toward autumn.

"All men are evil," he told his son. "There is none under Heaven who think any more of right and wrong. When this comes about we perish."

And he began to lose his wish for food and he worked less than he did and he had none of the old pleasure in harvest and planting that had kept him alive and young for his years.

This went on until Ling Sao grew frightened, for he was still more to her than all else besides, and she called her second son into the kitchen one day and she said, "You must think of some way to put hope into your father, for he is a man who has never before in his life given up hope."

"You ask a very hard thing, mother," Lao Er said sadly. "Where shall I find hope for us today? Can I buy it somewhere or find it lying on the ground to pick up like a jewel dropped? Hope must come out of what we have, or it is not hope, but a dream."

"Then your father's life is over," Ling Sao said weeping. "And our long battle is lost. Now the enemy conquers us." And she went away into her own room and closed the door and wept.

Lao Er took this very gravely and he set himself to find out if he could if there were anything good he could tell his father, but where could he find good?

Even in these times of evil men, Heaven could be evil, too. There had been the rains one year to spoil the land, and now the year just past was heaped with misery, for there was famine in the North once more and starving people drifted southward, from misery to misery. In other years they had so drifted, and

Ling Tan and others had helped them, but what help was there now, with half the villages destroyed by fire?

In the city that puppet sat on his seat, and sent out his little orders, and from abroad those nations which favored the enemy called him ruler. In the free land, it was true, they heard of a mighty army gathering, and yet they never saw this army and it remained only hearsay to these who lived here in bondage. For the enemy saw to it that no news came to them and the people still lived locked in silence from the outer world. Within this silence the grim enemy ruled, and still for nothing a man could be killed. Many were being killed even now, for some small fault or for none at all except an enemy's whim, and none could draw his breath with freedom. Slowly everywhere the hearts of men were being crushed, and many died from within and gave themselves up as one who drowns must first be willing to drown and cease his struggle to live before he can die. Many who had not been willing to smoke opium, now did turn to it.

Then searching everywhere in himself Lao Er thought of his old cousin whom in many months he had forgotten. He knew him to be alive, for now and again mouth to ear in spite of the enemy there would creep through the countryside some small piece of news, twisted and changed in the telling so that none knew by the time it reached the villages, what it had been in the beginning. And Lao Er thought, "I will go to that old bone, and see if he has any good to tell," and then he thought, "and I will ask my father to go with me, and if there should be something good he will hear it, too, and he will know I am not saying empty words for comfort."

So when Ling Tan's birthday came, and there was no feast beyond a fish caught secretly and hidden until the meal, when they had eaten it behind the locked gate, Lao Er said to his father, "Why should we not take a few hours for pleasure to-night and go into the city to that tea house and see our old cousin and hear again what he says?"

At first Ling Tan thought he would not go because he was weary and he despaired of hearing good, but he saw his son was urgent. So he changed the words he had been about to speak and he said:

"Though I have no zest for it, if it is what you want and since this is my birthday, I will go with you."

Thus it came about that once more Ling Tan and his son hid themselves among the others in the tea house. All went as it had before, and they went into the inner room. There after a while the old cousin came, thinner and more dried and drowsier than ever, and now if Ling Tan would have told him who he was that old opium eater could not have known him through the dimness of his dreams. But still he was clear enough for this one thing that he did every day because his opium depended on it, though anyone could see he would not live much longer to need it.

When the old man came in he sat down on his stool, and he spoke into his beard and in so low a voice that all must strain to hear him, and he said:

"I told you yesterday about that meeting between the two great white men, and it took place upon the sea. The one white man came from the country of Mei and the other from Ying, and they met together for a space. Today the one from Ying has spoken."

The old man fumbled in his bosom and brought out a small piece of brown-stained paper, and then his horn spectacles. With much trouble he put his spectacles on his nose and they fell off because his hands trembled so and he put them on again and again they fell off, and all waited in great patience until a third time he tried and this time they stayed. Then he lifted up the paper and read these words aloud:

"The ordeals of the conquered peoples will be hard. We must give them hope. We must give them the conviction that their sufferings and their resistances will not be in vain. The tunnel may be dark and long, but at the end there is light."

376

In this dark old room filthy with years and now with ruin, Ling Tan stood and heard these brave words. His heart was hungry as fallow land is hungry, and the words fell into his heart like seeds.

"Who is the man who said this?" he cried out. "I was not here yesterday—tell me today!"

The old cousin did not need to speak. Others were ready to tell what they knew, and one man and another, speaking together, eager to speak, full of hope and doubt because of long delay, they told Ling Tan that now at last there were those two peoples for whom this one man spoke, the Mei people and the Ying people. Ling Tan listened to this one and to that one, and he drank in every word, and those seeds in his heart took root.

"If those peoples are against this enemy," he said, "are they not with us?"

"Are they not?" others echoed joyfully.

Then out of his long weariness Ling Tan felt the slow tears come up into his eyes. All through the bitter years he had not wept. He had seen ruin in his home and in his village, and he had seen death everywhere, but he had not wept, and he wondered that now at this first good news that any had given him in more than four years, he had to weep.

"Let us go," he said to his son.

So his son followed him and they went out from the city and Ling Tan said nothing.

Soon they were beyond the desolate city, and the cobbled road grew narrow and wound its old way along the valley's bed. The hills were dark against the sky. This night there was no moon.

Now Lao Er had all this while been unbelieving, and it was in his heart to say to his father, "It is better for us not to count help sure from anywhere. Are there men who give their help for nothing?" But he had waited for his father to speak.

But when there was only silence he kept silent, too, and at last he thought to himself that he would let his father have his hope.

377

"I am young," Lao Er thought. "I do not need a hope. I can live."

And so with his heart cool and bitter within his breast, Lao Er let his father walk ahead of him and he saw him lift his head to look at the stars and put up his hand to feel the wind.

"Is there not promise of rain?" Ling Tan asked suddenly out of the darkness. There had been need of rain for many days.

"Only a promise," Lao Er said.